The Path to Paz

Book One

Written by
Jeremy Thelin

To find out when the next book in The Path to Paz series comes out, please visit www.jeremythelin.com where you can sign up to receive an email featuring his next release.

This is a work of fiction. All the characters and events portrayed are either products of the author's imagination or are used fictitiously.

Dedicated to:

My four children.
And all my nieces and nephews.
There are 16 on my side
And 24 on my wife's.

A special thanks to:
My wife.
She is literally the coolest person I know.

Afton Nelson and Chelsea Adams
For helping me believe this was possible
And then pushing me to make it happen.

My brothers
For always having my back.

My readers
Ashton, Kiara, Sam, Nipper, JaNea, Jerai, Calvin, Sue, Dennis,
MariAnne, Justin

A shout out to:
John Fallau
I honor you
And all servicemen and women
For your sacrifice and service

TABLE OF CONTENTS

CHAPTER 1

The Spoils

Toekin crouched behind a tree, masked and waiting, sling in hand. The guards of Abbadon didn't used to wear armor, nor did their detail always include an archer and three extra men bringing up the rear. And they certainly hadn't always trudged along in near silence, careful and cautious as thieves.

But that was before the attacks started.

They were close enough now that Toekin could see the white knuckles of the archer as he gripped his bow. The infinity symbol, engulfed in flames on his chest, marked him as the enemy.

These days, the Emperor's thugs were sober and careful. None bragged about their conquests, the families they split up or the lives they'd destroyed.

Scenes from the last time he'd seen his parents flashed through Toekin's mind and he squeezed his eyes shut to block it out. *Focus.* He reached into the sack at his waist and palmed three round seedpods—gathered from the unpredictable and dangerous Seivo Sangue tree—and placed one in the pouch of his sling.

The men walked with purpose, sure-footed and solemn. Their heavy armor belied their fears. However, their bare heads—the helmets piled up in the back of the cart—revealed they still suffered from arrogance. It was all the opening Toekin needed.

The sling in his hand began to spin, and with a quick jerk of his arm the projectile was gone. It landed in the middle of the archer's forehead, bringing him to his knees. Another black seed was already placed inside the sling and humming when they realized something was wrong. By then, another man was down.

The two rear guards turned at the commotion when the third Seivo seed found its mark and the sword, shield and body of the foremost man crashed to the ground. The remaining four soldiers raised their shields and scampered into practiced formation.

In the time it took his targets to blink twice, Toekin moved to a new position with unnatural speed. No one could have anticipated the direction the next hit would come from. Another one down.

Two of the remaining three took refuge behind the cart, crouching low, shield and sword at the ready.

The man in front dropped to the ground, covering much of his body behind his shield. "This is treason! We are Abbadon Guards! You will be punished by de . . ." He was down before he could even finish his speech.

Toekin raised his left hand high, gripping the final seeds, and extended two fingers upward. From the trees behind the soldiers, his crow, Corvo, sounded two, unnaturally loud cries. "CAW! CAW!"

The Emperor's men flinched and spun. One of them ducked his head and brought his hands to his ears, dropping his sword and shield in the process. Toekin used the distraction to move again, flashing like a black shadow from one location to the next until he was in a side flanking position, a perfect vantage to dispatch the remaining thugs.

Tha-DONK. The perfectly round seed glanced off the armored man's vulnerable head and ricocheted into the cart, lodging itself into the wooden siding. The guard crumpled forward onto his shield.

Giving into fear, the last one dropped his shield and sword and ran for his life—directly toward Toekin. He didn't get more than two steps before ending up face down in the dirt. Toekin crouched low, burying himself in the dark spot of a fallen log. He raised a finger in the air and made small circular motions and Corvo responded, circling the area, sweeping outward in far reaching loops.

He sat back against the log, taking slow, deep breaths, letting his heart rate return to normal. When Corvo landed on the cart and tugged at the canvas covering with his beak, Toekin knew all was clear.

The cart bore the flaming infinity mark of Abbadon, as did the wooden-spoke wheels, rimmed in purple steel. Everything was marked as property of Abbadon and anyone found in possession of it would be punished as a thief. It all had to be destroyed.

He looked up to find Corvo sinking his shiny black head into the various bags of taxes, and in short order, the bird came up with his prize—a bright red apple. "Did they bring us some good stuff this time?"

"Caw!" Bits of apple went flying and juice dripped off his giant beak. Toekin didn't know why his crow had grown so large. He'd found his abandoned egg right after his own parents had disappeared and he'd protected it until it hatched. In a way, he and Corv had grown up together. For a while Toekin had measured the length of his arms against Corvo's wingspan. Even though Toekin was as tall as most grown men, Corvo's wingspan had passed him up long ago.

Toekin dug through the cart and found sacks of grain, dried meat and more fruit. Several balls of cheese covered in red wax were packed tightly so they wouldn't roll around. He hadn't eaten cheese in years. After emptying the cart, he packed it back up with anything bearing the mark of Abbadon—that included the guards.

He cursed the addition of more men to each detail. He didn't enjoy dispatching so many, but it was necessary to cover his tracks. It was also necessary to exact the only measure of justice he knew how.

Years of climbing and hunting had made him strong but hauling the men into the cart should have exhausted him. He had no idea how unusual it was that he felt more hungry than tired.

He pushed the load off the main road 500 paces and parked it under a Seivo Sangue. With a quick burst of speed and a mighty shove he pushed it onto the circular pool of hardened sap, blood red and glossy, that existed beneath every tree of its kind. He heard the first bulb dump its boiling hot sap from high above as he walked away, not bothering to look back as the wooden cart started to smoke. It would take a few more dumps to completely erase it from existence, but erased it would be.

He returned to the bags of food to find Corvo slowly, but deliberately pecking away at another apple.

Toekin pulled off his hood, wiped his brow and said, "You gonna be able to fly, buddy? Because I'm not carrying you all the way back home."

Corvo seemed to glare back at him and Toekin laughed. "Hey, don't look at me that way. How many have you had? Four? Five?"

"Caw." It came out more pained than powerful.

Toekin chuckled, then looked into the sky. "The sun's moving. We better get going." He ate an apple, shoved some dried meat in his pocket, then said, "Ready?" He watched as the stuffed bird struggled to get off the ground.

"You better not throw up on me!" He shouted up to his friend. Toekin pulled his hood back over his head and swung the bags onto his shoulders and then took off at a jog onto the animal path that would keep him hidden from view.

While his efforts were probably no more than a small annoyance to the emperor, until he figured a better way to fight back, this was what he did. He was a bug, buzzing about the emperor's ear, always just out of swatting range. The fact that he would now have some cheese, jerky and fruit in his stores was no more than a delicious side benefit.

* * *

Toekin woke to the sound of a loud hiss followed by a wet, sizzling splat. He pulled his blanket up around his shoulder and rolled over, still content from the previous night's feast. Farther away, another hiss and splat echoed through the trees and Toekin felt a nip on his heel.

"Knock it off," he said into his mattress.

Another nip, this time to his ankle, with more feeling.

"The sun's barely up, you fool."

A moment later, Toekin felt Corvo's feet as he hopped off his perch at the end of the bed and landed on Toekin's back, kneading his sharp claws into his flesh.

"Okay! I'm getting up." Another hiss-splat rang through the air and Toekin rubbed his eyes. He'd gotten so used to the sounds of the nearby Seivo Sangue trees dropping their deadly sap that they'd become more of a soothing sound than a terrifying one. His body twisted into a yawning stretch and he stood up, reaching for the cord that pulled down a ladder. He climbed up, opened the hatch in the ceiling of his room, pulled himself through the opening, and righted himself. He breathed in the view from his tree; the only dormant Seivo Sangue tree in existence for miles. Probably the only dormant tree of its kind anywhere.

From his perch high in the air he could see the active Seivo Sangue trees jutting up above the canopy below. Corvo joined him and nudged his leg gently. In his mouth was Toekin's scope.

"We just did a raid a day ago. It's too soon."

The big black bird nudged his leg again, reaching up to him with the scope in his mouth. "Fine. I'll look. But I'm not making any promises."

Toekin held the instrument to his eye and toggled between the scope's series of red lenses until he focused in on what Corvo wanted him to see. When the lenses were set just right, he could almost see to Passo Fundo, a three-day journey on foot.

Today he didn't need to see that far to spot the detail of purple-clad Abbadon guards and their loaded cart. He collapsed his black scope, pausing to rub his thumb over the silver emblem of a dragon. "I don't know buddy. We need to be careful about how often we're doing this. We don't want to draw more attention than necessary."

Corvo hopped up and down like he had something to say.

"And we've got plenty of food to last us."

"Caw!"

Toekin felt the cool morning air. The seasons were changing and soon, the poor who lived and struggled in the hardscrabble cities would be struggling even more. Toekin sighed. "We could bring it to Favela . . ."

"Caw, caw!"

He drew his hand across his face, rubbing any remaining sleep from his eyes. It was risky. Staying hidden was his primary concern. Risks had to be calculated.

"We could get caught," he said.

Corvo nudged his leg, then flapped up onto his shoulder.

He pulled the scope to his eye once more and counted the guards. There were fewer than yesterday, but the haul looked as big or bigger. It shouldn't be too hard to take it. And he'd be careful. "You'll watch out for me, right?"

Covro gave a soft "caw" and nuzzled his silky head into Toekin's cheek.

Toekin swung open the hatch to his sap-bulb room and jumped back in. The warm air greeted him like an embrace. His parents had taught him how to put the Seivo Sangue in a state of dormancy, allowing him to drain the sap that flowed from the roots, deep in the ground, through the trunk and into every branch and sap bulb. What was left was a hollow trunk, big enough to store dozens of wagons inside, roots and branches that became hallways, and sap bulbs that became rooms.

He put on his shoes, grabbed his water skin, a few apples and tossed them in his satchel.

As Toekin walked away from his bulbous bedchamber, he trailed his fingers along the warm walls of the hollow branch until he came to the trunk of the tree, stopping only when the tips of his shoes tasted the ledge. He looked down. Golden light radiated from the inner walls of the Seivo Sangue and churned below him, warm updrafts displacing the mist in swirls. Steel cables stretched back and forth like spider webs cut across the trunk until they were too far to be seen in the dim golden light.

From his satchel he pulled out two grapples, each with a hook at the top, and slid them over his hands. Reaching out into the void he hooked himself into a steel cable and took one last look into the vast emptiness below.

Then he jumped.

Tears formed in the corners of his eyes as the warm wind raced past his face. The angle of the cable dropped almost vertically at first but quickly started leveling out as the opposite side of the trunk rapidly approached. Toekin squeezed the grapple in his hand to slow his speed just enough so he didn't slam into the wall.

He brought his legs backwards before swinging them forward in perfect timing, his feet landing squarely on the side of the tree, his body horizontal. In one fluid motion he relaxed his grip, releasing him from the upper most cable, while his other hand reached out and picked a new one.

He pushed off, and for a moment he was in free fall again. It felt like flying, unrestricted by the laws of nature. In no time he worked his way down the interior of the trunk to the base of the tree with Corvo alternating between diving and gliding to stay at his side.

At the base, large tubes, softly illuminated in gold, snaked out in all directions. Once a huge root system, they now formed tunnels, and his way in and out of his tree.

Toekin chose one of the side-roots and walked into it. Corvo flew past him, eager to be on his way. The hollow root tapered and Toekin crouched until he arrived at a wooden hatch that had been carved into the ceiling.

"Get back, Corv, unless you want to get dumped on again."

He pounded a couple times to loosen it and it popped open, dirt and rocks raining down on the crow despite his attempt to take cover. A shaft of light shot down into the tube, temporarily blinding both of them. Toekin listened carefully to the outside world while his vision adjusted, then poked his head out and looked around.

"All clear," he said, and Corvo was off, flying high into the trees and disappearing into the shadows.

Toekin emerged, closed the hatch behind him, and kicked some dirt and rocks onto it to make it blend in. He couldn't imagine anyone even getting close enough to his Seivo Sangue tree to see this hidden door. It still had the dried sap covering the base and looked like it was active. But if they did get close, he didn't want to chance anyone finding his secret entrance.

He thought about the people he would help today with the food and supplies he was going to take back from the Abbadon guards and felt a surge of excitement. Then he imagined the face of Emperor Beezul when he would learn yet another taxation cart had gone missing. Toekin smiled. Corvo had been right. He was going to enjoy this.

CHAPTER 2

The Ursmock

The trees shrank in size and grew farther apart as Toekin neared Favela. Mato Forest had once continued endlessly here, thick as a jungle and full of life. But the Second Great War had created great tracts of barren wasteland between sparse patches of forest. And the residents of Favela had paid the price.

At the edge of the forest, Toekin stopped and let the bags from the morning's raid drop from his shoulders. He sat down against a tree and watched the slow, steady midday pulse of the poorest part of town. Homes here looked like a patchwork of scraps, packed in tightly and held together with hope and tenacity. Corvo landed next to him and promptly fell asleep on two bags of food.

While he waited, Toekin helped himself to some spotted mushrooms growing at the base of an old tree. Since he was a little boy, he could never resist their rich, earthy, yet meaty flavor. Most people didn't dare eat them because they were often mistaken for deadly skullcaps, which caused almost instantaneous death. You never knew which you were eating until it was too late. *More for me*, Toekin thought, and silently thanked his dad for teaching him how to know the difference.

A woman came out of her home carrying a pan of dirty water. She tossed it onto sparse rows of carrots and lettuce that grew against the odds in a shaded patch of hardened dirt behind her house. It was already too late in the season for her crop to see maturity.

Toekin studied her movements, then grabbed a sack and ran toward the home as soon as she walked inside. He covered the distance in seconds and reached the front door, which stood ajar, then dumped the contents of the bag of food inside the threshold just as she was returning.

He didn't wait but turned and was off like a bolt.

He didn't doubt that if pressed by Abbadon guards, the villagers wouldn't hesitate to point a finger his direction. He was crazy to be taking this risk, he thought, folding up the marked bag and shoving it into his pocket. He would destroy it later.

He traveled along the outskirts of a less depressing part of town, adjusted his hood and tucked in his unruly sandy hair when he saw the orphanage.

It seemed to be comprised of three, sturdy log buildings connected by hallways with a large garden on the sunny south side. Toekin moved closer, three bags of food slung over his shoulders, keeping to the shadows in the trees that surrounded the property. There was a group working in the garden today, pulling up turnips and beets and piling them into reed baskets.

Perfect, he thought. He could get in and out while they were working, and they'd never see him. He just needed to get past everyone and he'd have a clear path. Luckily, they were more absorbed in the ground in front of them than they were in the outskirts of the yard where a few bushes, spindly trees and several handcarts were all that offered cover.

The orphans came in all sizes. Some were clearly quite young, while others looked like they might be his age. They all wore identical black robes, as if they were initiates in a religious order. Toekin moved from bush to cart, now as close as he would get to the group before rounding the corner and getting a clear shot to the main building. One was talking, a grown man who was probably their caretaker and most likely someone who would not take kindly to a mysterious stranger with a hooded face.

A shot of panic hit his gut as the memory of his mother's voice rang out in his head. "*Hide!*" Why was he doing this? People were dangerous.

He peeked out from behind the cart to gauge the timing of his next move and jerked back into hiding when he saw the same man, turned away from the working orphans, staring straight in his direction. The billowy hood of his robe was pulled over his head so that his face and eyes were lost in its shadow, but a long, white braided beard extended partway down his chest. It was impossible to know if he'd been seen. Toekin's heart raced as he considered his options. Should he dump the food here and make a run for it? Should he go back the way he came and try to drop off the food to someone else? The sun was sinking, and dark, ominous clouds were moving in from the east. He didn't have time to weigh out his options. It wasn't safe to be in Mato Forest after dark. It was now or never.

One more look, he told himself. If the old man still stared in his direction, he'd leave the food and bolt. Slowly, he leaned around the edge of the cart, expecting the bearded man be exactly where he'd been standing a moment ago. But he wasn't. Encouraged, he leaned forward a little more and searched. *Where had he gone?* The kids were still distracted with their work, but the bearded figure seemed to have disappeared.

Then he saw him, in the farthest part of the garden, kneeling on the ground assisting one of the smaller orphans, his back mostly to Toekin. How had he gotten over there so quickly? Regardless, this was his best shot to move unseen, and he took it. From cart to bush, to tree, and then finally out of view from the busy gardeners, all that remained was a straight shot to the door of the main building. From what Toekin could see, it appeared to be slightly open. *Perfect!*

He looked around, saw it was safe, and made a dash for it.

Once inside he knew he'd chosen the right place. The room was tidy, with rows of wooden tables indicating the many mouths that were fed here. A black cauldron hung over glowing coals in a fireplace at the end of the room. Nearly empty baskets pushed into the corners held a few potatoes and other root vegetables—not nearly enough to get them through the winter.

Shelves lining the back wall held several earthenware jars, three tall stacks of plates, and rows of washed and stacked cups. What would it be like to eat with so many other people? He imagined the room filled with the low hum of conversation punctuated with occasional bursts of laughter and suddenly the silence of his solitary life seemed to weigh on him.

Get in, get out, Toekin. Focus. He pulled his attention away from the details of the room and started to unload the contents of the bags on the table nearest the hearth. He was taking too long. If he wasn't careful, he was going to get caught. He turned to leave but stopped when he saw a beautiful carving of a dragon, its twisting body and tail covering the entire length of one wall. How had he missed it before? Each scale and claw were rendered with intricate detail and he recognized the creature instantly: Paz.

"Hello." The voice was cheerful, and welcoming, and made Toekin freeze in terror. *Slugs!* He spun around. The old man with the braided beard stood between him and the door at the other end of the room. He was trapped. He a made quick assessment: the windows were set high in the walls, near the top of the roofline. There was no way he could reach them. There were lots of doors along the wall opposite the Paz carving, but something told him they didn't lead out of this place.

"I see you've brought us some food. Thank you." His hood was pulled back now and Toekin could see his kind eyes set into a lined face that sparked with life every time he spoke or smiled. It should have calmed Toekin, but it had the opposite effect. His heart pounded in his ears. He couldn't be sure if his anxiety was from getting caught, or from another human actually speaking to him. He had to get out of here. *Now.*

The man stood slightly hunched and looked to be at least 80 summers. It would be a simple task getting past this artifact of a man. He tightened his grip on his satchel and took off for the door. He ducked to get around the bearded man, and he thought he'd made it. But, when he got to the door, the old man was there, waiting for him. Toekin backed up into a corner. This wasn't good. How had he moved so quickly?

"There's no need to be afraid. We are friends."

Toekin understood the word, "friends" but didn't know what it had to do with not being afraid. "Hide!" his mother had said, "hide!" He had to leave.

"You are welcome to stay or go. I'll not force you or anyone here against their will." He stepped out of the doorway and held his hand out in an invitation to exit.

Was it a trick?

"Of course. You're not sure you can trust me. I understand. Let me just give you some space." And just like that, the old man with the braided beard was gone. Vanished.

Toekin paused, confused and disoriented. What was this, magic?

"Don't worry. I'll just wait over here until you go."

He turned to find the old man sitting on the hearth, legs crossed and relaxed. How could anyone, but especially an old guy like him, move so quickly? Toekin surged forward, not pausing to worry about what he'd just seen, or not seen. He ran through the garden, almost running down a little girl with big brown eyes.

"Hey, who are you?" she said as he sped past. Then, turning to the others said, "Did you see that boy?"

He didn't stop running until he was well into the forest, off the main path, and tucked into the trees where he'd told his bird to stay. "They saw me, Corv." The crow hopped closer and put his head in Toekin's lap. "The old guy talked to me. I didn't know what to say." His heart was still pounding, his breath coming in short bursts. He ran his hand down the glossy feathers on Corvo's back, confused by the onset of panic.

"It's you and me Corvo. We only need each other, right? We're a team." He didn't belong at the orphanage. That was for kids who didn't have a home; who couldn't care for themselves. Not someone who had his own treehouse, could hunt and gather his own food and who was doing his part to redistribute the overzealous taxation of Emperor Beezul and his stinking thugs. Besides, those orphans certainly didn't need someone who was wanted by Abbadon, probably by the Emperor himself. Staying hidden was right. He knew that.

His heart slowed but was still pounding. "Let's get out of here, Corv." He stood up, grabbed his satchel and the remaining two bags of food. "I can't keep doing this all the time. I should just let people fend for themselves." Toekin grumbled as he made his way through the forest. Just one more obstacle to face and the rest of his journey home should be easy.

The Rio River cut the town of Favela in two, like a scar. Much of it passed through populated areas and had bridges covering the expanse, but Toekin was done dodging people today. He traveled out of his way to avoid human contact, to a spot in the river that was narrow and secluded, but also fast and dangerous. He would cross on foot.

Standing on the bank, Toekin picked out a route across some rocks. He'd crossed this spot before, but never holding two large sacks filled with food. The river was shallow, but it spat and roared as it rushed over the large boulders and smaller rocks. Any other time, a fall in the river would mean an icy inconvenience. But now, if he were to get tangled up with the heavy bags, a fall could mean death.

"See you on the other side," he shouted to Corvo, and turned his attention back to the river.

Boulders and smaller rocks created an almost continuous footpath across the river. He mapped his route, visualizing each step.

Toekin rocked back a step back, and then sprang forward.

His body moved forward with ease, but the heavy bags were a second behind, throwing their momentum into play as Toekin found footing on the edge of a wet rock. The swinging bags pushed him forward slightly, up onto his tiptoes, and he threw his arms out for balance, struggling to right himself before falling into the rushing water. Finally, he steadied himself, and let out a long breath he hadn't realized he was holding.

After adjusting his load, he timed the next jump better, working with the heavy bags, instead of against them. He landed softly on the next stone, crouching low and absorbing the weight on his shoulders. Most of the large rocks were close enough that he didn't need a running leap to close the distance between them, but just far enough that he still had to take things seriously.

He was almost across when he came to a rock covered in slippery moss and just a bit farther than he could comfortably leap. He eyed one spot free of moss and focused his attention there. It would be the safest place to land. But one false move and he'd be taking a bath.

He took a deep breath, reviewed the movement in his head once more and backed up. He took two running steps and launched himself over the rushing water. When his foot hit the rough, clean spot of rock, he relaxed and let the heavy bags finish their forward movement. He'd made it.

And then his foot slipped.

He jerked to keep himself upright, but the swinging bags threw him off balance. He struggled against gravity, valiantly at first, but the bags hanging off his shoulders swung around his arms into a tangled mess. Unable to loose himself from the dead weight he realized, with a touch of dread, that he was stuck with them.

Toekin sucked in a breath and braced himself, noting at the last moment the large rock just beneath the surface of the rushing water. He fell at an odd angle, his shoulder hitting hard, and then his head. All went black, except . . . he wasn't unconscious.

In the distance, he saw a light. He could neither look away nor keep himself from wanting to move toward it. He didn't think to wonder why his clothes were dry after his dunk in the river. He found his footing, and with every step he took, the pillar of brightness grew larger, like a blue flame rising to the heavens.

Urgency tightened his chest and he quickened his pace.

Soon he was close enough to see a dark silhouette within the blue blaze. It twisted and writhed, like a snake or . . . a dragon. As he approached, the dragon-like shape twisted again and Toekin focused on it, watching it curve and change form. He blinked, and it had become a person.

He took one step closer and the source of all the light and energy finally came into view. It was a girl.

Her eyes and mouth were closed as if she was asleep, and her skin shone with intense luminosity. Toekin was unable to pull his gaze away, transfixed by her beauty. Long, black hair hung straight and motionless, despite the surging force erupting skyward from her body. A line of freckles crossed her upper cheeks and nose, spotting her otherwise ethereal skin.

A thrum of unintelligible whispers surrounded him, hissing in his ears. Toekin felt an undeniable urge to save this girl—from what, he did not know. He took a step closer, and then another. One more and he would be within her wild aura.

He swallowed hard and took a long deliberate stride forward. As he stepped inside the blue wall of flames that encircled her, everything fell silent and warmth rushed over him. She remained still, at peace, and Toekin's mind filled with questions. What was she doing here? Who was she? How was he to get her out of here?

All at once the girl's eyes snapped open, beams of light bursting from them. Squinting against the brightness Toekin watched as her hair came to life, flowing and swirling with the power that emanated from her body. She looked straight at him and started to say something, and as her mouth opened, more light came pouring out. With unmistakable clarity, the words she spoke pierced his soul and sent shivers down his spine. "Save me!"

"Caw! Caw!"

Toekin swatted at his neck and shoulders. That noise! What was that wretched noise?

"Caw!"

Pain poured in upon Toekin and he cried out. He reached back to throttle whatever it was that refused to let him drift away and got a sharp jab to the hand.

"Caw!"

"Corvo?" he said, coming back to himself by degrees. "Slugs! What did you do to me?" He rolled onto his back despite stabs of agony and the wet sacks pinning him to the ground. Apparently, the bird had ripped through most of them to release Toekin from his bondage.

The crow stood right over him, beak to nose.

"I'm fine Corv," he finally said while trying to shoo him away with a few lazy fingers. "I'm not gonna die." He took a few deep breaths and tried to sit up, but the pain was excruciating. "What happened?" And then he remembered hitting the submerged rock with his head, but what hurt was his shoulders. He reached up to feel them and his hand came back sticky and wet with blood. He stared at it, then at the river, and then at Corvo's blood-covered toenails.

"You pulled me out of the river?"

The crow hopped a bit on his feet, then stepped toward him.

19

Toekin's mind was only able to guess at what it would have taken for his friend to pull him from the water, but the deep gashes in his shoulders gave him some idea. "You saved me."

Corvo pushed his head into Toekin's chest, nudging him before looking up with his bright, blue eyes.

"Thanks, buddy." He put his arm around the bird and pulled him close. "But you really did a number on me."

"Caw."

The bird's giant wings unfurled, and he dug his nails into Toekin's chest as he pushed off and hopped in a circle. He picked at his feathers, tucking them back into place, and then turned his blue eyes on Toekin as if waiting for an explanation.

"I had a weird dream," Toekin rubbed at his chest, easing the pain away while thinking of the breathtaking girl with light coming from her eyes, begging for his help.

"Caw!"

"It's not real. Nothing to worry about." That seemed to convince the giant crow, but deep down, Toekin wasn't sure. Everything had been so real and the girl, so desperate. But how was he supposed to help someone in a dream?

Toekin pulled himself up to sitting just in time to see one of the empty food bags dislodge from a fallen log and drift down the river, the flaming infinity sign face up for the whole world to see. Was it too much to hope that someone would fish it out of the river and burn it? Probably. Why did he bother helping these people?

"Slugs." Toekin let his arm drop from under him and he fell back to the ground. "Give me a few, Corv." He lay there adjusting plans in his throbbing head. Maybe he should take a break from the raids for a while . . . lay low; let the Abbadon Guards get a little more comfortable and less watchful. One thing was certain: he was done with his do-gooding for today. The pain in his shoulders was starting to ease a little and he turned his head to see Corvo laying strips of leaves across the open wounds for Toekin to use as bandages.

"Witch hazel?" Toekin said eyeing the oval greenery. "Smart bird." He pulled himself up and checked his satchel to make sure everything was still there, although all he really cared about were his scope and his sling. They were there, but he'd lost all his ammunition. He would need to gather more Seivo Sangue seeds on the way home.

Toekin folded the remaining Abbadon bags and shoved them in his satchel. A cold wind rustled the leaves on the ground and Toekin shivered in his soaked clothes. The dark clouds were almost on top of him. "Time to go."

Eager to beat the storm, he chose a shortcut that brought him within a stone's throw of the city. It was there he noticed the sign tacked to a tree. It was the pictures that first got his attention: the shining sun, bold moon and glittering stars. His education had been cut short, but he'd practiced reading from the one book he'd brought with him when he escaped—an exhaustive encyclopedia of animals his mother had painstakingly compiled from her own studies. He'd read it over and over, memorizing many of the pages.

On the sign, he recognized the words "Emperor Beezul," then picked out other words here and there until his understanding materialized. Beezul was looking for people with some kind of special powers. Did such people even exist? He thought about the old man at the orphanage. Could that explain why he was able to move so fast?

"Join the Army of Abbadon," the poster said. There was a picture of three people hanging from a gallows, eyes filled in with tiny x's. "Or suffer the consequences," the message finished. Toekin imagined an army of men that could move so fast you couldn't see them. They would be unstoppable.

"Caw!" Corvo called from the sky.

Toekin concealed himself and pulled out his scope. Far down the road a traveler plodded along, his beast laden with a mountain of bags. Probably just a merchant, he thought, stepping off the road. He picked his way through the underbrush until he was sure he wouldn't have to worry about seeing another person. It was then he felt the first drops of rain. Time to pick up the pace.

His injuries slowed him down only slightly and he ran through the forest, like a blur, heading toward his home. The rain was coming down steadily now and the winds howled, tossing small branches and leaves into his path.

Just as Toekin was about to enter the clearing, the place where he'd hidden the taxation cart with a block of cheese and sack of jerky from the morning's raid, he heard Corvo's warning. "Caw! Caw! Caw!"

One call was a warning, but three signaled retreat. Toekin stopped cold, but not before he saw what Corvo was squawking about. A full-sized ursmock was ripping into his sack of jerky, its claws tearing it to shreds, with what remained of his cheese spilling out of its gaping maw.

Toekin took slow steps backwards, careful not to make any noise that would turn the ursmock's attention his way. He was almost in the clear when the wind shifted, and the giant beast stopped and swung its head around, sniffing the air. The rain fell in sheets now, the long grey fur of the ursmock hanging like swamp moss, and the simian tail seeming to weigh heavier on the ground as it dragged through the mud. The creature leaped into the tree, digging its claws into the bark like a child digs fingers into soft clay. Then it spotted Toekin.

"Not good." He reached into his satchel and pulled out his sling, then into his pants for some ammo. Double not good. He had been so eager to grab his loot and get home, he'd forgotten to replenish his stock of Seivo seeds. He looked around on the ground and found three uneven rocks. They would have to do.

As he bent to pick them up, the ursmock jumped back down, rose up on its hind legs and let out a deafening roar.

Toekin loaded the sling and began swinging it in wide circles as his shoulders burned in pain. The monster dropped to all fours and roared one more time. Then it charged.

Fighting against the pain in his shoulder, Toekin steadied himself and took aim. He let the rock fly and it connected with the beast's shoulder, just short of the head shot he was going for. It barely slowed the lumbering pace of the animal and Toekin quickly loaded his sling again.

Corvo flew at the ursmock, diving talons-first and digging in about its back and neck. It was a valiant effort but had little effect.

As Toekin spun the sling, the pain was dizzying, but he focused all his energy into his next throw. If this one didn't fly true, it was all over. He released the sling, letting the stone fly. Immediately his arm and shoulder seized up in agony and he dropped to his knees, but his aim was true. The rock smashed the charging animal right between the eyes. Got him, Toekin thought to himself. The ursmock fell forward, plowing the dirt and vegetation in front of him until sliding to a stop in the middle of the opening.

Toekin breathed with relief. He had evaded death a second time today. He looked at the lump of fur lying close enough that he could smell its gamey musk mixed with the rotting flesh of other beasts it had devoured still lodged in the fur around its face. Then he thought he saw some movement. Had the rock not done the job? Before he could reach for his knife to finish the beast off, the thing had risen up again, full of unbridled fury.

Lightning struck nearby and Toekin was temporarily blinded. When the world around him came back into focus, he saw Corvo on the raging devil's back, his talons sunk into the flesh, ripping at the head and ears with his beak. The ursmock writhed and howled trying to free itself from Corvo's grip. It was a successful distraction, but nothing more. The massive beast dropped to the ground and began to roll. Corvo was big, but the ursmock was huge.

"Get off! He'll crush you!" Toekin yelled.

Just as the creature was about to flip onto its back, Corvo let go and made his escape. The ursmock rolled over, mud covered, with a thick stream of blood oozing down its face and looked directly at Toekin.

He loaded up his sling with the final rock and started spinning it. If this one didn't take the creature down, it was all over. This was his last chance. As the lumbering ursmock built up speed, so did Toekin's sling. But where should he aim? The rock to the head had only made it mad. Was there any killing this thing?

The ursmock leapt into the air, raising up a massive paw, swinging his finger-length claws into motion, and swiped downward at Toekin. Toekin took the only shot he could think of. He let the sling loose and watched as the black stone disappeared straight into its open mouth, striking deep into his throat. This threw the creature off, but not before his dagger-like claws raked down Toekin's chest, throwing him back several feet to the ground.

The ursmock stopped, stunned, and after a moment began choking and heaving, like a snow-cat coughing on a hairball that would never come up. It seemed to go on forever, this gradual suffocation. Finally, the beast's hacking slowed until it finally stopped and the ursmock collapsed to the forest floor.

Toekin lay on his side, propped up on his elbow. Blood puddled in the mud under him and his vision blurred when he saw it. His stomach buckled in pain and he glanced down at his chest, knowing he would immediately regret it. Four large open gashes stretched from shoulder to waist. A wave of nausea washed over him, and he coughed up blood. Corvo appeared with more witch hazel in his beak, but dropped it to the ground, seeming unsure where to start. It was bad.

Then Corvo did something Toekin had never heard him do before. He let out a long, piercing whine that sent a chill up his spine. Did he know something Toekin didn't?

He coughed again and tasted more blood in his mouth but knew if he was going to survive, he needed to get moving. He pulled off his hood, wadded it up and pressed it into his bleeding chest to try and staunch the flow, then pulled himself to standing and took one step. Then another. The rain was relentless, and his feet grew heavy with the buildup of caked mud.

Toekin walked on the main road, his mind slipping in and out of reality. Eventually the pain eased and was replaced with an overwhelming desire to sleep. He tried to lower himself to the ground. The soft mud would cradle him, and the wet leaves pillow his head. It looked so inviting.

"Caw!" Corvo swooped down and landed on Toekin's shoulder, bringing to mind an earlier injury that he couldn't quite remember the details of. The bird cawed and nipped at his ear until he finally gave up on the comfortable ground, deciding that somehow walking would be easier than dealing with that stupid bird.

As Favela came into view, a small surge of energy washed over him and his halting, unstable footsteps picked up slightly. He was close.

Toekin had never planned to be in this position: weak, vulnerable, and incapacitated. His pride and practicality warred with each other. He didn't need anyone else—could take care of himself. He always had, and he always would. Except for now, when he couldn't.

He stumbled forward toward the doors he'd run from only hours earlier, so close. We are friends, the old man had said. Was it true? Could he trust him? Did he have a choice? The questions exhausted him, and he wondered if he could close the last few lengths between him and the door. If not, would the orphans be troubled to find a dead body at their doorstep?

Just a few more steps . . .

He staggered, reaching for the knob, but missed and fell to the door with a heavy thud. The last thing he remembered was thinking he'd been right about the mud.

It felt wonderful.

CHAPTER 3

The Master

General Sem and his troops neared the city of Abbadon, carts loaded with the spoils of their raids. He'd called a halt to the procession just before entering the city so the men could pull themselves together for their victorious arrival. He ignored the moans coming from the caged wagons at the back of the column and instead focused on his soldiers.

"Full armor on everyone or you'll have me to answer to!" he barked, hitting a mug of ale out of the hand of one of the men as he made his inspection. "Fool! One more hour and you'll be sitting in the tavern ordering drinks on the house. Now is not the time. Dock his pay by half!" His eyes, black like marbles, darted to Captain Durman who nodded with acknowledgement.

"Durman." He said to his captain. "A word."

"Sir?"

The dark, leathery skin stretched across Sem's face, flattened his features and made it difficult to tell when he was relaxed and when he was about to swing a club at someone's head. He bent down and picked a mushroom from the ground and tossed it in his mouth, his black tongue darting out and licking the edges of his razor thin lips.

"Sir! Is that a . . . ." Durman's eyes were wide with fear.

"It's only a spotted shroom," Sem smiled. Or, at least he did what would have to pass for a smile. Durman recognized it and relaxed a bit. Shame more people didn't know how to tell the delicious fungus apart from its deadly doppelgänger. More for me, Sem thought.

The General swallowed and said, "The prisoners go to Nojento." Durman nodded. "I'll take them myself. I need you to see the troops to the barracks. It's been a tough month. They need a break. Get them all their pay and send them out to do as they will."

"Yes sir."

"And Durman. Give yourself an extra gold piece. Your service and loyalty have been . . ." Sem didn't finish, or couldn't.

"Sir?"

"Thank you. That is all." Sem stiffened and turned to face the capital, Abbadon. The setting sun bounced off the special steel used on doors, roofs and street signs, casting a purple glow. Its beauty was fickle and deceiving.

"Sir," Durman said, then adjusted. "Sem . . ." He tested the name as one would a cold stream with their bare toe. When his friend didn't object, he continued. "Why don't you come with me tonight. My sister can make her delicious meat pies; you can relax by the fire. You know my family has always liked you."

"Your offer is appreciated. I'll have to pass."

Durman gave Sem a look filled with memories and pain.

"We need to get going." Sem said. "We'll have the greatest impact if we arrive before sunset."

Durman lowered his head. "Yes, sir." If there was sorrow in his voice, Sem chose to ignore it. His captain turned and was gone. Sem returned his gaze to the city. The sun had shifted, and the once lovely glow had become cold and harsh, like a bruise. He jerked his head around, unable to look any longer and returned to his troops.

* * *

The steel rimmed wheels of their carts grated on the cobblestone streets of Abbadon, discordant and shrill, echoing off the walls of buildings that towered over the main thoroughfare. With six-dozen men and seven wagons, they were the spectacle they were meant to be. Shopkeepers stepped out of their shops as they passed, while citizens leaned out of their second and third story windows to shout insults and encouragement. It was unclear which was intended for Sem and his troops and which was intended for the wagon of ragged prisoners bringing up the rear.

Sem leaned his head toward Durman. "Provide some incentives."

"Incentives!" Durman shouted back, and immediately the armor-clad soldiers began tossing loaves of bread, bags of onions and carrots to the crowd. Sem saw long links of sausages fly through the air to a young lady in a low-cut dress hanging out of a second story window, and another handed a small cask of ale to a stunned shopkeeper, who took it greedily and ran back into his store, slamming the door behind him.

When overripe fruit and bad tomatoes landed on the street, many used them to pelt the passing prisoners—along with their cruel and filthy words.

The more the troops tossed food into the streets, the louder the chants for General Sem grew. Despite their seeming adoration, all gave him a wide berth as he passed, sometimes pressing themselves up against walls and slipping into alleys to avoid him. He knew he was a monster, but if fear was the citizen's way of showing respect, only the emperor was respected more in this town. Sem continually reminded himself that second to the emperor was not a bad place to be.

The crowds grew larger the farther into the city they marched, while the buildings gradually transformed from humble wood structures to impressive stone dwellings with statues and balconies. They were a testament to both the citizens' vanity and their knowledge that the closer they were to Beezul, both in proximity and alliance, the better off they'd be. Sem knew many of the residents of these buildings would disagree, but in his mind no splash of red geraniums out of a window box or shiny purple doorknocker could ever eclipse the beauty of the Seivo Salvador tree rising up in the northeast corner of the city.

The only thing taller than this five hundred-year-old giant was the emperor's palace—and that was not by accident. Beezul would have had it cut down long ago if the men he sent to do the task didn't keep getting themselves killed in steaming piles of hot sap. Of course, no tool or blade they used would easily cut through the scaly, black bark. The emperor finally gave up and added three extra floors to his towers so that everyone could be sure of whom they should bow to.

Still, the tree's silent majesty always left Sem in awe. There was one branch on the massive tree that was different from the others, growing upward instead of out. It was odd enough that people used to tell stories about it—that it was pointing toward heaven, or had some special meaning. Sem knew it was just one of those things but felt almost a brotherhood in the aberration. That there could be beauty yet in this branch that defied nature gave him hope.

They approached the moat separating the city from Beezul's compound. The dark, oily water was thick and stagnant. Rotting bird carcasses dotted the surface where the creatures had landed and become stuck in the mire. Sem had almost become used to the putrid smell and decided to ignore the troops who had to cover their mouths and noses with their hand to bear it.

"Banks! Scully! Stay with me. Captain Durman will see the rest of you to the barracks," he said. "I don't care what you do tonight, but if I don't see every one of you filthy rats at first bell tomorrow, I'll half your pay without thinking twice."

Durman nodded and peeled off with most of the company and five of the wagons, leaving the prisoners, Banks and Scully.

"Prepare the prisoners for Lord Nojento! Bring them along when you've finished." Sem strode off without waiting for a reply and mentally steeled himself for his meeting with the man who created him.

He entered the tower that was once his home. The spiral staircase that wound up the interior seemed to go on forever, but Nojento's lab was in the basement, a few floors down—too close for Sem, but probably just as far as the prisoners would be able to walk.

The door to Nojento's lab revealed everything one needed to know about the man. It was made from Abbadon steel that had been polished to an almost mirror finish. Purple filigree covered the door representing hours of forced labor. The only thing on the door that wasn't purple was the bright, silver doorknocker, a twisted human face captured in a moment of pure agony. Sem grabbed its lower jaw and knocked two times. A tiny hole opened up in the center of the door and a single eye peered through, before quickly disappearing.

Then the door opened, and a foul stench poured into the hallway. Sem tried not to think too hard about the smells. Identifying them would only make things harder. But before he could stop himself, he picked out the stench of burnt flesh and blood.

"Conk," he said with a quick nod acknowledging the lopsided hulk that let him in. Conk didn't nod back. He couldn't. His head, half of his face, and neck were covered in hardened, red, dragon's blood sap creating a permanent helmet, but rendering him motionless from the neck up. The sap continued down his back and half of his chest but left his arms free. Every breath was a struggle as his encased chest had little room to expand. Patches of sap covered his shins, thighs and parts of his arms creating a constant suit of armor—a gift from Nojento. A quick wheeze squeaked out as Conk lifted his disproportionate right arm, rippled with muscles and twice as big as his left, in a lazy greeting. Sem wondered if he didn't have the heavy mace he constantly carried in his left hand, if he would topple over.

In the corner another creature lurked. If Sem hadn't known him, it would have been hard to tell if he was man or an overgrown grindarr. Long brown fur covered his crouched body, sticking out like scarecrow straw under his Abbadon attire. His black nose pointed up and his nostrils flared as if he was picking out the source of an offensive smell.

Get a good whiff, you animal, Sem thought. His feud with the beast was nowhere near being settled.

Sem stayed well back from the creature. "Lobo," he said to him, a courtesy the barbarian barely deserved. Lobo's red eyes pulsed with energy and hate; his lips curled back revealing pointed fangs. A low, rumbling growl reminded Sem there were no alliances down here.

The room was filled with the stuff of nightmares: torture devices of every kind, one could only speculate their uses but thinking on the subject too long was not recommended. Vials and jars filled with strange liquids and embalmed body parts lined the walls. Nojento hovered over his exam table, his back to Sem. A human form lay before him and Sem could only guess whether it was dead or alive. Sem waited. He'd learned the hard way not to disturb the madman when he was in the middle of something.

"Just one more little sample, my dear," Nojento said, his voice a casual mock of the reality of the situation. He lowered his hand back in front of the body, his arm twitched and there was a muffled scream of agony.

So, it was alive, Sem deduced.

Nojento leaned his body forward, applying pressure to the human form, then jerked back, his right hand whipping toward the ceiling in an explosive movement. The struggling person stilled, gave a single cough, then fell silent. Blood dripped from the thing clamped in the tool held in Nojento's hand. A wave of revulsion washed through Sem.

As General, he had a reputation as a ruthless, cruel leader—quick to punish, slow to praise. But even he had his limits.

Nojento released the mass of flesh into a waiting jar, and then rolled the table over to an opening in the wall. Kicking a lever down below, the table tilted and the body slid, undignified, through the opening and out of sight. A low growl traveled up the chute followed by sounds of eager devouring.

"He loves it when they're still warm," Nojento said to no one in particular. "Conk, get over here and clean this mess up. You know I like to keep things neat and tidy." He spun around dramatically and saw Sem. "Darling! You're back!"

A spatter of blood bisected his hairless face at a disturbing angle, appearing black against his pale blue skin and cutting across his dark blue lips. He seemed unaware, or else he liked it there, as he made no effort to remove it.

Conk pushed a mop and bucket to the bloody walls and floor and began his slow, deliberate clean up. Without his mace the mop was not enough to balance him and he cleaned in ever narrowing circles that pulled to the right.

Nojento unbuttoned his blood-streaked lab coat and let it drop to the floor as he strode toward Sem.

Instinctively, Sem dropped to one knee and lowered his head. "Master."

"Oh, you!" Nojento extended a blue hand and trailed the backside across Sem's head and into his greasy hair. "I got it so right when I made you."

It was true. Sem was a result of Nojento's torture experiments, specifically designed to make him the ultimate warrior. Hand-selected for his natural gifts, Nojento looked with pride at the masterpiece he'd created. It was less complicated for Sem to feign gratitude in his master's presence than it was for him to confront the conflict of feelings he felt inside. He was a monster. He knew it, and no fawning by Nojento was ever going to change that.

"Arise," Nojento said, almost giggling, making light of the formality. At once his playfulness turned off like a switch and he lowered his voice to a whisper. "What do you have to report?"

Sem felt like a worm, wriggling on a hook. There was no way this was going to go well, but delaying the news would not help. "My search turned up nothing. I have no new information, my Lord."

Nojento said nothing for a moment while a vein on his forehead bulged and pulsed. His mouth turned down into a sneer of disgust and pure hatred as his eyes began turning red. Instability was his number one weapon and it could be deadly. Sweat beaded on Sem's brow and drops trickled down into his black featureless eyes.

Bang, bang! Echoes rattled around the room and Nojento's fiery attention turned to the door. He moved to Sem's side and lowered his head just inches from his face. "Expecting someone?" His voice was deep, angry and threatening.

"Yes, my Lord." Thank the sun! Just the distraction he needed. "I've brought prisoners in hopes you would forgive my failure. Some of them are even confirmed Zaints. Two of my men have brought them up."

It took a moment for this new information to register, but slowly Nojento seemed to relax, his burning red eyes cooling to a deep icy blue. "New test subjects? For me? Lobo, get the door, would you?"

Lobo, still crouched in the corner, lapping at a trail of blood that had trickled his way, looked up in irritation at the interruption. He had to obey. They all did.

"This is why I simply adore you, Sem." Nojento pulled back his lips revealing unnaturally white, overly large square teeth, and began using a long blue fingernail to pick between them, seeming to relish the bits he found. "Some said you were too young to work on, but they were wrong, weren't they my sweet? And look how you've turned out! Only seventeen. Who would ever guess?" So pleased was

32

he with himself, he skipped ahead of Lobo to be at the door when he opened it. "I'm that good, darling, aren't I. Made you look like a battle weary thirty-one-year-old and taught you a few tricks. Now you're Abbadon's greatest General."

Bang, bang!

"Lobo, please!" His eyes flashed red again, a warning. "I can not be answering my own door!"

Lobo ambled a little faster, his claws, not really meant for opening doors, scraping along the floor.

The light came back into Nojento's eyes and he returned his attention to Sem. "Such a transformation! My best yet." He glanced at Lobo and Conk with what might pass for regret. "Some might call me a genius, don't you think?"

There were lots of things people called Nojento, but genius was never one of them. "Yes, my Lord," Sem said as Lobo's claws tried to find purchase on the purple doorknob.

"Oh, Sem. Help him, would you? I can't wait to meet my new subjects!"

Sem obliged and the door swung open.

"Welcome, do come . . ." The words choked in Nojento's mouth when he saw who stood in the doorway.

Emperor Beezul.

CHAPTER 4

The Guests

Emperor Beezul's frame filled the doorway to the laboratory, his eyes dark with anger. Nojento, who had moments before, been filled with delight, seemed to shrink in both stature and demeanor. Sem took comfort in the scene, knowing there was at least one person who was able to subdue the maniac.

"What is the meaning of this?" Beezul's voice was hot and irritable. He waved his hand through the air, the enormous ruby on his finger catching the light and Sem's eye.

Nojento looked at the Emperor, his eyes flashing from blue to red and back again, and he bowed low to the ground. "Emperor Beezul. It is always a pleasure to see you."

Sem and Lobo knelt in respect while Conk fussed with the mop uncomfortably, unsure whether to take a break or continue cleaning.

Beezul's eyes narrowed in annoyance and he whipped around, walked back into the hallway and returned pulling a man by his hair. Muffled sobs and moans of pain escaped from under a large blindfold that extended past his chin. Beezul threw the man at Nojento's feet. "What is the meaning of this!" he repeated.

"Killing two birds with one stone," Nojento said, laughing at his own joke. "You know the work I do here. After I ask questions, I do my research. It saves having to round up more subjects."

Beezul was not amused. "So what information have you learned?"

Nojento stood a little taller. "Oh, there is so much I'm learning. I understand the limits of human pain. I've developed elixirs for strength and tonics of health . . ."

"Enough!" In fury, Beezul kicked the nearest thing his foot could make contact with, which, in this case, was Conk's mop bucket. "You know what I'm talking about, and it's not your deranged experiments."

Nojento looked hurt, but didn't press the Emperor. The prisoner on the floor moaned as bloody mop water started to seep into his ragged clothes.

"There is one thing that is more important than anything else. You know what that is, do you not?"

Nojento dropped his voice and said soft and clear, "the relic, Emperor."

"If the relic of Paz falls into the wrong hands, all will be lost." Nojento seemed to shrink at this reminder. "Your pathetic body modifications and artificial enhancements will be worthless." Beezul spit the word 'pathetic' out with disgust as he swept his eyes past Sem, Conk and Lobo. "You haven't turned up a single lead for six years. I fear I've left you unsupervised for too long; a mistake I need to rectify."

"My Lord! I am doing everything in my power to search the far corners of Enganoso." His words trailed off, weak and unsure.

"Everything?"

The question was simple, but the answer was not. Nojento squirmed, looking for the right words, but failed.

"You call this everything?" Beezul said, pointing a stiff finger at the quivering man at his feet. He grabbed the lump by its hair and pulled it up to standing. "This is your plan? To get information about the relic from this trembling fool and the others waiting in the hallway?" His words carried venom, filled with anger that matched the purple color that began blazing from his eyes.

"Well . . ." Nojento started.

"Silence!" He twisted the hair of the prisoner so that he could see his blindfolded face. "Prisoner, where is the relic of Paz?"

The man squirmed in his grip, and from behind the black rag covering his face, faint muffled sobs and groans emerged. Nojento raised a finger as if to interject, but one look from Beezul shut him up.

"I'll ask again," Beezul said with mock patience, placing a hand on the man's shoulder. "Where is the relic of Paz?"

The man shook his head and moaned.

The Emperor's hand gripped the prisoner's shoulder with more force and began to glow. A muffled scream emerged from beneath the blindfold. "I'll ask once more, and this time, I recommend you use words." Even as the Emperor spoke, the man was shaking his head. "Where is the relic of Paz!"

His head shook violently now, but no words came.

"Fool!" the Emperor shouted and the purple glow around his hand erupted into bright energy as he gripped the man's shoulder. The sound of bones grinding on bones overtook the man's stifled screams. Beezul released his grip and the prisoner crumpled to the floor.

The purple faded away from his eyes and hand and he settled into an eerie calm. He looked at Nojento but spoke to the heap on the ground. "To withhold what you know from the Emperor is treason, punishable by death." He wasn't here to get information. He was here to make a point—to punish Nojento. "Remove his blindfold."

Nojento reached down and untied the cloth coving his face. Tears flowed from puffy eyes, filled with fear. There was pleading in them as he groaned through lips, sewn together with thick white thread. Blood oozed from the fresh stitches, trickling down his chin.

Beezul glared at Nojento.

"I tried to tell you, my Lord, but . . ."

Purple light quickly consumed the Emperor, then exploded outward in waves. Neatly hung tools and instruments swayed on their hooks while jars and vials lining the shelves shattered in place. All but two of the torches lining the walls were extinguished, and they were left in a dim, orange light augmented by the sustained energy pulsating from Beezul.

Nojento cringed, looking from his destroyed laboratory, back to Beezul as if trying to decide between the warring emotions of horror and fear.

"Explain yourself."

"Well, my Lord," Nojento stuttered, clearly having settled on fear, "everything I do here . . . it's for you. The soldiers you've put under my command search endlessly throughout the land for any clue that would lead us to the relic. They are working tirelessly. But . . ." His eyes fell to the man on the floor as he chose his words. ". . . as you know, much more goes on here than simple interrogation." Nojento's confidence grew as he spoke. "Once we've questioned them about the relic, we cannot simply let them go. Rumors would spread; interest in the relic would grow. Someone might find it before we do."

Hate and anger continued to pour off Beezul in waves, but Nojento went on. He threw his arm out toward Sem, Lobo and Conk. "These men are ten, no . . . one hundred times more powerful than the common man. They are byproducts of your grace, my Lord. They are what will help us find the relic of Paz."

The Emperor showed no signs of being convinced or impressed.

"If, for some reason, we don't find the relic," Nojento shrunk as he spoke, as if expecting a blow from Beezul, "the powers I'm experimenting with, they too can be yours. As you know, my work extends beyond this lab to the isles of Normann Uaihm. Our research is paying off. Soon we will have a prototype for you— something spectacular. I know you will be pleased, Lord."

The waves of power blasted off Beezul causing Nojento to be pushed back, faltering, nearly falling to the floor. "You've been promising me results for years with nothing to show for it. For all I know I'm funding more of your demented perversions."

Nojento righted himself and focused his gaze more intently on the Emperor. "With this new invention, you will be unstoppable. Trust me. You will be the most powerful ruler anywhere." Nojento's eyes, which had begun flickering red and blue again seemed to have the desired, calming effect on the Emperor.

"And the matter of the little civil war we started among the Normanni will soon yield more recruits for our army than you can imagine."

"Of course we will continue searching for the relic. But in the meantime, I can build you the most powerful army in the world."

Beezul seemed momentarily dazed. He closed his eyes and shook his head. When he opened them, Nojento's eyes had settled back to steady blue. He shifted his attention to Sem who'd been enjoying this exchange from a safe distance. "You," he said, "General Sem." A sneer sat on his face like a snake, making clear his distaste for his modified state—as if he were less than human because of it. "What do you have to report? Have we suffered any more petty ambushes?"

"We've lost another taxation cart. Once again, it's simply vanished. Not a splinter of wood or morsel of food or hair of a guard's greasy head left behind. Vanished entirely." Sem stood firm. He'd learned the best way to deal with Beezul was to show no fear. It seemed to work.

"The loss of life and supplies are nothing to me. A small drop we can afford to sacrifice. These rebels might think they're hurting us, but they're not." When he mentioned the rebels, Beezul's fury began to flare. "But these nothing victories are something to them." The glow began to return, pulsing. But Sem stood firm. "Every successful ambush emboldens them, makes them stronger. Kimnar's rebels are weeds. Cutting them down is useless. They just come back stronger and more determined to take back my city for their weak king. They need to be pulled out by the root if they are to be stopped." Beezul's rage grew visibly as the purple glow intensified. "They will be stopped!"

Just then, with a bang and a flash of blue light, the door to Nojento's lab burst open and a dozen men and women rushed in. Sem recognized many of them as the prisoners he'd brought back from his campaign. Several vanished and reappeared around the room, leaving trails of golden light in their wake, while others became consumed in blue, white and yellow. Two rushed forward with swords they must have taken from their captors, their weapons taking on the glow of their bodies. They fell upon Beezul with a clasp like thunder, knocking him and Nojento to the ground.

Another, a Sun Slinger, was already at Conk. She stayed in his blind spot while he tried to wave her off like a bee, but she moved in blinks, her fists a blur of golden spray. Still, several others had cornered Lobo in a haze of clashing light. These Zaints were powerful. And they'd snuck their way into the Emperor's tower on his wagon of prisoners. This had been planned.

Nojento slunk back, away from the scene unfolding and watched with amusement.

Sem faded into darkness, invisible now to what was obviously Kimnar Rebels, and rushed over to Conk. The woman had slowed her assault, but the yellow light blanketing her fists was now larger and packed a crunch with each blow.

Sem pulled from inside and sent darkness hurtling outward like a black lightning bolt. The glowing light around the woman dried up and she took two steps back, now clutching her throat. Sem didn't relent until the woman dropped to the ground, dead. "Conk!" He grabbed the mace that had fallen to the floor with two hands and tossed it to him. "Go! Now!"

Conk snatched it out of the air and snapped to life, blue flames engulfed his body as he began swinging his mace wildly. Sem glided out of the way, reappearing in the corner by Lobo, just as the weapon came down on two of the rebels, taking them both out at the same time. Lobo had gotten the better of his attackers and was just digging into the meaty leg of one, collapsed on the floor in front of him. "Save the feast for later, you oversized rat." Sem said.

Lobo growled, pulled the body to the corner of the room, and then bounded out into the fray.

Sem turned to find five rebels surrounding Beezul, the two with swords swinging and stabbing, the others throwing blasts of fire and different colored light at him. Clad in a purple aura, Beezul, who hadn't even drawn his sword, looked almost bored as he dodged and deflected their blades. Finally, he redirected an incoming stream of fiery light, throwing the swordsmen and one other assailant into the wall where they fell into a crumpled pile, smoke rising from their chests.

"Don't kill them all," Nojento wailed. "Leave some for research . . . and questioning!"

The rebels brought the power of the sun, the moon and the stars in force, but it was a suicide mission from the start. Conk's mace continued to swing, destroying the few remaining parts of Nojento's lab that hadn't already been torn apart by Beezul.

Sem moved about the room unseen, using his dark powers to bore panic and fear into the minds of his enemies until they collapsed on the floor, when suddenly, he was hit in the face with a blinding light. How had he been detected? Before his eyesight could return, surge after surge of something slammed into him, knocking him to the floor. And then he felt it—someone's presence was clawing into his mind. As his vision cleared, he felt a foot come down on his chest and a hideous face materialized into view, eyes wild, a shoulder slumped, lips stitched closed and still dripping blood. Impossible. It was the first prisoner Beezul had drug in.

White light poured from the man's eyes. Sem yelled out and grabbed at his head. He could feel the stitched man's hate for Beezul as he pushed through his memories. Silver energy gathered around his clenched fist and he raised it, ready to deliver a devastating blow, but then he stopped. The hate faltered, and for a moment Sem thought he heard voices, like a distant memory. The glow around the enemy's hands fizzled and his eyes softened. Recognition flashed there. But recognition of what? Before Sem could explore this further, a giant beast jumped on the rebel's back and tore into his neck with powerful jaws.

"Alive, please," Nojento chirped. Lobo swung his head toward Nojento with a black look. "If you can," he added, with more humility, shrinking back into the shadows.

Sem rolled over and pulled himself up to his knees. The melee was under control, but there was still one fool who wouldn't give up, hurling shards of light over and over at Beezul like a bird repeatedly flying into a windowpane. His strength was waning, and it was only a matter of time before Beezul dealt the killing blow. Lobo wore a path in the floor, licking his lips and waiting to jump on the human at the Emperor's word. Conk too, stood by, mace at the ready.

The man seemed almost out of energy when he suddenly started to glow. His aura changed, burning bright, like a sapphire catching the sunlight, and swelled upward until it resembled a waterfall that filled room. From the ceiling it crashed downward, its pressure bringing Sem, Lobo and Conk to their knees, but the Emperor stood unaffected as it splashed off his violet radiance.

Sem gritted his teeth, trying to stand, but it was as if the weight of the world was pressing down on him. What is this aura?

40

With this fresh power, the man channeled his light into a large maul and ran straight for his target. Sem's eyes widened. A weapon of light? He'd never known such a thing was even possible. His maul met the Emperor's defenses, and Beezul was pushed back, but remained upright. He looked at the rebel in shock and for the first time drew his sword.

At that moment, a black cloud appeared just outside the room and grew larger until it extended nearly floor to ceiling. A dark red void appeared at its core, and the sorceress, Jade, emerged from it and entered the room. It was enough to momentarily distract the attacker, but with a final push that must have sapped all that he had, he charged straight for Beezul.

The Emperor seemed to relax and when the man took his final lunge forward, a dark red opening appeared out of thin air in front of him, greeting him with consuming flames. There was no way to avoid it, and it was too late to stop. He cried out as he caught fire, then disappeared through the portal, reemerging with his screams of agony on the other side of the room and falling face first and charred at Jade's feet. In one swift movement the sorceress silenced him by swinging her blade in an upward arc across the backside of his neck. She snapped her long, slender sword down, dispatching the blood of her blade to the floor, then returned it to its sheath.

"Hello, my Emperor," she said, surveying the scene in the room. Nojento rushed forward, wedging himself between the woman and Beezul.

"Empress Jade," Nojento said, his lips pulled down.

Jade ignored him and focused on Beezul. "Having fun, are you?" she said. Her long black robes trailed behind her as she stepped over bone saws and bodies. She fiddled with the gem nested in the top of her staff while taking in the carnage. The only thing redder than that impressive jewel was her hair, which fell past her shoulders to the middle of her back. Finally satisfied she turned her attention back to the Emperor. "Do I dare ask?"

"General Sem, where did you get these . . . prisoners." Beezul said not bothering to answer Jade.

"Triste, my Lord."

"Take the hairy one with you and go immediately back to Triste. See if you can root out the whereabouts of our friend Kimnar and his little band of rebels. And while you're there, look for any sign of the missing taxation carts."

"Yes, my Lord." Sem bowed his head.

"One more thing." Beezul set his jaw. "Find. The. Relic!" He pounded his fist on the wall leaving a hole in the stone.

"I will do all in my power," Sem replied.

Jade rolled her eyes and tapped her foot.

"Lord," Nojento said. "It was clear in today's skirmish that Kimnar's rebels don't have the relic. This is good news. It's still out there. We shall be the ones to find it."

Emperor Beezul paused at that, trying to hide his intrigue.

"Think about it. Killing you would be their ultimate accomplishment. If they'd had it, they would have used it today."

Jade shook her head. "Not necessarily. The may have it, but yet lack a Zaintozo to wield it."

Nojento shot Jade a dark look and was about to say something but he was cut short with a flicker of Beezul's gaze.

"Forgive him my Lord," Jade said. "As vexing as he may be, he does have his purposes." Reaching out, she caressed Nojento's cheek. "Although he'd be wise to remember the only Zaintozo that matters, is the one we serve." After a light slap, she turned away and used her staff to pick over bodies as she made her way back to the portal still open in the hallway. Whimpers were heard as a few of the rebels who hadn't been killed resurfaced to a terrible consciousness. Nojento tented his fingers to his lips and grinned.

"Lord Beezul. I have an important, private matter to discuss with you. Surely you will come with me." She held her hand to the portal and Beezul nodded moving toward the red vortex in the black, swirling cloud.

"General Sem," he said, just before stepping through, "I want this trip to be quick. Find out what you can and get back here. And don't fail me."

CHAPTER 5

The Evidence

Toekin opened his eyes to darkness and confusion. Where was he? He scanned the solid blackness, straining for anything that might clue him to his surroundings. And then he saw it. It was faint, but it was there. The blue light. He began moving toward it, slowly at first, then much faster.

Please let her still be there, he thought, closing the distance in a flash. As he approached he could see the dragon, twisting and moving within the light. Despite its familiarity, which he couldn't quite pinpoint, his heart sank a little.

"What did you do with the girl?" He spoke the words, but no sound came out. Still, the dragon seemed to understand; it wriggled and bent before his eyes. Then the girl was there, standing but asleep. He felt a burst of warmth in his chest. She was just as he had remembered. Her long dark hair hung straight at her sides and her skin was pale and smooth.

The blue light surrounding her pulsed and hummed with a power that almost seemed to repel him, but its warmth was inviting, and he longed to be within its embrace. He knew what to do. He pushed forward, reaching out for the energy.

"Save me," she had said, and he wanted to. Oh, how he wanted to. But how? Wasn't this just a dream?

There was something about this girl that made him want to get to know everything about her; to hold her hand and look into her eyes and count the freckles that dotted her cheeks. What was her name? Why was she here?

Finally, he was close enough. His hand reached through the blue. Gentle warmth crept up his arm, drawing him forward. At once he was inside, unsure whether the blue aura had reached out to enfold him, or if he had striven forward to be within it.

The girl stood still, eyes closed, lips soft and relaxed. She wore a simple, white dress, unadorned with button or ties, like something she'd sleep in. He wanted to wake her, to talk to her, but she looked so peaceful, disturbing her seemed cruel. He didn't mind just watching her. Not at all.

Without thought, he reached forward and took her hand in his. It was soft and warm, like pressing his palm against the warm wood of his Seivo Sangue tree, and he felt like his heart might explode. Light poured out as her eyes fluttered open and when she saw him, she smiled, then spoke. "At last. You're here." She said.

Before Toekin could even ask where here was, her hand slipped from his. The loss of her touch was like a punch to the chest and he winced at the pain. She began to rise from the ground into the blue light that seemed to go on forever. The higher she got, the sharper the pain to his chest became, until it was unbearable and she was undetectable in the abyss.

The feeling was more than he could bear and he cried out in distress. Then for a second time, he opened his eyes.

He woke in a dark, windowless room. A single oil lamp burned in the corner, casting a dim light that barely illuminated log walls and a small table. He tried to sit up but the pain ripped into him.

Where am I? He wracked his brain trying to pull up any memory that would put things in context and make sense of the scene. The log walls did seem strangely familiar. Think, Toekin.

There'd been the ambush, hiding the evidence, a picture slammed into his brain of Corvo devouring an apple, bits of fruit and juice flying in a joyful display. The food deliveries! Then his thoughts darkened. The fall in the river. His shoulders ripped to bits from Corvo's life-saving talons. Then the heart stopping realization that Corvo wasn't with him.

To be sure, he called out. "Corv? You here?" There was no reply. Slugs, slugs, slugs! This wasn't good. He returned to his thoughts, the trip home and then . . . yes, that was it . . . the ursmock. He placed a hand gently on his chest and felt firmly wrapped bandages. Yes. That was it, indeed. He lay back. Someone had found him and helped him. But who?

It returned in flashes, his push to reach the one place he thought he could get help. The orphanage. That was where he was. He looked around the room and the log walls seemed to close in on him. He had to find Corvo and leave, now. His bag was hung on the back of the door. He hoped everything was still there. Sitting up would be the hardest part. If he could just do that, he was certain he could walk out of here.

He clenched his jaw against the coming pain, counted to three and pulled himself to sitting. He wanted to scream as he felt a rip in his chest and his bandages became warm and wet. But he was up. He swung his legs over the side of the bed and rested for his next move. After a few breaths, he stood and took some careful steps. He reached his bag, checked for his scope and other things. All was as it should be. That was good. He wouldn't have to return and tear this place apart later.

He took his time opening the door. He wasn't sure what he'd find on the other side, not that it mattered. There was no other way out of this room, and he wasn't staying. It moved easily, the hinges well oiled, then it started to move on its own. Someone was pulling from the other side, and suddenly there was a small girl with wide brown eyes standing in front of him. She looked like she was seeing a ghost. "You're up." She said, her voice dripping with awe. "You shouldn't be up."

Toekin didn't bother replying, but he didn't need to. She turned on her heels and ran off, tripped over something on the floor Toekin couldn't see, then righted herself and continued in a streak across the room. He looked up, right into the wood carving of Paz. So it was the orphanage. The tables and benches stretched out before him, a few glowing embers were all that remained in the fireplace at one end, the door, his escape, waiting for him at the other. He took a step forward, ignoring the stabbing pain in his chest.

"What do you think you are doing?" Another girl, older and taller stood with her hands on her hips, while the younger one peeked out from behind. "And look, you've opened your wounds." She strode across the room toward him, tying a black robe over what must have been a nightgown. "Honestly!"

Toekin had faced down an ursmock, surely he could handle this girl.

"Let me help you back into bed," she said. When she reached him her hand flew to his butchered shoulder.

"Don't touch me!" He said.

"I've been tending to your shoulders." Her eyes flashed, as if stunned anyone would defy her. "They shouldn't hurt that much anymore."

"I'm leaving." Years of having only a crow to talk to had not left Toekin with the best communication skills.

The little girl's brown eyes got big and she ducked her head as she looked up at the older one, taking a few cautious steps away.

"Excuse me? I didn't just spend the last three days bringing you back from the dead to have you walk out of here and die." She planted herself in front of Toekin to block any attempt to escape. "You still have at least a couple more days of healing. Then you can do whatever you want. Now get back in there." She stuck her arm out, rigid, finger pointing to the bed.

The little girl was nodding and pleading with her eyes for him to obey.

"You can't keep me here." He knew she could, and it wouldn't take much. The little girl could probably do it with her pinky. Still, he didn't want to let on that this was the case. If she would just step aside, he could stagger out of there. But she wasn't moving. Still, Toekin had to try. He ducked around her, twisting his torso. The pain was excruciating, and the burning made his vision fade. He took one step toward the door and collapsed, his body finally making the call his stubborn mind refused to accept.

"Tessa, go get a fresh set of dressings." The taller girl said to the smaller one.

"I ought to let you just lay there." She looked at him with thinly veiled disgust.

"I can get up on my own," he said, but it came out in a slur.

"You've reopened your wounds. I'm going to have to redo all the dressings now." She paced back and forth while waiting, glancing down at Toekin every time she passed him. "Did that beast claw your brain too? Because trying to leave right now was completely stupid."

Who was this girl and who put her in charge of him? Where was the guy with the long beard? And why was everything getting so dark? So . . . dark . . .

* * *

When he next opened his eyes, the taller girl was standing over him, the smaller one watching from a corner. The taller girl's eyes were closed in concentration, blue light radiating from her hands pressed lightly into his chest. The strange thing was, it didn't hurt. It felt good. Really good. For a moment, he wondered if he were dreaming again.

Was this some kind of magic? It felt good now, but what if she was putting some kind of spell on him to make him stay? He wasn't quite ready to protest, enjoying a little more of the warmth that spread through his body. Then he saw a cage in the corner of the room and Corvo shoved inside with barely enough room to turn around.

"Hey!" He said, trying to sit up instinctively. "My bird! Let him out!"

At the sound of Toekin's voice, Corvo perked up. His wings were pinned to his side, but he shifted from foot to foot, which was about all the movement he could make in the small cage. This was torture. How dare they!

The tall girl dropped her hands and stepped back from Toekin as if she'd been caught doing something she wasn't supposed to; or that maybe she wasn't supposed to be seen doing. He tried to sit up, but the girl stopped him. "Please. Don't do that. You'll only hurt yourself."

"He doesn't belong in a cage," And neither do I, he thought.

"I need to change those bandages. Then we can let him out." She was firm and when Toekin looked down at his current dressing, blood soaked and starting to stiffen, he gave up.

"Fine. But I'm getting out of here as soon as I can."

47

"You can go whenever you want," she said gently pulling the bandages away from his chest. "Espero keeps no one here against their will."

"Who's Espero?"

"He takes care of us—teaches us."

Toekin thought of the old guy with the long braided beard that had seemed to disappear and reappear. "Why isn't he here instead of you?" He immediately regretted the phrasing.

The little girl, Tessa, stifled a giggle and the taller one paused and let out a frustrated breath of air. When she resumed removing the bandages, she did so with a little more gusto. "Trust me. I'd rather not be here, but Espero and Força left me in charge."

"And she's the only one that knows how to heal . . ."

"Heal-p people like you." The taller one shot a quick glance at Tessa, but Toekin didn't pay it much attention.

Instead, he felt the sting of remorse, along with the sting of stiff bandages being yanked from his tender skin. The girl now worked with a dispassionate efficiency. The thought of apologizing crossed his mind, if nothing more than to get her to go easier on the bandage removal. But he wasn't sure what to say so he gritted his teeth and tried not to grunt in pain.

"Hand me some clean bandages," she said as she cleaned his wounds with water that was conveniently on the cold side. She seemed to take pleasure in his discomfort. Tessa jumped up and grabbed a stack of greenish strips from the table and handed them to the girl.

"Can I help?" she said. "Força says I'm ready to start learning."

"Why don't you just hand me the bandages for now." She said, smiling down at the girl who nodded and tried to hide her disappointment.

She worked in silence. Toekin didn't dare say anything else.

He couldn't remember the last time he'd been touched by another person. It was both discomfiting and strangely pleasant. As the girl wound the pine-scented strips around his torso, he struggled to know which emotion he should focus on. He looked at the girl working with confidence and determination. She knew what she was doing, and she was good at it. Also, she wasn't hard to look at. He decided to relax.

As she worked, Toekin's thoughts drifted to the girl in his dream, bathed in a column of blue light. If he hadn't imagined it, it seemed similar to what this girl had done—felt similar to what it had been like in his dream: the warmth, the power, the overall feeling peace and contentment. Was it connected? "At last. You're here," she had said.

When she finished, she put the dirty rags in her basin and began to tidy up. "Tessa," she said, "do you think you can do it?" She inclined her head toward Corvo.

Tessa nodded, a big grin on her face, eager to finally help, and skipped over to the cage. She stopped short, as if second-guessing her enthusiasm, as Corvo hissed. Steeling herself, she reached forward to undo the latch, keeping her body as far away from the cage as possible. The door sprang open and Corvo wedged himself out the opening and was at Toekin's side in an instant.

"Here's a little porridge," the tall girl said, with a bowl in her hand. "You're probably hungry. It's been about four days since you've had a proper meal." As she approached the bedside, Corvo spread his wings and hopped forward, hissing.

"Corvo!" Toekin said.

The girl retreated into a corner, her confident façade replaced by a look of fear and caution. "You hand it to him," she said, pushing the bowl toward Tessa. "I'm tired of being attacked for just trying to help." She gathered her things and made a quick exit before Toekin could say anything.

"He wouldn't let her help you." Tessa said, handing him the bowl of grey mush and a spoon while keeping a nervous eye on Corvo. "Anytime one of us tried to get near you, he would do that." She nodded to Corvo who was still spread eagle, beak wide and ready to attack. "We had to put him in a cage or you would have died. If we'd had a bigger one, we would have used it." She seemed sincere.

"Your name's Tessa?"

She nodded as she covered an escaping yawn.

"Thank you, Tessa." Her smile warmed a place in Toekin's heart that hadn't felt warm in a long time. "Tell your friend . . ."

"Sister."

"Tell your sister . . ."

"Her name's Lua."

Toekin managed a weak smile. "Tell Lua thank you, too. I didn't mean to be ungrateful. It's just that I need to get home. You know?"

Tessa nodded. "Are your parents going to be worried?" Her brow furrowed with concern.

Toekin hesitated. "My parents were taken away by Abbadon Guards a long time ago. I'm all by myself."

Tessa's face dropped, and her eyes turned red. Was she going to cry? She stepped forward and laid herself carefully across Toekin and gave him a gentle hug. It was sweet and filled with innocence and love. To be honest, it also hurt like crazy. But he wasn't about to let Tessa know it. And then it was over. She stepped back and without saying a word, turned and ran out the door.

The feeling lingered, though. It felt like every part of his insides was warm and safe, and for the first time since he'd woken up in this place, or maybe the first time in a very long time, he felt . . . well, he didn't know. But he liked it. "What do you think about that, Corv?"

The giant bird hopped off his perch at the foot of the bed and picked his way across the blanket. He sat down next to Toekin and tucked his head under Toekin's chin. The quick thrum of Corvo's heartbeat calmed him even more.

"I'm going to be okay, buddy. Couple more days and then we'll go home."

* * *

He woke to Corvo nudging his arm. "Let me sleep" he groaned. Then he heard why the bird was trying to wake him. Someone was knocking at his door. "Come in," his voice cracked.

He was expecting to see Lua and Tessa again, but instead was greeted by the old man with the beard. What was his name again?

"Good Morning. How are you feeling?" His voice was bright and melodic and filled with optimism.

"Better." Toekin tried to sit up, but grimaced when he felt stabbing pressure on his wounds. "I think," he amended.

"Don't get up. Rest."

Corvo jumped on to Toekin's prone body and went into defense mode as the old man approached. "Caw!" He flapped his massive wings, snapped his beak and hissed. The bird did not hold back.

"Corv! Knock it off."

"Well hello to you too," the old man said. His voice should have been filled with fear, but it sounded pleasantly amused. "How long has it been since you've eaten?" He reached into the pocket of his long, black robe and pulled out an apple.

Corvo's wings retracted and the hissing stopped. He tilted his head, and then began hopping in the direction to where the old man held the apple. "Ouch. Easy!" Toekin said as the crow bounded down past the worst of his wounds.

"Why don't you eat it down here," he said, placing it on the floor. Then turning to Toekin said, "I'm Espero, in case the girls didn't mention it. I believe we've met before."

There was a twinkle in his eye and despite its friendliness, Toekin found it annoying. He was still sore about getting caught. "Yeah, that was me," he admitted. "Name's Toekin."

"Well, I'm not sure where you were able to get so much food," he paused and gave Toekin a look that said he knew exactly where he'd gotten it. "But I thank you for your kindness. We have had many winters where we've had to ration. This, thank the sun, will not be one of them. Our gardens produced bountifully."

Toekin thought back to his drop off just a few days ago, including the Abbadon Guard ambush that resulted in the big haul. The cart! The last piece of evidence that might tie him to the attack was sitting in plain sight at the edge of Mato Forest. He had to get rid of it.

Espero must have seen the fear flash across his face because his voice turned to one of concern.

"As Lua told you, you're welcome to go as soon as you feel ready. But you're also welcome to stay, if you'd like to. I think you'll find we have a lot we could offer you. You could hone your skills here."

Toekin had no idea what the old man was talking about. He could hone his skills just fine living in his tree. But not if he were going to be hunted down and killed by Abbadon Guards. "Actually, I just remembered something I need to do. It's important. I need to leave as soon as possible."

"Is it something to do with your food deliveries?"

Who was this guy? And how did he know?

"I just have to go, okay?"

"Certainly. Let me help you get ready." The tone of his voice reminded him of the time he told his mom he was running away from home, and she helped him pack. But this time he was really going. He had to.

Corvo, the traitor, was still working on his apple, trying to pick up every last morsel with his beak. Espero reached out and helped Toekin sit on the edge of the bed. He looked down at his bare chest, covered only in bandages. "Can I get my shirt?"

"It was in shreds. Beyond repair I'm afraid." Espero seemed sorry to be the one to share the news, but then perked up. "I'll have something brought." He opened the door and Tessa fell into the room with the grace of a newborn wood deer learning to walk. "Oh, Tessa. Just who I was looking for. Our friend here needs a shirt. Run and get an extra." He turned back to Toekin. "I had a feeling she'd be close by." He winked.

It didn't matter how friendly this guy was being. Toekin wasn't staying. He might not have had parents around for the last six years, but he remembered their tricks.

"Here's your bag," he said, unhooking it from the back of the door and passing it to Toekin. A quick search revealed everything was still where it was supposed to be.

Toekin stood and took a few steps. He felt better than last night, but still, each step was painful. He moved slowly across the room.

"Here," Espero said, beckoning Toekin to come toward him. "If you'll allow me, I'll teach you a way to ease some of that pain."

His smile was genuine, but it could still be a trap. Toekin hesitated.

"Okay." He backed up a wooden chair and sat, hoping that Espero would think it had something to do with his willingness, when really he was ready to collapse.

Toekin tensed when Espero moved behind him, but it was too painful to turn and look.

"Now take the deepest breath you're able to. Imagine breathing in health."

Toekin did as instructed, except the imagining part. He stopped well short of his lung capacity, not willing to risk tearing anything. There was a light touch on his back and immediately warmth pulsed into him, bringing strength and vitality. The stabbing pain eased into a mere tightness and for the first time in days, Toekin breathed in even more deeply. Espero continued doing whatever he was doing up his torso and onto his shoulders.

"Now let out your breath, slowly. Imagine letting out all the bad."

The feeling persisted, and Toekin started to think he could do anything. He followed the old man's instructions again, even the imagining part this time. There was a knock at the door.

"Espero? I brought a shirt." Tessa poked her head in and Espero broke off contact and the warmth faded from Toekin's insides. When Espero came into view he looked exhausted and about five years older.

"Are you okay?"

"Fine, son. Just fine." Something about the word, "son," pricked Toekin's heart. He pushed it aside. He didn't have time for these feelings. It had already been three days. Or had it been four? The cart may already have been found. He had to find out.

"The power of breathing." Espero winked. "Come in, Tessa. Thank you." He took the shirt and held it up in front of Toekin. "This should do," he smiled, but there was weariness to it.

Toekin pulled it over his head. "Come on Corvo. We need to get going."

"I'll walk you out," Espero said.

Tessa looked up at him in confusion and disappointment as he passed her, exiting the room. He turned away from her and focused on walking. He was still moving slowly, but the change was remarkable. No way it was the breathing, right? What had this guy done to him? And why couldn't he have done that from the start?

He stepped out into the main room full of kids of all ages finishing breakfast. "You're on dish duty." The voice seemed to rise above the din. "Get in the kitchen. The sooner you get started the sooner you'll be done." It was Lua, of course, directing kids and keeping order. "And you," she said, pointing to another. But she didn't finish her thought. Instead, her head swung around to follow the gaze of everyone else in the room as they turned to look at Toekin.

The door was on the opposite side of the room. He just had to make it that far and freedom was his. He dared a look back at Lua. She'd been nice, even though she was obstinate and annoying. Her glare, however, made him second guess his assessment. She looked like she wanted to strangle him. He casually turned to look at the other side of the room and caught Tessa's downcast face.

He just wanted to return to his life, what was so wrong with that? His shuffle got slower as he continued across the room, past the tables with dirty dishes waiting to be cleared, benches still filled with kids chatting, the wood carving of Paz, and then finally the door. Toekin felt like he needed a nap.

The sun was shining, but the air was crisp and cool, it was the perfect time to travel. He had the whole day ahead of him. He just needed to find the cart, destroy it, go home, and sleep for about a week. Everything would be fine.

Espero walked him a little farther down the path. "What do you know about Zaints?"

"What?"

"You know, the people the Emperor is looking for?"

Toekin remembered seeing something on one of the posters, but this hardly seemed like the time to strike up a conversation about it. He stopped and leaned up against the fence surrounding the garden. But a bench or rock would have been a better resting place.

"Do you know why he's looking for them?" Espero asked.

What was this guy going on about? "Listen, if I'm going to get my thing done, I need to be on my way."

"Where are your parents, Toekin?"

He hesitated. He didn't have to tell this guy anything. He didn't know him. This whole thing could be an act—a way to get information out of him and turn him over to the guards. Espero knew where the food was coming from, after all. His mind continued to assault him with reasons to keep his mouth shut, but his heart saw the man before him, kind, still weak from, whatever he had done. Besides, he'd already told Tessa. So, he spoke. "They were taken. A long time ago."

"And they never taught you?"

"Taught me what?" Toekin's patience was wearing. "Look, at the rate I'm moving, it's going to take a little longer to get to where I'm going, so I need to be on my way. If you don't mind."

"Of course not." Espero stepped aside.

Toekin shifted his weight off the fence. "Thank you," he said, then added, "for everything." The old man nodded and Toekin set off. They'd saved his life. He had no doubt. If they hadn't taken him in, he wouldn't be hobbling away right now. Maybe, years down the road, he might need their help again. It was good to know they were here, he supposed. Just in case.

"Oh, Toekin," Espero called.

He turned around. He'd only made it about ten paces and was already starting to think about when he'd stop for a rest.

"I just remembered . . . one of our men is heading into Mato forest. You could ride in the wagon if you're going that direction."

The thought of accepting help from this bunch yet again went to war with the very appealing idea of sitting. Besides, that was exactly the direction he needed to go. Sitting won. Toekin tilted his head up. "What do you say, Corv? Should we get a ride?"

Corvo, who had been hiding in the highest branches of a tall tree cawed and took flight high into the air. He'd get there his own way.

Twenty minutes later, Toekin was in the back of a wagon next to what looked like a one hundred-year-old woman. Maybe older. She was shriveled and tiny and had long wisps of hair that showed mostly scalp. Her skin looked dry, scaly and paper-thin, so white she was almost blue. She'd been lifted into the back by an intimidating hulk of a man named Força, heavy on muscle but light on words. His bald brown head shone in the morning sun and his thick beard muffled what little talking he managed. Her head hung, lifeless and Toekin wondered if maybe she was dead. If she wasn't now, he figured she would be before long.

"Keep that blanket on Freya. She gets cold," was all Força said as they set off. And that was just fine with Toekin.

CHAPTER 6

The Girl

"I know what you're doing." It was the first words Força had spoken in an hour.

"Excuse me?" Toekin shouted over the rumbling of the wooden wheels on the rutted and rocky road.

Força pulled back on the reins, and the old horse slowed to an eventual stop. He turned back and looked right at Toekin, his eyes dark and serious. "I know what you're doing. And I also know, you can't do it alone."

Who did this guy think he was? Toekin felt the grip of confinement tighten. Were they trying to entrap him? Force him to come back to the orphanage or else tell his secret to the Abbadon Guards? It had been a huge mistake bringing food to the orphanage—a mistake he would never make again. "Maybe you should just let me out right here." Toekin grabbed his satchel and started to rise. He could walk from here. This was close enough.

"Don't be a fool," Força growled. "You're barely well enough to make this trip as it is. I can help you."

Understanding crept in from the corners of his mind. "So this was a set up? You were never heading to Mato Forest, were you? It was just a lie to trick me?"

"Freya needed to get some fresh air. I would have taken her for a ride eventually." Toekin was furious. This was his business. Not theirs. He didn't need their help or interference.

"Espero knew the first time he saw you. You're part of the Waylayers. The ones who ambush the taxation carts."

"Waylayers?"

"It's the name the rebels have come up with for your group." By the look on his face, Força thought it a little ridiculous. "To rally people. And it's worked."

"Rebels?" Toekin shook his head. "I don't know what you're talking about." If he'd been well, this is the point he would have hopped over the edge of the wagon and put a lot of distance between him and this man. But he wasn't well, and the bumpy ride in the wagon had done nothing to ease his discomfort.

Força stared at him. His gazed seemed to penetrate Toekin and he had to look away. "You really don't know, do you?"

"Listen, you can either take me to the edge of the forest or I'll walk there myself. But I need to get moving, either way."

"We're on the same side, you know." He shifted his huge body and turned back to the horse, snapping the reins once and putting the beast in motion. He said nothing else until he found a secluded spot on the edge of town.

"Thanks for the ride," Toekin said, still not sure he should have accepted it in the first place. He groaned as he tried to haul himself out of the wagon.

"Stop."

The word reverberated in Toekin's chest and he looked up to see the same steely gaze and froze. So, this was it? The big man was going to turn him in here; guards were bound to crawl out of their hiding places any moment. He should have known everything was an act. The promise he could leave any time, and this conveniently helpful ride; all a ruse. His head sank, and he scrambled to formulate a plan.

"Let me help."

Toekin's head snapped up. "I don't think . . ."

"I told you. I know what you're doing, I know about your group. Me, Espero, we're part of the resistance too. We just have to keep a

57

low profile—because of our unusual talents." He hissed the words "unusual talents," as if he was worried someone might overhear.

Toekin was more confused than ever.

"Tell me what you need done, and I'll do it." Força said. "I just need you to stay here and take care of Freya."

"I don't think so." How big of a fool did Força think he was? The sooner he was away from him, and everyone else, the better. He angled himself to slip over the side of the wagon and stopped. A calm peace descended on him and he had the distinct feeling that everything would be fine. He shifted his balance and turned to Força, and for a moment he thought he saw a flash of blue light cross the brute's deep brown eyes.

"What do you need done?" He asked again. This time his voice was neither gruff nor annoyed, but washed over him like warm honey. He could trust this man.

"There's an Abbadon cart, due east of here. About a twenty-minute walk."

"I can do it faster," Força said as a matter of fact.

Toekin went on, not stopping to respond to this information. "It needs to be destroyed. I usually shove it under a fat Seivo Sangue bulb and let nature take its course. Or you can burn it, but the smoke might draw unwanted attention." Toekin felt so relaxed now, he eyed Freya and her blanket and considered crawling under with her for a little nap.

"Done." With a cat-like ease not usually seen in men of his size, Força hopped out of the wagon. "Watch Freya," he said again. "Don't leave her." And then he was off.

The warm calm stayed with him as he watched Força lumber off toward the forest, the very air seeming to sparkle in azure flecks, but as soon as he disappeared into the trees, Toekin's old concerns arose. He looked up and saw Corvo following Força from above. If there was any double-dealing, he'd let Toekin know.

He turned to look at Freya. She hadn't moved the whole time. Only the intermittent rise and fall of her chest was evidence she was still alive. *What's her story?* He wondered. And why was Força so protective? She seemed way too old to be his mother. His grandmother maybe? He looked more closely. In the jostle of the ride, her leg had slipped out from under the blanket. He reached to cover it up again and noticed large scale-like patterns on her shocking white skin. There was something wrong with this woman. She wasn't right, and she better not be contagious.

A scrap of hair had fallen across her face and Toekin reached to move it. But before he could, he went stiff with fear. Voices traveled up the road from around the corner. People were coming.

He couldn't leave this helpless woman, and even if he did, he wouldn't be able to run anywhere fast enough to hide. He tried to hide the panic pounding his chest. Then he saw who was coming. Abbadon Guards. *Slugs.* Had Força betrayed him after all?

"Well, what have we here," a tall one with greasy hair and a missing front tooth said.

"Looks like loiterers to me," said the shorter one, sniffing up a runny nose. His large belly quivered with amusement at his joke—which wasn't actually a joke.

Toekin didn't reply, but tried to appear small and weak, which he thought might be his best defense. It wasn't.

"What say you!" said the tall one, his face sharp and pinched, like a weasel's. He jabbed Toekin in the chest with the blunt end of his spear.

Toekin cried out as wounds opened and blood started seeping through his shirt.

"Looks like you've been in a bit of a," *sniff*, "skirmish. Maybe you were one of them rebels that escaped two nights ago?" Sniff, sniff.

Who were these rebels everyone was talking about? Força had said he and Espero were part of their group, hadn't he? Toekin found his voice. "No. I don't know anything about any rebels."

"Liar!" said the weasel. "I can tell just by looking at you." He slammed the staff into Toekin's ribs.

He doubled over, crying out in pain, certain at least one of his bones was broken. A burning hate rose in him and he envisioned burying the spear in the guard's heart. Despite his wounds, and now possible broken rib, he was sure he could get at least one of them before the other one took him down. But then what of Freya? He resisted the urge, for her sake, saving his anger for later.

"Please," Toekin said. "We're just farmers. We're waiting for our friend, who has gone to look for herbs in the forest."

"Oh yeah?" The guard wiped his nose with the back of his hand. "What do you got in that bag?" He pointed to Toekin's satchel.

Weasel used the end of his spear to drag it from Toekin's side, then reached in the wagon and grabbed it.

Please don't let them see my scope. Toekin chanted in his head while trying to keep a blank look on his face.

Freya sat there like a lump. Was she going to sleep through this whole thing?

Weasel upturned the bag and shook. Lots of things fell out: rocks for his sling, good string he'd picked up from the raid a few days earlier, some hard bread. But not the scope.

"Ooh, looky here!" The fat one picked up the sling with his snotty hand. "This is nicer than mine." He shoved it in his pants pocket while Toekin bit his tongue. His father had given him that sling.

They finished picking through his belongings, somehow missing the scope. "This string is better than that bunk you took off that kid yesterday." Sniffy said, full of ugly pride.

"What about this blanket," Weasel said, pulling the covering off Freya. "Winter is coming. Need to stay warm."

Sniffy laughed like it was a funny joke. Sniffy was an idiot.

"Hey," Toekin said, snagging a corner before it escaped his reach. "Let her keep it."

"Hand it over you little rebel dog." Weasel yanked back, but Toekin held firm.

"She needs it more than you! Look at her!" And for the first time, they did.

Weasel let the blanket drop from his hand and Toekin quickly pulled it back into the wagon. They stared at Freya, little more than a living skeleton, or a rotting corpse unable to die. A look of horror fell on them. "What's wrong with her," Sniffy said, snot running down his face.

"Leprosy," someone boomed from behind.

The two guards spun around to see Força standing, a full head taller and a half a man wider than Weasel, a small sack gripped in his fist. He was at once completely harmless and incredibly menacing. Toekin could learn something from this guy.

Força held up the sack. "Collecting herbs to help ease her suffering. A terrible way to go." He shook his head, his eyes downcast. Then he looked at each of them and said, "You didn't touch the blanket, did you?"

"He touched it," Sniffy said, pointing and distancing himself from his now terrified friend.

"Just on the end. And not for very long." Weasel seemed desperate for confirmation this would be okay.

"Oh dear," Força's voice dripped with mock concern. "Get yourself to a priest, and fast! It might be your only hope."

Weasel's eyes were huge with fear. "We better go!"

"You dimwit!" Sniffy punched Weasel in the arm. "Look at him. He's lying. That old crone has all her parts. Nothing's fallin' off. She's no leper."

Força's brows lowered and he looked like he wanted to take a swing at Sniffy. Toekin wished he would. "Don't believe me?" He said, instead. "Look at this!" With that, he pulled off one of Freya's boots to reveal a foot so dried and cracked it looked like it might crumble to dust. "It starts with the toenails!"

Sure enough, Freya was missing every single toenail. The guards recoiled in disgust. Even Toekin found it difficult to see.

"Now leave us and pray you don't get it too!" Força said as they scattered. He scooped up a few of Toekin's things, climbed into the wagon, and threw what wasn't his in the back.

"Yah!" Froça cried to the horse and the wagon jerked into motion. No one said anything. Every pebble and divot in the road sent Toekin into blinding pain and he gritted his teeth, holding in his grunts and moans while sweat poured down his forehead.

Finally, Força pulled the wagon off the road and came to a stop. He turned back to Toekin and said, "I took care of the cart."

"That was fast," *Too fast.*

"I told you it wouldn't take long. Your bird helped," he admitted with reluctance, "or it would have taken a bit longer. Showed me where to go."

Toekin nodded, still bothered by the abuse from the guards.

"Well, this is the crossroads," Força said. As good a place as any to part ways. He didn't acknowledge the new blood soaking Toekin's shirt, or the way he'd been hunched over to one side, gripping his ribs.

Toekin looked up and saw Corvo circling. He wasn't sure he could even get out of the wagon. Stalling he said, "The guards kept calling me a rebel. What did they mean?"

"You really don't know?" Força looked at Toekin with a skeptical eye, and heaved a sigh, as if he couldn't believe he had to explain this to anyone. "It was the systematic kidnapping and genocide of Zaints that caused them to organize—underground, at first. They were careful. Training, organizing . . . and then they started the attacks. There were little victories at first. Nothing that would bring Beezul to his knees. But they were making him nervous. And then the raids on taxation carts began—your group. That's why I assumed you knew. When rumors spread about the total disappearance of the guards, their carts and all their food, suddenly the rebels felt like they had a chance. I guess I just thought your group and the rebels were working together."

"There's no group." Toekin said. "I do it on my own."

Força lowered his gaze, staring at Toekin as if he could read his mind. Toekin would have squirmed if he could have managed to move. "Huh." Força rubbed his smooth brown head. "Impressive."

Toekin didn't know what to say. He wasn't the only one against the Emperor? The thought was powerful, motivating. He felt a surge of optimistic energy and was eager for his next ambush. He began to think of the villagers and townspeople he brought food to in a new light. Maybe they hated Beezul just as much as he did.

"Okay, then. I guess I'll be on my way." He rolled to his knees, took the deepest breath he dared and pulled himself up.

"So, lad," Força said, almost offhand. "You're a Zaint, right?"

Toekin breathed out in frustration. "I . . . I don't even know what a Zaint is."

"Come now, surely you're not carrying out all these ambushes on your own without a little help."

Toekin ignored him and pulled himself over the edge of the cart, landing in a painful heap. *I'm done*, he thought, pulling himself to his knees again, *with these people*. "I appreciate your help with the cart. I'll be on my way now."

Força watched as he crawled to the wagon wheel and pulled himself to standing, then paused to catch his breath. "Definitely sun. Every sun slinger I know is as stubborn as a mule."

Toekin glared back at him. Daring him to keep talking.

"You think I'm going to let you limp off like that?"

"Espero said I was free to go. You can't stop me."

Força let out a deep, baritone laugh. It was the first time he'd done anything but scowl all day. "Sorry lad. Have you seen yourself? I could make you do just about anything right now."

"I work on my own. I'll be fine."

Força jumped down from the wagon and covered the distance between he and Toekin in three easy strides. "Lad," he said, "Give Espero a chance to teach you a thing or two. You couldn't ask for better."

His mind flashed to the conversation he'd had with the old man earlier. What was it his parents hadn't taught him? Was that what Espero could teach him? He shook his head. He was nothing like these people. He turned away from Força and limped forward.

"Lad, hold up." The giant of a man, towering over him, was at his side, his hand on his back. Warmth flowed into him, just like when Lua and Espero had seemed to help him. He felt lighter and happier, his back straightened, and he stood a little taller. After a while, Força dropped his hand and he stepped back.

Toekin took an exploratory step. Better. A long way from perfect, but better. He was certain of it now—something was going on, and it had nothing to do with his breathing and imagination.

"Come and see." Força said. "One or two more days to heal up, then decide what to do."

It would still be a difficult journey. If he ran into trouble, he wouldn't be able to get himself out of it. Toekin nodded. He had already noticed the guards following them and knew they would go after him if he set off on his own.

Was he conceding defeat or making a strategic decision? He decided not to think too much about it and turned back toward the wagon. Freya still sat there, completely unresponsive. What was the point of dragging her out today if she didn't even wake up?

Back on the road, the slow rock and bump of the wagon had a calming effect on Toekin. The pain had eased, and he could sit more comfortably. He shouted up to the front. There was a question that had been bugging him. "Back there . . . how'd you know about the herbs?"

"What?"

"When you came back from the forest, you told the guards you were looking for herbs. It's the excuse I gave them, but I just made it up. How'd you know to play along?"

"Lucky guess." The broad back and shoulders shrugged once and then bounced in time to the movement of the wagon, but other than that, there was no other acknowledgement. Força, it seemed, had used up all the talking he would do today.

Toekin let the steady motion sooth him and began to drift off to sleep. He knew there would be decisions to face, and challenges that would arise—the guards were still back there, after all—but just for now, trusting Força to handle things while he napped was a luxury he allowed himself. In one moment he was still just conscious of his surroundings, and the next he was bathed in blue light, standing in front of the dragon girl.

He held both of her hands in his and was looking into her eyes, the smile on her face telling him everything he cared to know. And maybe this was all he would ever need to know. He could stand in front of her forever.

Who are you? He thought. His desire to know more consumed him, but he felt like speaking would break this spell. He savored the moment, committing to memory every detail of her face so he could recall it more easily when the dream was over. Finally, her lips parted. Blue light streamed from her mouth and she spoke.

"Help Paz. Help me."

He had been right about one thing. The talking broke the spell and her hands slipped from his as she pulled farther and farther away from him. The wagon hit a big rock and the vision ended.

He shook his head, reluctant to return to reality, especially when he saw Freya's nail-less toes jutting out from under her blanket uncomfortably close to his foot. He jerked his leg away. If he was going to make it through the next few days, he needed to be on high alert. Getting back to his tree was still his top priority. Although he couldn't help but wonder if he should think more about what the girl had meant. Toekin was nearly convinced she was more than just a dream, but what she said made no sense. Help Paz? The dragon from the bedtime stories? If she was truly desperate for help, she should give better instructions.

Far behind the bumping wagon, the Abbadon guards still followed. He shifted himself up toward the front and spoke up so Força could hear. "We're being followed."

"Yep." Força kept his eyes on the road ahead, unimpressed with the information.

"It's those guards from town."

"I know."

"You going to try and lose them?"

"Nope."

Toekin settled himself into the corner and wondered how concerned he should be about Força's lack of concern. The orphanage was Força's to protect. If he wanted to subject it to danger, that was his business. On the other hand, Toekin was now, at least for the next day or two, part of them. He'd given up control of his ability to stay hidden. Had he made the right decision?

He went over the events of the last ambush. Had he covered his tracks? Was it possible the guards were coming specifically for him? He didn't think there was any way they could tie the attacks to him, but he would not take chances.

Two more days. He thought. *Then I'm out of here.* Any more than that and he'd be compromising not just his safety, but also that of the orphans

.

CHAPTER 7

The Dragon

"You've returned," Espero said with a grin. He had been cleaning up the garden area with a tall boy who had white hair and looked to be about Toekin's age. The old man seemed joyfully delighted to see Toekin again.

"Just for a couple days," Toekin said, ducking his head to catch a glimpse of Corvo landing on the highest part of the orphanage roof. He was staying out of the way, not taking any chances of going back in the cage.

"Of course! Whatever you like." Turning to the white-haired boy he said, "Row, this is Toekin."

Row stuck out an eager hand and pumped Toekin's with enthusiasm. "Great to meet you." His skin was unnaturally white, with several even whiter scars running from his hairline, across his eye, and down his face until they were lost under his shirt. This guy had a story, but Toekin wouldn't be around long enough to learn it. He was okay with that.

"Dinner's in a few minutes. Come with me and I'll show you." Toekin thought he should probably mention something to Espero about the Abbadon Guards who had followed them. He turned back to Espero who was still grinning at him, then off to the distance, down the road, where Weasel and Sniffy watched with folded arms.

"I see them," Espero said quietly. "Do not worry. They pose no threat to us."

After situating Freya, Força had come back outside to take care of the horse. "Did you feed young Toekin while you were out, Força?" Espero said.

He grunted his reply as he walked the beast toward the stable.

"I didn't think so." Espero chuckled to himself. "Make sure you get enough to eat tonight, Toekin. Your body needs energy to continue healing."

As they walked toward the main building, Toekin looked back and saw Espero silently staring down the street toward the place the guards had just been. They'd disappeared, but something told Toekin it was not the last he'd see of those two.

"So, Toekin? Mind if I call you Toe?" Row didn't wait for an answer. "What's your story? You were in pretty bad shape when we found you."

Too many questions. "No story, just an unfortunate meeting with an ursmock."

"No kidding! How big?"

Toekin held his hand up just a little higher than his head.

Row let out a long whistle. "How'd you get out of that?"

"Suffocation, I guess. I shot a rock right down his throat and he choked." The thought reminded him of his stolen sling and his mood darkened. He didn't feel like talking anymore. He wondered if he could just get his food and take it back to his room—eat in silence.

"Hi!" He turned and saw little brown-eyed Tessa. "I knew you'd come back. I told Lua, but she didn't believe me. Hey! Is that blood?"

The red stain on his shirt had dried a rusty brown. Toekin didn't answer. The din in the room was overwhelming and he longed for a quiet meal in his Seivo Sangue tree with the only noise coming from the chattering squirrels and the occasional but constant hiss-splat of nearby sap dropping to the ground.

"We call this room the sun sala," Row said, sweeping his arm in a wide arc in front of him. It was the room Toekin was most familiar with. The one he'd dropped the food off in, and the one he'd tried to escape out of. The one with the large dragon carving of Paz on the wall. "We can sit here," Row said, pulling out a bench at one of the tables. "Close to the kitch'n, first to get fixin's. This okay?"

"Fine." Toekin sat and tried to calm himself with some of Espero's deep breathing—it didn't work. As soon as dinner was over, he was going to his room and staying there.

Tessa slid in next to him and looked up with excitement filling her eyes. "Can I sit next to you?"

"Sure." Toekin gave her a smile. She was sweet, and he wondered if this is what it was like to have a little sister. Probably not. She hit a cup with her elbow and it rolled to the floor.

"Oops," she said, reaching down to pick it up. She bumped her head on the way back up and laughed, rubbing the spot.

A young boy came to the table and set a stack of turned wooden plates in front of them. "Thanks Kai," Row said. The boy looked young, maybe nine or ten, with hair that flopped down into his eyes, which seemed to be trained on Toekin.

"You're here to help us." Kai said, looking right at him.

Toekin smiled. Maybe the kid would go away. But he didn't. He just stood there staring at Toekin like he was seeing a ghost.

"He's just here for a few days, kiddo. Recovering from an ursmock attack."

"I know," Kai said. "He ate your cheese."

Did he hear that kid right?

"Don't be sad," he added. "We have cheese here." He turned without saying another word and went to get plates for the next table.

"Don't let him creep you out," Row said. "He's harmless."

How had he known about the cheese?

"There you are Tessa. What are you doing over here with Row and . . . oh. It's you." Toekin watched as Lua's face changed from surprise, to something like happiness, and then settled on disgust as her eyes dropped to his shirt. "Opened those wounds again, did you?"

Toekin didn't bother telling her it was the guards who were responsible. He didn't think it would matter.

Lua sank down onto a bench next to Row. "I suppose I'll have time after dinner if you want me to redo the bandages. Well, at least you're alive. I assumed that after your trip, you'd be a lot worse." She turned her attention to Row and nudged him in the ribs. "Closest to the kitch'n, something, something about fixin's, huh?"

Row laughed. "I can't help it if I'm brilliant *and* strikingly handsome."

Tessa giggled, and Lua smirked. "You know kitchen and fixings don't rhyme, right?"

A gong sounded, long and deep, making Toekin jump. Espero stood at the end of the room, Corvo on his shoulder, apple bits stuck to the feathers around his beak. *Figures*, Toekin thought, resigned to his friend's easily bought allegiances.

"I'll give thanks for our meal and then we can eat," Espero said, then bowed his head. Toekin looked around and copied everyone else as they did the same. He felt awkward and uncomfortable, as if the eyes of everyone were on him, even though their eyes were closed.

The prayer finished, Espero said, "eat!" and the room descended into a managed chaos while everyone began reaching for food at the same time.

When dinner was over, Lua rose like a queen bee presiding over her hive and started directing everyone to his or her tasks. "Tessa, you're on dish duty. Zonks, you're clearing." She was firm, but respected, and kids scattered into their roles. "And Teagan . . . not so fast." Teagan, a girl with long blonde hair, turned just short of making her escape and rolled her eyes. "You're on . . ."

"I know," she said shuffling back into the sun sala. "Compost." She rolled up her sleeves and started picking food scraps off dinner plates. "This is so gross," she said, wrinkling her nose.

"What's your job tonight," Lua asked Row.

"Força and I have an errand to run." He gave her a knowing look.

"Right," she said, dropping the subject.

"In fact, I probably need to go. Nice meeting you Toe." Without another word, Row got up and left.

Lua watched him walk away and the look on her face told Toekin something was up. But before he could pinpoint it, she turned back and said, "You feel well enough to help out?"

"Uh." He wanted to say no. He wasn't feeling weak. In fact, he was surprised at how good he felt. Sore, but not in agony, like he probably should be.

The real reason he didn't want to help is he didn't want anyone to get used to him being here. *He* didn't want to get used to being here. Doing chores would ingrain him in this group, and he couldn't let that happen. He imagined Lua's response if he refused her. *After all we've done for you!* She'd say. And she'd be right. Helping out was the least he could do.

"What do you have in mind?"

"Bedtime stories."

Toekin started. "I don't know." He said, scratching the back of his head. "I only know one."

"Perfect," Lua said. "They're only allowed one." She smiled and trotted off to help some younger kids sweep the floor.

Toekin decided he'd try and find the big bird who had sold his soul for an apple. He was glad Corvo wasn't trying to attack people anymore. He just hoped the crow would leave with him when it was time to go.

* * *

"Settle down. Our new friend Toekin is going to tell you a story," Lua walked up and down the rows of beds making sure the children were tucked in.

"Will you give me a hug, Lua?" One little boy said. He couldn't have been more than four or five years old. What would it have been like if Toekin had been that young when his parents were taken? Would he have found a place like this?

Others called for hugs and Lua accommodated each one. "All right, hugs are done, now it's story time. Toekin?"

They were just a bunch of kids, but suddenly he felt hot. He took a deep breath. How had she wrangled him into this? Best to just get it over with. He started, "Four dragon brothers set out to explore the world, each traveling in a different direction. The great dragon Paz came to Enganoso."

There were twitters of excitement among the kids and Lua had to quiet them down. Memories of his own parents telling him this story at bedtime came flooding back along with the words of the story. Toekin continued.

"Out of all the places in Enganoso, Paz loved Mato Forest best. The trees were his playground and became his home. His favorite tree was the tallest in the forest: the Seivo Sangue. No creature in the whole land was more powerful than Paz. His teeth were sharper than daggers," Toekin snapped his teeth together just like his parents had and the kids giggled. "His claws could slice like razors." He raked his hand through the air with a growl. "And nothing could penetrate his hard scales.

"So strong was Paz, he would bathe in the very thing that would kill any other creature: the sap of the Seivo Sangue. With his razor claws he'd tear open a bulb, climb in, and let the hot liquid relax his tired, powerful muscles."

"That's why he's red!" a little girl said before being shushed by Lua.

"You're right," Toekin said, relaxing into his role of teller of tales. "He spent so much time in the sap, his whole body turned a deep, ruby red. Paz could have destroyed villages and even kingdoms if he'd wanted to, taking and keeping their riches for himself. But he was peaceful and only wanted to enjoy his beautiful forest home.

"One day, as Paz was soaking in his bath of sap, he heard a Bang! Bang! Bang! So, he went to see what it was. What he found were men chopping down his trees. 'What is the meaning of this!' he roared. The men didn't wait around to explain but ran off in fear. So, Paz flew to the village, right into the council of elders. 'Why are you destroying my forest?' he bellowed.

"He didn't mean to bellow, but it's the only way dragons know how to talk." Toekin winked at a child who'd been staring at him wide-eyed.

"All of the elders ran and hid, trembling in fear, except one. His name was Ganancia. He stood bravely before the dragon and said, 'Have you come to eat us?' His voice had only the slightest hint of fear.

"Paz laughed, and short bursts of purple flame and smoke escaped his mouth. 'I *could* eat you if I wanted to, but I'm a peaceful dragon, and have promised a powerful wizard I would never harm any creature. Should I do so, I would become his slave. But enough of that. Now tell me why you are cutting down my trees!'

"Ganancia stood a little taller, any trace of fear was gone from his voice. 'We are building a road so that we may better wage war on the cities to the north.' Paz roared, but this time it was in anger, not on accident. Flames shot out of his mouth, burning tables and making the elders uncomfortably hot. 'Remember your promise,' Ganancia said with a smile of pure evil on his face. Paz flew up to the ceiling, burst through the roof and flew off in anger.

"The next day, there were twice as many men and twice as many axes chopping down his trees. The following day, three times as many. Before long the road began to take shape, like a black serpent cutting through tall grass. Paz stewed in his anger. He felt trapped—a fool for telling Ganancia too much. He couldn't harm the workers, *but* . . . maybe he could trick them.

"That night, Paz flew down and stole all their axes so the next morning, the men couldn't work. The forest was quiet once again and Paz was happy. But the next week, they showed up with more men and more axes. This time, at the end of the day, they took their axes home. Paz stewed.

"The next day, the workers arrived to large casks of strong ale Paz had left for them. Happily, they drank until all of the ale was gone and the workers became drunk and fell asleep. And the forest was once again quiet. But three days later even were more men returned. Paz stewed.

"Finally, Paz flew to the scene of destruction, where his forest was being ripped apart for war, and landed right in the middle of the workers. 'You men are working hard. You are here early in the morning and late into the night,' Paz told them. 'Ganancia can't be paying you enough to come out here every day and risk your life. There's an angry dragon that lives in this forest, after all.' To make his point, he breathed fire onto a pile of felled logs and reduced them to ash.

"'The dragon has a point,' one said.

"'This *is* dangerous work,' another said.

"'We should be making more gold,' said someone else.

72

"So upset were the workers, they all walked off in anger, straight to Ganancia to demand higher wages. And the forest was quiet. No workers returned for many days.

"Weeks had passed in peace and Paz was soaking in a hot sap bath, enjoying his victory, when he heard it again: the chop, chop, chop of axe to tree. He rose from his bath and flew directly to the sound, dripping hot sap along the way. There he found Ganancia waiting for him while another man took timid chops at a nearby trunk.

"'Leave my forest alone!' he roared. Paz's tail thrashed about leaving great ruts in the ground where it came crashing down.

"'Dear Paz,' Ganancia said, his voice dripping with honey, 'I don't want to see this forest destroyed any more than you do. It's that fellow over there,' he said, pointing with his thumb over his shoulder. After every swing, the man glanced at Paz in terror, then went back to chopping.

"'He is the one who wants war, not me. He is the one insisting that we build this road. If it were up to me, I would never have chopped down one tree. If only there was something we could do to stop him.' Paz wondered if Ganancia was telling the truth. 'If only you could kill him, it would make all of our troubles go away.'

"'Fool!' Paz roared, 'if I kill him, my life will belong to the wizard.'

"'That's true,' Ganancia said. 'But what if he had an accident? As you can see, there is a Seivo Sangue tree in our path. That man wants to cut it down, but doesn't know how to cut through the thick, hard bark. If you tell him the secret, he will cut the tree, and before too long, he will be covered in sap and die.'

"Paz thought. Was it true that if this one man lost his life, the road to war would be stopped? He didn't want anyone to die, but maybe one person's death would be worth it to stop war. Finally, he said to Ganancia, 'Bring me his axe.' And so he did, and Paz touched it so that it glowed like the sun. Trembling, the man took his axe, walked toward the Seivo Sangue, stopping just outside the hard circle of glassy, red dried sap that pooled under the tree. 'Do it!' Ganancia demanded. And the man did. He stepped into the circle, approached the trunk and began to chop.

"The more Paz watched the man hack away, tears streaming down his face, the more he realized that Ganancia had been lying to him. But it was too late. Before Paz could save him, one of the sap bulbs burst, covering the unfortunate fellow from head to toe. Immediately, Paz was at his side, breathing purple flames to melt the dried sap in hopes that the man could free himself from its deadly shroud.

"A bolt of lightning from the clear blue sky crashed down beside Paz and out of a black cloud stepped the wizard. 'Paz the Dragon, your soul belongs to me now.' The wizard waved his arms and the glassy sap covering the man began to crack until he emerged like a bird from a shell, gasping for air. 'It was an accident,' Paz cried, as the wizard commanded the shards of red sap toward him in a swirling cloud. He waved his arms again, and the pieces came together in a tighter and tighter mass until a shiny, dragon-shaped flute fell into the Wizard's hands. He blew into one end and it made a single note, pure and clear. Then a black collar appeared around Paz's neck.

"Paz the Dragon,' the wizard said, 'until you right your wrongs, you will be under the power of this flute. But since you were tricked into harming this human, I will help you in your journey.'

"Before the wizard could say another word, a large knife came down in his back, killing him instantly. Ganancia, still holding the bloody weapon, bent down and picked up the flute and bound poor Paz to him forever. And Paz is still bound to this very day, until someone brave enough and clever enough, with just the right gifts, finds a way to set him free."

Toekin finished and the room was silent. All of the children were looking at him with rapt attention. He searched for Lua and found her sitting in the back, eyes red. She wiped at her face and said, "Okay, dear ones. Lights out." She extinguished a lamp in the back and walked toward the front of the room to get the second one. "Sleep well. You never know. Maybe one of you will be the one to help Paz."

Toekin and Lua exited the room and she closed the door softly behind her. "Are you okay?" Toekin asked.

"What do you mean?" Lua sniffed, pushed her brown curls behind her ear and tipped her head his direction.

"Is this the first time you've heard the story of Paz? It's just a kids' story. It's not real." He was thinking of his dreams and about the beautiful girl who had begged him to help Paz. It had felt real, but he knew it couldn't be.

Lua took a seat at one of the tables and Toekin sat down next to her. "I'm very familiar with the story." She looked up at the carving on the wall. "Although the version I know is . . . a little different."

"How so?"

There was some commotion in the kitchen and the door burst open into the sun sala. Two Abbadon guards strode across the room, knocking over benches and pushing stacks of plates to the floor. Weasel and Sniffy were back. "Go tell the old guy we're here on business of the Emperor," Sniffy said.

"We have reason to believe you're hiding someone." Weasel raked his hand across a shelf holding cups and they clattered to the ground. He kicked a basket of potatoes, then onions, which rolled across the floor.

Toekin's heart seized with fear. They were looking for him—for the ambushes—he just knew it. What should he do? If he ran now, he'd only look suspicious. Best to try and sneak out while they were preoccupied elsewhere. He watched for his moment.

Dorm room doors started to open, and kids peered out curiously before ducking back inside. "We're coming in there next you little snot-faced brats." *Sniff.*

He should talk, Toekin thought.

They burst into the room of the littlest kids who'd just heard the story of Paz. Cries and whimpers and sounds of scattering children could be heard.

"Can't we stop them?" he asked Lua.

"It's best just to let them look around, and then clean up when they're gone."

"They've done this before?" Toekin's anger grew. "And where's Espero? I haven't seen him since dinner."

"I'm here my son."

Toekin spun around to see the old man who'd seemed to appear out of nowhere. "We can't just stand here and let this happen." A cry escaped from the kid's room and Lua ran forward into the room.

Espero followed. But Toekin ran to the kitchen and grabbed the biggest knife he could find. Then followed Lua and Espero.

"I saw this kid moving too fast. He thought I didn't see him, but I did." Weasel had the little four or five-year-old, who had been the first to ask Lua for a hug, in his grasp. Lua had run to help him, but Sniffy had caught her and had her in his meaty paws. The boy looked furious that tears were streaming down his face, betraying his fear. He was trying so hard to be brave. "You're coming to Abbadon with us you little Zaint." Weasel twisted his arm and the boy cried out in pain.

There was that word again—*Zaint*. But Toekin couldn't take it any longer. Was Espero really going to let them take this kid? His anger boiled over and he felt the world melt away the same way he did when he ambushed the taxation carts. In an instant he was at Weasel's side, one arm thrown across his chest like a vise, and the other holding the knife to his neck. "*Let him go.*"

"Do you know what the punishment is for attacking an Abbadon guard, you little worm?" The man hissed, despite the crushing pressure on his windpipe.

"Let him go!"

"I'm on the Emperor's errand, fool. You let me go!"

Power surged through Toekin and he felt invincible. One fast draw across this scum's neck and he could be to Sniffy and do the same before anyone could blink. Abbadon guards would be no loss. They could dispose of their bodies tomorrow and no one would ever know. He gripped the knife and was about to slice when Espero appeared at his side, gripping his arm with unexpected strength.

"Stop." His voice was calm and warm and yet commanding. Toekin couldn't help but obey. "This is not how we do things."

It wasn't until Sniffy pointed to Espero and shouted, "He's a Zaint! We can take him too!" that Toekin realized the old man's eyes were glowing yellow.

One by one, the children came out from hiding, each lit up with a brilliant, glowing aura. Others from adjacent dorm rooms had come too, joining the show of power. Tessa was there, radiating a most beautiful blue light. Kai, the kid who knew about the ursmock attack, stepped forward, bathed in bright white, and approached Toekin and Weasel.

As he got closer, white light from Kai's eyes slithered through the air like yarn on a windy day, and found the guard in Toekin's grasp. Toekin felt the man relax in his arms and he instinctively lowered the knife and stepped back. He looked at Lua while Kai's white light formed a connection between both Sniffy and Weasel. Lua stepped back, unsurprised by this sudden development. What was happening?

"Zonks?" Espero nodded to the lanky boy standing by the door, and he ran out of the room. "Okay children," he continued. "Back to bed. We'll be around to check on you in a few minutes."

Everyone dispersed, including the kids who'd been sleeping in the room, and Toekin was left alone with Espero, Lua and the two guards. "We appreciate your concern," Espero said to the guards who seemed like they were just snapping out of a daydream. "It makes us feel better knowing you're around to keep things safe."

What was he talking about? These guys were the problem, the ones to be afraid of.

Espero walked the men from the room, a hand on the shoulder of each. They passed through the sun sala and into the kitchen. Zonks appeared with a basket overflowing with loaves of bread, cold storage apples, potatoes and turnips. "Please, accept this food with our thanks."

"You're too kind," Sniffy said, stiffly.

"Yes. Thank you." Weasel added in a drowsy monotone.

Toekin caught a glimpse of his sling tucked into Weasel's belt. He may not have been sure what was happening, but he recognized an opportunity when he saw one.

"And thanks for returning my sling!" He said while yanking it free.

Weasel nodded politely as Espero guided them to the door at the back of the kitchen and ushered them out. "Stay warm out there," he chuckled, waving as they faded into the distance.

Toekin blinked and tried to clear his mind. What had he just witnessed? The rest of the orphans had either gone back to bed or were heading there without drama or distress. What was this place?

"Why don't we talk," Espero said to Toekin. His robes fluttered in the wind as the door to the kitchen was pulled shut. "Let's sit by the fire though. That draft has left me a little chilly."

"What just happened?"

Espero looked up from his lap where he was rubbing his hands together to warm them. He waited for Zonks, the last person in the room, to leave before beginning. "Everyone who lives here at the orphanage is gifted. All of us are Zaints."

There was that word again. He remembered Força telling about how people had been killed for being a Zaint. Why would anyone want to be one?

"It's a gift," Espero said, and Toekin wondered if he could read his mind. It wouldn't surprise him after what he'd witnessed tonight. "We are either blessed with the gift of the sun, the gift of the moon, or the gift of the stars. Each grants us specific abilities."

Toekin nodded. Why was he nodding?

"You've seen me disappear and appear somewhere different? That's called gliding, and it's something people with the sun's gift can do. Our dear Kai has the gift of the stars and can influence people's minds. Tonight he caused those guards to forget everything that happened here."

That cheese kid? "Can he see things too . . . things that are going to happen?"

"Yes, that's something that few people like him can do. He's special." Espero looked at Toekin carefully, possibly assessing how he was doing with this new information before deciding to go on. "Lua and Força have gifts of healing. That's from the moon."

Toekin twisted his sling around his hand, drawn into the crackling fire. He should be running for the hills, but somehow things made sense, or at least felt right.

Toekin shook his head. "It's a lot to digest," he said.

"There's more." Espero turned a critical eye on Toekin.

"Is it about me, isn't it? Do I have one of these gifts too?"

"Not exactly."

He'd said it warmly. Kindly, even. Still, Toekin's heart sank a little, and it surprised him. Had he been secretly hoping he'd have one of these powers? He wasn't even sure.

"You don't have *one* of these gifts, Toekin. You have all three." He paused to let it sink in. "It is very, very rare."

He didn't know what to say. Espero's arm came around him and filled Toekin with comfort. Finally Toekin said, "What does that mean?"

"Right now, it doesn't mean much. You haven't been trained. Although, some of your abilities have developed naturally. The fact that you've been able to survive on your own since, I'm guessing, a very young age shows great use of your gifts."

"It does?"

"Yes. And your unusual friend Corvo . . . the power, which you received from the moon, made him into what he is."

Toekin didn't remember doing anything special to Corvo. He just loved him and had desperately wanted a friend.

"I can teach you so much Toekin, if you'll let me." Espero's arm dropped. "I know you're eager to be on your way, and I respect that. But . . ."

"But what?"

Espero hesitated, then said, "I don't want my will to interfere with yours, Toekin. I don't want to make you feel like you were tricked into staying here." There was a sincerity in his eyes that Toekin instantly trusted, then suspected.

"You're not using some power on me now, to try and influence me, are you?"

"You'd be able to tell."

"Well, then, what is it? What do you want to tell me?"

Espero took a deep breath and said, "Only a Zaint with all three gifts can summon and control the dragon Paz."

Paz. The girl's voice echoed in Toekin's mind. "But that's just a made-up story. There's no dragon."

"Oh Toekin," Espero's smile was filled with pain, "the story is real. Very real. The emperor is too powerful. Using Paz might be the only way to defeat Beezul and bring peace again to Enganoso." His voice dropped in volume and he leaned closer. "You could be the one to make that happen, my son."

CHAPTER 8

The Clue

General Sem rode hard for Triste, making the four-day journey in just two, pushing his horses and his men to their limits. "Hold up!" Sem shouted just outside the city, bringing his company to a halt. The horses' breaths blew out in heavy clouds of steam and the men took the opportunity to warm their hands inside their jackets.

He rallied his men and went over the mission. "The people here are hardened, rough, and for the most part, despise the emperor," he said. "But they despise their poverty more. Use this against them. Bribe them to get what you want, but feel free to play on their fears as well. Root out any rebels—any whiff of a Zaint and I want to know about it. They're our best bet for leading us to the rebels, and the relic."

Sem thought back to the rebel prisoners who had turned on them a few days earlier. Their boldness, despite its ineffectiveness, was disturbing. What might they try next? "Also, keep your eyes and ears open for any leads on the ambush of taxation carts."

From the corner of his eye he caught glimpses of a figure hidden in the shadows at the edge of the forest. Lobo had easily kept up with them on foot thanks to Nojento's *gifts*. One of the many side effects of these modifications, however, was Lobo's hatred and distrust for almost everyone. He preferred traveling in solitude, away from the pack, and more and more, he seemed more comfortable in the wild, like a true animal. Sem could tell he was the only one who even knew he was there.

"We'll ride in together, a show of force. Remind them who is in charge." Sem looked around at his best soldiers—the ones he reserved for missions like this. "Then we'll break off, two by two. Durman, you're with me. The rest of you will head out and see what you can find, then meet back here tonight."

There were nods, but no words as they grabbed the reins and continued the ride into town. Situated on the southernmost border of Enganoso, Triste was more of an outpost than a town. Bordered by sea to the east, mountains to the south and the Mato Forest to the north, it was secluded and remote, and the residents didn't expect or welcome outsiders. Especially ones from Abbadon.

As they trotted down the muddy road filled with potholes and puddles, doors slammed shut, windows shuttered, and people disappeared like roaches running from light. Ahead, a little girl darted into the road, trying to beat their procession and make it to the other side. Her foot hit a slick spot and she slipped. She looked up, dazed and dirty, tears welling, recoiling as General Sem and his horse stopped inches from where she sat. The whole detail ground to a halt behind him, horses snorting and stomping in their irritation.

What would it be like, he wondered, to *not* be a monster of children's dreams? He dismounted, boots landing with a splash in the mud, and approached the shivering girl. She looked no more than eight.

"Ana!" A woman screamed. She had started to run into the road, then stopped, fear-stricken and wide-eyed when she'd seen the General.

Sem reached out to the little girl, but she inched back, unwilling to meet his hand with her own.

"Let me help you," he said, but even as he did, he imagined how his black eyes and his grotesque face might look to this child. *He* wouldn't reach out to someone like him.

"Marcus, no!" the woman who had stopped in the road pleaded through sobs. Sem looked again and saw her holding back a man who was straining in his direction.

"Your papa?" He said to the little girl.

She nodded, tears escaping her eyes and leaving clean streaks through the mud on her cheeks.

"Why don't I bring you to him. Come." He held his hand out once more and this time, she responded. She was slow, at first, watching his eyes for any change of temperament until finally her hand was in his. "There you are, brave girl." They took two steps, and then she broke loose and ran into her mother and father's arms. Sem turned, unwilling to wait for the thanks he knew would not be offered.

* * *

After a long day of attempting to gather information, Sem and Durman approached the tavern. The only luck they'd had was from an old man who assured them he knew where the relic was, but also insisted on wearing a chamber pot on his head to explain its location. He also claimed he could turn cow manure into purple steel.

Upon entering, they were assaulted with the usual noises: bellows and hoots of men enjoying their drink, the clank of tankards pounding the table, the din of mundane conversation of crop yields and animal husbandry, and under everything, the whine of a fiddle coming from some unseen corner. As the two made their way into the room, heads turned, and one by one hissing whispers and stares replaced the more familiar sounds. All except one: The sound of a truhko game gone bad.

"You little cheat!" An Abbadon Guard accused a tall, greasy-haired man in a worn-out tunic and breeches with holes in the knees. Sem didn't recognize the guard as one of his own; probably someone who'd been stationed here for a while.

"The cards don't lie," he said, almost as a taunt. He turned to his companions and grinned in premature triumph.

"The cards don't, but you do!" The guard grabbed the man by his shirt and yanked him into fist range.

"What's going on here?" Sem stood like a statue of living stone, imposing and cold. The room went silent.

The guard turned in surprise. "General Sem, Sir!" He released the accused, saluted and then settled into a more confident stance. "This man cheated. I want my money back." He turned to the greasy man, cracked his knuckles and said, "He must be punished." A grin spread across his face indicating punishment was a foregone conclusion and that he would enjoy it very much.

"You have proof?"

The guard's head snapped back to Sem. "I don't need proof. I'm an Abbadon Guard. And this man's reputation as a crook is well-known. Ask anyone here and they'll tell you. He'd cheat his own mother if he got the chance."

Every head in the room suddenly turned away from Sem and the scene unfolding before them, clearly unwilling to be called to testify.

Sem turned his black eyes onto the man, his attempts at bravado suddenly quelled. "Did you cheat?"

"No, General Sem. I would never cheat an Abbadon Guard. Never!"

"He lies, Sir."

"Where is your proof!" Sem brought his fist down on a nearby table, crashing cleanly through the broad planks and sending tankards of ale flying.

The guard was now the one to cower as the man with the greasy hair slowly backed away from the unfolding scene. "Sir," he said. "It is well known."

Sem turned to the accused cheater. "Get out of here!" By now he was closer to the door than he was to the General. Still, he hovered in a corner to watch things play out. There were a few snickers and the whispers started up again. The guard looked around the room, the red in his cheeks rising with his apparent fury.

"Sir," he hissed angrily into the hole that used to be Sem's ear. "I've kept this town in line for over ten winters. They fear me. Tonight, in an instant, you have undone that. And all because of a known liar. I'll be a laughing stock now."

Durman had stood by as Sem dealt out his form of justice, but at the guard's foolish rebuke, even he started to distance himself from the scene.

"How dare you question my authority!" In an instant, Sem's sword was at the guard's throat, a thin trickle of blood running from the point of contact down his neck and underneath the purple collar.

Frozen and afraid to move the man cried out. "Please. Forgive me, General."

Sem's sword dropped and the guard relaxed momentarily. However, terror quickly registered in the guard's eyes a black tentacle-like cloud seemed to seep out of Sem's fingers, getting bigger and bigger until it engulfed the guard. He cried out in pain, his sobs and pleas seeming to only encourage Sem's assault. The guard crumpled to his knees, screaming and the cloud grew even darker, denser.

Onlookers turned away in horror. Serving girls huddled together in fear and several patrons ran for the door, but Sem was oblivious.

His eyes narrowed, and his efforts seemed to intensify. The guard's screams turned to moans and he fell forward retching, his eyes rolling back into his head. Finally, he collapsed onto the floor, lost to all consciousness. Slowly Sem seemed to return to himself. He stepped back, looked at the guard on the floor almost as if seeing him for the first time, then quickly recovered his own senses.

"Residents of Triste," Sem said. "Abbadon wants you to be safe, not oppressed. Guards like this one can't be left unchecked to wield authority with impunity. If you have information on abuses of power, or any other things that might disturb your peaceful existence, you may give me your report. Emperor Beezul rewards the citizens of this realm when they are loyal—and helpful."

Silence still blanketed the room as half seemed to be staring at Sem and the other half at the guardsman on the floor. "Now, who will bring some ale for me and my captain?"

The sound in the room rose gradually until everyone had reengaged in their previous activities. Sem and Durman found a quiet table out of the main commotion and someone dragged the prostrate guard out of the room.

"You scare me sometimes, you know," Durman said taking a drink of ale.

"It's what I am now." Sem didn't want to talk about it. There was no use wishing for things past.

Durman's eyes narrowed and his mood darkened. "I would like to see Nojento dead for what he did to you. And the others."

Sem replied by taking the whole of his tankard in one, long quaff. Most of the time, he agreed with this sentiment, but what would that change? He would still be the same terrifying creature whose greatest weapon was using people's fears to crush them.

"What do you think of those two over there?" Durman tipped his chin toward a spot in the room behind Sem.

Thank the sun, he'd changed the subject. He turned around to find a young man with unusually white hair and skin, apparently doing very well at a game of truhko. The boy drained his cup, showing off a long white scar that ran from his hairline, all the way down his face as he threw his head back. He called for more drink from a passing girl with a tray and threw his cards on the table with flair. "What about him?"

"I don't know. Something about him seems off. And his friend too."

"His friend?"

"Check out the muscle sitting at the other table. The dark-skinned fellow with the beard."

Sem looked at the man who's hulking body made the chair he was sitting in appear to be that of a child. He wondered what would make Durman think they were together, but after watching them for a few moments, it became clear. The man with the beard was keeping an eye on the card player, and his other eye on them. When he ordered another round of drinks after winning a big hand, the large man signaled to the serving girl to give him some weaker ale. He watched the other players in the game and how they reacted to the white-haired man. They *were* together.

Sem turned back to face his friend. "What do you make of it."

"They don't fit."

Sem turned back around. Staring would only draw their attention. "Keep an eye on them."

A serving girl brought two wooden bowls of meaty stew and a warm loaf of peasant bread. Sem ripped into it right away. "Compliments of my father." She spoke in short, nervous bursts. "If there be anything else you need, we are happy to oblige." Sem looked into his bowl of stew, unwilling to meet her eyes. No need to make this harder on the girl than it already was.

"Thanks to you and your father, Miss." Durman said. Relations with the public were best left to him. The girl scurried off and the two turned their attention to their meals. After a while Durman said, "Well, look at that?"

"What is it?"

"Someone just whispered something in the bearded man's ear."

"You think they're up to something?"

"Could be." Durman kept his eye trained on the man and reported to Sem. "He's getting up now, going over to the gaming table."

Sem finally turned around, leaving behind all stealth and subtlety, and watched as the man with the beard, approached the white-haired man at the table. They argued for a moment and finally the white-haired man leaned forward and pulled as many of his winnings as he could into his arms and left a table of angry, poorer men, shaking their fists in the air.

"Let's go," Sem said, and they rose, leaving their meal unfinished, and started to make their way through the crowded tavern. The bearded man ducked, fitting his large frame through the door after the white-haired man, and they were gone.

Sem didn't have trouble clearing a path. People moved out of his way whether he demanded it or not. Still, by the time they got outside, the two men had disappeared.

"They could be anywhere. Should we start looking?"

Sem chewed on that, then said, "We'll hold off for now, but stay aware." Maybe they were just travelers. But something told him there was more to their story.

"Excuse me, sir?" A timid voice came from the shadows. It was the greasy haired man from earlier.

"I thought I told you to get out of here."

"I know, and I was just on my way." The man had trouble looking Sem in the eyes. "But I remembered how you said, the emperor would reward people who were loyal."

"What about it," Sem growled.

The man shrank, then seemed to steel himself and said in hushed tones, "I have news about the rebels."

Durman stepped forward. "What do you know?"

The man ignored him, pulling a hand through his thin strands of hair. "I was wondering what exactly you meant by, 'reward.'"

Sem pulled a pouch out of his pocket and shook it. Coins jangled, and the man's courage seemed to double.

"I can tell you when and where they'll be gathering tonight."

"How certain are you of this information?"

"Quite certain, sir."

"I can offer you one silver piece now, and three gold ones if your information proves correct."

The man's eyes got big and he nodded.

"And if the information you provide turns out to be false, I'll hunt you down and get my gold back." Sem's smile was an uncomfortable warning slashed across his face. He grabbed the man's wrist and the smallest amount of black mist escaped, engulfing his hand. He whimpered as tears beaded up in the corners of his eyes.

Sem held on for a moment longer, then released his grip. "That is just a taste of what will happen if you're lying."

"You have a deal," he cried, cradling his hand against his chest as he shivered. "They're meeting just south of here, down by the Rio River. Should be about three or four men tonight. They'll be there by second watch, so you might want to get there a little early . . ."

"Thank you," Sem interrupted, pulling a coin out of his pouch and flipping it to him. "I think I can figure it out from here."

"Of course, General." The man bowed, backing away. "You won't be disappointed."

After he'd slunk off, Durman said, "I don't think we can trust this guy."

Sem took a drink from his flask and thrust it in Durman's direction but he shook his head. "We can't," Sem said. "It's a set up."

"What makes you so sure?" Durman said.

"That greasy rat never asked how to collect his remaining gold. He's expecting this to be a one-way trip. Besides, he really was cheating inside. I saw his memory of it when I . . ." There was no need to explain. Durman knew when.

Durman shook his head and smiled. "What's your plan?"

"Go meet the rest of the men at our rendezvous location, then bring them down by the river. I'll take care of the ambush and meet you there later."

"Sir. Don't go alone. You're powerful, but you don't know what these men might have up their sleeve."

"I'll be fine. It's a couple of men. Just go to the meeting spot."

"Sem! Please. Let me go with you."

"Rendezvous. That's an order."

"Of course," Durman nodded, resigned to the pig-headedness of his friend. Then a half smile crept onto his face. "You always were a stubborn git," Duramn said. "At least Nojento left one aspect of the old you intact."

* * *

Sem approached the clearing under cover, quietly picking his way through the trees and underbrush down to the river. It wasn't long before he found who he was looking for.

"I thought you'd never get here," Lobo said, his voice gruff and impatient.

Sem ignored the taunt. "What have you learned?"

"I've learned you're in over your head." Lobo pawed at the ground with impatience.

"I don't have all night, dog. Give me some information I can use."

Lobo growled and bared his teeth, saliva dripping from his gums. "There's a sun slinger."

This complicated things, but it certainly didn't make them impossible. "That can't be it. What else?"

"There will be about forty other men."

Now that was indeed bad news. Sem couldn't manage that many men *and* a sun slinger. He reformulated his plan. "You handle the Zaint and I'll take care of the rest."

Lobo growled, angry and vengeful. "Who do you think I am? I'm not your little pet to command. Maybe I'll just let them have their way with you." Lobo howled with dark laughter. "It would be . . . entertaining to watch you die."

The threat didn't surprise Sem, nor had it come as a first. "We have more to gain by helping each other," Sem said. "If I die, Nojento will create again and you may find yourself wishing I was still around."

A low thrum rumbled in Lobo's chest. "I will help." He snapped his jaws, as if he wished to retake his words. "I'll do it," he repeated, his eyes flashing red, "but I want the sun slinger."

"That was the plan I proposed." Sem swore, Lobo had lost more than his humanity in Nojento's experiments. His intelligence had taken a hit too.

"No, not to fight. I'll do that, and I'll win. But when I do, I want him for myself." His lips pulled back and more saliva dripped down his chin.

Lobo didn't need to say more. Sem had a picture in his head of what this entailed, too detailed for his liking.

"And no mind games either," Lobo bared his angry teeth. "I get him, and I get to do what I want with him."

"Fine."

Lobo grinned. "The slinger has long, blonde hair." And with that, Lobo disappeared in a blink, leaving behind a trail of red light that faded into the darkness. Within moments voices could be heard coming into the clearing. The three or four had, as Lobo said, become closer to forty men. Most kept back in the trees, as if Sem wouldn't know they were there.

He searched for the man with the blonde hair, but they were still in the shadows and hard to see.

Four approached the clearing. "We need to plan out our next ambush," one said.

"Beezul will never see it coming," another replied.

The group dialogue was ridiculous, obviously scripted, and an attempt to draw him out. And then he saw it. Light gathered around a man as he moved barely visible through the trees. First gliding to one spot, and returning to where he'd stood a moment before, then gliding elsewhere. Over and over he repeated this pattern and then Sem realized why: he was searching for him.

He sank back, deeper into the foliage, pulling darkness around him. It would only be a matter of time until the sun slinger found him. Time to act. Black waves of energy pulsed outward from his eyes and fingertips as he focused on the group of men.

"It feels like it's getting darker," one said. "But that doesn't make sense. It's already night."

Some of the men turned toward the edges of the clearing, positioning themselves for attack. The group hiding in the trees finally came forward, adding to their number in a weak show of intimidation. Some pulled their weapons. Sem continued to gather darkness until it was nearly as black as the deepest corners of a cave. The Zaint widened his search, gliding farther and farther out from the group.

One of the men screamed, falling to the ground, writhing in pain. Then another. Confusion broke out and those still standing drew their swords, watching, waiting for whatever might be out there to attack. More men dropped to the ground. One cut down two of his comrades before others could react. He cried out in agony when they brought him down, all while the sun slinger was getting closer and closer to Sem's hiding place. He didn't have much longer.

Where's Lobo?

"Stand your ground!" one man yelled.

"What's happening?" another cried in fear.

Confusion seemed to multiply as more men collapsed in pain. Some tried to run, smashing into trees and doing Sem's job for him. Then the sun slinger glided back into the center of the group, bright light gathering around his eyes as he stood with his sword in hand.

Blast that wolf! Sem was going to have to take care of this himself. He pushed the blackness forward, snaking through the air like tendrils of despair, but the Zaint detected the energy and traced it back until his eyes rested on Sem. The man dropped into the stream of light and was immediately before him, sword drawn. Sem barely had time to draw his own and deflect the attack.

And then he was behind Sem, his blade crashing down toward his head. *So fast!* There was no way he could move quickly enough to defend the blow. He braced himself for death.

Instead of the sword, however, Sem felt something hot on the back of his head. He turned around to find Lobo wrapped around the man, his powerful hairy arm had stayed the sword, while his

91

razor-sharp teeth were sunk deep into his neck and blood pumped out in thick waves. Lobo stared down at Sem with dark red eyes, and then bit even harder. There was a crunch and a popping noise and more blood splashed across Sem's face. Finally Lobo stepped back, letting the man drop into heap before him.

Sem reached up to his face and brought his hand back, covered in the man's blood. Lobo was bent down, low and protective over the body and growled a warning at Sem just for daring to look. Sem turned away in disgust, but not before seeing the broken man being pulled into the bushes. *He's getting worse*, Sem thought.

"The darkness . . . it's gone!" someone shouted and Sem returned to his senses. He shook off the knowledge of what Lobo was doing but couldn't keep the hate from welling up inside of him. Hate for Lobo, but ultimately hate for Nojento and what he'd forced him to become. Blackness poured from his eyes and he drew his sword, finally revealing himself to the rebels who were still standing.

Some stood their ground, others drew crossbows, but most scampered away like the rats they were. It was no use. In a matter of moments, every single one was either dead or passed out from pain. But he had ended it too quickly. Now there was nothing to prevent him from dwelling on the hate and self-loathing he felt. Thankfully, however, his next distraction came in the sound of a low rumble of horses' hooves that grew to a thundering roar as his own men rode into the clearing.

Durman surveyed the scene and then looked at Sem. "Sir, you're covered in blood."

"Not mine," he said, stiff and cold, his emotion spent. "Take all these bodies to the river. If they're dead, throw them in. If they live, hold them for questioning."

"Yes Sir," Durman said, and the team began hoisting bodies onto the backs of their horses for the short haul.

Sem hoped Lobo was far away by now. He had saved his life tonight, yet somehow, Sem detested him more than ever. He walked down to the river, taking time to unwind and clear his mind. At the water's edge he bent down, dipped his hands in, and began cleaning off the blood. The icy water sent shocking chills throughout his body and he welcomed the discomfort which brought the realization he could still feel.

He focused on the swoosh and gurgle of the river as it flowed freely, letting the rhythm of it calm him. That's why, when the rhythm changed, he noticed it. Something was restricting the movement of water and he looked up to confirm his suspicions. A dark form had lodged between some rocks. Giving into his curiosity, he stepped into the numbing water and waded closer to the spot. It was one of the dead bodies, sent from upriver by his men, which had become stuck.

Sem cursed under his breath. He should probably dislodge him. He waded deeper until he could reach the body, then unpinned his leg from under a log and released him back into the current. That's when something else trapped by the log caught his eye. He pulled it out of the water and turned it over to reveal the infinity symbol engulfed in flames. The brown burlap sack was empty, but Sem knew exactly what had been in it.

He also knew that, unfortunately, he wasn't done with Lobo's services for the night.

CHAPTER 9

The Game

"I can't believe you've healed so quickly," Lua said, removing the last of Toekin's bandages. "Even with the moon's light, most people would have taken twice this long." Corvo hopped from one foot to the other on his perch at the foot of the bed, overseeing Lua's work.

Toekin took her word for it. He figured he was lucky that in all the years on his own, the ursmock attack was the worst injury he'd ever had. Besides that, it was scrapes, bruises and minor cuts. He didn't pay attention to how fast they healed. Didn't really think of them again after sustaining them. They just seemed to take care of themselves.

Since he was doing so well, Espero said he could begin lessons today. Toekin reasoned that a few weeks exploring his newfound gifts would be enough to get him going, then he could return home and take over his own training from there. He looked down at his chest at the wounds that were, just over a week ago, a potential death sentence. Now they were nothing more than pink scars that would serve as reminders for the rest of his life. There was still some soreness, but only when he played pig ball with the littles, or carried in heavy loads of root vegetables and cabbage from the garden.

"Do all the kids train, then?" He asked, trying to keep the concern out of his voice. He imagined five-year-old Enzo out-performing him and cringed inwardly.

"Yes," Tessa said, taking the used bandage from Lua's outstretched hand. "That way the older kids help us younger kids when we get stuck." Of course to her, training with the older kids would be a huge positive.

It made sense, but didn't calm Toekin's worries.

"There. All done. Lua stood back and looked at her work, which was really just Toekin's bare chest. She looked a little too long and Toekin's cheeks turned red. Lua looked up in time to catch him.

She laughed, punching him lightly on the shoulder. "Don't flatter yourself." The way she said it was warm and friendly. Safe. "I'm just making sure you're really ready to go bandage free. It's still a little hard for me to believe you're healed. Here." She handed him his shirt and he put it on. "Tessa, would you go put those bandages in the laundry, and let Espero know I'm done?"

Tessa ran off, the long bandages trailing behind her and winding around her feet.

"She's going to trip," Toekin said, shaking his head.

"You don't have to be a seer like Kai and Row to make that prediction." Lua cleaned up her supplies and gathered them into a bag. "If you notice any redness or unusual pain, let me know right away." She looked into his eyes, letting him know she was serious.

"Promise," Tokin said. She had been good to him. Everyone at the orphanage had, and he still struggled to understand why. What were they getting out of it? What was their motivation to help other people? For Toekin, it had been to enrage the Emperor. The more he could be a thorn in his side, the better. Delivering the food was simply a way to get rid of the evidence. Nothing more.

These people confused him, but for the most part, he'd given up on trying to understand. He would learn what he could and get back to his life. A few weeks off from ambushing the taxation carts would do him good and confuse Abbadon. A win, win.

"You nervous about the sun lessons this afternoon?" Lua leaned back against the table and folded her arms.

He hadn't told her he would be learning the moon and stars too, and he didn't think Espero had said anything either. "A little," he finally said.

"I'm sure you'll pick it up quickly. You've probably been doing more than you realize. That's how it is with most of us. When we're kids, we have no idea that not everyone can feel the pull of the moon, or the power of the stars like we can. We just think it's normal. Once someone points out that it's not, it's easier to recognize."

"Our patient is ready?" Espero said, coming in through the open door. Tessa came tripping in behind him.

"Ready for what?" Toekin said. What did they want him to do now?

"I thought you and I might take a walk. It's a nice day. We could cover some of the basics before class."

Toekin felt a nervous load lift. Now maybe he didn't have to look like such a fool in front of everyone later. "Sounds great," he said.

"Yeah, I bet it does." Lua folded her arms smugly. "You were supposed to be on lunch duty later this morning."

"I'll do it!" Tessa said, raising her hand with pure enthusiasm.

This seemed to satisfy Lua.

"Can Corvo come with me?" She turned to Toekin and pulled open the pocket of her apron to reveal a red apple.

Toekin chuckled. "Corvo, you're becoming a bit predictable."

"Caw!"

"Sure, he can go with you. He'll probably be more trouble than he's worth, though." Toekin said.

"Thank you, Tessa dear." Espero said. "Now Toekin, shall we?" He held his arm out, an invitation for Toekin to lead the way. They exited through the sun sala and out into the actual sun. It was low on the horizon, its winter perch, and Toekin raised his arm to shade it from hitting him right in the eyes.

"As you've seen, we don't need to be outside to harness the power of the sun, moon or stars, but I thought being out here might help you better understand what that feels like, so when you are inside, you'll be able to tap into it more readily."

"Have you told anyone else that I'm—what did you call it?" There were so many new words and ideas; he was having trouble remembering them all.

"Zaintozo," Espero said. "That's what we call someone who has all three powers. And no, I haven't. They'll find out soon enough." Espero didn't seem particularly worried about it. Toekin wasn't sure how people would react to the news. Would they be happy? Jealous? He tried to think of how he might feel but had no context to put that feeling into.

"I want to cover gliding," Espero said, "because I'm certain you've done it before without knowing it."

Toekin nodded.

"This is when you move so quickly, it looks like you are disappearing from one place and reappearing in another."

"I'm pretty sure I've seen *you* do that, but I doubt *I* ever have."

"Think about it. When you and Corvo travel, you're able to move quickly, are you not?"

"I just run. Nothing special."

"When you've ambushed the Abbadon Guards, you're able to move so fast they can't even pinpoint your location. Correct?"

"I guess."

"You feel a surge of energy right before this happens, right?"

"Yeah. How'd you . . ."

Espero held up his hand. "Light is moving all around us. However, most people don't see it that way. They notice light, or the absence of it, and that is all. But the sun seeker can see light everywhere, even when it appears dark. Light's movement is obvious. We can see it *and* we can use it."

Toekin nodded. This made sense.

"When we glide, we simply ride that moving light from one place to another, stepping in and out of the flow. But do not force yourself on the light. Rather, let it take you, guide you. The better you get, the easier it will be to glide. You won't have to feel a surge of emotion, like anger or fear, to tap into it."

Toekin laughed. It appeared Espero knew him a little too well.

"And you won't have to even think about what you're doing. It will become effortless. Now try it. Focus on the moving light around you, where you want to go, and step into a stream of it and go there."

Toekin wasn't sure he could do it with out the intense feelings of hatred for the guards. If he'd done it, he'd never done it any other way before. He calmed himself now, and tried to bring the moving light into focus. Suddenly, there it was, more recognizable then when he'd been attacking the guards. How had he never seen it before?

He glided from tree to tree, watching Espero's face warm with joy. He couldn't believe he was doing it, and how natural it felt to move with the light. When he finally came to a stop, Espero patted him on the shoulder. "Well done! You're even better than I thought you'd be," he said. "Let's try it again, but this time I'll add some challenges."

Toekin started gliding and suddenly Espero was in front of him. He slammed right into the old man. But instead of knocking him down, Toekin fell back while Espero looked as if nothing more than a tiny woodland bug had pestered him.

"You weren't paying attention, were you?" Espero looked so pleased with himself, Toekin was a little annoyed. He stood, still stunned, and wondered if he would need Lua's healing hands again. "I suppose I wasn't playing fair. I created a layer of dense, pure light around myself like a shield. We call it pele. Works great for striking too, without hurting your hand." He laughed at his joke.

Toekin rubbed at his temples, trying to stave off a headache.

"I'll teach you how to do that later," Espero said. "Not as hard as it sounds. In the meantime, you need to learn to avoid obstacles, so let's practice that again."

"How am I supposed to get out of the way when I'm going that fast? I can't just stop."

"Train yourself to be ready to slip into another light stream in an instant. Always be aware—ready for anything. I'll go easier on you this time."

They practiced again and Toekin gradually improved. The morning slipped away and so absorbed was he in his lesson, he barely felt time pass. He was now able to re-route his glide with ease to avoid running into Espero, or whatever other obstacle he put in his way.

"Well, what do you know? He's still here!" Row and Força approached, their traveling bags still on their backs.

Toekin replied with a raise of his chin.

"And you're a sun slinger, I see." Row turned to Força and hit him playfully on the shoulder. "I wanted to wager on it with him, but he wasn't interested."

Força sighed and rolled his eyes.

Toekin took Row's outstretched hand and shook.

"How was your journey?" Espero said.

"Productive." Força spoke as if each word cost money he was loath to part with.

"Good, good." Espero smiled, looking from one to the other, as if more explanation would come. When none did he said, "You've guessed correctly, Row. Toekin is indeed gifted with the sun. We've been practicing all morning."

"Is he ready to spar with me?"

"Not quite yet." Espero said, pausing. He gave Toekin a knowing glance, then turned back to Row and Força. "He must first learn to control the light of the moon and stars too."

Row's mouth dropped open and his eyes got big. Toekin thought he saw a shadow of pain cross his face, but it quickly turned. "Really? A Zaintozo, you say?" He gave Toekin two enthusiastic pats to his back and slung his arm around his shoulders, although his smile didn't quite reach his eyes.

Força was simply nodding, looking thoughtfully into the dirt at his feet. Espero watched him for a moment and then said, "I'm sure he would appreciate your help with his training."

"You got it, Toe." Row had yet to release his friendly hold on Toekin's shoulder and Toekin wanted to shake him off, but something in the grip told him Row needed the human contact more than Toekin needed to be free of it.

"Of course," Força said.

The sound of the gong rang out.

"Sounds like lunch is ready." Espero said with a cheer that felt subtly forced. There was something these three weren't telling him.

"Before we go in," Força said, rising to the change of subject. "I need to tell you, we got word of Kimnar's location."

"This is good. You should visit, pass on our support, and learn of any plans." Espero seemed pleased.

"There's more." Força's eyes narrowed and he ran his hand over his long, thick beard, thinking carefully how to proceed.

"We saw General Sem." Row said, glancing quickly at Força before continuing. "He was in the tavern one evening. Just rode into town that day. Word was he was looking for rebels and asking questions about the relic."

"He took the opportunity to make a public example of one of the soldiers stationed in Triste. It wasn't pretty," Força said, shaking his head as if he still couldn't believe what he'd seen.

"He's got some kind of power that we've never seen before. It's like a blackness." Row, shuddered. "He covered the guard in it, and it looked like he was being dealt the foulest of torture. It kind of reminded me of the light of the stars, but the exact opposite. The guard's screams were . . ." Row trailed off, shaking his head.

"I've never seen the like." Força said.

Espero seemed lost in his thoughts. "I see," he finally said.

Toekin struggled to keep up with the conversation—the implications. Since he'd come to the orphanage, things he'd thought as constants, as basic truths, had all been turned upside down. There was a whole world outside of the one he'd lived in, and he hadn't even realized it. How could he have thought on such a small scale? The battle was bigger than he had ever imagined.

"The visit to Kimnar and the rebels has taken on a bit of urgency, Força. Prepare yourself to leave in a day—two at the most."

Força nodded.

"Things will begin moving quickly. We need to prepare." Espero's voice was measured, lacking its usual levity. He looked at Row, then Força. "I fear we can no longer passively teach our children how to use their gifts. Have Lua teach the moon children while you're gone, and Row, you will work with the seers. I'll take the children of the sun. It's time our young ones truly learned how to defend themselves—how to fight."

* * *

Toekin sat on a bench in the sun sala, stroking Corvo's head. He had some decisions to make. Trouble was coming, and he needed to decide if he was going to be part of it, or if he was going to strike out, chipping away at the Emperor's wicked rule in his own way. He would have more freedom of movement and total control if he were on his own—responsible only for himself.

But, if there was another ursmock attack, he thought, or worse? Who would be responsible for him? Working with others, he could wield more power over Beezul—strength in numbers. But if what Força and Row had said was true, the Emperor had some dangerous weapons at his disposal. Maybe unbeatable weapons.

"Hey! There you are." Lua saw Toekin from across the room and covered the distance between them in just a few angry steps. "Why didn't you tell me?"

"Tell you what?" He'd only interacted with girls for a few weeks now, and so far found them to be pretty confusing. Especially Lua.

"That you're Zaintozo," she said, as if it were obvious.

"I didn't know I was supposed to make an announcement."

"Not to everyone. But at least you could have told me. I thought . . . I mean, we're friends, right?"

"I don't know. I've never had a friend before. Besides Corvo." Living with other people was so complicated. He put that on his mental list as one of the reasons to return to solitary life.

Lua sighed, checking herself. "Right. I keep forgetting." She looked Toekin in the eyes. "We're friends, okay? I helped you heal—although it seems like you might have been fine without me. And you would help me if I needed something. Right?"

Toekin thought before answering. What was he committing to? "I guess. Sure."

"Then we're friends." She smiled and patted his arm, then reached for Corvo. The bird hissed low, warning her away. She sighed. "I just can't win that bird over."

"Corv," Toekin chided, laughing under his breath. Was this true? Were he and Lua friends? "Sorry," he finally said, then added, "that I

101

didn't tell you. All this stuff is so new to me. And I'm not really used to being around people."

"What do you mean?"

"I've been on my own a long time. I've always gone and done exactly what I wanted. Part of me really misses that."

"You're not going to leave now, are you?" Lua's eyes flashed icy blue and her brow furrowed, daring him to confirm it.

"All this talk of Paz the Dragon being real. I don't know if I can be the person you need me to be—the person Espero thinks I should be." And, he thought, he didn't know if he could be the person the girl from his dreams wanted him to be. But she was just that—a dream. Wasn't she?

"One of the great things about being part of a community is that we help each other. You can be better than your best self when you work with others."

Toekin thought about it. He supposed it could be true.

"Is Toe telling you how he's going to save the world?" Row came across the room, stopping by the fire to warm his hands. "Zaintozo. That's something, isn't it Lua?" A look passed between them so quickly Toekin wasn't sure he'd seen it.

"It's something," she said. There was sadness in her voice, but a smile on her face. Just like when Força and Row had found out.

"Is there something you aren't telling me?" Toekin asked. He was getting tired of being on the outside of so many secrets.

Row looked at Lua, silent communication passing between them.

"You know what? Forget it," Toekin said. He was an outsider and always would be. "This is your world, not mine." He got up and started toward his room. Corvo followed, hopping off the bench.

"Toekin, wait." Lua called out. He stopped.

"We're sorry. You see, we had a friend who was Zaintozo, and she . . . got sick. We miss her. That's all."

"Yeah," Row, for the first time since Toekin had met him, looked serious, sincere. "It's still kind of hard to talk about."

"So is this something that happens to Zaintozos? Do all of them get sick?" Was that why they had seemed hesitant to talk about it?

They stood there, unsure of what to say next.

"Oh! I almost forgot why I came up here in the first place," Row said. "I was supposed to get Toekin and show him the training area. It's time for some lessons!"

They were dodging the question, but part of Toekin didn't know if he really wanted to hear the answer. "So this is where I get to look stupid in front of everyone?"

"No way," Row said. "You're going to do great."

"Hold on," Toekin said. "You just said you came *up*? This place has a downstairs?"

"Wait till you see it!" Lua said.

Row led the way across the room to one of the doors Toekin had assumed was another dorm room. Instead, behind the door was a hallway. They followed it around a corner and came to a corridor with no windows. Lit torches, set in wall sconces, were the only source of light. Row stopped about half way down the hall where ornate carvings of the sun, the moon and the stars decorated the wall.

"Here we are," Row said, grinning at the puzzled look on Toekin's face.

"Row," Lua chided. "Here, let me show you. Find your symbol—mine's the moon. Well, I guess yours is all of them. Anyway, you just . . . go like this." She placed her hand on the beautiful moon carving and blue light gathered around her fingers, spreading outward until it rippled across the entire surface. There was a soft *click*, Lua pushed, and a door opened, revealing a staircase that descended down.

"How big *is* this place?" Toekin said, amazed at the secret passageway.

"Big enough we can hide what we're doing from the Abby Guards." Row winked. "But, Lua," Row said. "I don't think that was very helpful. You didn't even explain how to make your light into energy."

Lua shook him off. "You just . . . do it. I don't know how to explain it."

"Look, Toe. You need to visualize." Row closed his eyes to demonstrate. "Imagine seeing all the light within yourself. Since you're Zaintozo, it's probably good that you start trying to identify the difference between the three types of light. Once you've found the light of the sun, which is what you'll need to open this door, picture it flowing into your arm, your hand, and finally your fingers." He said this as if it were a simple thing, but Toekin still had no idea what he was talking about.

"Try it," Row was encouraging. "Don't worry if you don't get it at first. I guarantee, after a couple times, you'll have this thing down."

Toekin took a deep breath, closed his eyes and placed his hand on the sun. Nothing happened.

"Visualize, really search yourself," Row said.

"Sorry to be the one to tell you this, but there's no power inside me."

"You just have to find it," Lua said. "It's there."

Toekin tried again. This time he reached down deep. He remembered making his first ambush, getting all that food and finally not having to eat slugs to survive. How he hated slugs. He thought about the day Corvo hatched. He remembered his parents telling him the story of Paz before he fell asleep at night, warm and safe in his bed. And there it was. He could even feel the difference in the types of light. The light of the sun was the easiest to distinguish, it easily occupied ten times as much space within him than the other two combined. He imagined it rising, feeling it ascend from the bottom of his chest, higher and stronger, traveling into his arm and finally, through his hands and into his fingers.

"Whoa!" Row said. "Easy! You only need a little."

Toekin opened his eyes to see the whole door lit in warm, golden light.

Lua's eyes were big with giddy excitement. "See, I knew you had it."

The door clicked and Toekin pushed. A similar staircase lay just beyond.

"And that's your first lesson." Row said.

"Is there going to be a big need for unlocking doors when we fight Beezul?" Toekin said. He may have rolled his eyes.

Lua stepped forward. "This is just the first step in being able to do a lot more. When sun slingers get good enough, you can use it to make fire, either for warmth, or for battle." She said this last part in hushed tones, as if speaking out loud would bring conflict on much sooner. "Espero will teach you more." She held the door for Toekin and he walked through, taking the stairs down to who knew where. It was dark, but he could see more torches up ahead. Lua and Row followed.

As they got closer, Toekin could hear Espero's warm, encouraging voice, along with the occasional, "gotcha" of one of the kids. He rounded the corner with Lua and Row to see a game in progress. The kids moved in blurs in and out of spinning obstacles.

"Welcome," Espero said, making his way to Toekin while still keeping half an eye on the game. "Lua, Row, I trust all went well at the sun door?"

"Better than well," Row said, not holding back his amazement.

"Good. I'll take the training over from here. Will you two be okay with your groups?"

Lua nodded.

"Have fun, Toe." Row patted him on the back and then he and Lua left.

"The children are playing a game called Sun and Seek."

Toekin could see flashes and blurs and the kids moved around the room, hiding behind obstacles while trying to tag other players out.

"Got you!" Enzo shouted, and Teagan halted mid-glide and sulked to the sidelines.

"He's one of our best players." Espero said with pride. "We're almost done with this round. I think Enzo only has two more people to tag, then you can jump in."

"Uh, I don't know if I'm ready to train with the others. Can't I just observe?"

"Nonsense. You performed splendidly this morning. This game is nothing more than gliding." Espero stood with his arms folded, as if there were nothing to it. "Well," he said, as if suddenly remembering something. "I guess there is another small detail."

Toekin arched his brows and gave Espero a skeptical look.

"You must learn to hold back your light in order to conceal yourself from others. It's very simple. Just imagine your energy is behind a big dam. When you hold it back, you will be harder to see.

When you let a little flow out, you can glide to another hiding location. The more you let out, the easier you are to see."

"I'm probably going to get beat by a little kid."

"Everyone is getting beat by a little kid," Espero laughed. "Dear Enzo, here, is Sun and Seek champion." It was just then that Enzo tagged the last person and came gliding over in two short bursts to Espero.

"I'm done! I got everyone!" He said like a puppy with his tail wagging.

"Should we play one more time?" Espero said.

"Can we!"

"You'll go easy on Toekin though, won't you child? This is his first time."

"Sure I will. Come on Toekin!" Enzo grabbed his shirtsleeve and started pulling him toward the stage where the game was played.

"One more time!" Espero shouted to the others.

"The secret is," Enzo whispered, "to find a good hiding place and then hold back your light." He hopped with energy still unspent. "You can do that, right?"

"We'll find out." Toekin rubbed Enzo's head, making him laugh.

"Watch out for Teagan, too. She's really good."

"Begin!" Espero shouted and everyone was off.

Toekin dropped into the light and entered the field of spinning panels that were taller than he was. Gliding was beginning to feel very natural, and fun. He moved quickly in small, short glides looking for a good hiding place, but there didn't seem to be one. Everything was painfully exposed. Then he looked up. What if he climbed on top of one of the obstacles?

He found a panel on the perimeter of the stage and when there was a break in the gliding, he pulled himself up. From here he could watch the whole game. Now to conceal himself. He thought about what Espero had said and tried to imagine a big dam. It started to work, and he felt himself fade slightly. But it wasn't enough. What did he do when he was ambushing guards? The feeling came to him, and he reached out with his mind, gathering in darkness from the corners of the room that weren't lit with torchlight. He pulled some from under a table and the shadows of the spinning panels. He even felt like he pulled some from within himself.

That was better.

From his perch he watched the game, seeing different strategies at play and learning. The children were amazing to watch, vanishing and reappearing in golden trails of dust. Enzo was good, but so was Teagan. Soon, they were the last two left. Toekin watched as Enzo hid and concealed himself, then channeled his light just as Teagan was gliding by. "Got you!" he said.

Teagan stomped her foot in frustration. "One of these days I'm going to beat you." She said as they walked off the stage.

"The game is not over," Espero said. "Toekin is still out there."

"I didn't see him," Enzo said. "I thought he was out already."

"Well, kid," Teagan said, "you're the only one who wasn't tagged out. You go back in and get him."

Enzo spun around, smiling big, and glided off. He didn't need someone to tell him twice.

This is my chance, Toekin thought. All he had to do was drop down behind Enzo and tag him. He'd never see it coming. He waited, watching the little kid zigzag across the stage in growing frustration. He imagined his surprise if he suddenly appeared behind him and tagged him out. He played the scene out in his head and realized Enzo would, at the very least, be disappointed. He'd worked so hard to win. Toekin suddenly didn't feel quite right sneaking up on him like that.

He dropped moments before the child glided into his path. "Got you!" Enzo said, pure glee overtaking him. He hopped over to the sidelines chanting, "I got him! I got Toekin!"

Yeah, that was worth it, he thought, as he made his way off the stage.

"Where were you?" Teagan said. "I didn't see you the whole time and I looked everywhere."

"It seems that Toekin found a hiding place not one of you has yet discovered." Espero shot a knowing look Toekin's way.

Of course! Espero would have seen him on top of the panel from his position at the edge of the room.

"We'll let him keep his secret, in case he wants to use it again. But, remember children, when you do what everyone else is doing, you get the same results everyone else is getting. Don't be afraid to think differently."

There was some muttering, kids asking if anyone had seen Toekin's hiding place, and one person suggested maybe he wasn't playing fair. Espero ignored the chatter and clapped his hands. "Let's dim the lights and practice eyelumination." Several kids ran to extinguish torches.

"Toekin," Espero said, lowering his voice, "tell me. How *did* you conceal yourself so completely up on the panel?"

Toekin thought about it. "Just holding back the light didn't seem like enough." He said. "I don't think I'm good enough at that yet. So, I imagined covering myself and my light with a blanket of darkness."

"How did you do this?"

"I don't know. I just sort of imagined pulling it from different parts of the room." A look of concern flashed across Espero's thoughtful face. "Was that okay?"

"Of course," he said. "It's so good to see you learning to use your gifts. You are more talented than you know."

Something told Toekin this wasn't exactly what Espero was thinking, but he decided not to push further. "What are we doing now?" He said. It surprised him, his sudden excitement for learning. He was eager to see what else he could do.

"Eyelumination," Espero said. "This will help you see in the dark."

"How do I do it?"

"It is the same as the other things you've been doing. Focus, draw upon the sunlight within you, and lead the power to your eyes. Give it a try."

Kids were laughing and bumping into each other as they practiced the skill. It looked like it could be fun, joining the others. Just not right now. Instead, Toekin chose an empty, dark corner of the room and cleared his mind of everything except the well of light within him. He was getting better and better at accessing it quickly. He followed Espero's directions and gradually, the room brightened.

It was still dim, but as he looked he could see things in greater detail that had moments before been invisible to him.

He saw kids laughing over a joke, the stage where they'd played Sun and Seek, and in the back of the room he saw Espero, watching him very carefully.

CHAPTER 10

The Stars

"Why won't you help me? Help Paz! It's almost too late!" The girl from his dreams stood before him. She was more beautiful than ever, but her face was drenched in sadness. Toekin wanted to pick her up and start running, save her from whatever this place was, but somehow, he knew that wasn't possible. Her normally serene face had dropped into a look of despair that made him feel physically ill.

"I don't know what to do!" He said, pleading. "Tell me and I'll do it. Anything!"

"Help Paz," was all she would say.

He looked at her, imploring for more, but nothing came. Then there was a flicker, and for the briefest moment she disappeared. It happened again, and then again. Each time the flicker lasted just a little longer and Toekin wondered if she'd return, or simply be gone forever. A panic rose in his chest. He was running out of time. She flickered once more and this time, when Toekin saw her again, she'd become a dragon. The beast's eyes were fierce, full of fury. It opened its mouth wide, bearing its razor teeth, then lunged at him.

Toekin bolted up in bed, panting, drenched in sweat, and trying to figure out which reality he was in. He hadn't been eaten, that was good. He gripped the sheets in his fist, letting his heart rate slow from the pounding gallop to a less painful trot. He heard noises coming from the sun sala. People talking, trying to keep their voices down, but failing; shuffling; doors opening and closing; someone bumping into one of the benches and hitting the floor with a thud.

"I'm okay," came the muffled voice.

Tessa. *What time is it?* Toekin got out of bed, threw his shirt on, and cracked open his door. Lua was just coming out of one of the rooms. "What's going on," he said, stepping out into the big room. He spoke in hushed tones. It was still dark, maybe the second watch.

"It's Freya," she hissed. "She's not doing well."

Toekin didn't know what to say. She hadn't looked right to him, well . . . ever. It was more of a surprise that she still lived.

"Força's still gone and we don't know when he'll be back." She grabbed his hand and pulled him along. "Come," she said simply.

He stepped into the room dimly lit with oil lamps and disappointment.

"If she could just hang on until Força returns. He will never forgive himself if he's not here . . . and something happens." Lua choked on the last word, turning away from Toekin so he wouldn't see her cry, but being betrayed by her sniffles.

Freya was motionless, as usual. But now she was sucking in gasping, ragged breaths way too infrequent, each one breaking a morbid bubble of suspense.

"I got him," Tessa said, dragging Espero in by the robe. She glanced at Toekin with sad eyes and crossed the room to his side. Toekin remembered the hug she'd given him when he told her about his parents, and put his arm around her shoulder, drawing her to him.

Golden light gathered around Espero's hands, brightening the whole room. He placed them on Freya's head and closed his eyes in concentration. The light came in brilliant, rhythmic pulses. Freya's breathing calmed and quieted, returning to a less dramatic cadence and Espero removed his hands and stepped back. "It is all I can do." His voice was weary. "We will have to hope Força returns soon."

Lua nodded, seeming unwilling to risk speech.

They began filing out of the room, but Toekin turned back. He looked at the human form, withered and weak, a dried husk of a person, lying on the bed. It should have been a mercy to wish this woman's quick exit from life. Let her go to whatever reward the afterlife had for her. Yet, somehow, Toekin felt a deep sense of longing. It didn't make sense, but he wanted her to live. Not just for Força, but for Lua and Tessa. For Row and Espero. And yes, even somehow, for him. Why wasn't he learning how to heal? Maybe he could help?

"She will make it through the night," Espero said. "We can discuss her care in the morning. Get some rest." He turned and disappeared behind one of the doors.

"Sorry we woke you up," Tessa said. "I was trying to be quiet."

"I was awake anyway." Toekin smiled.

Lua gave him a grateful smile and followed Tessa back into their room.

* * *

Breakfast was bone broth and mashed turnips. It was warm and filled Toekin's belly, but it was easy to see he wasn't the only one disappointed by it. The children ate out of pure duty, some putting a spoonful of turnip mush into their mouths, then washing it down with the broth. Others simply held their noses while they ate.

Lua was seated across from him and was doing a much better job at hiding her disgust. "How's Freya?" Toekin asked.

"Her breathing still sounds good." She brought a spoonful of turnip to her mouth, then stopped, dropping the spoon into her bowl. "But that was so scary last night. The thought of losing Freya . . ." She looked down into her bowl, not thinking about turnips at all anymore. "I'm just glad you were there."

"Me?" Toekin said, tipping his bowl of bone broth into his mouth to get the last drops. He didn't care what anyone thought. This was still loads better than eating slugs. "I didn't do anything."

"You did. Somehow." She shook her head as if she didn't quite understand it and pushed her last spoonfuls of turnips around in her bowl. "As soon as you came into the room . . . I don't know . . . I just got the feeling she was going to be alright."

Toekin didn't have much time to think about how little sense that made before Row took a seat across from them with his breakfast. "How are you enjoying our end-of-cycle menu?" He loaded about twice as much mashed turnip on his spoon as it was meant to hold and shoved it in his mouth, smiling.

"End-of-cycle?" Toekin said.

"We're scraping the bottom of the barrel," Row said with a mouthful of mush. "Except for a few bones, the meat's gone, our grains are tapped out, and cheese is just a distant memory."

Maybe Toekin needed to get back to raiding taxation carts a little more quickly than he'd planned.

"Every new moon we go into town and trade for more. Remember how we had cheese when you first got here?"

How could he forget! Toekin nodded.

"That's because you came at the beginning of the cycle, after we'd just done our trading."

"So," Toekin asked, "someone going in to town today?"

"Yep. Cart's already loaded with all our surplus from the fall harvest, and it was a good one. I should be able to trade for tons of good stuff. Maybe even some jambu fruit or pomelo."

"You? You do the trading?"

"Of course! I am an excellent negotiator, Toe! The best."

Toekin was getting used to Row's bravado. He chuckled, "I'll be glad to see what you bring back then."

"Especially after this meal," Lua added still rearranging the last two spoonfuls of mashed turnip.

"Good news, Toe!" Row laid his hands out flat on the table and leaned forward. "You don't have to wait until I get back to see my haul. You're coming with me."

A wave of alarm came over Toekin as he remembered his last trip away from the orphanage. Abbadon Guards were everywhere, and even though he'd covered his tracks, the more visible he was, the greater the chance he'd eventually be found out. "I don't know," he finally said. "I think I should stay here."

"Nonsense! Come with me. We'll have a great time." Row looked at Lua for confirmation. She replied by eating the last of her turnips.

He shouldn't go.

"I do this every cycle. I never have any trouble. Besides, you can't stay shut up in this orphanage forever."

"I lived by myself for six summers and was perfectly happy," Toekin countered.

"I can give you some tips at being a seer. There's no one better to learn from." Row's toothy grin was infectious and Toekin suspected he was used to getting his way.

"That's true," Lua said. "When it comes to the stars, Row *is* the best."

"Fine," Toekin said. "I'll go."

"Great!" Row slapped the table, closing the deal. "We'll leave just after lunch. I still have a few more preparations to make." Then turning to Lua, he said, "Don't worry. He'll still have plenty of time for his chores."

Row jammed the last of his breakfast into his mouth and jumped up and started toward the kitchen to gather empty bags and baskets. "Prepare yourself for adventure!" he turned and called out before disappearing behind the door.

"Do me a favor," Lua said, ducking her head close to Toekin's. "Make sure you trade away every, single, turnip we have."

* * *

It didn't take long for Toekin to figure out why Row had wanted him along. He stood behind the crossbar, next to Row, pushing. The cart felt like it was loaded down with thirty grown men. Row chatted away, clearly glad of the company, but Toekin wondered if he was pushing at all.

He felt exposed, vulnerable, and sensitive to every movement. As they came around a corner they unknowingly flushed a family of quail out of a bush. The group beat their wings loudly as they took flight across the road. Toekin jerked and his heart pounded. He tried to play it off.

"Don't they have quail where you come from?" Row joked. "They make good eating when you can get them."

The bridge over the Rio River lay directly ahead with several guards monitoring the crossing. Toekin felt his chest tighten. He'd never left himself so exposed to his enemy.

"Relax," Row said, low and serious. "I've done this many times. I just throw them a bribe and they let us through. No trouble at all. Just let me handle everything."

Toekin half-expected to see Weasel and Sniffy, but these guards were completely unknown to him.

"Halt!" one of them said. "What is your purpose in Favela today?"

"Just doing a little trading in town." Row said.

"What products are you carrying?"

Toekin wasn't sure why the guard was asking. The other two had already taken the liberty of searching their load, opening bags and rummaging through baskets.

"Just our fall harvest; mostly potatoes and turnips." One of the guards wrinkled his nose in disgust. "Oh, and we have one bag of apples," Row said, his voice bright and clear.

"Where? Where's the apples?" one of the two rummagers said.

"I kept them up front," Row said. "You fellas like apples?"

"Show me." The main guard said. Row held open the bag, revealing beautiful, red fruit. Was this what he was going to give the guards? What a waste!

One of the rummagers came up behind the main guard and snatched the bag out of his hand. "We'll take this," he said.

"And you're welcome to it!" Row said as if he was talking to a good friend and not a sworn enemy.

The main guard waved him through while the other two guards bit into apples.

Toekin gritted his teeth in anger as they pulled their load onto the bumpy timbers of the bridge. He couldn't wait to get back to raiding the taxation carts. He felt a surge of energy building that made pushing the cart much easier.

"See? What did I tell you? Easy."

"You gave them our only bag of apples!"

"No," Row laughed. "I gave them one of our many bags of turnips . . . with a few apples on top. The rest of our apples are back at the orphanage. How do you think we plan on keeping Corvo from attacking us?"

"Huh," Toekin said, thinking. "I guess that's pretty smart."

"You guess? It's genius, and don't forget who masterminded the whole thing." Row leaned into the crossbar to push the wheels off the last timbers before they were back on the road.

It felt good to be back on the winning end of an encounter with the Abbadon Guards again, until Toekin saw a problem. "What happens when we come back? They're going to remember us and they won't be happy."

"The guards will have a shift change before we return. Nothing to worry about."

Toekin was worried though. And besides that, he felt the distinct feeling he was being watched. He glanced into the trees on either side of the road. No one was there, but he couldn't shake the feeling.

They rolled through town while traders tried to entice them both with their claims of generous rates and the highest quality of meats and dairy. "Why aren't we stopping at one of these places?" Toekin asked, when someone claimed to have a whole pig haunch.

"I have a guy," was all he said.

They finally found Row's guy at the edge of town, down an alley, and behind a closed tea shop. "Arik!" Row called out to a short bald man with a plain brown vest pulled over his shirt.

"Row! My favorite client. How are you?" He tamped out his pipe and crossed the yard, a purple chain that started at a buttonhole and ended in his vest pocket moved like a snake across his belly as he walked.

"We had a great harvest," Row said, "wait til you see our onions! As big as a baby's head." Row waved his hand toward Toekin. "This is my friend Toekin. He helped me with the cart today." He leaned into Arik and said in an exaggerated whisper, "Don't tell him, but I was hardly pushing." They laughed and Toekin found a place to sit. Probably best to stay out of the way.

Row went through the cart, swapping red potatoes for cheeses and carrots for bags of oats. Slowly, the cart was being unloaded and reloaded with different food. There was even dried meat and a large jug of honey. Toekin was truly impressed.

It bothered him, however, that it was taking a little longer than he'd expected. The sun was quickly sinking in the sky. Nightfall had never been his friend in Mato Forest, and his instincts kept telling him it was time to go.

"Now Arik, several vendors on our way in offered to trade a pig haunch for much less than that!"

"They are lying! There is no way I can accept less for a piece of meat this fine."

"I've been visiting you for three summers now. Only you! You know I bring the best produce. Just look at the onions! No one else will have onions that big except you, Arik. Babies' heads! You owe your reputation to the food I trade with you. But I could easily bring my produce to someone else. Philo, perhaps?"

"Philo! That lice licker! I wouldn't get near his store, and neither will anyone in this town."

"I don't know. His store looked pretty busy when we passed by."

Arik huffed and kicked a rock across the courtyard. Row took the opportunity to shoot a glance at Toekin, wiggling his eyebrows and grinning. He was loving this.

Arik turned back to Row. "I won't do it." He said. "No deal."

"Well, I'm sorry to hear that, Arik," Row said. Then, looking up to the sky, he raised his left arm high. White light formed around his skyward fingers. His right arm reached over his shoulder as if it were drawing an arrow from an imaginary quiver on his back. He continued the pantomime, pretending to nock the arrow in the bow. When he pulled back a shaft of white light formed like an arrow, dim at first, but quickly growing in intensity until he let it fly. White energy from Row's fingertips shot out right into Arik's forehead.

It was finished before Arik even knew what was happening.

"What are you doing?" Toekin said, standing. He didn't know if he should be impressed or mortified.

"You seeing this?" Row turned and said to Toekin. His eyes were pure white, glowing with power. "This is your first lesson as a seer."

He turned his attention back on Arik, becoming still and focused. A beam of light from Row's pointed fingers linked him to Arik, right between the eyes. For several moments Row didn't move.

Toekin didn't either. Then the white connection between the two broke and Row turned and said, "See? That's all there is to it."

Toekin wasn't sure what he'd done, let alone how he'd done it.

Arik shook his head like he was waking up from a daydream. "Let me go and get that haunch for you," he said. "You sure I can't throw in an extra side of bacon too?"

"No, no, Arik. You are generous enough. Please, just the haunch and we will be on our way."

"I feel like I'm taking advantage of you!" he laughed as he walked into a smoking shed to fetch the meat. "All those turnips for just one piece of meat?"

"It is a fine piece of meat, and you are a fine friend. It's a fair trade, Arik." Row kept looking over at Toekin. If he kept wiggling his eyebrows and grinning like a fool, his face was going to freeze like that.

"Of course, my friend." Arik came out with a large bundle wrapped in paper and string. "Let me load this for you. Oh!" he said, suddenly remembering something and running into the back of the tea shop and out again. "Take this." He thrust a box into Row's hands. "For the guards. A few sweets from my lovely wife's tea shop. Wouldn't want them deciding your pig is a worthy bribe, now, would we?" He arched his brow and whispered conspiratorially, "if two of those pastries aren't in the box by the time you get to the bridge, I'm sure those good-for-nothings will never know."

They covered their load with oilcloth and said their goodbyes. "See you next cycle!" Airk said, waving.

They hadn't traveled too far before Toekin turned to Row. "What was that all about?"

Some of Row's self-assurance had disappeared. "I changed Arik's mind about the pig," he said, matter-of-factly.

"If you were going to cheat him, you should have just done it from the beginning. Could have saved us all a lot of time." Toekin had a bad taste in his mouth.

Row's smile was weak but sincere. "I didn't cheat him. It was the only fair deal I got."

"How so?"

"He over charged me on everything, but I was playing the game. I knew I wanted that meat, so I took the bad deals, knowing the good one at the end would make up for all of it. Normally he would have taken the offer, without the additional motivation."

"Oh," Toekin said, thinking back to that stream of light between Row and Arik. "So, how does it work? How did you convince him to change his mind?"

"It's like being able to see his thoughts. I see everything about him that makes him who he is and find out what's keeping him from being fair. Then I just do a little adjusting here and there." He paused, and after a while he said, "He hit his wife this morning. Left a bruise on her face. She wasn't able to open her teashop. But in the end, I made a few adjustments that she might like too."

The bad taste was gone, and Toekin was glad for it. They pushed the cart in silence, Toekin thinking about what that must be like, to see into someone's mind. He wondered if he would ever be able to do it.

"You mind if I duck my head in here? It'll only take a minute." They'd stopped in front of a tavern, still not busy at this hour.

"I suppose. But hurry. We're losing daylight."

"Great, keep an eye on the cart."

Toekin watched the towns-people as he waited, coming and going, being about their business. Not one of them seemed to notice him. Yet, the feeling was still there. Someone, not these people, but someone was watching him.

He scanned the buildings, the alleyways and the side streets. Where were they?

Toekin shivered and noticed the patch of sunlight he'd been standing in had disappeared, gone as the sun dipped behind the tavern. How long had Row been in there?

"There you are!" Row said, coming out of the tavern. He seemed to be in a much better mood. "Sun's setting. Espero doesn't like it when I'm late!" He got behind the crossbar and started pushing. Really pushing this time.

Well, this is an improvement. Toekin thought. But Row's energy didn't last. Before long, he was lagging and stumbling. "Stop," Row said. "Stop. I gotta stop."

"You drunk?" Toekin asked.

"A little." Row said. "If I can just rest for a little, I'll feel better. Give me a second."

"How about you rest *after* we pass the guards on the bridge."

"Relax." Row wobbled to the edge of the road and lay down in the grass. "Those guards are push overs. They always do what I say."

Toekin rolled his eyes. What was he going to do with Row? "Why don't you jump in the cart. I'll push. You can sleep."

"No!" he said. "That's not fair. I made you push by yourself the whole way out here." He shifted and fussed and tried to get comfortable in the grass.

"If you feel bad about it, then get yourself in the cart so I don't also have to lift you into it."

Z z z . . .

You've got to be kidding me. Toekin felt anger rising inside of him. The kind of anger that, he'd learned, brought on his powers even before he knew he had them. He could use them to push the cart, but Espero had showed him a better way. He brushed off his anger and reached inside. This time he remembered how good it had felt to train with Espero. He thought of Enzo's face when he won Sun and Seek. And there it was. Lua had told him the light of the moon gives strength, so he focused on the blue light within. Warmth rose inside of him.

He walked over to Row, felt strength surging through him, bent over, and picked him up. He was light, like a sack of feathers. Maybe this would work after all. He secured him in the back of the cart, threw the oilcloth over the top of him, and set off. The cart was still heavy, but Toekin was able to easily push it along at a steady jog.

He reasoned away his suspicions about being watched, convincing himself that it was nothing more than his anxiety. In his head he could hear Row telling him to relax. So he did.

The cart thundered across the bridge as the first stars were appearing. *Sorry Row!* Toekin thought as the cart bumped along at an uncomfortable speed. His heart picked up its pace as he approached the booth. He tried to remember where that box of pastries had been stashed. He replayed Row's earlier interactions with the guards in his head and tried to rehearse the lines.

Here they came. "Good evening," he said, forcing levity he did not feel.

"It's *you* again."

Toekin felt his stomach drop, straight down into the icy river below. The darkness had hid the truth, and now it was too late. There had been no change in guard.

"I brought a little something for you." Toekin's voice was as shaky as his hands as he pulled back the oilcloth. He thanked the stars when he saw the box was in just the right place.

"Here you are."

The guards yanked the box from his hands and tore into it. "After what you pulled with those turnips, you got a lot of nerve thinking you can buy us off with . . . what are these? Sticky buns?" the guard slurred.

They're drunk too?

"No," another guard said through a stuffed mouthful, "these are cardamom sweet rolls. I can taste the cardamom."

Maybe he could just sneak past them?

"You! Where do you think you're going!" Quicker than he could react, the guard had his spear out and was pointing it at Toekin. Well, mostly pointing. It wobbled quite a bit. The guard began jabbing erratically, coming dangerously close to stabbing Toekin in the face.

Moans and a grunt came from the back of the cart as Row rolled over in his sleep.

"He's got someone in there!" The guard shouted. "Ambush!"

The other two guards wielded their spears with equal lack of skill or grace, one focusing on the still sleeping form of Row, while the other doubled up on Toekin. "We are authorized by Emperor Beezul to kill, on sight, anyone attempting to ambush Abbadon Guards," one said. He seemed particularly excited about the killing part, then Toekin found out why. "I think we got two of the Waylayers, boys!"

Toekin could glide out of there. These guys were slow from drink, he could probably just duck and run. But he had a cart full of food, and more importantly, he had Row. Something, a feeling, drew his eyes to the quickly darkening sky. The new moon gave no competition for the stars and they seemed to shine brighter than ever. He had to act. An idea came, then a feeling compelling him to trust it.

121

He promptly raised his left arm in the air and focused on the light of the stars, both from within and from above. Cool warmth rushed into his arm and over his whole body. He mimicked what he'd seen Row do, producing a white arrow of light, and then two more. He nocked the arrows as he pulled back the string of his imaginary bow. The arrows flew past his outstretched arm, each trailing a shining line of energy that connected him to his targets. Bull's-eye.

Time seemed to slow. The river below crawled instead of crashed, moving so slowly it was barely noticeable. He felt the will, desire, and thoughts of the three men flow into him. From there, the images came fast: A mother senseless on too much ale and a father he never knew; a fight in the street, horrible accusations and broken bones; years of starving, going through trash, sucking the juices out of an old fish wrapper; inner demons, tormenting; and then the dark cloud.

It dropped fast and thick, covering completely, filling lungs; suffocating. Then pain so exquisite, so specific. Toekin pulled back and before the vision was over he saw a creature, black-eyed and deformed. Skin, tanned like leather, stretched over a skull so tightly as to leave only one expression permanently affixed: pure evil.

He searched desperately until he found the place in their minds where he thought he could have the most influence on the guards, made his suggestions and broke the connection just before collapsing to the ground.

"Have a good evening," one guard said down to Toekin, using the pointy end of his spear to tip his hat. The other two guards turned and wandered noiselessly back to the booth, tucking themselves inside without a word. "Let me help you up," the guard said, extending a hand.

He took it and rose, holding onto the cross bar on the cart for support. His body felt slack, as if his bones had turned to jelly. He tried to tap into more of the light within, for strength to get home, but just didn't have it in him. He felt dark, corrupted and heavy, like a load of bricks had just been piled upon him. He looked back at Row, happy, asleep, and wondered if this was what it was like every time he went into someone's mind. If there had been a tavern in front of him, Toekin would have gone in and drunk away this feeling too.

The guards paid him no attention, just as he'd instructed them, so they didn't see the slow pained steps he took with the cart. I'm never going to make it back to the orphanage, he thought. And then that feeling again: He was being watched. He couldn't deny it any longer. He dropped the crossbar and the cart rotated forward, the axle for the giant wheels acting like a fulcrum. Row tumbled out but Toekin paid him no attention. "Who's there!"

His lonely voice echoed around him until a figure emerged from the darkness, walking toward him. Immediately he realized his folly. He was weak and there was nothing he could do to defend himself. Still, he stood his ground as the figure came closer, into the light. He was huge, muscles rippled across his arms and torso, and on his chin, a dark, thick beard.

"Força?" Thank the stars. Toekin nearly collapsed again, this time in relief.

"Looks like you can use a hand," he said, circling around the cart to reload Row.

Toekin stood there, just focusing on remaining upright. "I thought you were . . . I think someone is . . ."

Força walked over to the cross bar and lifted it up. "Here," he said, handing him a beautifully carved staff he'd been using as a walking stick. "Maybe this will help."

It did. Toekin wrapped his hand around the wood and noticed it was adorned with an intricate carving of a Seivo Sangue tree. He was bombarded memories and sounds and smells and feelings. But one feeling hit him harder than all the others: He was homesick.

CHAPTER 11

The Departure

Sem swallowed back a sense of dread as he lifted the grotesque doorknocker at Nojento's lab. Durman's words at their last parting rang through his head. His friend had never hidden his hate for the deranged creature and his inhuman experiments, but this time his warnings had been different.

"Your alliance with him is becoming dangerous," Durman had said.

"He is my master. Even Beezul understands that. What would you have me do?"

"Your life has been all but claimed by that madman. He's taken nearly everything. If power shifts, you need to make sure you are aligned with the right person."

"I appreciate the reminder," Sem growled, and turned to leave.

"Wait," Durman said. He grabbed Sem's arm and pulled him back. "There's one thing he will never have unless you give it to him." His eyes were sincere and full of concern. "He can never have your will," he said. "You still have choices. Just . . . think about that." He dropped Sem's arm, gradually turned back to the troops and began barking orders.

So, here he was once again, returning to Nojento like an abused dog to his keeper, and he hated himself for it. Durman hadn't the first idea what he was talking about. Nojento owned him. All of him.

The eyehole slid open and a single red eye appeared. It quickly turned to blue and the door flew open. Nojento pulled Sem into his lair, closing the door quickly behind them. "Lobo already returned with the news." His blue skin fairly glowed and his hideous grin displayed every one of his gleaming teeth. "I'm beyond thrilled. Tell me everything." He started to pull Sem over to a metal chair that looked to be made of femurs and tibias, with a full set of ribs to support the back.

"Wait," Nojento said, stopping suddenly. "Your movement is off. Have you been injured?"

Injured, or four long days on horseback. *What's the difference*, Sem thought. His neck and shoulders were a steel trap, holding all the tension and anxiety of the last week while his lower back absorbed the shocking stabs of pain that came with every step. He'd tried to hide it, knowing that even the most minor infirmity would catch Nojento's attention and lengthen this interview. He did not want to be here one second longer than he had to.

"It's nothing." He said. "Let me tell you how I found the sack of . . ."

"Stop." Nojento held up his hand. "Not one more word. I can tell you're in pain."

"Really, I'm fine."

"You are so stubborn! I really should see if there's a modification for that." Nojento's wink did nothing to settle Sem's nerves. If anything, it put him more on edge. "Come," he said, leading Sem to an examining table and patting it to indicate where he wanted him to lay. "You can tell me about it while I fix you up."

Nojento's moments of lucidity were tenuous. Sem had grown used to the insanity. He could deal with that. This side of his master was more confusing—more dangerous. He figured it was best to yield, and got on the table.

"There." Nojento moved his hands up and down Sem's back as if he were feeling for something. "Now . . . the sack."

"We had just defeated the rebel ambush when I noticed it lodged under a log in the river. It was a bit of luck, really."

"Your vision has always been superior. Ah, yes. Here it is," Nojento said, his hands hovering over Sem's lower back. "Roll to your side."

He did as commanded. "I had to wade out to get it. Lobo was able to pick up a scent. He left that night to track it."

Nojento placed a hand on Sem's hip and another on his shoulder. "Lobo was . . ." Nojento started to say, suddenly shoving Sem's shoulder back while yanking his hips forward, ". . . wildly successful."

Sem held his breath, unsure of what had just happened, but also, anxious of what would happen next.

"So tense. It's as if you've got the weight of the world on your shoulders. Roll to your stomach. And keep talking. Were you able to bring me any more experimental subjects?"

"Yes, although, many of the rebels did not survive the fight. I was able to bring you five healthy men." He had thought it would be enough to appease him, but when Nojento reached a hand around his head, grabbed his chin and started twisting, he was sure he'd angered him.

"Relax. This isn't going to work if you're all clenched up. Trust me."

Sem hesitated, then said. "It's a little difficult when it seems like you're about to rip my head off." He watched in terror as Nojento's eyes flashed angry red, probing for a moment, then finally, settled into a bright blue.

"Oh Sem. You're jesting!" He laughed lightly, as if he finally understood the joke. "This is why you're my favorite." He jerked Sem's chin in one direction and then the other producing a loud crack with each twist. "All done." He looked smug and clearly proud of himself. "How do you feel?"

Sem was dazed from the experience. What had just happened? He lay there, unsure of what to do.

"Get up, silly." Nojento said lightly as he floated over to his bone throne and took a seat.

Slowly, Sem rose. The pain in his neck and shoulders was gone, as was the stabbing pain in his back. He stood, twisting from one side to the other, quite amazed.

"Don't act so surprised. Now get over here. It's my turn to talk."

Once again, Sem obliged.

"Lobo has tracked the scent to an orphanage in Favela," Nojento started. "I know. Orphans seem like the last people we should worry about. But what a brilliant cover, wouldn't you say? Who would ever suspect them? Lobo says at least two of them are Zaints."

"What would you have me do?" Sem knew what Nojento wanted to hear.

"Nothing with the wretched orphans for now. I've taken precautions." Nojento's eyes narrowed. "The relic, however, is a different story."

"We still don't have any leads."

"Nonsense. We are closer now than we ever have been. It is only a matter of time." Nojento's eyes turned blood red. "I must have it, you understand."

Sem nodded, unsure of where he was going with his line of reasoning, but unwilling to risk questioning.

"I can not allow Beezul to get it first." His voice had dropped to an ominous tone. "Lobo and Conk already have their orders. They know what to do. But you . . ." He paused.

It was as if Nojento was waiting for something. Something from him. Then he remembered. He pushed the chair back, dropped to one knee and bowed his head briefly. "Anything, master."

Nojento, smiled, baring his square top teeth. "I need you to be my eyes and ears with Beezul," he said. "Stay close to him. Make sure you know all of his plans, his every move."

Durman's words came rushing back. *You still have choices.* But did he? It didn't feel like it. Betray Beezul and he could expect to die a slow and painful death. Betray Nojento and it could be that—or worse.

"What is your answer?" Nojento said, his voice heavy with menace while his eyes flashed steady blue and red. Sem struggled to stay in control of his thoughts.

"Of course." He bowed his head to break eye contact with his master. He needed to stay in control of his mind. "I am, and have always been, your faithful servant."

"Oh Sem!" he practically squealed, "I knew I could count on you. We really are quite a team, aren't we?"

The thought of he and Nojento being aligned in anyway caused a wave of nausea to sweep over him. He said nothing. He used to revel in the power Nojento had gifted him; the way he could bring men to their knees. He had more gold than he knew what to do with, a home with every luxury. Merchants threw their wares at him, begging him to take them, telling him it would be an honor if he rode in their finest saddle, carried their exquisite broad swords or drank their best ale. At one time this was sufficient to make him happy; his forced connection to Nojento was nothing more than a distasteful necessity.

Now, none of those things could erase the self-loathing he felt for who he'd become. And he laid the blame directly at Nojento's feet.

"You will report to the Emperor. Tell him that you've located those responsible for ambushing the taxation carts." His excitement built as he unfolded the plan and he paced with nervous energy as he explained. "Tell him you will take him there. Lobo will lead you from the shadows. I will handle everything else."

"Yes, master."

"But you must remember all. You will be my eyes and ears." He grabbed Sem's wrist and a howl of excitement escaped. "This is happening, Sem. I will have the relic and Paz for myself!"

When Nojento dismissed him, Sem made a quick exit and worked his way up the long spiral staircase to Beezul's chambers at the top of the tower. Openings covered with clear glass appeared every tenth step and the higher he climbed, the more expansive the view became. Finally, just before reaching the top, he stopped to look across the land of Abbadon and farther out into Enganoso.

The forest spread across the land to the north until it faded into dark nothingness. What if he were to set off on his own—lose himself in the woods? Go someplace where he could live out the rest of his days alone? Was there any place he would be safe? Somewhere Nojento or the Emperor wouldn't find him? His gaze returned to Abbadon and the majestic Seivo Salvador that stood unbothered and alone on the south end of the city. No one dared approach it for fear of the deadly sap. It was left completely to itself. *Lucky tree.*

He was escorted into the emperor's quarters by a guard, but instead of Beezul, he found Jade, the sorceress, stretched out on a fainting couch, her hand lazed over the side, stroking the head of the emperor's black panther, Gunju. The beast's red eyes glowed with fury that seemed only temporarily subdued by Jade's touch.

The hood of her cloak kept her eyes mostly in shadow, but Sem felt her gaze heavy and judging upon him, as if she could see his soul. Her lips, painted red, matched her hair that dropped in waves over her shoulders. Sparkling gems—rubies by the look of it—studded her belt and matched the fist-sized stone in her staff, resting beside her on the couch.

Rising from her seat, she motioned for Sem to follow as she walked out to a balcony overlooking the city. Emperor Beezul stood alone, his back against the rail, his cape dancing in the wind.

"Leave us," Beezul said to Jade. She paused a moment, then turned and left with a sneer, the unnaturally large cat trailing behind. "You have news?" His voice dared Sem to disappoint him. He began a deliberate pace back and forth across the balcony never taking his eyes off Sem, as if he was just waiting to pounce.

"We have located those responsible for the ambushes." Sem said.

"The *Waylayers?*" Beezul spat. "I believe that is what the traitors call them. Who are they? Disgruntled dockworkers who, despite their ineptitude, have managed to organize themselves? Farmers with pitchforks?" His laugh was spiked with anger and hatred.

"Orphans, your majesty."

Beezul was silent, but Sem could see a storm raging in his eyes. *Say something*, he thought.

"Children?" Beezul's voice was ice, sharp and frigid. "Are you certain?"

"Our best tracker found them. He is never wrong."

"They must be Zaints. There is no other way they could have gotten the best of my Abbadon Guards."

"At least two have been confirmed as such."

Beezul turned and walked to the edge of the balcony, splaying his hands on the railing and then pulling them into tight fists, his knuckles whitening. "You will lead me there. We leave immediately," he said, turning to face Sem. His voice was dangerously under control, dark and ominous. "Ready your troops. I will make an example of these orphans. The rebels must know there are consequences for crossing me." He paced. This time there was anger with every step and he lost himself in his building rage.

Emotions warred inside of Sem. The rebel attacks on the carts had plagued him for over a year, every lead eluding him. He was as eager to punish the criminals as Beezul. There was something, however, about the bloodlust pouring off the emperor now that left him feeling disconcerted.

"What are you still doing here?" he spun to face Sem as if just realizing he hadn't dismissed him. "Go!"

"Yes, Emperor!" Sem stalked out of the room, not even pausing to notice if Jade and Gunju were still there.

* * *

Before the sun had passed its zenith, two hundred of Sem's men had mustered in the courtyard beneath Beezul's tower. The wind had begun to pick up and dark clouds crept in from the horizon. His elite team had rested enough and were each seated on a fresh horse, while the remaining men were packed into carts with supplies and weapons.

Durman readied them for inspection while Sem oversaw the operation with an eye toward Beezul's carriage. The emperor had insisted Sem ride with him and he'd agreed, even though he preferred to travel with his men. He would use the time to listen to the Emperor's plans so he could prepare his troops.

He saw Jade and Beezul approach the carriage and decided he could wait no longer. He gave a curt nod to Durman and made his way toward the enclosed transport. He'd hoped to have had a few days to rest before setting out on another campaign, but maybe this was for the best. These offensive maneuvers kept his mind occupied and his skills honed—less time to brood.

"General," the emperor said dispassionately as he approached.

Sem dipped his head in acknowledgement, and then both he and Beezul turned at a noise behind them.

"I suppose this will do, although I'm used to a little more luxury when I travel." Nojento said as he swept over to the threesome. "Sorceress Jade," he said with a curl of his lip. Conk followed close behind carrying a large trunk.

"You're not coming with us." Beezul said through his teeth.

"I would use my own sedan, but one of my carriers recently had an unfortunate turn in his health. Good carriers are so hard to find. Just set my things on the back, would you Conk."

"You are not part of this campaign." Beezul turned and began to walk away, not interested in further discussion.

"I disagree, my Lord," Nojento started. "You need me. I can be of great help to you."

Jade stepped in front of Nojento, blocking his passage to Beezul. "Your *help* was supposed to be providing Emperor Beezul with a weapon that could subdue the Zaints, and you failed," she said, not bothering to hide a satisfied smile that crept onto her face.

"Lovely Jade," Nojento started, "if only you were powerful enough to transport this whole army to Favela through your little portal. Weak as it is, even you have chosen to forgo your little trick and travel like the rest of us."

The wind was growing stronger and it gusted as Beezul shouted, "Enough!" He turned and walked back to Nojento and Jade. "I have spoken, Nojento. Abide or suffer the consequences." A cold blast hit Nojento in the face and Jade wrapped herself tighter in her cloak against the cold.

"My Lord," Jade said, her eyes turning dreamy and her voice quivering. "A snow storm approaches. If we leave now, it will travel with us all the way to Favela."

"A storm will not favor your advances," Nojento said. He must have sensed an opening because he pushed himself in front of Jade, faced Beezul and set his eyes to flickering. "Wait for the storm to pass. Your success will be guaranteed if you aren't fighting in a blizzard."

"Fool!" Beezul said, sweeping Nojento out of his way with his arm. Nojento stumbled and then regained his balance. "Have your accursed eyes made you blind? The winter storm will hide our face from our enemies until we are upon them. Their escape will be impossible."

Nojento backed up like a scolded dog as Beezul spoke.

"We leave now." Beezul pulled himself into his carriage with Jade following.

Sem signaled Durman who motioned to the trumpeters. A shrill sound rang through the air and controlled chaos immediately transformed into order. Wagon drivers took their seats, men bundled up in the back of wagons, and riders mounted their horses and pulled into formation. Sem glanced back at Nojento once more before climbing into the emperor's carriage. A figure stood beside him now, heavily cloaked, a hood completely obscuring his face.

Unless one was familiar with the distinctive hunched posture of the half-beast, as Sem was, no one would have guessed it was Lobo. Nojento's face was a mask of calm and cunning as he handed him what looked to be a letter. And then Lobo was gone. Sem wasn't sure what game his master was playing, or if he wanted any part of it. One thing was certain. He was going to need to tread very carefully in the days ahead.

He pulled himself through the carriage doors and into a shocking, but welcome warmth. A brazier pushed off to the side held glowing coals and the carriage seats were lined with plush cushions, while light from oil lanterns bathed the interior in a golden glow. Sorceress Jade was already covered in a blanket of fur and another waited, folded on the seat for Sem, should he require it. He could get used to this. But he probably shouldn't.

"A little nicer than your usual mode of travel?" Beezul said.

"Very much so. Thank you, my Lord." Sem relaxed into the thick cushions, suddenly aware that he hadn't had a good sleep in weeks. He blinked his eyes, forcing himself to focus. "Shall we discuss your plans for the attack?"

"There will be time enough for that." Beezul said, lazily, seeming to fall victim to the soft cushions himself. "There is one thing, however, that I would like to know first."

"And what is that?"

"How long has Nojento been planning to betray me?"

Suddenly, Sem was no longer sleepy.

CHAPTER 12

The Newcomer

Her image was faint. Toekin could hardly see her anymore—a mere ghost of herself. "What's happening?" He said out loud, but she didn't respond. She just stood there in the blue light, her hair fanning out around her in waves of energy. He stepped into her aura and reached out to touch her, but his hand failed to grasp anything but empty air. He panicked.

"Wake up! Talk to me!" He reached for her hand again and this time clenched his fist around where hers might have been. "Please." He closed his eyes against the panic that pierced his chest. Had he lost her forever?

"I'm here." She finally said. It was weak and barely audible, but Toekin's eyes snapped open and he felt a wave of relief wash over him. Though it was hard to make out, her tired, beaten-down expression told him she was exhausted and weak.

"What's happening?"

"It's almost too late. Soon I'll be gone forever." Her face drooped with disappointment.

"Where are you going? I don't even know who you are!"

"You didn't help Paz. You didn't help me."

"You're just a dream. Paz is a bedtime story. What am I supposed to do?"

She looked at him with deep sadness but said nothing.

"How am I supposed to help you if you won't tell me what to do?" Toekin clenched his fists tighter as the girl seemed to fade even further into nothingness.

"Goodbye," she said.

It was soft, almost unintelligible. In fact, it could have been anything: a surge in the energy whooshing around his ear, or a whisper from some unknown being. Deep down though, Toekin knew it was her—knew this was her farewell.

"Argh!" He slammed his fists into his mattress and sat up in bed. Another dream. His heart pounded, and he felt sick at the thought of losing this girl—of not being able to save her. He knew she had to be real.

Corvo, perched at the end of the bed, shifted with a grunt before tucking his beak back under his wing and returning to his slumber.

It was dark, but Toekin didn't feel like sleeping any more. He got up, threw on his shirt and stepped out into the sun sala. The fire in the hearth was down to barely glowing embers. He grabbed the poker and stirred it, kicking up sparks and a little warmth.

He thought back to the night the guards raided the orphanage. Espero had spoken of Paz like he was real. Lua and Row seemed to think he was too. Could this be true? And if so, where was that dragon?

Toekin heard a loud thump coming from the kitchen, as if something big and heavy had fallen against the outside of the building.

"What was that?" Lua poked her head out of her room.

Slugs! She's a light sleeper. "I don't know?" Toekin rose to investigate and Lua followed. The inside of the kitchen seemed undisturbed as he made his way toward the back door. He reached for the knob.

"Careful," Lua said, but it was too late. As he pulled the door open, a man, who had clearly been slumped against it, fell inside, his head hitting the floor with a crack. "Oh dear. That didn't sound good." Lua reached under the man's arms and started to drag him out of the way. "Get the door, would you? It's freezing."

She strained and struggled and barely moved him enough for Toekin to close it.

"Is he okay?"

Lua shrugged her shoulders while trying to examine him in the darkness.

"What are we going to do with him?" Toekin asked.

"Bring him down to the moon room," said a deep voice. Both Lua and Toekin turned to find Força standing in the doorway, looking over the scene.

"We'll take care of him there and then figure out what to do." Força turned and headed for the secret hallway that led downstairs.

Toekin grabbed the man around his waist and hauled him up, over his shoulder. He was heavy and as he lugged him out of the kitchen and across the sun sala, he thought, not kindly, how Força would have been the better person for this job.

"He needs to save his strength for healing," Lua said, as if she were reading his mind.

Força pressed a glowing hand into the carving of the moon on the door that led down into their training room, and then held it open for them.

There didn't appear to be anything physically wrong with the man, other than being unconscious. He carefully descended the stairs with his load, trying not to let the shifting weight throw him off balance.

"Put him here," Força said, pointing to a large tub of water.

Toekin leaned forward and the body fell into the tub, splashing an icy spray back on him.

The man shuddered and started to come to, but Lua's already glowing hands found his chest and he suddenly relaxed and seemed to fall into a peaceful sleep.

"Water amplifies healing," Lua said before Toekin had a chance to give voice to the questions running through his head. "The light of the moon gives us power over water, just as the moon controls the tides."

With the person laid out before him, even in the dim light coming from the torches on the wall, it was clear he was young, probably about his own age.

Força's hands moved slowly and methodically across the young man's body until they came to his head. "Here's the problem," he said. "He must have been hit. Pressure is building up and I need to release it. And quickly. Lua?"

Without another word from Força, Lua's hands, radiant with blue light, manipulated the bathwater so it pushed up and over the young man's head. A thin layer covered everything except his nose and mouth.

"Hold it there." Força's eyes became filled with bright blue. He placed his palms together and pulled apart. Thin strands of azure light appeared between his hands and Força gently pushed the tip of each of them into the side of the young man's head with his fingertips. Then, strand by strand, he carefully pulled them out while Lua struggled to maintain her hold on the shroud of water. Beads of sweat gathered on her forehead.

Blood started to seep from the spot in a slow trickle, rolling down the side of the young man's face.

"Hang in there," Força said to Lua. "It's almost cleared out."

Drops of blood mixed into the water Lua held steady around the boy's head. "Just a little longer," Força said, "There's something else in here." His focus intensified, and soft blue light spread over his whole body while waves of it poured from his eyes. The light around his hands grew brighter and his face twisted with concentration. He eased back with a hand and a tiny object emerged from the man's head. Força retrieved it and held it in his palm.

"That will do, Lua," he said finally, and she fell back with relief as she broke contact. The water sloshed down into the tub and she took a few heavy breaths.

"What is that?" she said, finally.

Força held it up in front if his eyes, examining it closely. It looked like some sort of tiny dark red shard, thin like a needle, but maybe half the size. "Look," he said, pointing to the wound in the young man's head. Blood was flowing freely now, leaving a pink cloud in the water below. "It's like this thing was holding back the flow."

"Don't you need to stop his bleeding?" Toekin said. It looked like a lot of blood.

"It needs to drain," Força said. "It will slow down soon, and then clot."

"Here," Lua said, handing Toekin a pale green bandage. "Once it's done draining, use this." Her eyes sagged, and her movements were slow.

"What is that thing?" Toekin asked, as Força held the red object in the palm of his hand. There was a strange familiarity to it he couldn't place.

"Not sure. But I don't think it's good." He pulled a cloth out of his pocket and placed the red piece inside, carefully folding up the edges and replacing it. "Toekin and I will finish up," he said, turning to Lua.

She nodded, gathered up the unused bandages, and climbed the stairs back to the living area and, Toekin guessed, her bed. After tonight, Toekin knew he'd never see her the same way again. She was strong and powerful, capable and confident. He had so much to learn, and he hoped some of it would be from her.

He wondered, for a moment, if he should tell her about his dreams. Maybe she would know how to help, if it wasn't already too late. Or, maybe she could just confirm what he already thought: that they were not messages from some trapped girl, but just dreams—nothing to worry about.

"Help me get him out of the tub and undressed," Força said once Lua was out of sight.

Toekin grabbed the young man's feet while Força took the other side and they carried him over to a blanket. "How are we going to get these wet clothes off?" He said. "They're stuck like sap."

Força pulled a dagger out of the back of his breeches. "Here," he said, handing it to Toekin handle-first.

He took the blade to the pant-leg and slid it all the way up the side without any resistance. "Is this what happened to my clothes?"

"Yep. Too hard to get off otherwise."

Toekin cut up the other side as Força pulled dry towels and some clean clothes from a cabinet in the corner. Força's curt answers made him long for the easy conversation he knew he'd be having with Lua if she were still here.

"What happens if this guy wakes up?"

"He won't. Lua put him to sleep for a while."

"Really? She can do that?"

"Yes. She had to. He's not gifted. Can't have him learning about what we do here."

"How can you tell he's not gifted?"

"You can't?"

Toekin thought about it. There was no light around the man. His aura seemed dull and muted. He'd grown used to the subtle glow all the orphans here seemed to have. Their whole person just seemed brighter and more vivid. Now that he thought of it, it was clear this man didn't have that. "I guess, maybe I can tell." He said.

"We'll have to send him on his way as soon as possible. When he wakes up in two days, preferably."

"What if he has nowhere to go?"

"How long do you think before he notices that strange things happen around here? All he has to do is talk to Kai and he'd know something was different about us. And of course, there's your giant crow. How would we explain him?"

"I see."

"Zaints like us are wanted by the Emperor either to exploit or to torture. And sometimes both. I've seen the results of his work and they're terrifying and disgusting. We can't risk this guy giving us away."

Toekin understood. Something inside him made him feel like he understood better than most, but he couldn't put his finger on why. He used the dagger to cut the wet shirt off the young man's torso.

"When I was pulling that red shard out of his head," Força said. "I could feel more. I'm not sure why, or what they do, but someone put them there for a reason."

"Can't you get them out?"

"I can't," Força said as he pulled a dry tunic over the young man's head. "I would need at least two other healers as strong as me. Lua is good. But she's not there yet."

"Is there anyone else?"

"Yes, but I haven't seen them for years." Força got a faraway look in his eyes. There was a story, but Toekin was sure he wouldn't be hearing it tonight. "They were master healers, both of them. Last I heard one had traveled to the top of Mount Devoto."

"What about the other one," Toekin said, when Força trailed off.

"Abbadon." He said the word like he was speaking of a killing plague, and for a moment, neither of them said anything. "Help me get him upstairs to a bed." Força didn't stand as tall and moved much slower than he normally did.

"Let me get the arms," Toekin said, and Força did not protest.

"He's going into Kai's room. That means Kai is going to be rooming with you now."

Toekin thought of the strange little boy and tried to hide his disappointment.

"Don't worry. He sleeps on the floor and he's gone most of the night. You'll never know he's there."

Gone most of the night? Toekin wanted to follow up on Força's comment, but his focus quickly shifted to the heavy load as they lugged the young man upstairs. Toekin almost regretted taking the head, but when he saw how Força struggled with the feet, he decided he could handle it. He searched for his inner light, something that was becoming more natural to him every day, and felt a surge of energy, and noticed his hands and arms took on a faint hint of blue. Força looked up at him with gratitude as he felt the load lighten.

"One more thing," Força said when they were finally setting the young man down in Kai's bed. "Espero's been gone in search of that rebel outpost a little longer than I expected. I'm heading out at first light to see what I can find."

"Does Lua know?"

"Yes. She and Row are used to running things while Espero and I are away."

Toekin nodded. He was sure this was the most unusual group of orphans he could have happened to stumble upon. But something told him danger was coming. He could tell Força was holding something back.

"Continue your training. Don't stop while we are gone." The dim light from the oil lamp cast heavy shadows on Força's face. His eyes were like dark caverns that went on forever, making his suggestion feel almost ominous.

A shiver snaked down Toekin's spine. "I wasn't planning on stopping."

"Good." It looked like he wanted to say something else, but he simply repeated himself. "Good." He turned and left without another word.

Toekin looked at the young man, now warm and dry and resting peacefully. Who was he? He hoped they hadn't erred in bringing him into this place. But if Força was right and this guy was going to stay asleep for two days, there shouldn't be anything to worry about. Yet.

While returning to his room, he heard the creak of the kitchen door and someone come in. He ran across the sun sala, positioning himself where he could pounce on whoever it was. He hadn't practiced battling with his developing gifts of light yet, but he reached down into his reserves anyway, just in case.

His heart rate climbed with the approaching footsteps and with his rising adrenaline he almost failed to recognize how soft and small they sounded. No effort was being made to conceal them. This wasn't someone who was sneaking. Toekin peered around the corner and saw a boy. A white haze of light clung to his body.

"Kai!" Toekin hissed. "What are you doing?"

"I'm going to bed," he said without fuss.

Toekin was astonished. It was late. This kid should have been in bed a while ago.

"Don't worry. Espero and Força said it's okay for me to go outside at night."

Toekin remembered the young man in Kai's bed. "Well, don't go to your room. We had to use your bed."

141

"I know about him already," he said. "He wants to be good, but he can't." He shuffled off to Toekin's room without another word, while Toekin looked on in wonder. That kid had issues.

* * *

Everyone had left the training room long ago. Little Enzo had even brought Toekin's dinner down so he didn't have to stop practicing. He was getting good enough at faísca, as Espero had called it, that he could create and throw balls of fire from one end of the room to another. It was becoming harder and harder to practice outside without drawing attention to himself or burning down a large swath of land. The training room for sun slingers was going to have to do for now.

With Lua and Tessa's help, he'd been able to strengthen his control of the moon's light. And just now, he'd been able to keep the flow of both sun and moon continuously without as much strenuous concentration. He'd noticed that when combining light, they formed different colors. The golden glow of the sun and the icy blue of the moon, made his light manifest in shades of green. It felt like everything was becoming a natural extension of who he was, and that felt good.

If he was being honest with himself, a side benefit to all his training was the alone time. It's not that he didn't like the others, but he found the noise of all of them together, sometimes, more than he could bear. Now that the harvest was over, they were inside and all together more and more. It was a relief to sequester himself and not have to struggle to make conversation or stumble over social rules he didn't understand.

In time, he would ask Row to help him learn to channel star light and learn some defensive and offensive moves. For now, however, he was content to work on his skills by himself. In streams of gold he glided from one side of the room to another, delivering attacks of blue moonlight to the thick shields in each of the four corners. Faster and faster he moved until the noise from the attacks sounded like one loud burst of sound instead of four separate ones, and the light around his hands sparked green.

When he finally quit for the night, he was drenched with sweat. Upstairs it was dark and quiet; everyone had gone to bed. Looked like Lua had given him the night off from chores. The dying fire still cast a faint light on the sun sala, but the corners were bathed in darkness. He wove through the rows of long tables and then froze when he saw a door open.

It was Kai's room, but it wasn't Kai coming out of it. Enhancing his vision with eyelumination he could clearly see it was the young man they'd healed the night before. He must finally be waking up. "Hey," Toekin said, trying to get his attention. He knew how disorienting it could be to wake up in an unfamiliar place. The man must not have heard him. He walked along the edge of the sun sala with purpose, seemingly oblivious to Toekin's presence.

"Hey!" This time he said it a little louder. Still the man gave no hint that he'd heard him.

He looked like he knew exactly where he was going, and it appeared he was headed straight for Espero's room. He reached out and grasped the doorknob and started turning. Why was he trying to get into Espero's room?

"What are you doing?" Toekin crossed the room. He wasn't too worried. Espero kept his room locked when he was gone. But, this strange behavior bothered him.

When he couldn't open the door, the young man took something out of his pocket and began working at the lock.

"Hey!" Toekin hissed and grabbed the young man at his shoulder, pulling him around so he could see his face. When the man swung around, his eyes seemed glassed over and distant. Then Toekin saw what he was using to try and force Espero's lock: two knives.

He thrust the knives out blindly but Toekin dodged them easily. He stepped forward, continuing to stab the air with his knives. Toekin recognized the weapons from when he'd been on dish duty: They'd been stolen from the kitchen. As the swipes continued, it was clear the young man could not see him very well, but it was also clear by his stance, and the way he swung the blades, that he had had some type of training.

Is this the thanks they got for saving his life? Anger rose in Toekin's chest. He needed to put an end to this fellow's treachery. The man's arm jerked as he threw one of the knives at Toekin and this time it was going to hit its mark. But Toekin was already a step ahead, the light of the sun flowing through him. In a flash he had moved to the side and watched as the knife went flying past. Except the knife didn't fly past him. It crawled through the air, so slow that Toekin reached out and snatched the handle. Enough of this!

He lunged forward, but the man pulled another knife out and took on a different fighting stance Toekin was not familiar with. He kicked out in an attempt to sweep Toekin's back leg from under him, but once again, Toekin easily avoided the blow. Tired from his day of intense training, tired from saving this ingrate's life the night before, and now, tired of this blatant disregard for the orphanage's hospitality, Toekin balled his fist, swung and connected just under his ribs. The follow-through carried the punch straight up into the young man's lungs.

He dropped the knife, then dropped to his knees, gasping for breath. Toekin reached down and recovered the weapon, giving him a quick pat down to make sure there weren't more.

"What's going on?" Row appeared in the hallway in his drawstring drawers with Lua close behind him, throwing a robe over her nightgown.

Toekin held up the knives. "I caught him breaking into Espero's room, then he tried to attack me."

"Hope you weren't too hard on him," Row said with a dark chuckle and looking at the lump on the floor. "Lua, didn't you give him a dose of your sleepy-time moonlight?"

"I did," she said. "He should have been out until at least tomorrow morning."

"Well, he's up now," Toekin said.

The young man began moaning and rolled over to a sitting position. "Where am I?"

Toekin lit several of the wall torches using faísca. The room, and their guest-turned-thief came into better view.

"I think the more appropriate question is 'who are you?'" Row said. "And why were you trying to break into one of our rooms?"

"What are you talking about?" The confusion in his voice seemed genuine. Toekin had to admit, this guy was a good liar.

"I hit you in the gut, not the head. You can cut the dramatics."

The young man shook his head, as if trying to clear it. "I'm serious, I don't know what you're talking about. I just woke up, in pain, on this floor in front of you. Truly, I can't remember how I got here."

Toekin, Row and Lua all looked at each other. "You think he's lying?" Row said.

"Probably," Toekin said.

"What's your name, and why did you come here last night?" Lua said.

"Last night?" Now the young man looked not just confused, but also scared. "I . . ." he paused, his mouth opening and closing like a fish with each started and discarded sentence.

"Fine. Just answer the easy question. What's your name?" Lua shoved her hands onto her hips. She clearly was not used to being defied.

"I don't know!" the man cried. "I can't remember anything." He put his face into his hands. They were either dealing with a highly skilled stage player, or this man was truly as harrowed up and terrified with his reality as he seemed.

"What are we going to do with him?" Row said, not a little annoyed.

"Can you . . . you know . . . get in his head a little?" Toekin said under his breath.

"Not a good idea with his head injury. Maybe if he had a day or two of healing, but not now."

"I guess we let him stay. At least for the night." Lua said.

"Okay thief!" Row said. "We're too tired to deal with you now, so it appears this is your lucky night."

The young man moaned again, this time holding his hands against his head where it had been bandaged.

"We'll let you stay, but tomorrow we talk. And we'll expect answers."

"How can you trust him to stay in that room?" Toekin said to Row. "I don't know what happened tonight, but he seemed to be under some kind of influence that wasn't his own. It could easily happen again."

Row cocked his head in the young man's direction and Lua was standing over him, hands—glowing blue—pressed to his head. He was already out. Asleep or unconscious, Toekin didn't know. But the thief, as Row called him, looked more peaceful and relaxed than he'd looked all night.

"You grab his arms and I'll get his feet," Row said.

Toekin rolled his eyes at Row. He remembered well the heft of this guy as he'd lugged him around with Força.

"Come on. Just over to Kai's room. You can go that far, right?" Row winked and launched into an exaggerated display of arm stretching and leg lunging before picking up the light end of the body.

"Fine." Toekin growled. He was liking this thief less and less.

CHAPTER 13

The Sap

After two long nights with little sleep, Toekin found Corvo's morning wake-up call absolutely unwelcome. The bird stood on his chest, hopping up and down while nipping his ear with his beak.

"Enough!" Toekin said.

"Want me to let him out?" came a small voice from down below.

Toekin shot up, causing Corvo to flap in a frenzy in order to stay upright, and peered onto the floor. *Oh, right. Kai.*

"I'm getting up," Toekin grunted. Living among so many people after years of solitude was still an adjustment. Having someone sleep in the same room, regardless of how low a profile this kid actually kept, was too much. He felt a longing to get back to his tree—just he and Corvo, free and unrestrained.

His feet hit the floor and he stepped over Kai to his shirt and trousers. He dressed silently, self-conscious of carrying on with the usual banter he had with his bird each morning, feeling more and more stifled.

"Where do you go at night?" Toekin said when the silence had started to feel awkward. Feeling awkward: that was another thing he wouldn't have to deal with if he left this place.

"I visit my friends." He said as if the answer was obvious.

"Friends?"

"The stars. They teach me. They tell me things."

"Oh, they do, do they?"

"Yes. They have a lot to say, but most people don't listen."

"And what do they tell you?" Toekin tied the belt around his waist and tried to smooth the wrinkles out of his shirt before giving up.

"They say to get ready." Kai had started folding his blankets and stacking them in a neat pile out of the way.

How could one so young be so mysterious? Toekin felt like he was playing a nursery guessing game. "Ready for what?"

Kai had finished tidying up and walked to the door. He turned back before leaving and said, "For cold, and change, and . . ." He held Toekin's gaze for a moment, a flash of pain crossing his face, then closed the door behind him leaving Toekin alone with Corvo. Finally.

"I don't get that kid," he said.

"Caw."

"What do you think? Should we go home? Better to travel before the snow comes."

"Caw!" Corvo jumped on Toekin's shoulder and began tugging at his shirt.

"I'm all better, Corv. They're just a few scars now."

Corvo nipped at his shirt.

"It's you and me, buddy." He slid his shirt back onto his shoulder. "I almost forgot. Can you stay out of sight today? There's a visitor here that probably won't understand giant crows."

"Caw."

"I'll sneak you out. Maybe you can scout the area. See if it's a good time to travel." Toekin cracked the door and peeked out into the sun sala. Kai sat alone, eating his morning meal while many of the other children went about their chores. No sign of their nighttime visitor. He slipped out with Corvo on his shoulder, past the rows of tables and the warm fire, into the kitchen and out the back door. A blast of cold air hit him in the face. He thought of his warm Seivo

Sangue tree. There wouldn't be many more days to gather food, but his stores were full. He was prepared for winter.

With a sharp thrust to his shoulder, Corvo lifted off and flew for the trees. If there were any apples left, Toekin would have one for him when he returned.

"Hey, what are you doing out here?" It was Tessa with a bucket of potato peelings and parsnip ends to dump onto the compost pile. "It's freezing!"

"Just coming in," he said, running to hold the door for her as she fumbled with the large bucket.

"Your breakfast is waiting for you, but it's a little cold." She said. "You sure sleep late," She looked up at him with her sweet, brown eyes full of innocence and life.

Toekin smiled. He would miss her when he was gone. "I'm sure I can warm it by the fire," he said.

"It's better when it's hot, though. You should get up and eat with us." She set the bucket down in the corner and grabbed a covered wooden plate off the counter and handed it to him. "Actually, it tasted horrible even when it was hot," she whispered, hand raised to shield her mouth.

"Food is food, right?" It had been one of the luxuries of being here, not having to prepare his own meals. The taste was almost secondary.

"I guess. But whenever Força is gone, Zonks does all the cooking. He's even worse than Força." She giggled conspiratorially.

"I'll be the judge of that," he said, taking a lump of something cold and beige off his plate and popping it into his mouth. His eyes went wide, a show for Tessa to be sure, but there was truth in them.

Tessa's giggles doubled as she tried to hide them behind her hand. "See?"

It was truly awful. But, Toekin reminded himself, still better than slugs. He gripped his chest in mock disgust, swooning a bit before collapsing onto the floor at Tessa's feet.

Unable to hold it in any longer, she let out a chorus of sweet belly laughs, prodding him with her hands to try and get him to stand back up.

"Are you working or playing, Tessa?" Lua said, coming into the kitchen. "Oh, Toekin. I didn't know you were in here."

He jumped up and brushed off his pants. Falling onto the floor before it had been swept for the morning maybe wasn't the best move. "Just getting my breakfast," he said, grabbing the plate and putting another beige thing into his mouth. "Yum." He tried to be convincing, but it was no use.

"Please. You're not fooling me. It tastes awful. I know. We all know. Even Zonks knows and he's the one who made it!" A tall skinny boy with long floppy black hair scrubbing dishes in a basin turned and gave a weak wave to him. Lua grabbed a broom and handed it to Toekin. "Make yourself useful, will you, or we won't be cleaned up before it's time to start lunch.

There was a crash in the sun sala and Lua turned at the noise. Seconds later, she was knocked to the floor as someone pushed by, running at top speed. It was their visiting thief.

"Hey!" Lua rubbed at the spot on her shoulder where he'd slammed into her.

Before Toekin knew what was happening, the young man zoomed past and was out the door. "You okay?" He said, pivoting on his feet to give chase.

She didn't get a chance to answer. Row plowed into the kitchen, nearly hitting Lua again, in pursuit of the man. "Go!" She said to Toekin.

He turned and ran, following at top speed.

"Don't let him see you glide," Row said, panting as they headed straight into the woods.

Toekin's extra training had increased his endurance and he pressed ahead, closing the distance between him and the nameless man.

But the man never seemed to tire, running in and out of the trees. Toekin's lungs burned and he wondered how much longer he could keep this pace without gliding.

Finally, the man stopped. Toekin ground to a halt and Row nearly plowed into him as he too came to a quick stop. The poor guy had come to rest right under a Seivo Sangue tree.

"Leave me be!" he screamed, then grabbed his head in agony. "Make it stop! Please!" He seemed to struggle, as if his feet were already glued to the ground in hardened sap. He moaned and sank to his knees.

"Are you crazy? Get out of there!" Row said, craning his neck to look upward at the lowest branch.

A heavy sap bulb high above seemed to pulse above him. "When that thing goes, you're going to die." Toekin said. "Just get away from there and we can talk."

"I don't want to die!" He sobbed. Then in the next breath he said "Die!" through clenched teeth. He grabbed his head again and wailed, "Stop talking!"

Toekin looked at Row. "Something's wrong."

"Yeah! In a second he's going be covered in dragon's blood." Row said, shaking his head in disbelief.

"Can't you do something? Get in his head. Convince him to walk out of there?" The sap bulb looked even fuller than just moments before. On the backside of the tree, another one hissed and dropped its load.

"Aah!" the young man screamed. "Help!"

Row closed his eyes and reached his hand out toward the man. No sooner than the trail of white light from Row found the thief, Row was pushed back, stumbling and falling to the ground. "Something's blocking me. I can't get in."

Toekin didn't take another second to think. He glided, leaving a trail of golden light from where he disappeared. He reappeared in front of the man, and clamped his fist on his forearm, and tried to pull him to safety. But he couldn't get him to move.

"It's about to go!" Row shouted. "Get out of there!"

The young man pleaded with eyes full of fear, even as he said, "Leave me to die!"

Toekin clutched his arm tighter and tried to glide away with the man but felt his grasp rip free and crashed to the ground while the man remained, unmoved.

He glanced up—he had one more chance. Maybe. He glided back to the man and grabbed both of his wrists. This time he strengthened his grip by bringing the light of the moon into his hands. Blue light burned around them, and he clamped down so hard the man yelped in pain.

"Toe! Watch out!" Row yelled.

He looked up to see the bulb, high above, venting open and sap beginning its deadly rain. With a final effort he dropped into a stream of sunlight, starting to glide backwards, and held on with his might. Toekin got several body lengths away from the spot before the young man was torn from his grasp. When they broke contact, Toekin flew back onto the ground, rolling to a rest at Row's feet. The young man, however, fell face down at the edge of the hardened red surface, safe from the cascade of hot sap, but not from the splatter.

Large and small globs splashed onto his clothes, quickly drying to a dark, blood red lacquer. "Get it off! It burns!" he cried.

Toekin ran forward, grabbed his hand and dragged him out of the danger zone. "Get his shirt off!"

Row was one step ahead of Toekin and, with his knife, had the shirt sliced and peeled off within seconds. "Get your pants off!" He said.

The young man pulled the drawstring and the pants and jerked one leg out with a quick hop. The other leg—heavy with sap—however, was not coming free. The young man reached down and tried to pry it from his skin, crying out in agony.

"Stop!" Row shouted. "It's too late." The sap had dried to an unbreakable, inflexible new exoskeleton that covered the bottom half of his leg, ankle and heel.

He clawed and scraped at it in a maddened panic, but it was no use. Finally, he fell back to the ground, nearly naked and defeated.

"What were you thinking," Row said quietly, "standing under a Seivo like that?"

The young man didn't answer—just laid there, despondent.

"Something was holding him there," Toekin said. "You saw. I couldn't pull him away. Even when I used the light of the moon like Lua showed me, he would barely budge."

The young man's eyes snapped open and he stared straight up into the canopy of trees above him. "What are you?"

Row cleared his throat. "Who me?" He chuckled good-naturedly. "Some say I'm a handsome devil, other's say I'm a madman who can't handle my own genius." He ticked the list off on his fingers.

"Not you, ghost-man. Him!" The stranger lifted his arm, a circle of sap now fused just above his wrist and pointed at Toekin.

"And, now, some say I'm a ghost-man." Row said, his head down as he shuffled his feet behind Toekin.

"How did you disappear and reappear . . . out of thin air." He turned his head slowly and glared at Toekin. "And just now, you were talking about using the light of the moon. You're a Zaint, aren't you?"

Row and Toekin looked at each other. "We should get you back to the orphanage." Toekin said.

"Here." Row pulled his shirt over his head. "You can wear this." He held it out with a helpful smile.

Toekin had never seen Row with his shirt off and couldn't help but stare. His friend's markings, or scars, or whatever they were, didn't only go from his hairline, over his eye and down his face and neck, but they lead to his heart, where other markings from his hands and arms and below his belt all converted into a twisted knot of swirls.

Before he could think more about it, their visitor, gone thief, gone suicidal, spoke. "I'm not going back with you."

"I'm afraid you have to, now." Row said.

"We can talk back at the orphanage," Toekin added.

"We can talk here." He said, turning to his side and sitting up. He snatched Row's shirt out of his hand and put it on.

"Fine." Toekin said. "Who are you and why did you show up at our orphanage. The *truth* this time."

"I'm telling you—I don't know. I can't remember anything: who I am, where I came from, why I'm here."

"What about the voice in your head?" Row said, looking at him from under a lowered brow.

Toekin shot Row a questioning glance and the young man said, "How did you know about that?"

"I heard him. I was in your head. He was telling you to kill yourself."

The young man put his face into his hands and sighed. "I don't know who it is, or how it got there. But when he starts talking, I can't stop doing whatever it says. No matter how much I want to."

"That must be why I couldn't pull you out from under the Seivo." Toekin said, looking first at the stranger, then at Row.

"We're both Zaints." Row said, finally. "And since you aren't in control of your actions, I think it's best to keep an eye on you."

"I promise I didn't want to do any of the things it made me do."

"I believe you, brother." Row said, standing over the young man, offering him his hand.

He grasped it and stood up, hobbling a little on his new, sap covered leg. Then he took inventory of the rest of the damage. Besides his leg, and the large patch that traveled across the entire length of one of his forearms, and the small glob above his other wrist, it had appeared the rest of him was untouched. Until he craned his neck around to try and see if any had landed on the back of his body.

"Uh, there's just a little . . ." Toekin started, not sure how to finish.

"Yeah, it's just," Row patted the back of his head.

The young man's eyes widened. "What?" He touched his hand on his head and felt the now partial helmet of sap that would be with him for the rest of his life. He hung his head. Toekin couldn't tell if he was trying to come to terms with his new fate or planning to finish the job back under the Seivo Sangue. In the distance, hisses and splats were a reminder it would be no trouble for him to do it.

"Hey. Don't worry about it," Row said, his voice filled with a compassion that was unfamiliar to Toekin. He put his arm around the young man and said, "At least now I know what to call you: Sap Head."

Toekin looked at Row and shook his head while the young man covered his face and moaned.

"Kidding," Row said. "But if you're going to come with us, we need to figure out something to call you. At least until you remember your own name."

"Who says I'm coming with you?" There was more depression in his voice than defiance.

"There are people there who might be able to help you," Toekin said. "Maybe they can figure out why you've forgotten everything and how to fix it."

"And truly, you don't have a choice." Row said without a hint of sympathy. "We can't let you go, now that you know we're Zaints. You must understand."

"I do," he said. "I suppose I can't set off like this anyway," he said, indicating his lack of pants.

"Let's go," Row said, turning back toward the orphanage. Toekin kept pace with the limping stranger, mostly to offer support, but part of him still expected this guy to bolt. "We really do need a name for you," Row said, glancing back at the two of them. "Any ideas?"

There was a loud "Caw!" and Corvo floated down out of the trees. His outstretched wings and pointy feet made it look like a monster was descending upon them.

"Cheepers!" the young man yelled and dropped to the ground, covering his head. Corvo came to a rest on Toekin's shoulder and he laughed out loud.

"If there's one place you don't need to protect anymore, it's the back of your head!"

"Good one, Toe," Row said.

The young man peeked out from under his arms and looked in awe at Toekin and Corvo. "What in the world . . .?"

"Great news," Row said. "I've come up with a name for you." He helped the poor guy up once more and threw his arm around his shoulders. "From here on, you shall be known as Cheep!"

* * *

Lua came running out to meet them as they got close to the orphanage. "Oh, thank the moon! I was so worried."

"Worried? About us?" Row scoffed. "Whatever for?" He smiled and threw his arm around Lua's shoulders.

"Ouch. It's a little tender," she said, massaging it.

"I did that, didn't I?" Cheep sounded disgusted with himself.

Lua nodded.

"I'm sorry, I didn't mean to, it's just . . ."

155

"We'll fill her in, Cheep," Row said. Lua looked at him, the obvious question plain on her face. "Yes. That's what we're calling him. Cheep." He smiled and walked past her in through the kitchen. "Anything to eat? We're starved. Cheep? You haven't eaten for a couple days. Let's get you some food and talk."

Força and Espero suddenly appeared in the doorway to the sun sala and everyone stopped. They took in the dark red sap with a critical eye, and then Força said, "Tessa, why don't you run and get our friend some pants. And while you're at it, a shirt for Row."

Toekin hadn't noticed Tessa but saw her now, peeking out from behind Espero and Força, mouth agape.

"Tessa," he said again, when she failed to move.

She turned and ran, the sounds of stumbles and bumps following her.

"Cheep, is it?" Espero said, gesturing toward the sun sala. He led them to a table near the warm fire and pulled out a bench. "I am Espero, and as long as you mean no harm to us, you are welcome here."

"Thank you. I think." He said, taking a seat.

Toekin and Row sat across the table and Zonks brought out plates of what looked like something Tessa would throw on the compost pile. He threw a handful of forks into the middle of the table unceremoniously. Toekin took a deep breath. *Better than slugs*, he told himself. Row didn't even bother with taking a fork, but let the plate sit, untouched, in front of him.

"This is what we know," Espero said, sliding a folded-up cloth onto the table in front of him. He pulled back the edges one at a time to reveal the glassy red shard. "This was inside your head." He held it up and it glowed in the winter sunlight streaming in through the high windows. "Força here," he said, gesturing, "found others inside your head—six, maybe seven—that he was unable to remove."

"What are they?" Cheep said.

"We believe they are what has caused you to forget your past," he said. "Also," he added, "because of these pieces, someone has been able to control you. Lua told us about last night—you trying to break into my room."

"And just now," Row said. "He tried to get himself killed under a Seivo Sangue. I could hear the voice in his head telling him to do it."

"It was nearly impossible to pull him away." Toekin added.

Espero looked at Força and nodded. "Even if we had the skill to do it, the sap on your head will now make those tiny pieces impossible to remove."

"I'll never get my memory back?" Cheep's face sagged in devastation.

"I'm afraid not," he said softly, as kindly as he could. "However, my guess is that whoever was controlling you, will no longer be able to do so. The dried sap on your head is like a protective shield. That is good news for both you and us."

The news *was* good, but not enough to cheer Cheep up.

"We have never had non-Zaints live among us." Espero continued. "However, we are willing to give you shelter."

Cheep nodded.

"There are a few conditions, though," Força added with haste as if he was unwilling to let anyone be too comfortable for too long.

"Right," Espero continued, a warm smile crossing his face. "We require an oath."

Cheep nodded again. "I'm willing, but what good would that do if whoever was trying to control me, does it again?"

"I might be able to put in some safeguards." Row said. "But I would need to try and go into your mind again."

"You would need to agree to it, though," Espero said to Cheep. "That's part of what makes the binding on the oath so strong." Espero stroked his beard and scrutinized Row. "You sure you want to do this, son?" He said to Row.

Row nodded. "I'm sure."

"Cheep?"

"I don't really understand it all, but I'll do it. Anything that makes it harder for that guy to talk in my head again."

"Alright then." Espero said. "Cheep, do you promise to be loyal to those in this room, and all those who live here, to always have their best interests in all that you do, and to defend and protect all of us to the best of your ability, or forfeit your own life."

"I promise," Cheep said, though his face paled, like he was just realizing what it was he was agreeing to.

"Very good. Now, Row."

Row reached across the table and grasped Cheep by both wrists. "Better grab mine too. This might get rough."

He held back, seemingly thrown off by Row's warning, but then he gave in and gripped Row's wrists and nodded, perhaps sensing that it was too late to back out now. "Go ahead."

Row closed his eyes in deep focus. Cheep shifted uneasily in his seat but then recovered, bowing his head toward the table, steeling himself toward the occupation of his mind.

Before anything appeared to have started, a trickle of blood came out of Row's nose and a pained look crossed his face. Still, he remained calm, focused, his eyes closed. White gathered around his body, pulling into him slowly at first, but gathering momentum and energy as it sucked in on him like a whirlwind. Cheep opened his eyes and seemed momentarily filled with reverent wonder.

Then unexpectedly Cheep pulled back and yelled out in pain, trying to break contact with Row who still managed to hold on with one hand. Cheep gripped his head and blood seeped through the bandage from his wound.

Row continued, gritting his teeth and growling with the effort. He leveled his head at Cheep, his eyes filled with pure white light and held the gaze. Sweat beaded on his brow and he began to tremble.

Toekin wondered if Espero would step in and put a stop to it. Row looked like he might be going too far. Finally, he slumped forward onto the table while Cheep fell backwards to the ground. It was over.

Toekin didn't know what had just happened, but it was a show of pure power; a power he wanted to learn to control.

"What was that?" Row said into the table while Força helped Cheep off the floor.

Everyone looked at Cheep, waiting to see what he'd say. He looked over to where Paz graced the wall of the sun sala. "The dragon thing?" he asked, rubbing at his temples.

"Yes," Row said, sitting up. "The dragon thing. How do you know about it?"

"I have no idea. It just kind of showed up in my head. I got the idea that is what I was supposed to look for, when I was trying to break into that room last night." He turned to Espero. "Sorry," he said.

Both Espero and Força seemed to perk up. "Really, a dragon? What did it look like?" Força asked. Row cocked his head and raised his eyebrows. Something unspoken passed between them.

"I don't know. It was small. It fit into the man's hands."

"Did you get a good look at the man? Where was he?" Espero seemed almost as interested as Força, leaning forward on the table, eager to hear any detail.

"It was just the tiny dragon in the hand," Row said. "That's all we could see."

Força relaxed and seemed almost disappointed.

"You're sure you've never seen it before in your life?" Espero said.

"I don't think so," Cheep said. "I wish I could remember."

"Me too." Espero patted him on the shoulder.

"Ahem," A little voice came from behind them. Tessa stood, eyes covered with one hand, a bundle of clothing in the outstretched other. "Here's some pants," she said. Her cheeks were flushed and when no one immediately grabbed them, she inched forward, peeked to make sure she wasn't going to bump into anything, set them on the table and ran away.

* * *

Toekin figured it was time to tell Lua and Row his plans to head back to Mato Forest—his home. The three of them sat and talked at an empty table in the sun sala. Dinner was over and cleaned up and some kids were playing games, while others were sitting around talking. Cheep was moping near the fireplace while Corvo hopped back and forth in front of him, almost as if the bird was trying to cheer him up. Cheep had been caught earlier trying to burn the sap off his arm but had only come away with singed hair and a lecture from Espero.

"Seems like snow will come any day now," Lua said.

159

It was the perfect opening to tell them his plans, but at that moment, Força came out of Freya's room, shutting the door behind him quietly. He pulled a cloth from his pocket and wiped his eyes and nose.

Lua jumped up and ran to him. "What is it? Is she . . ."

"She lives." He said. "But just barely." His tough veneer was still intact, but his beard, wet with tears revealed it was thinner than ever.

"What can we do?" Row said.

"Espero and I have looked everywhere. If we don't find it in time . . ."

"Can I go in?" Lua asked. Força nodded. Row followed and then it was just Toekin, standing alone with Força. He didn't feel like going in. He didn't know this person at all. Besides, she was hard for him to look at. Someone so old and frail, her body so broken and used up, surely deserved to die.

"She's your mother?" Toekin asked, growing uncomfortable with the silence.

"My daughter." Força's eyes were fixed on nothing in the corner of the room. He spoke as if in a daze.

His daughter? That old woman? Impossible. Surely, in his grief he'd misspoken. Before he had time to ask another question, Kai came out of his room holding a potato sack packed full of who knows what, and a stack of folded items.

"Do you know where I can get a sack for these things?" He asked Força. It looked like he had a blanket or two and a change of clothes.

"Check the kitchen for an old flour sack." It was obvious to Toekin Força's mind was somewhere else, but Kai was oblivious.

"Do you want me to get a flour sack for you too?" he asked Toekin.

"Why would *I* want one?"

"Because we're leaving tonight," he said, as if it were obvious.

"What makes you think that?"

There was a loud pounding on the door at the end of the sun sala. A hush fell over the children and everyone turned their attention to the door, afraid to move.

160

"That's why," Kai said, staring at the unopened door.

"Children, to your rooms," Espero said, as he suddenly appeared at the door. "Quickly." They all went, but all the doors were left open just a crack.

"Stay here," Força's voice rumbled low and deep as he put a massive hand on Toekin's arm. "Just in case." Lua and Row slipped out of Freya's room and joined them, and they moved closer to the door, flanking Espero on either side.

Espero turned and smiled, then opened the door. What stood there was a creature so disturbing, it was hard to tell if it was human or animal. He wore a heavy cloak, the hood concealing most of his face, but Toekin could clearly make out a hairy snout and sharp, pointy canine teeth.

"Leave here at once," the creature said in a deep growl.

"Why would we leave? We are very happy here," Espero replied.

The thing at the door stepped backwards, lowering himself into a crouch like a threatened animal. When he raised his head, his eyes blazed red and furious from inside his hood. "This is a warning, old man. The only one you'll get." He pulled a folded piece of paper from inside his cloak and flung it toward Espero. It rode the wind, twisting and turning wildly in the air until Espero caught it with precision, but did not open it to see what message it contained.

"Fool!" the visitor barked. "An army of more than two hundred soldiers, led by the Emperor himself, will be here by day break. He yanked a piece of cloth from his belt and threw it on the floor. "This is the proof."

Espero breathed slowly in, then out. His happy eyes that were usually pressed into slits from all his smiling were now wide open and began filling with yellow, then orange light. His jaw was rigid and stern. "Are you threatening my children?" His voice rumbled with all the power of distant thunder and the accompanying danger of a deadly lighting strike.

For the first time, Espero radiated something Toekin had never felt before. It wasn't hate, or death. It was the will of someone who would do anything to protect those he loved, plus the power to actually follow through.

"No threats. Only warnings!" he barked again, then shrunk even farther, growling and cowering before Espero.

"Be gone, beast!" Espero said, his pointed finger unleashing a blast of dazzling light that sent the creature yelping back into the night.

Big flakes of snow had begun swirling in the air, some twirling into the orphanage through the open door. A storm was coming.

CHAPTER 14

The Destination

"Lua! Organize the children." Espero's robe swung in a wide arc as he turned and began giving instructions. His voice was calm, but powerful, leaving no doubt that this was a time for action and not questions. "Row, you and Zonks will pack provisions from the kitchen." Row and Zonks ran to their duties as if it were a drill they'd practiced dozens of times.

"How do you know we can trust this guy?" Toekin said. "What if he's just leading us into a trap?"

Espero whooshed toward Toekin, handing him the folded piece of paper as he passed. "Força, the carts, please."

There was nothing written on the sheet of paper. Just a crudely drawn map of Enganoso with x's crossing out different villages. Favela, however, was circled.

"It's all the places we've tried to hide." Força said before Toekin even had a chance to ask. "Only the Emperor's army would have this information."

"Why do you need to hide?"

"Have you not figured it out yet? We're part of Kimnar's rebels. We used to play a much bigger role in the fight against Beezul, and because of it we've had a bullseye on our backs ever since. There are many rebel groups, but not all have Zaints among them. We, on the other hand, are a whole group of them. Every single one of us. We pose a special threat to the Emperor."

Toekin eyed the Abbadon taxation sack still lying on the floor where the strange creature had thrown it. Recognition hit him like an angry slap across the face. It was the bag he'd lost when he fell in the river. Somehow, they'd connected it to him and found him here.

"I don't know if it's you the emperor is after," Toekin said.

"You saw all the crossed-out places on that map. That's how many times the emperor has come for us," he said. "Come, help me get the wagons. There's no time to stand around and chat."

Toekin turned to follow as Força brushed past toward the door. He bent down and picked up the sack. "This," he said, waving the bag at Força as he ran across the snow-dusted yard, past the garden, to catch up. The big man turned. "This is a taxation bag. Abbadon guards fill it with the food and supplies they steal from citizens of Enganoso."

Força looked at Toekin, impatience and lack of understanding flaring in his eyes.

"After an ambush, I'm very careful to cover my tracks—destroy all evidence. That's why I was so eager to get rid of that cart when I first got here."

Força nodded.

"I dropped this sack. It floated down a river when I was injured. Now they've found it, and somehow, I don't know how, but they've tracked it back to me. Here. I'm the reason the Emperor's army is on its way. Me."

Força didn't say anything.

"I should be the one to go. I've been ready to leave for a few days now anyway. I even had Corvo scout our route this morning. I'd be much faster than an orphanage full of kids. You could even point the army in my direction. Let them try and track me. I'll be well hidden."

"You think Beezul is going to call off his army because we tell him you're gone?" Força said. "He and Espero have a long, prickly history. He knows what we're up to. He will not hesitate to attack. He will spare the little ones, only to bring them back to Abbadon where they will be subjected to cruel experiments and body modifications. Their gifts will be exploited, and just as the creature at the door has been abused and malformed, so will they."

Força didn't stop there. "The older ones, if they survive the battle, will be tortured for information about the rebels and their whereabouts. It doesn't matter that they don't know. The torture will continue, slowly and painfully, until they are dead."

Toekin listened. His dropped bag had put everyone in the worst kind of danger. He thought of little Enzo, so sweet and eager, as a tool of the emperor, and his guilt grew heavier and more smothering.

"Even if Espero and I survive, we would sacrifice our lives in pursuit of any children claimed by the emperor. Running is our best option for survival. We'll fight another day—a day when these children have grown and become stronger in wielding their light. One day they will be powerful weapons in the fight against Beezul, but not today."

Toekin's grip on the taxation bag tightened and he felt glued to his spot, unable to move for the shame and regret of what he'd done. Força must have noticed.

"This is no time for assigning fault or self-pity. The emperor would have found us eventually. Now we must act. Are you going to help me get the carts or not?"

He followed Força in silence, well beyond the boundary of the orphanage. They passed through a grove of trees and onto a neighboring farm. "Where are we going?" he asked, after a while. In the distance, he could barely see the outline of a large building.

"Someone sympathetic to the rebels lives here. He's old and too weak to be involved in the cause, but he has allowed us the use of his barn to store our wagons and carts."

They crunched over dry stubble, a remnant of the last harvest, and continued across a field to the barn. As they approached the building, Força reached out to raise the cross bar and open the door when a figure jumped out from around the corner. He held a lantern and Força threw up his arm to shade his eyes. Toekin was temporarily blinded but within seconds, a man came into view, wielding a small dagger.

"I don't care for trespassers," he said waving the knife around in front of him. Then he paused and moved the lantern closer to their faces. His countenance softened, and he said, "Força, is that you?"

"Yes, Abel. It's me. We're moving along tonight. Trouble is coming."

The old man lowered his knife and held out his light. "Take this. It's dark in that barn. I'll get my boys out here to help move the carts."

"Better not. We don't want to bring trouble your way. But the light sure would be appreciated."

"You only brought one to help. I'm already here and still strong enough to push a cart."

"Okay then." Força said. "But just help us move them out of the barn. We can take it from there."

Abel swung open the cross bar and pulled the door open. When the inside was illuminated, Toekin couldn't believe his eyes. "What are you doing with so many carts?" There must have been nine— maybe ten.

"I told you. We move a lot."

The three of them began moving the carts to the patch of dirt outside the barn. The work kept Toekin warm as snow started falling in heavier, fatter flakes. Each cart was similar to the one he and Row had used to bring their harvest into town: nimble and easily maneuverable with two large wheels and a bed resting on the axle. Long pull shafts extended off of each side and a cross bar connected them both in the front, allowing the cart to be pushed, or pulled.

"You sure you've got these?"

"We will be fine, Abel. Get in the house before your wife starts to worry." Força reached out and grasped the man's hand with one of his and patted him on the back with the other. "May the moon always shine upon you."

"And you too, brother."

Abel left and Força started positioning the carts, one behind the other. "See here?" he said. "There are pegs in the back. Use them to connect the carts. I'll take five and you can take four. Use your light so we can move quickly. The sooner we set off tonight, the more distance we can put between us and Beezul's army."

166

Once his four carts were connected, he did as Força instructed, focusing on the moonlight within him. He felt power and warmth surge into his limbs. He looked over at Força and saw a blue aura intensify around him. Suddenly he remembered the girl from his dreams. At the thought that she might be lost to him forever, he felt an overwhelming desire to hurry. If he couldn't save this girl, he could at least help save his new friends. A storm rose up in him and he took off running.

As he and Força cut through the woodland, there was a rustle in the bushes and a man emerged, bent over and wiry, red eyes gleaming in the darkness.

"What are you doing here?" Força said, his voice thick with revulsion.

It was the visitor from earlier and Toekin still couldn't tell what he was.

"You've done your job. You've warned us, and we're leaving. We have no quarrel with you."

The man-beast approached, bounding forward on two legs like a creature more accustomed to four. His only reply was a low, rumbling growl.

Força regarded the creature critically. He'd removed his hood to reveal a flattened nose and long, spiky teeth. His ears were pointed back and covered in hair and more hair sprouted from his neck and face. "Who is your master?" Força asked with more than just curiosity. It seemed like he was seeking confirmation on a hunch.

"My master is none of your concern." His hands flexed and for the first time Toekin saw the claws, long and brown with dried blood. He licked his lips and grinned.

"I warn you," Força said. There was darkness in his voice. "If you do this, I won't hold back."

The creature roared, saliva spraying into the air as he barked with laughter.

Intense blue light engulfed Força and Toekin thought he saw him grow just a little taller, his muscles a little bigger. His aura seemed to spread like fine mist throughout the area as he reached for a long, straight branch on a nearby tree about the same thickness as

Toekin's forearm and yanked. It came free with a loud crack, and Força had himself an improvised staff.

"You are no match for my powers, mooner." The creature disappeared and reappeared behind a thicket of trees. Toekin could barely track his movement. A moment later he was gone again. Toekin tried to follow with his eyes but lost him.

Confused, he looked at Força for reassurance, but he didn't get any. Força's eyes had grown large and Toekin felt hot breath on the back of his neck. Now he knew where the creature was.

Before Toekin could glide away, the beast wrapped his arm around him, claws digging into the muscle. The beast smelled of rotting flesh. The breath on the back of his neck got hotter and Toekin struggled to know what to do. He'd never let an enemy get this close before, nor had he faced one so dangerous.

In an instant, the beast was gone and Força's staff swung within inches of Toekin's head.

"Be ready," Força said under his breath.

Toekin was already on it, reaching down into the depths of his connections. He felt the power of the sun rush into his limbs as the beast glided to a position on the outer rim of the meadow. He could follow its movements now. His senses were heightened, and his thinking more finely tuned. He watched the trail of red light that tailed the creature as he circled, then stopped right behind Força.

Before Toekin could act, the monster had sunk his teeth into Força's large neck, digging his claws into his arms. He shook his head about, like a starving animal rending flesh. Toekin's fingers itched for his sling, his body eager to let loose a few well-placed projectiles, but he had to work with what he had. His fingers warmed, and he looked down to see a ball of fire he had created, almost without thinking. He sent it flying toward the creature, aiming for the hairy neck.

But, at the last minute the beast swung out of the way, still clinging onto Força, and his fireball missed its mark, igniting a nearby tree instead with explosive flames. Just as Toekin readied another blazing ball of faísca, Força reached up and caught hold of the creature's arm, whipping him off his back and thrashing him forcefully to the ground. Bones snapped where Força still gripped his arm as he whirled him around and threw him, head over heels, straight for a large tree. There was no way he would survive the impact.

Somehow, though, the beast twisted unnaturally and glided in mid-air, throwing off its destined course of death and crashing into a thick group of bushes instead.

Toekin looked at Força, expecting to see blood gushing from his neck. But to his surprise, there were only a few cuts and scrapes. Before he could say anything, a loud roar echoed through the woods. "Get ready," Força said, moving in front of Toekin.

Now a ball of hot swirling light spun in each of Toekin's hands. They had never come as easy before.

The beast came bounding back into the clearing, howling with rage, holding his broken arm tight to his chest and a long dagger in the other hand. He glided closer to Toekin and Força, dropping into a crouch, like a wild animal ready to pounce.

Toekin felt the sun's power more keenly than ever. Every shift and adjustment manifested as movements in the air. Energy flowed into his hands, building the power of the fire he held there. Força's massive body was a wall in front of him, shielding, hiding and turning him into the perfect element of surprise.

"You will be mine!" the beast roared, and then charged.

Força lifted his staff and Toekin knew exactly what to do. The enemy's movements seemed to slow. Everything came into sharp focus. He aimed his hands for the creature's head and with a force he'd never imagined possible, he sent the balls blasting forward. He saw the beast's pointed ears twitch in his direction at the last minute. He'd been noticed, but it was too late.

The man-beast started to glide out of the way, but before he disappeared completely, the fire caught him squarely on the knee, obliterating joint and bone. He yelped in pain as his body came crashing to the ground, landing face-first in the snow. He sat up quickly, his eyes furious but fearful, red light leaking in all directions. With his dagger still clutched in his grip, he pushed himself away with one arm and one leg. He tried gliding backwards, but only stumbled into what appeared to be a painful heap.

He was weak and vulnerable. Toekin fought with his desire to eliminate him now, while they had the upper hand. Two more fireballs itched his palms, eager to fly. Something, however, told him to wait, to follow Força's lead. Had being in the orphanage made him soft? Força stood his ground, staff in hand, not moving to finish the job and end this threat.

The beast writhed on the ground and struggled to find footing. "I will feast on flesh tonight!" He yelled, and suddenly, despite his shattered leg and broken arm, he launched himself off the ground and flew toward Força, fangs and claws bared.

In one swift motion, Força thrust his staff forward, catching the monster under the right arm as he sailed toward him. Toekin watched as his body blurred in and out of clarity, his silhouette flashing red, then yellow, then orange as he failed to glide away, the staff protruding from his back.

Força pushed the branch forward, sending the animal stumbling back. His fist opened, and the dagger fell to the ground as he gripped his chest and the branch poking out of it. He wobbled, unsteady on his feet, and fell to his knees. Toekin thought he heard the creature whimper and figured it would only be a matter of time before the beast-man died. His head drooped and took sucking, deep, deliberate breaths, as if each one might be his last.

Toekin looked at Força. Someone needed to put this creature out of his misery, but before either of them had the chance, the creature grunted, then let out a blood-curdling howl. In one quick movement, he yanked the branch from the side of his chest. Blood came rushing out of the gaping wound and the animal ripped his shirt off, shoved it in the hole, dropped to all fours and ran away.

Toekin stared in awe. Unsure if he'd really seen what he'd just seen. A big hand came down on his shoulder. "It's over," Força said. "For now." He walked over and picked the dagger up off the ground, turned, and handed it to Toekin. "Not many can throw faísca like that," he said. "Your aim may have saved us."

The cold snow pelted his face like icy darts that melted immediately and dripped away in rivulets. He took the long dagger, turning it over in his hand. The fine purple blade was free from nicks or scratches. Ornate carvings and scrollwork adorned the handle, worn smooth to the touch with years of service. The end of the handle was inset with a large, multifaceted red stone. It looked valuable. He imagined the beast had stolen it from a wealthy person he'd killed.

Toekin nodded his thanks to Força, tucked the blade into his belt and rounded back to the handcarts. He double checked to make sure they were all still hooked together and began pulling. He couldn't shake the images he'd just witnessed. While his ambushes of taxation carts had been quick, clean, and precise, this had been a vicious and bloody mess. He looked over at Força's neck, amazed that his injuries were not more severe. Still, thin trails of blood trickled down his neck and soaked into his linen shirt.

"We need to pick up the pace," he said.

"Right." Toekin shook his head to clear the images.

"You okay?" There was a softness to Força's voice that Tockin hadn't heard before.

"Fine," he said. Saying it out loud helped him to believe it.

"We were lucky to take care of him when it was just you and me. Things could have been so much worse if he attacked when we were moving as a group." The blue glow returned to Força and he broke into an easy jog.

Toekin matched the pace. "What was that thing?" Out of everything that had just happened, the strange creature's appearance was the image that lingered. "The bent back legs that couldn't stand fully upright, the hunched shoulders, the inhuman sounds it made as it ran off into the woods . . ."

"One of the emperor's experiments." Força said. "Rumor is he's found a way to take parts of animals—the parts that would be best in enhancing a human warrior—and blends them with people. Sometimes the changes work, and other times they don't. This guy? I suspect he wasn't a complete success. Probably part grindarr."

A shiver traveled down Toekin's spine at the thought of being turned into a wild animal. He asked no more questions, and the two traveled in silence. Even loaded down with carts, they returned to the orphanage in half the time it took them to get to the barn.

"Pull your carts around by the kitchen," Força said. "We can load out of both doors." He did, unhitching and pulling them apart when the door opened.

"Just in time," Zonks said, carrying out bags of potatoes and onions. "You better go inside. Espero wants to talk to you."

Toekin nodded and walked in through the kitchen. Row was pulling things off shelves and shoving them into sacks while Cheep was pulling dried spices off the drying racks and bundling them up. Each time he brought a bundle down, he would rub the leaves and sniff, then either set it aside to leave behind, or add it to his growing bundle, taking care to wrap it separately from the other items.

"Espero wants to . . ." Row started to say.

"I know," Toekin said. There were no jokes, no smiles—just a dogged determination to break down and get moving as soon as possible. When he entered the sun sala, Espero was sitting by the fire, talking to Kai, who was adjusting a thin leather cord around his neck that disappeared down the inside of his shirt. It was a harsh contrast to the hustle of everyone else around him, and at first, Toekin couldn't help but feel a sting of resentment.

"Toekin," Espero said warmly. "Come. Sit."

Toekin wanted to shout and scream! Did he have any idea what was waiting for them if they didn't get going? And they could have used his help against that . . . *thing* in the woods! How could he be so calm? Instead, he took a deep breath and sat down across from Kai. The little mop-head looked perfectly relaxed as well.

"I need to plan our route tonight. And to do that, I need to know where we are going."

Toekin nodded. This made sense. Espero and Kai both looked at him as if he was supposed to interject something at this point in the conversation. Instead, he waited for Espero to continue, and after an uncomfortable pause, he did.

"Kai says *you* know where we're going."

Toekin nodded again, then Espero's words sunk in. "Wait, what?"

"My friends told me you'd know," Kai said. His potato sack full of the belongings he'd packed before anyone knew they were leaving sat in his lap, neat and ready to go.

"Your friends?" Toekin asked. "Are you talking about the stars?"

"Yes. They said that you would lead us to where we need to go." Kai and Espero both looked at him as if he was holding back important information. Except he wasn't.

"I'm sorry, but I think *your friends* are wrong. I have absolutely no idea where we're supposed to go."

"They're never wrong." Kai said. His big eyes were innocent, and at the moment, Toekin didn't know what to make of it.

"You might not know now, but think about it. Maybe it will come to you." Espero patted him on the shoulder with a smile. Toekin couldn't take it anymore.

"How can you be so calm?" He shook his head with disbelief and maybe a little disdain. He was their leader, and he was sitting around chatting! "We have got to get out of here. Shouldn't you be getting ready?"

"Kai, I think the carts are out back now. Why don't you load your belongings," Espero said. Kai nodded, picked up his potato sack, and left. "Toekin, I am so grateful our paths crossed. The sun brought you to us, I don't doubt it. There are great things in you yet to be seen. Always remember that."

"Are you saying goodbye?" On the other side of the room, Força entered Freya's room, speaking in low, sweet tones that Toekin couldn't make out.

"I *am* saying goodbye. But just for now." Espero said.

He watched as Força emerged, carrying a heavily bundled Freya as if he were handling his most precious possession.

"What do you mean?" Toekin felt hints of panic take root in his gut. Certainly Espero was a hands-off leader who showed great faith in his young charges by giving them weighty responsibilities. He was often gone; doing things Toekin could only guess. Above all, he was mysterious, and Toekin suspected the cheery persona was covering up something much more powerful. Despite all of that, he was undoubtedly their leader. He should go with them as they relocated. More than that, he should pick a place to go rather than listen to the flighty imaginings of a little kid. They needed his direction now, more than ever.

"When the army comes, I will meet them and hold them off as if I'm protecting everyone inside. It will give you and the rest more time to disappear into the woods. Possibly hours."

"You? Against a whole army?" This did not sound like a very good plan.

"You let me worry about that. You need to worry about which direction you will be heading." Espero smiled but Toekin wanted nothing more than to grab his shoulders and shake him. How was he supposed to know where to lead an entire orphanage of children?

"We leave within the hour," Força announced. "Get your things to a cart and find your groups."

"I guess I need to get packed," Toekin said. Lucky for him, he only had one bag, but what he had really wanted was an excuse to end his conversation with Espero—it was turning his thoughts and emotions inside out.

Tessa emerged from one of the rooms, her arms loaded with bulging bags and a wooden box balancing on top. She sidestepped, trying to peek around her load and not bump into anything.

"Let me help," Toekin said, jumping up. He glanced back at Espero who gave him a confident nod. It did nothing to calm his nerves. He grabbed the box and several bags out of Tessa's arms. "Where are we going with these?"

"Out through the kitchen," she said, gratitude filling her voice.

"You sure you need all this stuff? We're limited on space, you know." Toekin winked, but it was true. Some of the smaller children would ride in the carts to speed their flight. Older ones, especially ones possessing the light of the moon, would be expected to push and pull using every power they possessed.

"It's medical supplies, you goof," Tessa said, incredulous. "You think I would have this much stuff?"

Toekin peeked in the wooden box and saw tiny bottles filled with what he assumed were healing ointments and medicines. "I knew that." She laughed at his smirk, which told Tessa that was not the case.

There was a bustle of activity around the carts and Toekin was impressed everyone had come together so quickly and effectively. Corvo oversaw the production, hopping around looking for dropped food or other treasures. When he saw Toekin, however, he flew directly to him.

"Caw!"

"Come with me to get my stuff."

Corvo hopped on his shoulder and they headed toward the room. When he got there, Kai was waiting for him. Corvo hopped down and swooped over to his perch at the end of the bed.

"Do you know where we're going yet?" Kai asked.

Toekin closed his eyes, hoping to tap into some unknown power of patience. "I don't know where you got this idea that I know where to go, but I don't, okay? It would have been better if you hadn't said anything because for some reason Espero believes what you said and is relying on me to come up with a solution."

"Don't worry," he said simply. "You'll remember."

Toekin sighed. "I wish you would stop saying that." He grabbed his satchel off the back of the door where it had hung for the weeks he'd been at the orphanage. He brought it over to the bed and started going through the contents. His sling was there, along with some sturdy rope. But the thing that made his heart soar was his scope. He had scarcely looked at it since his arrival.

He kept it deep inside the bag so Kai wouldn't see it, and reached in to examine it. The weight and size felt good in his hand and he remembered the days, standing atop his tree house, his Seivo reaching high above the forest, using it to look for changes in the weather or approaching enemies. He thought of his old room, the warmth that radiated from the floors and walls, the golden glow. He longed for his home—he had since the day he arrived. But he was surprised to realize that for the last few hours, he'd completely forgotten about his desire to leave this place and return.

He had made up his mind to leave, but now he didn't know if it was his sense of guilt, because of the taxation bag, or something else that made him determined to see his new friends to safety. Or maybe he was growing accustomed to being around other people, to working together toward a greater end? Whatever the reason, he realized for the first time that he was committed to this group. Maybe even part of it.

He closed up the satchel and threw it over his shoulder. Kai still sat, legs crossed, on the now empty tabletop. He had grown to like this place and would miss it. The warmth of the fire in the sun sala, the regular meals, the steadiness with which everyone went about their routines: it would probably be a while before he enjoyed those kinds of luxuries again.

"We're going to be in the same hand cart group," Kai said. "Tegan told me."

Toekin smiled. The kid was cute, even if he was a little irritating. "Anything else you know that you'd like to share?"

"Yes." Kai said.

"Well? Spit it out."

"We shouldn't be afraid of the dragon's blood, right?"

"Now Kai," Toekin said, "I don't know if that's very good advice. Did your star friends tell you that?"

"To your carts!" Força's voice boomed through the mostly empty orphanage. "Everyone, to your carts!"

"Yes. They did." Kai hopped down from the table and walked to the door. "And they're never wrong."

Toekin motioned for Corvo to fly to his shoulder and together, all three walked out of their room for the last time. "I've seen what dragon's blood can do to a person. You've seen Cheep, right?"

"Sometimes what hurts you, can save you." Kai said.

Toekin rolled his eyes. This kid had the strangest ideas. How could something that hurt you, also save you?

And then he knew.

"Kai?" Toekin said, relief and purpose filling his soul. "I know where we're going."

CHAPTER 15

The Exodus

"Where's Enzo!"

Toekin watched as Lua ran from cart to cart in a panic, crunching through fresh snow and leaving foot prints everywhere. Some of the white eyed seers looked on with irritation and quickly worked to recover her tracks and hide their movement.

"I wonder why she needs Enzo so badly?" Toekin said. He and Row had set a fast pace through the forest and they were making good time. Morning light was just starting to filter through the clouds.

"I don't know. Probably wants to give him a chore." *Sniff.* They both laughed, the mood had lightened now that they'd put so much distance between themselves and the old orphanage. Confidence was also building the closer they got to their destination. "So you say there will be enough room for all of us?"

"Plenty of room," Toekin said. "More than we'll need."

"You got a castle you didn't tell us about?" *Sniff.* Row wiped his nose with the back of his hand.

"You'll see. You feeling okay?"

Row shrugged, wiping at watery eyes. "Ragweed and I don't get along, but I'll be fine."

So far, the exodus had been surprisingly uneventful. Toekin expected they'd make it to their destination by late afternoon.

Finally, Lua reached the front of the caravan of carts. She was out of breath and had a desperate look in her eyes. "Please tell me you've got Enzo in there." She said, looking at their cart. There were two younger kids bundled up between the sacks, covered in blankets.

"Not here," one of them said, while the other shook her head.

"Look under the covers. Maybe he fell asleep behind something." She started yanking blankets off the kids and lifting packages out of the way.

"Why do you need him so badly?" Row asked. "Let him rest, wherever he is."

"Where he is," Lua said, her voice rising in pitch and hysteria, "is not here."

"What do you mean, 'not here?'" Toekin stopped the cart and the rest of the company came to a gradual halt.

"I mean, I think we left him back at the orphanage."

Força walked up to the front. "He wasn't in Teagan's group?"

"She thought he was with Zonks! And he thought he was with you!"

"Can he catch up with us when Espero comes?" Row asked.

"Stalling Beezul's army will take everything Espero has," Força said. "But if he has to protect young Enzo at the same time . . ."

Lua's knees buckled, and she grabbed onto the side of the cart for support. "What are we going to do?"

"I'll go back," Toekin said without hesitation. "I know the forest, and I can get there faster than anyone else if I cut through it."

Força pulled at his beard, looking like he might object.

"And I can out-glide everyone here."

"He's right," Row said.

Força's expression softened. "Beezul could already be there," he said. "You need to be cautious. Some in his army are Zaints, and others, something else altogether."

Toekin nodded.

"And if you see a guy with black eyes and a mashed-up face," Row said, "don't get near him."

The description made Toekin think back to one of the guard's memories he'd seen. He scrunched his nose in disgust.

"He's hard to miss," Row said.

"You going to be okay with the cart?" he said.

Row shot him a look. "You know how many offers I've had to be the strongman in a traveling sideshow?"

Força rolled his eyes. "None," he said, shaking his head as he returned to his cart.

"Well, I could," Row shouted after him. "He has no faith in me. None at all."

"Just keep heading northeast." Toekin said, "I should be back with Enzo before we have to turn off the road." He patted Row on the back and readied himself to glide.

"Toekin?" Lua's voice was small and broken. "Thank you."

He reached out and gave her shoulder a squeeze. "I'll bring him back. Don't worry. Just keep moving forward."

He found a stream of sunlight and stepped into it, disappearing into the forest. Trees, bushes, logs, even the ground itself, ran like wet paint before his eyes as he pushed the boundaries of what his body could do. Though he was beginning to feel drained, he couldn't believe how fast he made it back to Favela. Not knowing what to expect, he decided to take his glides in shorter bursts as he neared the orphanage. It wasn't long before he heard a deep, resonating voice shout, "Fire!"

Toekin crept closer until the orphanage came into view and what he saw both terrified and amazed him. Beezul's army was fanned out in formation while archers from the rear let volley after volley fly at a solitary person: Espero.

The old man stood in fiery splendor, his arms splayed. Sunlight pierced a small slit in the cloudy sky, descending in a transparent wall so large it encompassed both him and the orphanage. It vaporized every arrow into ash and it appeared the army couldn't even approach it without getting singed.

Espero's robe had fallen off and his shirt was open to the waist, revealing rows of well-defined muscles. He'd been holding out on them, Toekin thought, thoroughly impressed. He figured Enzo was still inside, but if the soldiers couldn't get in, Toekin didn't think he'd have much luck either.

After a few more rounds of fire, the captain called for retreat, but Espero's wall of cascading light remained in full force. It was then Toekin noticed an extravagant carriage, with purple steel wheels and ornamentation behind the bulk of the army. The door opened, and a tall man stepped down onto the snowy ground. He was bald, with a full black and white beard hanging off his chin. He wore a high collared purple cloak over black clothing. The toes of his boots were encased in purple steel and looked like they were made for kicking in doors, or teeth. Toekin knew at once—it was the emperor.

A woman followed, accepting his extended hand, stepping down carefully to avoid the hem of her long cloak. Her hood partially shaded her eyes, but her red lips and matching red hair stood out in stark contrast to her pale skin. She carried with her a long staff and even from his great distance, Toekin could see the giant red stone that glinted from the top. She scanned the scene before her, sweeping across the landscape with her eyes, which didn't stop at the edge of the clearing, but continued into the trees and seemed to rest, momentarily on Toekin. Her gaze felt invasive and penetrating. Surely she couldn't see him, could she? Fear gripped his heart until he remembered playing Sun and Seek and pulled a blanket of darkness around him just like he had then.

She turned to Espero as a terrifyingly large cat exited the carriage at her heels. It stood as tall as the woman's waist and Toekin remembered from his mother's book that it was a panther. But for the life of him, he thought they were supposed to be much smaller.

Toekin shook off a shiver that ran up his spine and steeled himself. He needed to think of a way to get to Enzo. He watched as Beezul and the woman approached Espero.

"Hold fire!" The captain shouted and at once the army stood down.

The woman wasted no time and thrust her staff into the ground sending red bolts of energy out in all directions. The ground began to shake and soldiers fell, gripping the ground with their hands, holding on to whatever they could find. The orphanage roof began to collapse and Toekin lurched forward, wanting to run to Enzo, but unable to stay upright. Espero stood firm, the powerful shield still protecting him and keeping the soldiers out of the orphanage.

"Stop!" Emperor Beezul bellowed, shoving the woman so that her staff broke contact with the ground and shaking ceased. "Or there'll be no one left to interrogate, fool."

The woman looked away, clearly disgusted. The soldiers took to their feet again and the emperor began waving his hands in the air, as if stirring the very elements. All at once, a great stream of yellow and red light burst outward like living flames of raw power. Toekin had never seen its equal. It battered the wall of light and Espero looked like he might falter.

Beezul pulled away and the beam of energy ceased. A fireball formed in his palm, bigger than the biggest gourd Toekin had ever seen. It grew yellow, then red, pulsing and humming. The emperor's body glowed blue and his hand turned purple where it met the orb. With a mighty throw, Beezul hurled the fireball toward Espero and it crashed into the shield with a thundering boom, the explosion showering the area in flaming remains that rained down like comets.

More support beams of the orphanage crashed down, and a few teetered precariously over the entrance. Then Toekin's heart dropped. The doors to the orphanage pushed open, and Enzo stepped out, rubbing his eyes. The beams rocked and then started to slide. There was no time to think. No time to come up with a plan. Instead, he reacted, gliding out of hiding. He wondered if he would be vaporized like the arrows he'd seen hit into Espero's wall of light, but just before he passed through it, it vanished.

Mid-glide Toekin glanced at Beezul, and for a moment time seemed to stand still. The emperor, who was already building new balls of light into his palms, caught his eye, looking at him as if he were no more than a passing fly. But then an evil smile spread across his lips. With sickening realization, Toekin knew why—Espero's defensive wall of light was down.

When he reached the porch he yelled, "Glide!" He grabbed Enzo's wrist and pulled, and Enzo followed, beams crashing down just behind them. Toekin turned back to the battle in time to see the emperor hurl two more fireballs at Espero. In a blink they crashed directly into Espero's outstretched hands.

"No!" Toekin yelled, grabbing Enzo and crushing his face into his side in a fierce hug so he wouldn't have to witness the scene. But to Toekin's astonishment, Espero caught them with his hands and crushed them together between his palms, setting his whole body aglow when the fireballs were no more.

Beezul's army took no time to celebrate the fall of Espero's wall. A black-eyed general, who Toekin recognized immediately from Row's description, sent a detachment into the partially crumbled orphanage to search while the rest of the army stood in position, at the ready for whatever may come.

A muffled voice came from Toekin's side.

"Sorry," he said, releasing Enzo.

"What's happening?" Enzo said, all innocence and wonder. "Where did everyone go?"

And then Espero was beside them. "I'm getting too old for this," he said, sidling up next to them.

Enzo threw his arms around Espero but broke his embrace with a start when a shouting soldier emerged from the orphanage.

"Sir! The place appears to be empty!"

The black eyed General turned to Beezul for direction.

Beezul's gaze, trained on Espero, darkened. "Send scouts!" he said, motioning to his troops. "I want two riders searching in every direction."

Finally, the emperor pulled a sword from his scabbard. The purple steel began to glow as hot flames licked the blade. With the flick of Beezul's head, his General stepped toward them, his pitch-black eyes oozing darkness. He pushed his hands forward and thick shadows streamed outward, twisting and multiplying in droves through the air. His power swelled high over their heads like a wave of midnight, crashing down upon them and engulfing them in total obscurity. However, what should have been terrifying to Toekin, wasn't. Instead, the darkness brought him an odd familiarity, resonating calm within his body. He felt hidden here. Safe.

"Remember," he heard Espero say, "Light will always chase the dark; never the opposite."

A small spot above them began to glow dark red, then orange and finally yellow. Sunlight burned through the black ceiling, pouring down in a tight circle around Toekin, Espero and Enzo. The darkness lifted like mist to the wind, disappearing faster than it had come. Toekin looked up. Somehow the clouds had parted just enough to cast a bright column of light upon them. When he followed its path from the sky down to where they stood, he saw the emperor bringing his sword down upon him. He nearly jumped back, but Espero caught ahold of his shoulder.

He blinked twice. Just outside their ring of light was a furious Emperor Beezul, slashing down with his sword. His mouth was open, as if yelling, while his eyes and body vented volumes of unmoving purple flames.

"What's going on?" Toekin asked.

"I wouldn't do that." Espero said, grabbing Enzo's outstretched hand before he could touch the circular wall of light.

Toekin looked around. The General of Darkness stared at him without moving, his hideous face twisted in confusion. Flames on nearby homes stood still and snowflakes hung motionless in the air.

"You can . . . freeze time?" Toekin took a timid step toward the emperor and examined him more closely.

"Time and light . . . they are difficult to understand." Espero said. "I've spent most of my life studying them, but my knowledge is like a tear drop, falling into the vast ocean."

"Then, what's happening right now?"

"Even if I had all the answers, we would not have the time to discuss them. If you pay closer attention, you'll notice that time has not stopped at all. It has merely been slowed down, or perhaps sped up, it's hard to tell."

Toekin looked again at Emperor Beezul's glowing sword. It hung suspended in the air, dangerously close to the barrier of light—then he noticed.

"It's moving!"

"Prepare yourselves to flee," Espero said. "I will stay to fight the emperor."

"But they know nobody's here, and they're already setting out to look for us."

"This is true," Espero conceded.

"Then why stay? Why not come with us? We need you." Enzo nodded with enthusiasm.

"I will join with you, Toekin, but now is the time for you and Row and Lua, and you too Enzo," Espero mussed Enzo's hair. "to find out what you're made of. I have faith in you."

"But I just found out about my powers. I still have a lot to learn. I'm not ready." Had he really been thinking of returning to a solitary life just yesterday? It felt so long ago, and he couldn't imagine why he had spent a moment considering it.

"Many will step forward to teach you, but there's something you must do."

Toekin nodded, listening.

"Go to the sun temple. Study everything you can there. This is where your true training will continue. There is much more I would tell you. But alas, we are out of time."

"Why don't you just tell me later, when you join us." Toekin said, sure he was exposing Espero in some great scheme.

Espero simply smiled and put a hand on each of their heads. "Here is something I *can* give to you," he said.

Toekin felt warmth envelop his body. There was a lightness that made him feel like he could fly. He quivered as every part of his being felt more aware, more alive. He looked at Enzo who had a big smile on his face along with a strong golden glow that covered him head to toe.

Too soon, Espero's hands dropped away. "I have given you a portion of my light. Use it to glide to safety. Use it to protect your friends."

Enzo nodded, satisfied. But Toekin wasn't. This was happening too fast. He wasn't ready.

"My son," Espero said to Toekin. "Promise me you will seek out the sun temple."

He nodded. He wished Espero would say something different. This felt too much like a final goodbye.

"It is the first step you need to take to truly be able to develop all four of your gifts."

Toekin nodded. The old man was repeating himself now. Except . . . "You mean three gifts. sun, moon and stars."

"I was correct the first time," Espero said. "I became sure of it when you played Sun and Seek and hid so that no one could find you. In addition to the three, you also have the gift of darkness."

Toekin stared at the smash-faced general, tendrils of dark still hung from his fingers and eyes. "Like that guy?" Toekin said. "I have that in me?"

"You choose how to use your gifts, Toekin. A dark power doesn't make a dark person. Remember that."

"This is not the kind of news one should give at parting," Toekin said.

Espero smiled. "Very true." He turned to look at Beezul's sword which was now so close that the walls of their sanctuary began to hum and vibrate. "Our time is up, but we will talk more about this when we meet again."

Toekin nodded.

"Now, go!"

"What about you?"

"Don't worry about me! Go as quickly as you can. You will only have this one chance for a safe escape."

Toekin and Enzo held hands, looked at each other, and set off. He didn't remember hearing the clash of energy between Espero and Beezul as their battle resumed, but its force pushed against his back as homes and buildings lit up in a brilliant blur of purple and yellow. For the first time, he appreciated Enzo's speed and agility. All those games of Sun and Seek had paid off for the little guy as they now hurtled out of Favela and l   into Mato Forest.

A deafening shrill pierced the air and Toekin ground to a halt, concealing himself behind some underbrush. He looked back toward the sound and pulled out his scope. Somehow it allowed him to see through or around the trees and buildings blocking his view. Finding the battle was easy. Great blasts of blue and red erupted from the ground as Beezul advanced his relentless attack. Orange flames licked out of the upper windows of the orphanage while countless soldiers flanked Espero, at the ready.

With each blast from Beezul, Espero lost ground, his strength and energy waning. Toekin watched as Beezul swung his glowing sword and Espero parried his blows with flashes of yellow light, but he was not fast enough. Then the emperor pulled his sword down in one swift blow, connecting with Espero's arm.

The last thing Toekin expected to see was Espero's defeat, so it shook him to the core to see his arm fall to the ground. Even more, Beezul's attack seemed to vaporize Espero himself, reducing him to nothing more than a pile of clothes.

Toekin couldn't breathe. It felt like he'd been punched in the gut. A cloud of hopelessness descended and for a moment he wasn't sure if he could go on.

"Toekin?" There was a hand on his shoulder and a small voice bringing him back to reality. Toekin jumped, quickly stuffing his scope into his satchel. "I thought you were right behind me." It was Enzo. "Come on. We have to go."

He was right. Toekin nodded and turned, putting more speed into his glides than he had before. He had to get back to his friends. He had to tell Força.

Espero was dead.

As they neared the caravan of handcarts, he spied the men on horseback who'd been sent to track them. They were getting close; pounding down the very road the slower moving orphans were occupying a short way away.

"We've got to warn them!" he said, and the little boy nodded. Toekin felt a surge of pride at Enzo's strength and courage. This was no helpless kid, but a brave warrior in a tiny body. The landscape blurred again and within moments they'd reached their group.

"Oh, thank the moon!" Lua came running and swept Enzo up in a big hug, but he shook her off.

"We have to hurry," he said.

"Scouts from the army are almost upon us," Toekin added. "We need to get off the road, now!"

Força turned to Row. "Gather all the seers and get our trail covered. We'll need to work fast."

Toekin grabbed his handcart, and got to work, holding nothing back. He couldn't glide with the cart, but he was moving fast enough.

Força passed him pulling two heavily laden handcarts, hooked together like they had been that first night. He was surprised to see that even Lua and Tessa managed a handcart each. The snow reached past their ankles now and seemed even deeper between the trees.

"Try to stay in my tracks," Toekin shouted to those behind him. "Less to cover up!"

Força ran past him, to retrieve another cart, and before too long, Toekin found a secluded spot to hide the group. He left his cart and went back for another. Most had been moved a good way off the road already, so his return trips got shorter and shorter until all the carts were hidden. He glided back toward the mounted troops to check on their progress, staying parallel to the road. They were within minutes of the place where they had pulled off. He glided back to find Row and the others still covering the tracks.

"They're coming! You have to leave."

"Kai, you and the rest run to the carts. Hide there. Toekin and I will catch up in a minute." Row breathed deep and doubled his efforts as the smaller kids ran off. "Just a little farther and they shouldn't be able to see our tracks from the road," he said under his breath, between sweeping arm gestures that stirred the snow and allowed it to resettle naturally.

"Forget about the tracks. They're going to see *you*!" Toekin ducked into some bushes and looked nervously down the path. He pulled out his scope and adjusted the red lenses for shorter distances. There they were. Close enough that they would surely notice a dark figure waving his arms frantically in the distance. "Get down," Toekin said, grabbing Row and pulling him behind a tree.

"Really, Toe. If you wanted to be alone, you should have just said." There was a touch of annoyance behind the joke and Toekin gave him a withering look. Within seconds they could hear the muffled pounding of hooves in the snow.

Just ride on by, Toekin willed.

Closer and closer they came, the pattern and tempo of hoof-beats staying comfortingly consistent as they got louder and louder. Toekin held his breath. They were going to pass. Everything would be fine.

He looked at Row, whose nose was scrunched and his eyes squinted closed. He was pointing at the bush next to the tree—ragweed—and holding back a sneeze. Before Toekin even had a moment to think, Row let it go, trying to bury it in his hands. It wasn't the noise, as much as the jerk forward that made Toekin's heart rate race. Had he slipped out of the tree's cover enough to give their location away? Maybe not.

The pounding pattern rang out in his ears. This was it. Surely they would pass them and move along. But the hoof beats changed, and the horses slowed and then came to a stop, the metal on the bridles jangling with the horses' unspent energy. "It was right there," one of the men said. "I thought I saw something."

"That far off the trail? Probably just a tree fox. They're everywhere out here."

"No. Didn't seem like a tree fox. Something else." The one soldier dismounted and walked, cautiously, into the woods.

"There's not even tracks out here. Are you sure?"

"Let's just check it out."

The other one dismounted and followed. Toekin panicked and did the only thing he could think of. Gathering darkness from nearby shadows he pulled it toward both himself and Row, covering them in a dusky cloak.

Feet made heavy crunching in the snow as the men neared their hiding place.

"It was right here," the soldier said, and he began circling the tree.

Toekin held his breath and clamped onto Row's forearm, a signal to hold still.

Just inches from the two of them, he turned to his companion and said, "There's nothing here. Let's go."

They were just about to leave when the nosier of the two soldiers spotted something. "Wait. What's that?" He pointed farther into the woods. Does that look like tracks?"

"Probably just animal tracks."

Yes, thought Toekin. Animal tracks. Go!

But the one would not leave it alone. He drew his sword and started further into the forest, toward the tracks that hadn't been covered; toward the waiting handcarts and kids. Toekin tried thinking of his next step. He needed to do something to protect the others. He could dispatch these men, but if they went missing Beezul would know in which direction they went.

"Caw!" The sound came like a gift from heaven, descending quickly. "Caw! Caw!"

Back on the road, the horses, nickered and neighed, stomping their hooves in irritation at the diving scavenger.

"Caw!" The ear-piercing calls were relentless, and the horses' displeasure exploded.

The soldiers turned to watch just as Corvo dove, feet first, digging his sharp toenails into one of the horse's rumps. It bucked violently, kicking the other horse, and sending them both running, back down the road in the direction they'd come.

"You didn't tie them up?" The nosy soldier said to the other one.

"I thought you did!" They both took off after their beasts, cursing at each other until they were out of earshot.

Row gave Toekin a questioning look, and after a couple minutes, Toekin let the cloak fall back into the shadows and stood up slowly, checking to make sure the men were out of sight. "It's clear," he said. "Let's get back to the others. The snow will have the rest of these tracks covered before they get back."

He took a few running steps before realizing that Row was not with him and turned back to find he hadn't moved. "What was that?" Row said, looking at Toekin like he was seeing him for the first time.

"Come on! Those guys are probably going to come back. We need to get out of here." Toekin wasn't sure what to tell Row about his control over darkness. He wasn't sure he understood it himself.

"I've seen that before, you know. That flat-faced man with the black eyes could do it. I saw him cover some guy in darkness." Row shivered, and not from the cold. "It was horrible."

"Look, I don't know why I can gather darkness that way. But Espero said a dark power doesn't make a dark person."

"Espero knows about this?" Row shook his head, unbelieving.

Why had he mentioned Espero? The final scene played out in his mind again and he felt the same punch to the gut, the same overwhelming hopelessness. He shoved it down. There was no time to mourn. "We've got to go. You can follow me, or you can stay here. But if we don't get moving soon, we're going to put the whole group in danger." Before Row could ask another question, he took off.

They found Força keeping everyone on high alert, ready to run away if the soldiers happened to find them.

"Well, it's about time!" The show of emotion from Força surprised Toekin. "When you didn't come back with the others, I thought . . ."

"The scouts are gone. For now." Toekin said. "But we need to keep off the road." His skills from years of living and surviving alone were coming back to him and he started to think more strategically. "I know of some smaller trails, animal paths . . ."

He started to say more, but at that moment, the air ripped open, directly in front of him, sparking and crackling with energy. Toekin stepped back and the children hid behind their carts. The rip grew until it was the size of a small door, glowing with red light. First a foot emerged, and then a whole leg. Within seconds, there was a woman standing before him, wearing a long flowing cape over her corseted battle gear. Red hair cascaded over her shoulders matching the red stain on her lips. The hole in the air closed behind her. It was the woman from the battle.

"You must have fought hard to win that," she said to Toekin as she eyed the dagger stuck in his belt. She surveyed the company with eyes full of greed and disdain. "Well, Força," she said, running her eyes up and down his body. "Still running around with a bunch of brats?"

Força said nothing.

The woman turned quickly, the hem of her cape swinging out in a wide arc and started pacing. "Just give me what I want, and I'll be on my way."

"We don't have it, Jade," Força said.

"Don't tell me lies. I will take it by force if I must."

"It's no lie. Now return to your master and leave us be," Força said, his voice low and threatening.

Jade's eyes narrowed, leaking red light that matched the fury of crimson coming off her in waves. The air began to rip apart, but instead of one large portal, there were many, smaller openings. Several appeared in front of Toekin, while others popped open right in front of some of the smaller children. The woman drew a long sword from a scabbard at her waist and thrust it through one of the openings in front of her. The blade took some invisible journey across the clearing and shot out in an opening right in front of Kai. Lucky for Kai, Força had been standing next to him, and picked him up, swinging him out of the way just in time.

"I'll kill these children if I must." She said, returning to her pacing. "It would drive Beezul to madness, and I so love seeing him go mad."

Força wasn't listening. He was helping children crawl to protected spots behind rocks and trees. But as fast as the children scurried for hiding places, the portals would reopen within striking distance. Jade's face darkened.

"This is no joke. Hand it over, or," she jabbed her sword through an opening, barely missing Enzo as he glided out of the way, "die!" She thrust her sword again, but this time, when it appeared, Zonks hit it out of the way with a long tree branch he'd found on the ground.

"Row, Lua!" Força shouted, but they were one step ahead of him, each guarding two openings, hiding the children behind them for protection. Toekin felt his anger get the best of him. He pulled the long dagger from his belt and charged Jade, gliding past the portals and employing a frontal attack. Their weapons clanged in the forest, and within his first few strikes he could tell her weapon and swordplay both surpassed his, but he had her beat in speed and fierceness. Now engaged with fighting off his advances, she had no more time to attack the children. The openings in the air around them began closing and reopening in a cluster around Toekin instead.

Jade retreated a few steps and took aim at one of the portals in front of her. She jabbed her blade at Toekin, and he defended himself from the same direction, but half of her sword vanished and reappeared at his back, just nicking the top of his shoulder.

Toekin shouted, more from surprise than pain, and turned to see that Row and Lua had come up behind him: Row with an arrow nocked in his bow, and Lua with a decent looking sword that she apparently knew how to use, judging from the way she swung it in an impressive display before assuming her fighting stance. *Where had that come from?*

Jade continued her attack, focusing now just on Toekin, while Lua defended Toekin's backside from the portals and Row unleashed a current of white light. She glided back to avoid Row's light, but Toekin followed. He lunged forward and sliced through the fabric of her pants, leaving a trail of red oozing from her thigh.

Her anger intensified, and she renewed her efforts with the portals, moving them constantly so it was impossible to know which starting point led to which end point. She lunged ahead, pushing Toekin back, her blade never coming from the same direction twice. She was so focused on hurting Toekin, she didn't see Row with his arrow nocked, pointing right at her head until it was almost too late.

Row let the arrow fly with a whoosh and Jade turned, suddenly aware. She opened a portal directly in front of her face and the arrow disappeared into it, immediately reemerging behind Toekin. It hit with full force, sinking into the meat just under his shoulder blade.

He cried out, dropping to his knees and Row rushed to his side. Lua's eyes turned pure blue, shining bright while she wielded her sword like a woman possessed, leaping forward again and again until she was sword to sword with Jade; no portals. Lua attacked with strength and viciousness, Jade evading over parrying, but after one misstep and a quick kick to the chest, Lua was sent stumbling backwards. Jade opened up a portal behind her and Lua ended up on the other side of the clearing where she stumbled backwards over a fallen log and hit her head on a rock.

But Lua's attack had given Toekin just enough time to stand and he squared up to the sorceress once more.

"Move your head to the right." Row's voice came into Toekin's mind. He listened, and an arrow hissed passed his ear but was quickly met by a stream of fire from Jade's outstretched hand. The shaft and feathers turned to dust in the air and the arrowhead harmlessly bounced off her shoulder. She tilted her head to the side, getting a better look at Row who had already nocked another arrow.

"I didn't recognize you at first," she said. "Are those markings from that day?"

Toekin knew he was no match for her, but he had to try. He dug deep, pulling all the light he could from within—the sun, the moon, the stars. Suddenly the pain in his shoulder subsided, and he felt light on his feet again. He knew he couldn't sustain the feeling, the power, so he pushed the pace, pursuing her trail of light and wielding his dagger without relent. New portals opened so closely around him that he felt their heat radiate against his face.

Fire from her hand erupted into one of the openings, resulting in an inferno of unexpected flames, exiting various portals and coming at him from all directions, but the events were moving slower for Toekin again. She screamed when Toekin chased his own light, gliding around her in a tight circle so quickly that it caused the torrent of fire to bend inward on her. Parts of her hair and robe sizzled and smoked, and Toekin finally saw his chance to deal the final blow.

He lunged forward, or at least tried to, but a stabbing pain in his foot glued him in place. Looking down he saw a blade protruding up from the toe of his boot. While impaled in place, the sorceress quickly brought her staff whirling down over Toekin's head. He raised his blade in time to stop it from crushing his skull, showering the area in bright golden sparks, but the impact was dizzying.

Jade wrenched her sword from the portal she'd made, and it slipped out of Toekin's foot, leaving a growing red bloom in its place. Then, just as quickly, all the portals converged into a giant one behind her and she stepped through. Before he fell to the ground, Toekin used the last of his strength to throw the dagger, end over end, into the hole after her. And then it closed, and she was gone.

Row was there first. "I'm so sorry! I didn't know . . ." Toekin gauged his expression as his eyes traveled from his foot, to arrow in his shoulder, then back again. Toekin could tell by Row's expression—it wasn't good. Adrenaline had taken care of the worst of the pain. Up until now. It came in one giant wave that increased in intensity. His vision blackened at the edges and he thought he heard Row say something.

"I'll do it fast," he said. Toekin had no idea what he was talking about.

"Wait," Força said, somehow joining the scene. Tessa was there too, worry etched in her brow. Corvo landed next to him, back from scaring the horses, and nudged his silky head on Toekin's chin. The faces hovering above him grew in number and as the pain became so great it started to go numb, he found himself thinking how different this was from the last time he was injured: Alone, completely on his own.

This was nice.

Someone was saying something, but he couldn't quite make it out. They wanted to know where to go. They wanted to know how to get to his house.

Corvo laid his head on his chest and Toekin could feel the rapid thrum of his bird heart beating in his bird breast. *Nice bird.*

Still, the faces wanted something. What was it? Oh, right. "Corvo," he said. His voice was weak and not enough to appease the faces. "Corvo," he tried again. "Corvo."

This time they heard, but something told him they didn't understand. *Oh faces. Leave me alone.* The curtain was dropping and Toekin welcomed it. But there was one more thing he needed to do. He called to the last few drops of energy and feeling he had left.

"Corvo. Show them. Show . . ."

And then all went black.

CHAPTER 16

The Toes

Toekin woke to find Força's wild face about an inch from his. It was terrifying. He was patting his cheeks and saying something. *Slugs*, his breath was bad. Why couldn't he just let him sleep? He was so tired.

"Your bird has stopped." Força said. Toekin tried to roll over but the blasted giant wouldn't let him. What was he saying about a bird?

"We need you to tell us where to go," he said.

Toekin tried to sit up but a stab of pain shot through his back. Where was he? He looked around at the boxes and bags that surrounded him, then up at the trees quickly fading in the late afternoon.

"Don't try and sit up, lad. But if you can just tell us where to go . . .. Corvo's brought us to a patch of these accursed devil trees and he's going to be covered in dragon's blood any moment if he doesn't watch himself."

Lua's face came into view, hovering like a determined bumblebee over Toekin. A light green strip of cloth was wrapped around her head. "It's going to be dark soon, and I think we might have gone the wrong way."

It came back to him in bits and bursts; the fight with the woman Força had called Jade; Espero, holding off the emperor's army; the nighttime flight from the orphanage. Toekin was leading them to his home. His Seivo Sangue tree. He focused on the line of treetops around him—the way the bird calls echoed through the wood. He recognized the needleless giant spruce resting against another like a favorite brother. They'd arrived.

"It's right there," he said. He tried to point, but pain kept him from raising his arm.

"He's not totally awake yet," Lua said to Força. "Maybe give him a shake?"

"I'm awake. And we're here." He said. "Corvo is standing in front of it."

"Toekin." Lua's voice was loud and steady, like she was speaking to a dimwit. "Where is your home?" She made a tiny roof with her hands in case he'd missed her meaning. This was going to take forever.

"Get Row," he said. His voice was rough, and his head swam. He needed to tell them how to get into his tree before he passed out again.

"Row!" Lua turned and shouted, "He's asking for you. Hurry!"

Força shook his head and gave Toekin a sympathetic look.

"Hey Toe." Row skidded into his line of vision, a little out of breath. "Sorry about shooting you back there. We got you all fixed up though. You're going to be just fine."

Something hit the back of Row's head and he flinched with irritation. "We don't have time for this. His house. Ask him about his house," Lua said.

"Row, listen to me," Toekin said, struggling to focus. "My house is that tree. Corvo is standing on the entrance."

Row looked at Força, then at Lua.

"See? What did I say? Totally out of it." Lua turned away and shouted, "Get away from Corvo! He's too close to the Seivo! Everyone, stay behind the handcarts," and then left to deal out her discipline.

"The tree is safe," Toekin said to Row. "I lived here long before I came to the orphanage. It's dormant."

Row didn't look convinced.

"Just walk over to where Corvo is. He'll show you the hidden latch." Talking had become too much of an effort. "Just look at the tree," he said, pausing to catch his breath, "have you seen any bulbs burst? Just trust me . . ." he broke off.

"Well, I suppose I kind of owe you one. You know, for the arrow." Row smiled and put a hand on his shoulder. "I'll do it."

Toekin winced, and a wave of blackness clouded his vision.

"Sorry. I forgot that was the bad side."

"They're both the bad side." Força's voice was soft, but firm. "One from your arrow and the other from that witch's blade."

Row ducked his head, then was gone.

"You really lived inside a Seivo Sangue?" Força asked.

Toekin was too fatigued to speak and hoped his weak nod was enough to convey his answer.

Força shook his head and a low chuckle rumbled in his chest. He was either impressed with his genius or surprised that despite his stupidity, he hadn't gotten himself killed years earlier.

He must have seen in his eyes the question Toekin couldn't bring himself to ask because he said, "Don't worry, son. You'll heal. I'll see to it myself." His smile was genuine. It was the most regard Força had ever shown him. "Because, if we actually get into this devil tree of yours alive, there will be questions I'll need answering." Força turned his head sharply toward the tree, his face a momentary mask of amazement. "Well, I'll be . . ." he muttered.

In the distance there were cries, not of relief at finally being at their journey's end, but of fear. He could hear someone—Lua maybe—trying to calm everyone down. "I'm sure it's a mistake. We will find someplace soon; a cave or maybe we'll get lucky and an old forest witch will take us in."

Toekin couldn't have heard that right. His tree house would be a wonderful place for everyone to stay. He wondered how Row was doing getting the trap door open. He wanted to caution him to duck so he wouldn't hit his head on the low knot sticking out of the top of the root. He needed to explain how to climb the branches to get to the upper sap bulbs and where he kept the extra grapples so people could use his cable system. What if they couldn't find which bulbs held his food storage?

He watched for someone, anyone, to pass him by, to explain. But keeping his eyes open became a burden, and soon, staying awake did too.

* * *

"It's you!" She said. She looked radiant.

"I thought . . . you're still here!" Since the last time he'd seen her, the change in the mystery girl had been phenomenal. Her energy pulsed and glowed and when he stepped inside her aura, she was more vivid and real than she'd ever been. He wanted to take her in his arms and bury his face in her soft dark hair and breathe in the scent. Her eyes sparkled, and her smile sent his heart racing. "You were so weak last time. What happened?"

"I was going to ask you the same thing! You must have found the relic."

Regret replaced joy and gripped his chest. "I haven't. I don't even know what it is." He thought of Jade and her demands that Força give her something. Beezul too was searching for something, besides Zaints to turn into soldiers. Even Espero, with his frequent travels, had seemed to be looking for something more than just the rebel leader.

"I can show you what it looks like," she said. "Just close your eyes." She placed a soft hand on his cheek and all rational thought flew from his head. "Focus," she said.

How was he supposed to focus? Still, somehow, a picture started to take shape in his mind.

"Are you feeling better?" she said.

"Great," he said through his grin.

"Do you think you can sit up?" she asked.

"Sit up? I'm already standing." He heard soft laughter and the vision that was coming together in his head began to dissipate. "Wait, I can't see it . . . it's fading."

"I think he's dreaming." It was a male voice that spoke now, a cruel jerk back to reality.

Toekin cracked open his eyes.

"There he is!" It was Row, of course. "Finally."

How was he supposed to learn how to save this girl if he didn't have more than a few moments to talk with her? He closed his eyes again for a moment and steeled himself for whatever reality awaited. He glanced around at the familiar softly glowing walls, the inside trunk of his tree. Gentle warmth emanated from them, wrapping him in a sense of security. He was home. "You guys got in." Toekin beamed. "Was it hard to convince everyone?"

"Some of the younger kids were a little worried," Lua said, "and Cheep, as you can imagine," she added under her breath.

"And you!" Row said. "Don't pretend you weren't ready to live just about anywhere else."

Lua blushed. "Fine, I admit it," she said. "Toekin, what is this place?"

"It's pretty amazing, isn't it?" Lua and Row both helped as he struggled to sit up. They were at the base of the tree, a room that easily held all nine of the hand carts and still had space for almost everyone's bedrolls. A delicious scent, full of spice and flavor filled the air. "What smells so good?"

"While you were napping for two days," Row said, "we discovered that Cheep is a bit of a wizard in the kitchen." He looked across the great hall to where Cheep labored on the far end. "That *is* your kitchen, isn't it?"

Toekin looked over to the natural alcove coated in hardened red sap. Before Toekin had fixed the tree, the branch above it used to drain sap back inside every time the bulb swelled, creating a neat fireproof coating. Now, the hollow branch also acted as a convenient smoke hole for the fire built underneath. Toekin nodded.

There was a whoosh and then a buzz from above and Toekin looked up. Two children zoomed down the wires from branches higher up while Corvo drifted down along with them.

Lua followed Toekin's gaze. "I hope that's what those were for. The kids have been exploring a bit."

"They climbed up on the outside branches?" Toekin was amazed they figured out how to do that so quickly.

Lua nodded. "I tried to keep them inside, but they were getting antsy after a while. I've at least restricted them to only the lower half of the tree."

"Tell them to be careful. The branches can get slippery in the winter."

"Also, in case you've forgotten, we're in hiding." Força was holding a bowl of something warm and steamy. "Feel like eating?" he said, handing it to Toekin and taking a seat on the floor next to him. "Have you two told him?"

"Told me what?" Toekin looked at Row, who wouldn't look him in the face, and then at Lua, who seemed to have her gaze fixed on his bandaged foot.

Força sighed. "The good news is we got that arrow out of your shoulder just fine. Thank the moon it got you right in the muscle. Just a matter of healing up."

"And you heal so quickly," Lua pointed out, a little too enthusiastically.

Toekin knew they were trying to soften a blow. "What about the foot?"

"You're short a few toes." Força's bluntness was appreciated, but his lack of follow up, not as much.

"Just two," Lua said with a sympathetic smile. "And they were the little ones."

Toekin took in the information along with a bite of stew. It was amazing. "I should be able to walk, right?" At the moment it was what he was most worried about.

"Oh sure," Força said. "I knew an old smithy that got his foot crushed while re-shoeing a horse. Lost all but his big toe and he got around just fine."

Lua winced.

"And," Row added, "as an apology to you, since I . . . you know," Row gestured toward Toekin's wrapped shoulder, "I won't bother you by coming up with any annoying nicknames." He folded his arms and nodded as if making a formal decree.

"Well, that's some good news," Toekin said.

"Besides, 'Toe' works even better as a nickname than it did before!"

Lua punched Row in the arm and Força rolled his eyes.

Toekin looked at his foot, bandaged and healing. It would probably be a few days before he felt like putting weight on it. His mind flashed to the moment he had looked down and saw Jade's sword sticking up through his shoe and shuddered.

"What's wrong? Are you cold? I can get you another blanket." Lua started to rise, but Toekin motioned for her to sit down.

"It's not that. It's just . . . that woman."

"You mean Jade?" Row said.

"Yeah. She just appeared out of nowhere."

"That's her specialty," Força said. "She is a sorceress who has many tricks."

"What is to keep her from showing up right here? Right now? How can we be sure that won't happen again?"

"I've been thinking about that. I believe it was the dagger from the beast we fought," Força said. "When she appeared, it was right next to you, and she looked surprised to see you. I caught her looking at it, tucked in your belt. I think it made some kind of connection for her and those portals."

Toekin thought about it. She had also looked right at him back in Favela when she stepped out of the royal carriage. He hoped Força was right. He remembered throwing the dagger after her as the portal closed, thanking the stars he had. He wouldn't mind never having to see her again.

Lua ran her hand along the inside of the tree. "It's so smooth," she said. "I never would have guessed this is what it would be like in here. What makes it give off light?"

The warm, golden glow from inside of his tree was one of the things Toekin had missed most while he was away. It always felt welcoming here. His tree was strong and protective, giving and safe, and almost as much his family as Corvo was. "I'm not sure."

Toekin stuffed more stew in his mouth and thought of his mother's book, filled with animals of every kind, the last few pages dedicated to the Seivo Sangue, almost as if it were an animal itself.

"Sap isn't made anymore, yet warmth still circulates throughout the tree. But the light . . ." He shrugged.

"Maybe the tree's alive, like an animal," Row said. "And it glows because it's filled with the same stuff as fireflies."

"But then the light would be seen on the outside too, not just the inside." Toekin said.

Lua looked high up toward the top of the tree where the glow faded in the distance. "Are all Seivo Sangue trees like this on the inside?"

"No," Toekin said. "This one has been changed. I sort of tricked it into thinking it was over heating."

"How in the world did you do that?" Força said.

"Family secret," he replied. If he had told them how he'd done it, he'd have to tell them about his scope, and he wasn't ready to do that yet. In reality, it wasn't too difficult though. All one had to do was locate the heart of the tree—an old knot of wood that was always located on the aberration branch, the one branch that looked different from all the others. Using his scope, he'd focused the sun through the lenses into the knot. It was the only way to generate enough heat to tell the tree it was too hot, and once it lowered its temperature, sap stopped being produced.

Somehow that small change was enough to set the rest in motion. He didn't exactly understand how it all worked, and he was grateful that they didn't press him for more.

"My mom always said that the Seivo Sangue trees would save the world." Toekin said. "I remember that because I always felt like this one saved me."

Lua smiled. "And now it's saved all of us."

"That it has," said Força.

Toekin finished the last bite of his stew and set the bowl aside. "I feel so much better," he said.

"Do you feel like getting up? Maybe a little stroll will do you some good?" Row said.

"I don't know. I don't think I'm ready for that."

"Oh come on," Row held his hand out to him. "Just lean on me."

"Yeah," Lua said. "Let's take a little walk. There's someone you should see."

Força smiled, clearly following their line of thinking. Toekin let Row pull him up and he paused, getting his balance on one foot before testing out the other. He tried a little weight on it and quickly returned to his whole foot. "I better stick to the good one."

Row threw his arm around Toekin, and Toekin gently swung his arm over Row's shoulders and together they made it to where most of the kids were gathered around the kitchen fire. There was a makeshift bench someone had fashioned from one of the handcarts. A low chatter of conversation buzzed as they approached, but then Tessa turned and saw them.

"Toekin!" She stood and stepped over the bench and ran toward him. Toekin drew back, waiting for her to trip on her skirts and fall right into him. She didn't. She stopped in front of him, reached out and hugged him around the waist. "Thanks for saving us from that lady. She was horrible."

"I had help you know, but you're very welcome," he said, rubbing her head.

"Hey, I love your tree!" It was Zonks, and before long, everyone was gathered around him, asking questions about how he knew it was safe to live here, did he really make that cable system all by himself, which sap bulb was his room? He laughed at the barrage, then noticed one person still sitting on the bench in front of the fire. Her back was to him so he couldn't be sure, but he only knew one person with long white hair.

"Is that Freya?" He said, looking at Lua.

She nodded. "Come on." Row helped Toekin hop over and sit down across from her. She still looked like an aged woman. Her skin was still dry and scaly and so white it was nearly blue. But now, she looked . . . alive. "She's still not talking, but she can sit on her own, and will eat when we feed her."

Lua's expression of joy was so pure, but it couldn't beat Força's. He came around and sat down next to her, pulling her close to him with his giant arm. It was true she still looked like a thin rag doll, but the best version of a thin rag doll she could possibly be.

"What happened?" he said. "Did your healing her finally work?"

"It wasn't that," Força said. "Almost as soon as we entered your tree, she began showing signs of improvement. I don't know what to say about it."

"Well, you could stop calling it a devil tree," Toekin suggested with a smile.

"Never again!" Força raised his hand as assurance and laughed.

This felt right, Toekin thought, to have all these people here. First, his friends, now, his family. This tree had always been his house before, but now, it felt like home. Teagan, Cheep and Zonks conversed easily, while Kai listened to whatever Tessa happened to be saying with devoted interest. Toekin smiled.

"When is Espero coming?" one of the little children said. It was a simple question, asked in innocence, and one that was probably on everyone's minds. Still, the mood turned, and the happy chatter was cut short as everyone turned to Toekin.

He thought back to the clash with Beezul's army and Espero's power and strength in holding all of them back for so long. And then the arm. He remembered it falling to the ground: a clean cut, seared and bloodless, laying atop a pile of empty clothes. Had Espero survived? Or, had he been vaporized by the blazing violet weapon wielded by the emperor? Only his scope had made it possible to watch. Now he wished he hadn't.

"I don't know when he's coming," Toekin said.

"But he *is* coming, right?" Tessa said.

Toekin looked at Kai. This would have been the perfect time for one of his eerily accurate, but equally confusing predictions. Kai remained silent.

"I don't know."

Toekin looked at Força who nodded with quiet understanding. Lua's head dropped, hiding her face and Row stared, emotionless, into to the fire.

"Something tells me," Toekin continued, "that Espero had things to do that would keep him away for a while." He saw the faces of the children look up in hope. "He said that we needed to find out how strong we were on our own. He told Enzo and I that he had faith in all of us."

There were weak, accepting smiles and Lua nodded at him, her face full of gratitude.

"I think it's time the little ones got to their beds," Lua said. There were groans and mild protests, but all knew there was no use arguing with her and they slowly made their way to the perimeter of the room where the bedrolls were laid out.

Cheep busied himself wiping out the bowl Toekin had eaten his stew from and went back to cleaning up the rest of dinner.

"Hey, Toekin," Zonks said, sliding onto the bench next to him and Row. Teagan plopped down next, taking the seat next to Freya that Lua had vacated.

"Glad you're feeling better." Teagan said. "And thanks for bringing us here. It's amazing."

Toekin nodded.

"I can't believe we're actually inside a Seivo Sangue tree," Zonks said. He had a chunk of wood in his hand and was working at it with a small knife.

"What's that," Toekin said, pointing to it.

"This? Just a little something I'm working on." He held it up to reveal the crude, blocky shape of a dragon.

"Paz?"

Zonks nodded. "I gotta keep my hands busy and since I'm much better at wood carving than I am at cooking," he chuckled, "this is what I'm doing. It can replace the one we left behind."

"Zonks did that big carving at the orphanage, you know," Teagan said. "He's good."

"Really?" Toekin was surprised, but then realized he hadn't taken a lot of time to get to know Zonks back at the orphanage.

"Yeah," he shook off Teagan's praise. "Just a little something my dad taught me, before . . . you know."

Toekin knew. Every orphan had a story.

"He still has all his tools and everything," Teagan said. "You did bring them, right?"

"Course! I couldn't leave those behind. They were my father's." Zonks smiled and pulled a smaller knife out of his pocket and attacked some of the finer detail on the dragon carving.

"You ever worked with Seivo Sangue wood before?" Toekin asked.

"Nah. Too hard. And I've never even seen a piece of it not attached to the rest of the tree. Folks don't cut these things down."

"It's not hard on the inside," Toekin said. "Feel it."

Zonks got up and did as Toekin instructed, taking his time, running his hand over the wood like he could read it. He knocked at the wood with his fist and listened, then ran his fingers along the grain, rubbed them together and sniffed. "It's beautiful," Zonks said.

"You think you could carve with something like that?" Toekin said.

"Yeah, if I'm ever lucky enough to get a chunk of it. Like I said, no one cuts these things down."

"Well, you've got the biggest chunk anywhere right in front of you," Toekin said. "You feel like doing a bigger version of Paz?"

Zonks's face lit up. "You serious?"

Toekin nodded, then smiled when Zonks looked at the space near the fire pit. "I could probably do it there. It's where everyone will naturally gather." He said, seeming to look at everything now with a critical eye.

"So you'll do it?" Toekin said. "A new carving of Paz, for a new home?"

"Yeah!" Zonks's grin stretched from ear to ear. "I'd love to."

"Make it as big as you'd like." Toekin said.

Teagan whooped, earning her a 'shhh' from Lua, and ran over with Zonks, who began evaluating the wall, stretching his arms wide to judge the space.

It was good to see Zonks doing something he loved. And Toekin was particularly glad it was no longer cooking.

"We need to talk about what's next," Força said, coming up behind Freya. "We can't hide out here forever. We're going to need to locate Kimnar and the main group of rebels."

"What about looking for the relic?" Toekin said.

"What do you mean?" Força shot a concerned look at Row.

206

"I may not know what it looks like, or what it is, but I know it's what everyone's been looking for—Jade, Beezul, even Espero. Clearly, finding this thing is a big deal."

Força and Row exchanged nods.

"Alright then. It's time you knew." Força cleared his throat. "Whoever has the relic will gain power—too much power. There will be no defeating him. If Beezul or any of his ilk find it first, we can look forward to endless oppression. There's nothing he wouldn't be able do."

"Why would you want any one person to have that kind of power, for good or evil?" Toekin said.

"I think Kimnar would want to use the power of Paz, but not all of us want that . . ." Força broke off and looked at Row just as Lua walked up.

Row looked at Toekin, his eyes were full of purpose and conviction. "We want the relic," he said, "so we can free Paz the dragon."

The words struck Toekin like a bucket of cold water to the face, and the truth and importance of the task sunk deep. Espero had said the dragon was real, but had never mentioned the relic and Paz were tied together. This is what he needed to do. It was as if he'd always known it. Now all of the things the girl from his visions said made sense. He looked at Row, and then at Força and Lua, but they were all staring at Freya, their eyes huge and mouths agape.

Freya had stood on her own, and was taking lurching steps forward, right toward Toekin. Row, Força and Lua all stood in shock, their arms out stretched, unsure if they should help her, but clearly unwilling to let her fall. With one reeling step after another, she crossed the distance between the two benches toward Toekin.

What was she doing? Where was she going? He watched with uncertainty, taking his cues from the others, but at the last moment her strength gave out and she stumbled, falling right into him. He reached out to catch her, but the moment they touched, his world disappeared.

He was already within the column of blue light, and her soft hand was clamped around his wrist. "I'm right here! In front of you! Please tell me you see me." She said. "Say something, please!"

"I see you," Toekin said. "I *definitely* see you."

"Oh, thank goodness. I feel like I've been shouting at you for days!" her sweet smile and the relief in her eyes melted Toekin's heart and he reached out, taking her in his arms, finally.

But the look on her face changed from pure joy to one of horror as she was pulled backwards and out of his grasp.

He blinked and now Força stood before him, holding a silent, glassy-eyed, and very old looking woman he had once claimed was his daughter.

"Are you okay, Toekin?" Lua asked. "She didn't hurt your shoulder when she fell, did she?" She fussed around, checking his shoulder dressing and looking at his foot, a mess of nervous energy. "I can't believe she walked. Can you believe it?" she said to no one in particular.

"You're alright, aren't you?" Força asked as a matter of courtesy, clearly more concerned about Freya than Toekin.

"I'm fine," Toekin said. "But Força . . ."

"Yes?" He set his daughter back down on the bench like she was a porcelain doll.

"It's time you tell me the truth about Freya."

CHAPTER 17

The Truth

"It's true. She is my daughter." Força spoke softly so those who slept would not be disturbed, but it added a reverence to the tale that Toekin didn't doubt it deserved. "She too, is a Zaintozo like yourself. So, when the relic fell into our hands, she was the only one who could use it. She was young—only eleven—the youngest to try in hundreds of years."

Toekin still didn't understand how someone who looked so old could be his daughter. Row's head hung as he listened to Força's tale while Lua stared straight ahead, unmoving, her emotions hard to read.

"What do you mean, she used the relic. What is the relic? What does it do?"

"Think back to the story of Paz. When Ganancia tricked the dragon into taking a man's life by killing him underneath a Seivo Sangue, the wizard appeared and bound Paz to him. The wizard pulled the sap from the man, and used it to form a glassy red flute, which had power to control the dragon. The flute is the relic."

Could it be true? All of it? It was one thing to believe that Paz was real, but the whole story? The thought that the flute was out there, somewhere, suddenly excited him. And if Força was to be believed, at one time, they'd had it! Thoughts and questions overwhelmed him, and he didn't know what to ask first, so instead he listened.

"The person who holds the flute . . ." Força's voice caught and he paused, cleared his throat and continued. ". . . can blow into it to summon Paz. When he appears, he is bound to do their bidding." Força cleared his throat again but was unable to go on. He hung his head and swiped at his eyes with an old cloth pulled from his pocket.

"We were being attacked by Beezul's army," Lua said. "It was the only chance we had at not being destroyed." Lua's eyes glistened with tears, but she continued. "Freya called Paz, climbed on his back, and commanded him to drive the army away. And for a while it was working. But then something horrible happened." Now Lua broke off, unable to continue. Força handed her his cloth and she blew into it.

"Paz fell out of the sky," Row said. "And Freya came with him. When they landed, she couldn't separate herself from him. It was as if she were being pulled right into the dragon itself." Row looked to Lua and something passed between them. "I ran to help her, but she was already starting to change . . . turning into," Row gestured toward Freya, "this half-dead shell of a human. Sorry Força."

"'Tis what she is, son." He nodded.

"Because I was holding on, trying to pull her off, some of the effects fell upon me. My hair turned white, and I got these." He touched his face near the long scars that disappeared beneath his shirt. "If I hadn't pulled her off, she would have been connected to Paz forever. Just like the others."

"The others?" Toekin wasn't sure he liked where this was going.

Força took a deep breath and exhaled. "Every person who's ever used the relic has at some point ended up stuck to Paz's back, where they are cursed to ride him, ghost-like, both living and dead, forever."

Toekin took a moment to think about what they'd just told him. The fire popped and hissed, and no one said anything. "Does anyone know why this happens? Is there a way to prevent it?"

"If there is a way, I'm not aware of it." Força said.

Toekin nodded, his understanding coming into focus. "And this is what you wanted me to do? Because I'm a Zaintozo? You wanted me to use the relic, call Paz, and turn into that?" He pointed to Freya, his anger rising.

"I hoped you'd want to try and find a way to free my Freya," Força said.

"But it's never worked before," Toekin said. "And it probably won't work now. How many bodies is Paz carrying around now?"

"Counting Freya, nine," Row's voice was soft and sheepish.

"Unbelievable." Toekin said. "That's why you've kept me around, offered me food, a roof and training? It's not because you wanted me to be part of you. You just wanted me to doom myself to an eternity stuck on the back of a dragon for a lost cause." Toekin had to leave, but there was nowhere to go. They were in one giant room. When he quickly stood up, he remembered his foot was still healing from his recent loss of toes. He stumbled backwards and caught himself.

"Here," Row said, offering an arm. "I can help."

"Don't bother." His mother's nagging voice had told him to hide; to stay hidden. He knew better than to trust people. What had he been thinking? And now he'd let them into his home. Toekin got four defiant hops off his good foot before his strength gave out and he fell.

Lua was at his side in an instant. "Don't be stubborn," she whispered. "Let me help you." She pulled him up and wrapped her arm around his waist. "Just lean on me."

She wasn't as steady of a crutch as Row had been, but she would have to do. When they got to his spot, she helped him as he stretched out on his bedroll and covered him with a blanket. "May I," she said, holding bluish glowing hands out toward his injured foot.

He nodded. He knew he was acting harsh, but *slugs*, had they really expected him to risk turning himself into something like Freya?

"This will relieve the pain, so you can rest." Her hands moved with expert precision over his foot and lower leg. She seemed to be lost in the healing and totally focused. Finally, she held her hands around the end of his foot letting the blue warmth penetrate them. She looked up and said, "I don't think you should use the relic, if we ever find it."

"You don't?" Toekin was surprised. Wasn't Freya her friend? Didn't she want him to try and release her from the dragon's grasp?

"It's too dangerous. No one has ever succeeded. It's just not worth the risk." Pain receded beneath her healing hands.

"I wish there was something I could do, but it just seems so dangerous." Tokein said. "Maybe if Força understood more about how the relic works with Paz . . . but he doesn't seem to know anything."

"We do need to find the relic, though," she said. "It needs to be destroyed so that it stays out of evil hands." She shuddered and looked away so Toekin couldn't see her face.

"What is it?" he said. "There's something you're not telling me."

She shook her head, her eyes glistening with unspent tears.

"If I'm going to get mixed up with the relic—finding and destroying it—I have to know everything. Something happened when Freya and Paz fell out of the sky, didn't it? I saw that look you gave to Row back there." He rose up on his elbows, determined to catch her words both spoken and unspoken.

"We were so young. It was mostly Freya in the fight. I was just a healer and working with the injured. When she fell, though, she came down close to where I was—close enough that I could see her struggling. I would have run to help her, but someone appeared. At first he just stood there and watched with wild excitement." Lua shuddered and squeezed her eyes shut at the memory that must have been flashing across her mind.

"His skin was light blue, and his eyes . . . they flashed back and forth between being blue and red. I was terrified. He towered over me, and when I tried to run and help Freya he held me back with some power I didn't understand. But then Row came. He saw Freya and grabbed onto her, trying to keep her from going into Paz like the rest of those awful beings. When the blue man saw what he was doing, he lost it and his power over me turned into something more like torture. I mostly remember screaming. I couldn't move, and my head felt like it was going to split in two."

Toekin watched as Lua spoke. Pain at the recollection was evident throughout her whole body. Her warm hands had dropped from his injured foot and were now clenched at her sides.

"Row turned and saw me, but he couldn't leave Freya. We would have lost her. The blue man's eyes were on Row, but his torture did not let up. All I could do was scream. Then there was a burst of light, and Freya was free. Row had her in his arms. She looked dreadful, but he'd saved her. And then they collapsed to the ground. The blue man turned back to me, but not to me exactly. He looked up the trail, as if in fear. Then he fled, and the pain stopped. Moments later, Espero appeared and Força came running down the trail. He told us later they thought all three of us had died. I couldn't move, Row and Freya were unresponsive. It's something I never want to witness again."

Toekin was quiet. It was a lot to take in.

"We need to destroy the relic, not just to keep it out of Beezul's hands, but so that no one else will be hurt by it." She picked up Toekin's foot again and resumed her healing.

"Makes sense," Toekin said, lowering himself to his back. He felt warm tingles in his foot and his breathing slowed, then deepened. His last thoughts, before drifting off, were of Freya. She had pleaded for him to save her. Maybe she would know what to do.

* * *

Row brought him his meal the next morning, a warm bowl of steeped grains and honey with jabu nuts and dried pennfruit. "A peace offering," Row said.

"Cheep made it; you just walked it over here." Toekin sat up and took a bite. It was delicious. He knew he wouldn't be able to stay mad at Row for much longer.

"Listen," Row said, sitting on the floor next to him. "You're my friend whether you try to figure this relic thing out or not. In fact, you could leave now and if we never saw you again, I'd still consider you a friend."

"You mean leave my own tree?" Toekin said, raising an eyebrow. "Just turn it over to you and everyone else? You'd still like me then?"

Row shoved his palm into his forehead at the gaffe.

"How very generous of you, *friend*." Toekin grasped Row's forearm and shook vigorously, a smile creeping on his face.

"You know what I mean. It was never just about the relic."

Toekin sighed. "I just don't see the purpose in trying to summon Paz when we don't even have a plan on how to rescue Freya—let alone not end up like her."

"You're probably right." Row nodded, thinking about it. "But we don't even know where the relic is, so it doesn't really matter."

"Lua thinks we should still try and find it, and I agree."

"If we don't, someone else will."

"Exactly. Where was its last known location? Or, who had it last?" Toekin said, taking another bite.

"As far as I know, we were the last ones to have it. Força gave it to a trusted friend, a man who used to stop by the orphanage from time to time. We tried to ask him about it, but despite our best efforts to find him, his whereabouts are still unknown."

"Okay," Toekin said, scratching at his healing shoulder. It itched like crazy. "I was also thinking, that if we want to know more about how to use it, maybe Freya might know."

Row laughed. "Have you met Freya? In case you didn't notice, she doesn't talk much."

"I can talk to her."

Row scoffed but Toekin held Row's dubious gaze in his own. "Wait, you're serious?" he said, his eyes wide.

"When we touched last night, when she fell into me, we made a connection. We . . . communicated."

"Why didn't you say something?"

"I needed some answers first." There were the dreams too, but he wasn't ready to share those yet. "There have been so many secrets—so many things I don't understand. I needed to know everything."

"I can't believe this. Força is going to have a fit! We have to tell him."

* * *

Freya was beaming. Literally. Shafts of light streaked from her joyful eyes and her sweet mouth, open in a wide smile. "My father is with you?" She said. "I'd almost forgotten him. It feels like I've been so long in this place."

"He says it has been six years, and he has missed you every day."

"I want to get out. I want to see him again." There was so much hope in her voice, Toekin's heart nearly broke. What could he say? That they didn't know if it was even possible? How could he crush such undiluted optimism?

"We are looking at all our options. We're not really sure how to do it. But the first step would be finding the relic. Força's been working on that. But after, we need to know what to do to help Paz. That's where you come in."

"What can I do?"

"What help does Paz need? Or what can we do so that if I use the flute I don't get absorbed into his body?"

Freya squinted her eyes in concentration and the streams of light from her eyes turned into slivers, fine and piercing. "I don't know," she finally said, shaking her head in quiet despair.

"Is it possible for you to probe with your mind? Maybe get into Paz's head a little?"

She brightened. "I can try."

"Great!" Toekin gave her hands a gentle squeeze. "And maybe try to get a sense for if the relic is close to you, or far away. You think you can do that?"

She nodded, her eyes filled with gratitude. "Toekin," she said. She stood on her tiptoes and pressed her lips to his cheek. "Thank you."

The pleasant shock sent his heart racing and all words lost their meaning so that it became impossible to choose two to string together for a reply. He must have had quite a look on his face because Freya covered her mouth and giggled. Then she started falling backwards. Or was it Toekin who was falling up? Before he could decide, Freya was gone and Força's big face was staring him down.

"What did she say?" He asked, his voice full of desperation. "Did you tell her I love her and miss her?"

Toekin rubbed his cheek and blinked. That feeling lingered, though Força was quickly chasing it away. He felt out of breath and lightheaded; a little like when he'd held his breath for too long at the bottom of a river. "I did. She said she loves you, and misses you, too." He decided to leave out the part about almost forgetting him.

215

Força sat back, his relief apparent in the way his shoulders relaxed, and his breath came out all at once. "She's going to try and search Paz's mind—hopefully she'll learn something useful. Maybe we can figure out what to do differently this time."

"What I wouldn't give to have her back," he said, stroking his beard.

Toekin felt a stab of guilt. He was getting pulled into this, and he still wasn't sure he wanted to. Saving Freya would be amazing, though. The idea had been part of his thoughts for a while now. The chance to get to know her outside of that realm excited him. But to give his life, when saving her might not even work, that didn't seem good for anyone.

He wondered how long he should wait to see her again. He still felt the press of her lips on his cheek and wanted to go back. Right back. But he probably needed to give her time—to see if she could connect with Paz. Toekin sighed and Força gave him a curious look.

"Tell me about the relic," Toekin said. They needed to talk about something besides Freya. "When is the last time you had it?"

"After the battle, and the accident with Freya, we gave it to a trusted friend. Along with Espero, the three of us decided to bring it to King Kimnar and the rebels. They could keep Beezul from obtaining it and using it against us. And Turbin agreed to be the one to deliver it."

"I'm sorry," Toekin said. "Turbin?"

"Yes, Turbin Salazar—a secretive, but good man. We'd known each other many years. And when Espero and I started the orphanage, he would often stop by to visit during his travels. Sometimes he would stay one night, other times several days. He was very active in our cause."

Toekin said nothing.

"Son, what is it? You look like you've seen a ghost."

He wondered if he'd heard Força correctly. He hadn't heard that name for many years and hearing it now brought back a rush of complicated emotions. "Turbin Salazar," Toekin said. "That was my father's name."

He'd clearly shocked the big man because his eyes widened, and his mouth dropped open ever so slightly. "You don't say." Força looked at him with a critical eye. "You don't suppose there might have been more than one?"

"Did he have a tattoo on his forearm?" Toekin asked. Over the years he'd found it harder to remember what his father had looked like. The tattoo was one of the few things he could still envision.

"He did. Right about here," Força said, tapping his forearm. "A rose, about yea big."

Toekin felt numb. "My mom's name was Strella Rose."

"I've always wondered what had happened to him," Força said, his mood turning somber. He rubbed his beard again. "I gave him the relic, then never heard from him. And Kimnar said Turbin never made it to him."

"My dad was . . ." Was what? Toekin didn't even know where to begin.

"Your dad was a great man, and powerful." Força shook his head. "He wasn't a Zaintozo, but he was stronger than me with moonlight, and easily Espero's equal with the sun. There was not much that could stop him when he had it in his mind to do something."

Toekin was silent, fighting back emotion while thinking of the last time he saw him. His memories of that night were patchy—little bits here and there with big empty spaces in between.

"What happened to him?" Força asked in a way that showed he knew it might be painful to talk about.

And it was. "I had just turned eleven," He said. "I remember because my father gave me my first knife as a gift. I loved it." He paused, steeling himself before moving on. "It made me feel grown up, like he trusted me to care for the family in his absence. But when the Abbadon Guards came, I didn't feel like a man. They took my parents away, and then I was alone." Toekin let the anger he felt toward the guards replace his sorrow and shook his head to see if any more memories would shake out. "That's all I remember."

"The timing's about right," Força said. "You say you are seventeen now?"

Toekin nodded.

"Do you ever remember seeing a shiny red dragon flute in your home? Did he hide it there, maybe?"

"I just can't remember," Toekin said, unsure if he was trying hard enough. "It's possible." It had always bugged him, these gaps in his memory. Even his journey from his home in Abbadon to Mato Forest was spotty, almost as if he'd made the trek in a dream.

"And do you remember where you used to live?" Força sounded like he was holding onto his last straw.

"Yeah." Toekin said, slowly finding his past easier to discuss. "We lived in Abbadon. I still can picture the exact place. We had a lovely view of the Seivo Salvador from our front window." It had almost been like a picture, framing in the whole majestic thing.

"You think you could find it again?"

"Sure. But what are you suggesting?"

"Go back, have a look around. See if you can find the relic, or maybe a clue to its location," Força said, his mood brightening.

"You realize someone else probably lives there now."

"Sure."

"So we'd have to prowl—maybe break through a window or pick a lock."

"Or," Força pointed out. "Maybe they are the type who don't lock their door. You know, *trusting.*"

"Don't you think in six years they've probably found the thing if it were there?" Toekin said.

"We would know if they had. No doubt your father hid it well. He knew the consequences of it falling into the wrong hands. Do you remember any special hiding places that only your family knew about? Hidden holes, nooks, crannies?"

Toekin thought. What was his problem? Only old people were supposed to have problems remembering things. He'd always felt like there was something wrong with him, but now, faced with Força's line of simple questioning, he was really starting to believe it.

"That's okay, son," Força said when Toekin failed to answer. "Maybe once you get there, things will start coming back. That happens sometimes, you know."

Toekin nodded. "So you really think I ought to go back?"

"Not just you. Lua and Row should go as well."

Toekin cringed inwardly. Lua and Row couldn't glide, which meant he wouldn't be able to either. His foot hurt just thinking about all the walking. Although having his friends along would make the journey a bit more enjoyable.

"While you're healing, we will take the time to plan and gather supplies. I'll make sure you have everything you need."

"Then what?" Toekin said. "What if we don't find anything? It's a long trip to Abbadon just to have a look around."

"I feel good about this," Força said. "When I think about Turbin, it seems like something he would do."

"What do you mean?"

"I told you he was powerful, did I not?"

Toekin nodded.

"There is no way your pa would have let a few Abbadon Guards take him and his wife away. Overpowering those goons was all in a day's work." He shook his head and looked thoughtful. "No, if he was taken, something went wrong. I bet he knew and secured the relic before his capture. I'm certain of it."

"Say we find it in the house—what then? I'm not ready to commit to summoning Paz when we don't have a plan that keeps me from being his eternal slave."

"Let's secure the relic first. Then we will worry about what to do with it."

Toekin thought about his father. The fading picture of him he'd kept in his heart had seemed to become nearly unrecognizable within the space of an hour, now filled with details of a man Toekin wondered if he had ever truly known.

"Trust me," Força said. "It will work."

Toekin wished he could be so sure.

* * *

He took a careful step, his good foot shooting out in quick bursts to compensate for the three-toed one's inability to take weight for more than the shortest amount of time. His hand slid along the smooth wall as support.

"You're doing really well," Tessa said. From anyone else, the over-positive encouragement would have driven him crazy, but there was something about Tessa's sweetness he couldn't resist, and he allowed her to stay and cheer him on. "Before you know it, you'll be running all over the place, just like Enzo."

Toekin smiled and watched as the little guy glided around the great room, much to the chagrin of—it appeared to be—nearly everyone. His grins and laughter made it clear he was having a great time. He took another step and thought about Freya. He wished he could visit her alone, without having Força waiting nearby to pull him back from his trance. It felt like having a chaperone.

"Keep going," Tessa said, "You've almost made it back to the fire pit." He was exhausted, but would finish for her.

He thought of his upcoming trip back to Abbadon. It would be the first time he'd returned in six years. A wave of panic washed over him. "Hide" his mother's voice came, unbidden, to his mind, almost as if she were still trying to keep him away. Her voice had been the thing that had kept him hidden all these years. Surely it was okay to disregard now. Surely she didn't mean for him to stay hidden forever.

"Just a few more steps." Tessa reached out her hand. "Want to see if you can make it without holding the wall?"

"Sure," Toekin said. "I'll give it a shot." He took her hand and left the safety of the tree trunk. If he slipped, he would surely take her down. He focused on placing his foot carefully, so as not to put pressure on the area where the toes had been severed, then quickly transferred to the other foot.

"Good."

Hide, he thought. Why did that word keep invading his thoughts every time he thought about leaving? And why couldn't he remember simple things from before? Had he forced himself to forget painful memories?

"I need to talk to Row," he said as an idea sprang up like the unchecked sun over dawn's horizon, and he found an extra spring in his step. "Let's head toward those benches."

"That's a little bit farther. You sure you can do it?" Tessa's eyes narrowed, and she seemed to evaluate him, and the prudence of this request.

He smiled, "With you by my side, I could walk all the way to Abbadon," he said, smiling down at her. She was going to make an excellent healer one day.

His compliment hit home and Toekin could practically see the pride swelling in her chest. She stayed by his side until he was seated and settled next to his friend.

"How'd he do, Healer Tessa?" Row said with genuine deference.

"I predict he will be walking on his own in no time. Now," she said, waving a finger at Row, "he's worked hard and needs to rest. No running around, you two, okay?"

Row pounded his fist over his heart in salute. "Yes, ma'am, Healer Tessa."

She left, satisfied with his answer, and wandered over to where Kai was sitting.

"She's strict!" Row joked. "Maybe a little too much like her older sister."

"She's great." Toekin replied. "Hey, listen," he said, changing the subject. "I had an idea—about the relic."

"Let's hear it," Row said.

"We need to find the relic, but we're not sure where it is." Toekin said, setting up his defense.

"True."

"And as we've recently learned, as crazy as it sounds, my dad was the last known person to have it."

Row nodded.

"One would think I might have a memory of seeing it at some point before my parents were taken."

"I've wondered as much." Row was starting to look suspicious. Had he figured out what Toekin was going to ask?

"For years I've wondered why I can't remember simple things; things like whether or not I had any siblings, or my favorite food." He paused while Row caught up with him. "When my parents were taken I tried to never think about it, but what if I tried so hard to forget that I actually did? So, I was thinking, maybe we could learn something important if you probed my memories?"

"Bad idea," Row said, shooting it down immediately. "Going back that far in someone's memory can mess them up. Permanently. That's like, five years," he said.

"Six," Toekin corrected.

"Even worse! And I'm not even sure I could do it. I'm good, but going back that far takes a lot of skill. It's like I have to go through more and more doors of your memory, but I have to hold each one I go through open so that I can find my way back out. It'd be nearly impossible for anyone to do alone."

"Then why don't you let Kai help?"

Row huffed and shook his head. "It would still be very dangerous. Not for us, for *you*."

"I'm willing to let you try. If it means learning something about the relic, and helping Freya, it's worth it."

Row gave him an appraising look. "You serious?"

"I am." If he was going to walk back into Abbadon on one bad foot, especially while being wanted for raiding the capitol's taxation carts, he needed as much information as he could possibly get. He needed to be prepared.

"Let me think about it."

Toekin smiled and patted him on the shoulder. "You'll do it. You owe me one." He said, gesturing with his eyes toward his own shoulder.

Row gave a disapproving grunt and threw his hands in the air. "*Fine*. But if something happens and you come out of this all muddled in the head, that's on you."

Toekin smiled. "I trust you, Row."

CHAPTER 18

The Expected

As if time was unraveling in reverse, events unfolded in rapid succession. His battle with Jade; subduing the guards on the bridge to Favela; waking up in the orphanage; the fight with the ursmock; picking off Abbadon Guards with his sling; sliding down the cables in his tree; a tiny beak breaking through an egg; eating slugs. Each memory was more vivid than the last until he saw himself curled into a ball, pressed up against a log, and forcing himself not to cry.

The forest floor was cold and damp. A moldy leaf stuck to his cheek. In the distance he could hear the strained barks of a grindarr pack, tracking him through Mato Forest. For a while, their yips traveled away from him, but suddenly they turned back. They were getting closer.

He jumped up and ran.

"We're not deep enough yet," he heard someone say. "We need to keep going farther back."

Toekin's heart pounded as the grindarr's barks intensified. The trees went by in a blur as he raced through the forest. If he could just get to the clearing . . .

And then he was in his room with his mother. She kept a hand on his mouth and placed a slender finger across her lips until he nodded his understanding.

"You." He heard his father's voice, strong and gruff.

"I didn't like the way our last visit ended." The strange voice was unfamiliar to him; it seemed too high to be a man's but too low to be a woman's. It gave him the chills. His mother motioned with her hands for him to stay put, then crept to the door to peek out. In the dimness of candlelight, Toekin watched her study the scene before her. Without taking her eyes off the events beyond his room, she reached up and pulled a satchel off the back of the door. A moment later she was at Toekin's side.

She took his hand and led him, silent as a thief, across the room. Pushing a finger into one of the knots on the paneled wall; a section slid open. She reached inside and pulled out her book of animal sketches and put it in the bag. She added a dagger and a rope and then held out something Toekin had never seen before. It was small and dark and had the image of Paz carved into the side. She kept it in her hand and positioned the satchel over his shoulder.

"I need you to listen very carefully." She said. Pain rang through Toekin's head until her words faded with his sight. Pressure pushed down on him, harder and harder. He felt like a hard-shelled beetle under boot, whose insides were about to burst out, but then the boot lifted, and the pressure was gone. He could hear voices again coming from downstairs, though he couldn't make out what they were saying.

"Toekin, focus on me."

He didn't want to look at his mom, at least not while she was like this. He'd never seen her act this way before, nor look so tired. There was something different about her—the warmth and color in her eyes had paled, making her look like part of her soul had suddenly died.

"Your father and I love you very much." She clasped her hands over her mouth and nose as tears began streaming down her face but quickly shook her head until she was back in control.

"Tell me what you're going to do," she managed to say.

"Hide."

"And?"

"Wait until everyone's gone and get to Mato Forest."

"Good, what else?"

"Find the heart and change the tree."

The voices from the other room grew louder, making it hard for him to think.

"And?"

"But I can't climb a Seivo!"

"Yes, you can! Your father's done it, and I know you can do it too!"

"He has?"

She nodded. "Trust me, you're stronger than you know. If only there was more time . . ."

"You can't have him!" His father's voice boomed through the house, making his mother flinch. For a moment her eyes watered again, but she kept her gaze trained on Toekin.

"What else did I say?" She said.

Toekin shook his head again, holding back tears. He couldn't think of anything; his mind was blank and his head was starting to hurt.

"Don't let anyone see you." His mom tried to start him off, but all he could do was nod. "Don't trust anyone." Toekin kept nodding. "And never, ever let anyone see this." She held up the dark cylinder with the dragon on the side before dropping it in his bag.

"Infinity plus one," she said, gazing upon Toekin as if it would be the last time.

"Infinity plus one," Toekin responded automatically, then a sound like thunder shook the house.

"Now hide!" His mother's voice pierced his soul. But more than from her voice alone, Toekin felt an overwhelming desire to hide come over him. In a blink, she was at the bedroom door, and when she looked back, her eyes were filled with bright yellow.

She smiled, and then she was gone.

Toekin's mind seared with pain once more until his world became lost in a sea of white. But as quickly as it had come, it was gone again. He was still in the same place, his parent's bedroom, pressed into a corner. In front of him stood two hooded figures. One carried the limp body of his mother under his arm, and his father over his shoulder. Blood dripped off his father's head. "Who's the most powerful *rascal* now?" he said. A laugh rumbled somewhere deep inside him and rippled out through his shoulders in careless jolts and shudders making his father jiggle like a worm on a hook. Then he turned and left, taking his parents with him.

Why was he just sitting there, doing nothing? Why didn't he get up and run after them?

Hide! Her voice still rang through his head. He was in plain view in the dark corner, yet he still felt, somehow, hidden. He held his breath, terrified to move.

The other hooded figure in the room seemed more like a creature than human. It was hunched and crept around like an animal on the hunt. When his gaze fell on Toekin, red eyes glowed in the dim light. The thing snuffled as he looked under the bed, tore off the covers, then overturned the bed. Toekin was screaming on the inside and crying in terror. But for some reason he was staying calm and quiet on the outside.

"Something's not right," the animal said, its man's voice coming as a shock to Toekin. He tilted his head up and sniffed several times, then lowered his head, looking right in Toekin's corner. He took a few silent steps in his direction, then stopped, staring directly at him, but still, somehow, not seeing him. It was as if Toekin were invisible.

The second man came back into the room, blue eyes beaming intently beneath his hood. "We're leaving," he said. "The house has been searched. There's nothing left for us here."

Voices echoed in his ears and he felt himself pulling away from the room, being dragged toward two white lights. They grew in intensity until he found himself in the great room of his tree, leaning up against the warm trunk.

"He's back," Kai said.

"Good." Row's voice was strained. He clutched his stomach and Kai thrust a basin his way just as all the contents of his lunch came up. When he'd finished, Kai got up without a word, grabbed the basin, and carried it away.

"How are you feeling?" Row managed to say.

"Better than you, apparently." The mind flay hadn't been pleasant. His heart beat with all the same anxiety he'd relived in his memories and a cold sweat coated his brow. Still, he had to wonder if Row had gotten the worst of it.

"That was intense." Row's voice was weak and he coughed and spit into a rag. "I've never seen memory locks like those."

"Memory locks?"

"Someone, I'm guessing your mother, put very powerful blocks on your memories. If Kai hadn't been there with me, I wouldn't have been able to get into any of them. Even with his help, some are far beyond me."

"You mean, there's more?"

Row nodded.

"Why do you think she did that?"

"Clearly, there's some stuff she didn't want you to remember."

"Like the secret panel in her room?"

"Maybe." Row balled up one of Toekin's blankets and used it like a pillow as he curled up against the wall of the tree.

Toekin thought of the strange animal sniffing him out in his parent's room and wondered. Could it be the same being he and Força had encountered in the woods just a few weeks before? And who was the strange man with blue eyes who had talked about being a dangerous rascal?

He pulled his satchel toward him and reached inside. Without removing it, he grabbed the scope, turned it over in his hands, and examined the engravings: The dragon on one side and infinity plus one on the other. He played with the lenses, swinging them in and out of alignment. It had been useful in seeing great distances, but it had also been invaluable as a fire starter. Even on a cloudy day, the powerful lenses could focus the light of the sun enough to set a pile of dry tinder aflame. And of course, he'd also used it to burn the heart of his Seivo Sangue, turning his tree into a home.

Toekin nudged Row, whose snoring had become reminiscent of a stampeding pack of woolly kullmhorinn, and he rolled over and returned to quiet breathing.

Searching his memories had been a sacrifice for his friend, but for the first time he felt a calm assurance about the trip back to Abbadon. Now he had a plan. Now he knew where to look.

* * *

Almost two weeks later, Toekin, Row and Lua arrived at Abbadon's city gates near sundown. They carried bags over their shoulders with a few necessities and the instruction to blend in with the locals. Row wore a leather cap to cover his white hair and the three of them attached themselves to the end of a large group of traveling entertainers and snuck through the gates.

Lua flirted mercilessly with one of the hands while Row chatted up a cook's girl keeping her goats in line with a long switch. Toekin pretended like he knew what he was doing and before he knew it, they were standing in the main plaza.

The rounded cobble stones brought a familiar feel beneath his feet as he watched merchants offering their wares under the bell tower, and citizens trickling down the steps that lead toward Town Hall. From out of the normal din of voices and clopping hooves, greetings and goodbyes, Toekin heard the cry of a baby. He turned to see a mother, carrying a child on her hip while pulling another along with her other hand. It was a simple scene, but brought an unexpected rush of vivid memories to him like a fist to the face.

The cries of children multiplied, their shrieks filling the air. The acrid smell of smoke filled his nostrils as the wind shifted and he coughed. Someone was pulling him forward by the hand, but who? The crush of the crowd kept him from getting a good look at anything besides the backsides of other people. Finally, they emerged from the throng, to see flames licking the base of a platform where a man and two women had been chained to stakes. He turned to see who belonged to the big, warm hand that held his and saw a rose tattoo. Father!

"Treasonous Zaints!" a voice called from the top of the steps. "For your crimes against Abbadon and the land of Enganoso, Emperor Beezul has sentenced you all to death by fire!"

There were cheers and screams as the flames rose higher. Toekin glanced at his father in time to see him turn his face away from the scene, preparing to plung them back into to the mob in order to make their exit.

"Come along," he said, but it hadn't been to Toekin. He looked to see whom he'd spoken to, and that's when he saw that his father held the hand of another boy about his size. The boy looked up at Toekin's father with fear in his eyes, but also trust and love.

A goat bleated and Toekin shook his head, returning to his current reality. More unremembered memories. Had Row shaken something loose when he probed his mind? "Hello," Row said, waving his hand in front of Toekin's face. "Do you know which way we should go?"

"This way." Toekin directed them to a side street, his mind still running away with his father and the unfamiliar child. "My home sits just on the edge of town." He looked up at Beezul's tower, which seemed to follow them wherever they went. Would they ever be out from under its watchful eye? "A little farther."

By the time they reached his childhood home it was quite dark. They made several wide circles around the house, checking for signs of life, occupants or potential danger, taking care not to be seen. "It looks empty," Lua said. The windows were dark and there had been no movement inside the whole time they'd been watching. She reached for the handle. "Locked," she said, not a little disappointed.

"I've got this," Row whispered. He removed a small, drawstring bag from his pants pocket and reached in with two fingers. A slender rod came out, shedding grains of sand back into the bag. Row held the thing like a needle. "If I may," he said, squeezing his way past Lua and taking a knee.

He dumped the contents of the bag in his palm, which looked like nothing more than sand, then inserted the rod in the keyhole. His eyes began to glow white, then he closed them, and the grains of sand began rearranging themselves around the rod, fattening it up with tiny notches and ridges, appearing in what was hopefully all the right places. A moment later, Row turned his wrist, then opened the door.

Toekin held his finger to his lips, then motioned for them to follow. Six years had melted away, and despite the furniture being in all the wrong places, it seemed as if he'd never left. He pushed the door to his parent's room open, careful to take his time, remembering the squeaky whine that sounded when it was opened quickly. The room appeared vacant, but it was too dark to be sure. A soft tap on his shoulder brought his attention behind him, where he saw the soft blue glow of Lua's eyes—*of course, eyelumination.*

He brought light to his vision, surveying the room before beginning to move toward the back wall, tiptoeing across a floor littered with heaps of clothes, and bedding. A large chest stood in front of the spot on the wall he'd seen in his vision and Lua stepped forward. Her hands and arms glowed blue and she pushed it out of the way with ease, but a high pitched, quick scraping sound of wood grinding on wood rent the air as she did. The three of them froze and waited. From the next room, they heard a brief succession of creaks and cracks, as if someone had shifted in their bed. When it was obvious no one was coming, they continued, now taking more caution than before. Someone was clearly in the house.

Toekin found the knot in the wall, just as it had been in his vision. He reached out and pushed, and a panel swung open easily.

It was empty.

Toekin let out a long breath and turned to Lua and Row and shrugged. Then they heard voices.

Loud and boisterous, feet stomped at the threshold and lamplight seeped in through the crack in the bedroom door.

"Ezmae!" a man shouted, "Get out here! That lazy daughter. Nothing but trouble I tell you, boys!" Their laughter was cruel and dangerous.

Lua looked at Row and Toekin and held an invisible flask to her mouth and threw it back, then pointed toward the next room. They both nodded. The men were definitely drunk.

They shrank into the corner and Toekin pulled the shadows around them. He knew how to stay hidden. He'd been doing it for six long years. As he was gathering darkness, he caught the view from the window. The Seivo Salvador, stood majestic and proud, just as he'd remembered it; the biggest tree in the land. *One day, the Seivo Salvador will save the world,* his mother's voice came unbidden. *Be like the branch that points toward the heavens. You must always remember the branch.*

The voices in the other room turned from harmless and obnoxious to rough. "Look at her! Skinny as a wet cat. Good for nothing." There was a slap followed by a woman's startled whimper.

Lua looked at Toekin in shock. He shook his head and motioned for her to sit still. Wait it out.

"Kizzy, down at the tavern? Now that's a girl a father could be proud of," the man said to his friends. "Strong back, and not ugly like this one!" There was laughing followed by a loud crack and crash on the wall. "Did I see you give me a look?"

The sound of a chair skidding across the floor, then falling over, rang through the house, followed by stomps across the room. There was another small screech of terror, and nervous whimpers. "I didn't mean anything by it, honest," she said.

Lua flinched when she heard the hit, broad and clear. The girl, Ezmae, must have fallen to the floor because there was a loud thump.

"We better leave you to it," one of the men said.

"We'll catch up with you tomorrow," the other one said, and the front door closed with a house-shaking thud.

"Why do you always have to embarrass me in front of my friends." His voice was rising right along with his temper. "We just wanted a few more pints of ale before we called it a night, is that so hard?" There was a dull thud and Ezmae grunted in pain.

Lua jumped up. "I will not sit here . . .," she said, taking a step toward the door.

Toekin grabbed her by the arm as he and Row rose to their feet. "Together," he said, exchanging looks with them both.

She gave a solemn nod and as one, then burst through the bedroom door. "Enough, you brute!" Lua said before skidding to a halt in front of the man. He stood a head taller than Row and from the looks of the muscles on his arms, Toekin guessed he spent his days smashing rocks in the quarry with his bare hands.

The girl, Ezmae, lay curled up like a newborn baby on the floor, small and helpless.

"Well now," the man slurred, turning his attention away from the woman. "It appears I have some intruders." There was spittle in his beard and his eyes flashed a warning of instability and bloodlust.

Lua backed up until she bumped into Row and Toekin.

"He said this would happen one day." The man laughed like a madman while they stood there and watched, unsure what to do next. Maybe they should have planned something first.

Before Toekin could formulate a plan, the man spoke again. "Ezmae!" White light flew from his fingers, forming a stream between him and the girl. She rose from the ground. Blood dripped from her nose and mouth and a bruise was already forming on her cheek, but she moved as if she were injury-free.

"You take the white-haired one. I've got the girl."

CHAPTER 19

The Light

White light began pouring off the man in great gushing waves, and Toekin squinted against the brightness. He just needed to disable this guy, then they could figure the rest out.

"They're seers!" Row said. "Don't let them get in your head!"

Toekin was just about to reach for his dagger when his legs were swept out from under him and he fell on his back.

"Too late," Row said, looking at Lua and the string of white light that connected her to the man.

She stood over Toekin, ready to deal another blow.

"What are you doing?" Toekin said, his tailbone and pride severely bruised.

"He's in her head. She's not herself!" Row rushed his words as Ezmae came at him. He pushed both hands forward, though the surge of dazzling white energy came from his eyes. It crashed into Ezmae, who stopped her advance on him and turned, walked back to the corner, and sat down peacefully.

"Argh!" The man raged. "Useless girl!"

"Well! Get in *his* head! Make him stop already!" Toekin said to Row.

Lua's foot landed a crushing kick to Toekin's ribs and he curled into a ball, absorbing the pain and protecting himself from further attack. But after two more kicks he'd had enough. "That's it!" He jumped up and tackled Lua to the ground, pinning her arms to her side. She wriggled and kicked, screaming to get out of his grasp.

"Anytime now!" Toekin said. He had a good hold on Lua, but he wasn't sure he could last much longer.

"He's too drunk!" Row was bathed in white light, directing all of it toward his foe. "I can't keep hold of his thoughts!" Row's light brightened and intensified into a beam, but his enemy resisted. It looked to be a draw, until a volley of unexpected energy blasted into the man's side, turning him into nothing more than a shadow within an array of white. For a moment he struggled, pressing his hands against his head, and tearing at his hair.

"Devil girl!" he said, turning his full wrath toward his daughter. From her corner, she had pulled herself up and was glowing like Row, her fierce gaze and all her energy directed at her father. "I'll kill you!" he roared. Her light flickered and died, and she collapsed to the floor with a thump.

Row used the distraction to his advantage. He charged the man, and dove for his knees, crashing into them with as much force as he could muster. The man fell back and there was a loud crack as his head hit the floor.

"Toekin, get off of me!" Lua protested. "What are you doing?" He rolled over and Lua sat up, rubbing her head. She looked at the man lying on the floor, who groaned, and started to rise.

"Toe, watch out!" Row shouted from across the room.

Toekin felt a sudden void in his boot where he'd stashed the dagger his father had given him and turned to see Lua, glassy eyed and dangerous, bringing the dagger down in one powerful thrust. He brought his arms up just in time to block the blow. "Sorry, Lua," he said under his breath and twisted her wrist until the blade clattered to the floor. He pulled her arm behind her and pushed her to the ground, digging his knee into her back.

Row resumed his assault on the man, breaking his connection with Lua a few times, but only temporarily. Nothing seemed to hurt him. Nothing could stop him.

Toekin watched as Row struggled, this time not daring to let Lua back up until he was sure the man was subdued. He felt his knee rise and looked down at Lua. Her entire body was glowing blue and she started to break out of Toekin's hold. This wasn't good. He glanced back at Row, looking for help, and saw him struggling to keep his own hands from chocking himself. He followed a telltale path of white light to the girl in the corner, her glow giving away her devious designs. She had switched sides again?

The drunkard stood, laughing at the sight; relishing his upper hand. Lua bucked Toekin off and pounced on him, pinning him to the ground. Waves of blue poured off her. She felt so heavy. Her strength was overwhelming. She raised the knife and Toekin struggled to hold her back.

"That's it!" The man growled. "Kill him!"

Toekin's only hope was to get her to come to her senses. She was too strong for him. "Lua, no!" he shouted. "It's me! Stop!"

The vacant look in her eyes told him it was no use. The knife inched closer and closer, while Toekin's arms strained to hold her back, just a few seconds longer.

A chair smashed into Lua and she went skidding across the floor. Row stood, dusting off his hands. "Thank me later," he said to Toekin, still lying on the ground. He turned his body toward the drunk man and sent his white light shooting across the room.

Lua rose with a moan just as the front door swung open and two cloaked figures walked in, one dripping darkness in his wake. The other one lifted pale blue hands and pulled back his hood, revealing a smooth, hairless blue head and eyes that glowed like sparkling sapphires. His smile was filled with oversized, glistening white square teeth. "Good work," he said, sweeping through the room, sizing the man up like he was a cow at auction. "You've done well. I knew someone would return."

The man reached into his shirt and pulled out a red, glowing jewel hanging from a chain. "It's been a long time, Nojento," the man said, his voice wavering with fear. "I started to wonder . . ."

"Yes, well," the blue man said, running his long, dark, rectangular blue fingernail up and down the man's arm. "You should have known never to doubt me."

The girl, Ezmae, had been slowly backing away and was now huddled behind a sideboard. Lua, on the other hand seemed petrified and Toekin thought he saw a single tear slip down her cheek. The man's voice was familiar in the same way one would remember having the stomach flu: Toekin couldn't quite place it, but he knew it was bad.

"Oh, I never doubted you." The man's voice quavered with nervous laughter, "I am happy to be of service."

Don't let the dark one touch you. The words came, unbidden, into Toekin's mind. A faint, almost imperceptible, thread of silver connected him to Row, who inclined his head slightly toward the man dressed in black. He looked at Lua and she blinked and nodded subtly.

"When you gave me this pendant," the man swung the chain around on his finger, becoming dangerously relaxed, "you said there'd be a reward when the time came." He paused, gauging the blue man's mood for a moment before adding, "a *generous* reward, if I remember correctly."

Nojento said nothing.

"They broke into my house! Scared my Ezmae—which isn't too hard," he said, whispering behind his hand. "She's a bit of a mouse—really, no use to me at all."

Nojento continued to stare at the man and his silence seemed to play on his nerves.

"You could take her, if you want. Maybe she could be of some use to you. She's none to me. I'll just take my reward and . . ."

"Sem," the blue man's voice was sticky sweet. "Give the man his reward."

Sem moved like a shadow and was suddenly at the man's side. He placed a gloved hand on the man's shoulder, a seemingly harmless act that quickly became horrifying.

The first thing Toekin saw was Row, closing his eyes and turning his head away from the episode unfolding before them. The man gasped, his eyes wide, as tendrils of black snaked around his head and shoulder, slithering over his torso, arms and legs, until it had consumed him. A whine issued forth from his lips, which deepened in steps until it had become an unearthly howl. He dropped to his knees before falling over in pain. Tears poured from his eyes as he begged for mercy.

Toekin inched his way over to Lua. He reached for her and she pulled herself into him, burying her face in his chest.

The howling turned into screams and Toekin watched as blood dripped from the man's mouth, his nose, and finally his eyes. He thought of Espero telling him about this fourth gift he possessed: darkness. Was this what was inside him too? This ability to call up such pain and suffering—to kill with a single touch? The tendrils of darkness pulled away from the dying man, coalescing into a single cloud that seemed to penetrate Sem's chest, where it would live, waiting for its next victim.

With the final twitch of the man there was a gasp from the corner of the room. Ezmae fell forward onto her knees and white light lifted out of her, evaporating into the air above her head. She rose, examining her hands with wonder, standing a little taller than she had before.

Sem stepped over the man, lying in a pool of his own blood, and took several menacing paces toward the girl. "No!" Toekin said with a leap and put himself between the black-eyed man and Ezmae. "She's innocent! Leave her be!"

"Interesting." The blue man said as he drifted over to where Toekin and Sem stood. He looked Toekin up and down with a smug smile on his face and then did the same with Sem. But then his attention turned. "It's true Sem," he said. "He put her under oath to obey him, then controlled her with his light. A stupid brute like him could hardly rely on a child being loyal out of love and respect." He turned swishing his cloak and waving the black-dressed man to stand aside.

Lua ran to the girl and spoke to her in soft tones, helping her take a seat in a wooden chair. Row moved so that he stood next to Toekin.

"Allow me to introduce myself. I am Nojento, chief researcher to Emperor Beezul, and I know exactly why you've returned."

Toekin said nothing, already making the connection between the man who stood before him and Lua's tale of their battle with Beezul's army six years earlier. How many other blue-skinned, eerie madmen could there be?

"There is no need to fear me—it's Toekin isn't it?"

Toekin shuddered. "How do you know my name?"

"You see, when it comes to the relic, I make it my business to know everything. We actually have the same goals, you and me. We both want to keep it out of Beezul's hands."

"You'll forgive me if I don't believe one word of that." Toekin said. He wore self-possession like a shield but inside he was a storm of anger and fear.

"Oh, but you must believe me," Nojento said, pouring sugar on his already sweet tones. "I'm a man of science. I want nothing more than to study the relic, to experiment with it."

Toekin could hear Força's voice in his head, telling him about the torture in the name of science the Emperor allowed to be performed on children and prisoners. No doubt this, Sem, was one of the results of those *experiments* and Nojento, the man who carried it all out.

"If Beezul were to gain control of the relic, who knows what he would do with it, what evil would befall all of us should that happen." Nojento managed an over-played shudder. "I, on the other hand, would only study it. That's all. If you wanted to summon Paz, even to overthrow Beezul, this is nothing to me. We could work out a deal. We could form an alliance."

Toekin saw Row shake his head. "You're wasting your breath. We don't have the relic, but even if we did . . ."

"Oh, I know you don't have it, now. But I have a good feeling you will soon. And when you do, I want you to remember me." There was a dramatic pause, but no one said anything. Nojento tented his fingers and pressed them to his blue lips. "I can tell I haven't yet convinced you."

Of course he hadn't convinced him. These two looked like characters from stories parents told kids to scare them into behaving. And the dead man, lying in front of him on the floor, was reminder enough that he needed to tread carefully.

"How about this!" Nojento's voice rose and he began pacing, stepping over the girl's crumpled father with each pass, as if there were nothing odd at all about a dead body in the middle of the floor. "I know you've been trying to locate the whereabouts of our former king—your rebel leader—Kimnar. He is well hidden! But I know where he is." He stopped pacing and stood in front of Toekin, a look of excited anticipation on his face. "Even Beezul doesn't know this—and I would never tell him. But I'll tell you." He giggled like a little girl sharing a juicy secret. "He's in Passo Fundo."

He resumed his pacing, adding a little skip in his step, clearly delighted with himself. "You look surprised. You didn't know that, did you?" Sem stood like a statue in the corner, his solid black eyes making it impossible to tell where he was looking or who he was looking at. Still, Toekin felt certain he was staring at him.

"No deal, Nojento," Row said. "What you say may be true, but we'd have to be halfwits to believe you cared one bit about our interests. This is all about you. And when you get what you want, you will reward us just as you have this man."

"Fool!" Nojento shouted, his voice deepened, and his eyes burned deep red. "I have already saved you once before. Who do you think warned you of Beezul's approaching army?"

Was it true? Someone *had* warned them. Toekin thought of the beast-man, hunched and drooling, howling into the night as he ran away, injured and bleeding. It made sense that such an abomination would be this man's creation.

"And what thanks did my Lobo get for warning you? He came back to me nearly dead!"

"He attacked us." Toekin leveled an accusing gaze at Nojento. "He told us his *master* would have wanted him to have a reward for his service."

Nojento waved him off. "No harm done. You appear to be fine, and with my skills, I was able to heal my Lobo in a trice. All is forgotten."

Not even close, Toekin thought.

The blue man turned his smile back on and faced Toekin, covered in a veneer of concern. His eyes flashed in a smooth rhythm of crimson, then azure. "Find me the relic, Toekin. Bring it to me. Let me study it. Do this . . . and I will free your parents."

Toekin's breath caught and he felt as if his heart was being squeezed. Had he heard him right? *Free* his parents? Did this mean they weren't . . . dead? Hope must have shown in Toekin's face because the blue man's grin turned greedy, the cadence of his flashing eyes now frenetic.

"It's a lie," Row said. "Don't listen to him."

Toekin stepped forward, approaching Nojento but still keeping his distance. "What do you know about my parents?"

Nojento's smile showed every one of his dazzling teeth. "Beezul knew your father had the relic, and so he asked him for it. When asking nicely didn't result in answers, he had to apply some . . . pressure." Nojento looked at Sem, something resembling pity crossed his face, but quickly disappeared. For his part, Sem remained still, a smudged, dark monolith awaiting his master's command.

"I always thought they were hiding something. Their will power has proven quite strong. They've never let even a single hint slip. Remarkable, considering . . ." Like a trained rhetorician he let his words trail off, his awareness of their effects plain in the way he watched for Toekin's reaction.

"Give me the relic and I will unlock their cell with my own hands."

Lua had moved, soundless, across the room and now stood by Toekin's side. "It's a trap," She said. "We can't believe anything he says."

Toekin heard Lua, but he didn't. Hope had filled his heart. His parents were alive!

"We used to be friends, you know . . . Turbin, Strella and myself."

He felt like his heart was tearing open. To have this man speak his mother's name . . .

"The three *rascals*, we used to call ourselves. We would get into so much trouble." When he laughed, something flipped inside Toekin. The rip in his heart sealed shut and he felt like fire was running through his veins. *Rascals*. The way he'd said that word . . .

"I know you," Toekin said through gritted teeth. The memory of the night his parents were taken crashed upon him like a rogue wave and he was barely able to hold back his fury.

"Well, I'm not surprised," Nojento said, huffing on his fingernails and buffing them on his arm. "My reputation is well-known throughout Enganoso."

"Beezul didn't take my parents. You did!" The room waxed scarlet before Toekin's eyes as anger consumed him. He looked down at his hands. Light seethed off them in yellow, then dark orange, then red, until each palm held a violent sphere of swirling energy at the ready. Without thought he hurled them at the freakish blue body of Nojento, but just before impact, the dark figure, formerly rooted in place, stepped in front of his master and intercepted his attack, absorbing the flaming energy in a torrent of blackness, like a coffin of light.

"Toekin, no!" Lua screamed, but Toekin was beyond warnings. He didn't act when his parents were taken on that night long ago, but nothing would hold him back now.

Toekin glided around the room, sending fireball after fireball at his target. Each time Sem extinguished the attacks, his power whipping around like tentacles of the night. Toekin was going to have to take down Sem to get at Nojento.

He evaded Sem's assault and scooped up his father's dagger as he glided from one spot to the next. Nojento seemed both confused and delighted by the show, like a bored cat entertained by a desperate but dying mouse. Sem, on the other hand stood still, eyes focused straight ahead and breathing deeply, as if tapping into some unseen power.

Don't let those things . . . Row's voice jumped into Toekin's head but was abruptly cut off. He could hear Nojento's delighted laugh, and out of the corner of his eye, he caught him wagging a finger at Row. His fury doubled. Blue light emerged, mixing together with the red aura around Toekin's clenched hand until it burst into flames of purple. He lunged at Sem, but fell short when lines of darkness, unnoticed by Toekin until it was too late, wrapped around his body, and anchored him in place. Sem walked forward, spinning his shadowy web like a starved spider securing its prey, until he was an arm's length away.

Toekin fought to free himself, but Sem reached forward and grabbed Toekin's wrist. In an instant, his world went dark, the light extinguished. He was back in his parent's room, hiding like a frightened child, doing nothing while they were carried off. He was running through the forest, running away from, instead of toward his parents to help. All the shame his mother's memory blocks had kept at bay rushed forward, piercing him like a thousand knives. He heard the screams of tortured souls, rising from a pit of anguish and despair before realizing the screams were coming from him.

He dropped to the floor, warring with the shame of abandoning his parents and the anger over the foul creature that captured and tortured them. His screams sounded like those of the Zaints, burned in the town square. The vision came back, unexpected, and he looked up into his father's face, the licking flames reflected in his eyes. Then he saw the other child—the one whose hand his father held. The boy stared at him, and for a fleeting moment a feeling of affinity passed between them, but was dashed away when the boy's eyes rolled back and tears like tar streaked down his cheeks. His mouth snapped open and blackness poured out, engulfing Toekin with terrifying pain.

"Remember," he heard a familiar voice say, "Light will always chase the dark; never the opposite."

Espero. His memory and words warmed Toekin like the noonday sun. With all the intensity he could muster, Toekin pushed back against the veil of darkness he felt crushing his soul.

A single beam of light, tiny but true, broke through the black. Then, as if holes were being punched in a gloomy sky, another beam broke through, and then another. He opened his eyes and saw Sem's face inches away, his expressionless eyes somehow registering surprise. The site of his enemy incited Toekin's anger once more. He pulled from the smoky darkness puddled at his own feet and pushed it into Sem. The savage stepped back but did not release his grip from around Toekin's wrist.

Toekin gathered the evil cloud, still hovering near the dead man, the sick pleasure dripping off Nojento, and all the lies, ill-wishes and hate floating through Abbadon's night air. Great wisps of murk began swirling around him, bursting through the open door, collecting, growing. He forced the cloud onto Sem and he fell to his knees. The gash across his face that was his mouth opened and a bitter howl escaped.

Out of the corner of his eye he could see Nojento, looking on with sick fascination.

Toekin clamped his hand around Sem's, holding it to his wrist, refusing to let the connection break. Sem's cries intensified and he doubled over, retching at Toekin's feet. *Let him go.* Nojento's voice invaded his head.

No chance, Toekin shot back, but even as he did, against his will, his grip relaxed and Sem dropped out of his grasp.

"Interesting," Nojento said, waltzing over to the scene with the air of a battle instructor, ready to give his critique. "You're a Zaintozo, *and* you wear the crown of darkness?" he said to Toekin, holding his hand out for Sem. The dark man turned away from Nojento, refusing to take his offer of help.

Toekin didn't reply. What would he say? At that moment, even he wasn't sure what he was.

"This is more than I could have hoped for." Nojento said, swishing his robe in a big arc and leaving Sem to fend for himself. "We're finished here, Sem," he said, walking to the door. When his subject didn't follow, he returned, knelt beside him, and laid a glowing blue hand on his back until Sem shrugged it off. "There," Nojento said, "good enough to travel?" Sem stood on unsteady feet. "Really, I am just as surprised as you," he said to Sem.

Sem moved slowly at first, and then seemed to gain strength as he followed Nojento across the room. The blue man held the door for Sem and turned back. "Fate brings us together, Toekin. The stars say that you will bring me the relic. I have seen it. There is no use trying to do otherwise. Why not work with me instead of against me, hmm? Think of your poor parents . . ."

The moment the door closed, Lua and Row ran to Toekin's side.

"Brother, what in the starry skies was that?" Row patted him on the back, then thought better of it and backed up a pace.

"Are you okay? Did he hurt you?" Lua hovered like a nervous mother.

"I'm fine," Toekin said. "Are *you?*"

Lua hesitated, appearing to be caught up in old, and now new, memories of Nojento. She shook her head and tried to smile. "It's you I'm worried about."

"I just need to sit down."

"I thought we were goners," Row said, guiding Toekin to a wooden chair near the cold hearth. "How did you turn those shadows of death back on Sem like that?"

"I don't know." He didn't want to think too much about it—about what it meant, this power within him. He knew he'd felt the darkness, and he knew he'd controlled it. What did this make him?

"Don't worry over what he said about giving him the relic. He's full of lies." Row folded his arms as if to seal his judgment.

Toekin nodded.

A quivering cup of ale was pushed in front of Toekin. "Here you are." The girl's voice was small but certain. "Sorry about earlier," she said to Row. "I didn't mean to make you choke yourself. My father . . ." she trailed off.

"Don't worry," Lua said, glancing over at the slumped figure on the floor. "You helped us when you could. And, he won't be able to hurt you anymore."

Ezmae nodded.

"Do you have somewhere to go? Family?" Lua asked.

The girl shook her head. "They've all been killed by the emperor, charged with supporting the rebellion. It was him who turned them all in, guilty or not," she said, looking at her father. "He only kept me around to cook and clean for him."

"While you've lived here," Toekin said, "have you ever found anything unusual? Something that seemed like it had been hidden?"

She thought, then shook her head. "Nothing, and I've been here for several years now."

"Would you mind if we looked around a little?" Row said.

"Please, be my guest."

"Toe, you sit," Row said, "Lua and I will have a look around."

Toekin nodded. Standing up seemed like too much work anyway.

Ezmae walked over to a chest, pulled out a blanket, and returned, draping it over Toekin's shoulders. "You were strong. I've never seen anyone fight off General Sem."

Toekin nodded without enthusiasm. He didn't feel strong right now.

"So, you grew up in this house?" she asked, sitting next to him with her arms warpped around her knees.

"Yeah."

"I moved here when I was nine," she said, getting a distant, painful, look in her eyes.

"Did you ever slide down the railing on the stairs?" Toekin said.

Ezmae nodded and smiled for the first time that night. Maybe, Toekin thought, for the first time in months.

"I did too." Toekin said. The memory came back in bits and pieces at first—him straddling the dark brown railing, sliding backwards. His mom had scolded him when he'd done it, but his dad had always winked and smiled. "Did you ever hide something in the woodbox?" He asked.

"I found a lizard once and Mama said I couldn't bring it in the house. I put it in the wood box outside, but I could see him when I opened the little doors from inside. I named him Gil."

"Ah," Toekin said. "Very clever." He would have reached out and touched her arm, but his joints ached, and his energy was spent. The sky was starting to lighten. They would need to be leaving soon. He wondered how he would summon the strength to get up and move.

Ezmae smiled at the exchange, tears a blink away from running over. "I can't stay here," she said, answering the question Toekin had asked with his eyes. "I'll be suspected of his death. His friends were just as crooked and cruel as he was. They'll turn me in just to claim a reward. I don't know where to go."

Toekin thought. He wanted to help, but how? Invite her to join them so she could live a life of avoiding death by Beezul's hand?

"When I was younger," she said, "I would climb on the roof to escape."

Toekin smiled. He had climbed to the roof many times, but his escape had probably been nowhere near as desperate has hers.

She continued. "I went up there once, and I pretended I was in Mato Forest."

"Did you, now?"

"Yes. And I pretended the birds were my best friends, and they talked to me."

This was starting to sound familiar.

"And whenever there was trouble . . ." Toekin tried not to think too deeply about what kind of trouble she might be referring to. ". . . I imagined running to the Seivo Salvador, and that it would save me."

"Those trees are dangerous," Toekin said.

"Yeah, I know." Ezmae smiled. "But I pretended the Seivo Salvador and I were friends—that it would hurt other people, but . . ."

"Not me," Toekin finished as if in a dream. Through the window, Toekin watched as the light from the rising sun illuminated the giant tree. How could he have missed it? He felt as if his mother's arm was over his shoulder.

"It will be hard, but I know you can do it." She'd said.

"Really?" young Toekin had replied.

"Yes." Her voice was filled with certainty. "You know the secret now. The Seivo Salvador will always be dangerous to other people. But not you." She gave his shoulders a squeeze and the vision was gone.

"Are you all right?" Ezmae said, handing him a handkerchief from inside her sleeve.

Toekin nodded, tears streaming down his face. "That's a great story," he said, declining her offer and using his sleeve instead. "You still want to escape to Mato Forest?"

"Yeah, let's go," she said with a chuckle, but her smile faded to a questioning look when Toekin didn't give her any indication that he was joking.

"Well, we found nothing," Row said, interrupting their conversation. "Even looked in the woodbox."

"The house is pretty empty, actually," Lua added.

"My father didn't allow me more than a few personal items," Ezmae said. "Always figured it would work to my benefit one day if I ever had to leave quickly." She looked at Toekin, hopeful.

"Well Toe," Row said, "We should probably be on our way. It looks like the trip is a bust."

Toekin smiled and lifted his hand and placed it gently on Ezmae's arm. "No it's not," he said. "I know where the relic is."

CHAPTER 20

The Relic

"You're going to climb the Seivo Salvador?" Lua didn't just look shocked; she looked like she suspected Toekin of being a little off in the head.

"I know the relic is there," he said. When the others weren't looking, Toekin had spent most of the morning studying the aberration branch through his scope and was certain the sap bulb was dormant. But, it would be a good climb past many sap bulbs that weren't. He studied different routes and finally found one he thought was the safest. Still, his heart pounded as he gathered courage. His timing would have to be perfect.

"Are you absolutely certain?" Row said. "That's a dangerous climb, even without the possibility of deadly sap raining down on you."

"I'm sure." Now he knew: his mother had been preparing him for this moment. Her hints about the Seivo Salvador saving the world, helping him to know how to live in one, even her book of animals—which, now that he thought of it, might have been given specifically for the information on the Seivo Sangue she'd carefully recorded in the back—all were supposed to help him know how to find the relic at the right time. And this was the right time.

"What can I do to help?" Ezmae asked. She had needed no convincing to come to Mato Forest, even after explaining the risks of being associated with them. Over and over she'd thanked them, promising to help with sewing and laundering once they got to their forest home.

"I doubt Nojento went far. He's probably waiting to follow us right now," Toekin said. "We need a plan to distract him—to give me time to get up and down the tree."

"He's looking for three of us, right?" Row said.

"Right," Lua said.

"What if Lua, Ezmae and I pack up and go. Ezmae can dress up like a man. Your father has some extra clothes, right?" Row said. They'd thrown a blanket over the body, but he was still there, and they all avoided looking that direction.

She nodded.

"We can get on the road, draw Nojento away, and buy Toekin some time." Row said.

"She should wear my clothes," Toekin said. "And I'll wear your father's clothes, just in case Nojento has that dog Lobo tracking us."

Ezmae's eyes grew big when Toekin mentioned being tracked, but she nodded anyway.

"We'll head toward Triste, then when you get the relic, you can go straight home. We'll circle around and meet you in about a week."

"If I can glide, I can travel faster alone, too." Toekin pointed out. "I think this plan might actually work."

"Of course it's going to work." Row said. "It's my idea, after all."

* * *

"What do you think?" Ezmae stepped out of the bedroom in Toekin's clothes. She'd even been willing to chop off her long hair so that it looked more like Toekin's too.

"Wow," Row said. "From a distance, you'll easily pass. You didn't have to cut your hair though. You could have just worn a cap."

She shrugged and smiled. "This will be better."

Toekin rolled up the pants and sleeves on his new clothes, cinching the belt to keep his pants from falling down.

"If I had some time," Ezmae said, pinching the waist and tugging at the shoulders, "I could alter these for a better fit."

"It will be fine." Toekin said.

"Okay," Row said, going over the plan once more. "We pretend to hide a decoy relic in Triste, ditch these clothes for new ones, and head back to Mato Forest."

Everyone nodded. Row pulled up a chair and straddled it, facing Toekin. "Now listen," he said. "If anything happens—if this switch doesn't work, you have to do everything you can to keep the relic out of Nojento's hands."

"What Row means is, you can't believe his lies," Lua said. "Even if it's true and your parents live, you can't trust anything he says."

"I know," Toekin said. He wanted to believe Nojento—wanted to believe that seeing his parents again was as simple as unlocking a door. In his heart, though, he knew it was the cruelest of deceptions.

"And Toekin," Lua said, coming over to stand behind him, "be safe." She gave his shoulders a squeeze, then reached down and picked her bag off the floor.

Row patted his shoulder. "See you in a week."

"Got it."

"Be safe, and Toekin? Thank you," Ezmae said, fighting back tears.

The sun was just passing its peak when they finally left. They would make it out of the city and get on the road heading east. He just hoped Nojento would hold off his attack long enough for him to retrieve the relic from the Seivo Salvador. Otherwise, it would all be for nothing.

Toekin spent the time waiting for darkness to fall wandering the rooms of his home. Memories came back like warm caresses, slow and sweet. His mother cooking his breakfast over the fire, topping his porridge with honey; playing catch across the table with a woven grass ball; hiding in the wood box to surprise his father.

There had been love in this home and Toekin knew somewhere, either in or out of this world, the love remained.

The sun dipped behind the horizon and it was time. He swung his satchel over his shoulder and set off for the tree, stealing himself through the shadows of town. By the time he neared it was dark, but

The Path to Paz

the gibbous moon lit his way perfectly without giving up his location. The Seivo Salvador loomed over Toekin and the buildings came to an abrupt stop, giving the tree the wide berth it deserved. He pushed the sleeves up on his giant shirt and longed for his own, for more reasons than fit alone. The thought of wearing that foul man's clothing made him feel itchy and wrong.

He'd taken time to memorize his ascent path and now, as he approached the tree, he knew exactly where to start. He stood just outside of the hardened sap circle beneath the tree where it was still safe and examined all the bulbs. He could tell the one where he needed to start was close to bursting, so he waited, and when the hot sap came shooting out, he held himself back, counted, took his shoes off, and then ran straight for the Seivo Salvador.

The first branch would be the hardest to reach, but Toekin had had years of practice. His feet gripped the scaly bark but then slipped when the expected number of toes weren't there to do their job. He made a quick adjustment and kept going. Speed was his best tool. Pulling himself with his hands and arms and pushing with his legs, he reached the first branch in no time. His newfound gifts made accent so much easier than it used to be, but even after playing out the route in his mind over and over, there was no way to be truly prepared for spurting sap. He had to make on the run assessments with each new branch he reached.

The Seivo Salvador was taller than any other of its kind, and the target branch, higher than he'd ever climbed. He continued upward, just missing being doused with sap more than once. Finally, after climbing for what felt like forever, he reached the one branch that was different from the rest. While the other branches shot out rigid and firm to the horizon, this one sloped up toward the heavens with the sap bulb hanging out from the side.

Toekin had never worried about heights before, and Seivo branches were much wider than his arms could stretch, but as the wind picked up and he considered his path along the branch, away from the safety of the thick trunk, he felt his knees weaken slightly. He leaned back into the tree to steady himself, then took several timid steps onto the irregular branch with his hands extended wide for extra balance. *Psssh.* From high above a sap bulb spewed out its contents. He glanced up and jerked his arms to his chest, feeling the heat from the steamy sap as it poured down beside him. He thanked the stars it hadn't hit his branch and splattered. This was no time for a case of the nerves.

With his gaze fully fixed on the bulb in front of him, he took a step. Then another. He kept his eyes on the branch at his feet—no farther. There was no need to see exactly how far up in the air he was. One foot in front of the other; finally, he was at the bulb. The trap door in the top told him all he needed to know. His dad had been here. This was the place.

Relief washed over him as he climbed inside and planted his feet firmly on the floor of the sap bulb. The first thing he noticed, beside the warm glowing embrace of the walls, was the infinity symbol, with a plus one next to it, etched into the side of the bulb. "Dad," he said while running his fingers over it. Emotions swelled within him as he noticed how this side of the bulb, attached to the tree, glowed brighter than the rest. No doubt hot sap flowed just beyond. And then he saw it—the dragon flute—waiting for him to claim.

Timid, he picked it up and found it fit into his hand almost like it was meant to be there. The flute curved like Paz's dragon body, back and forth in a graceful wave. His head curled around so that the beast looked back at its tail. The dragon's mouth was open, its teeth bared and menacing as if waiting to bite off any music that dared escape. The flute shined a glossy red, the sap seeming to glow, jewel-like in his hand as if sunlight was hitting it at just the right angel. But there was no sunlight.

Eager to be on his way, he carefully placed the dragon flute in his satchel and reached for the opening in the top of the sap bulb. The trip back down Seivo Salvador went faster, his rhythm and timing seemingly synched with the giant's heartbeat. With each jump and glide he felt more and more part of the great tree. Finally, he reached the last branch and climbed the scale-like bark down to the circle of hardened blood red sap.

He put on his shoes, regarded the Seivo Salvador once more, then stepped into a long glide and was off. In the cover of night, he picked his way through Abbadon until the capital was soon at his back. It felt good to move this way again, unburdened by well-traveled roads and human contact.

Even in the dark, the familiar animal paths welcomed him with their promised protection. He spent the rest of the night gliding, fatigue coming from his lack of sleep as well as the constant use of his powers through the countryside. As the sun rose, he hit the edge of Mato Forest and his belly grumbled. He stopped to drink from his water skin and look for a few mushrooms. He'd be home before midday.

He hadn't found more than one mushroom when a growl ripped through the air and the half man, half grindarr stood before him, huffing and spitting. Toekin turned, hoping to escape through the copse of trees at his right, but Sem was there, and to Toekin's great astonishment, Lua struggled in his iron grip. To the left, another creature appeared, a hulking man with great patches of dragon's blood covering his bulging muscles and protecting his dim-looking head. In one hand he carried a mace and in the other, he held Ezmae, tucked up under his arm. He looked like a giant child bringing home a small creature for dinner.

"Looks like you're surrounded."

Toekin turned to find Nojento at his back, smug and giddy, with Row standing at his side, docile and dumb.

"Hand over the relic and we'll let your friends go. Simple as that."

"Don't do it, Toekin!" Lua shouted before Sem silenced her with a small dose of darkness. Her knees gave out and she whimpered. Only Sem's tight grip kept her upright.

"Try and run and they'll be dead before you're out of sight, and your cheap tricks won't work on Lobo. He can track you wherever you go. You'll never be safe."

Lobo pawed at the ground, sniffing the air as if something else had captured his attention. His body quivered as if he were eager to run.

"Lobo!" Nojento shouted. "Stay!"

The man-beast whined and settled onto his haunches.

"You're stuck. Give up," Nojento said.

Toekin looked at Lua's pleading eyes, her lips forming the word, *No.*

To his surprise, Ezmae looked serene, her face full of determination. She opened her palm toward Toekin, quick but deliberate. It was enough. Concealed there was a short knife—not a killing blade, but sufficient for a painful distraction.

Row's head lolled to the side, his eyes unfocused and dreamy. Then he blinked, and his gaze sharpened before dropping to the ground. Behind him, grains of dirt and sand came to life, rising in a steady, nearly invisible column up into his cupped hand, which hung innocently by his side. His gaze leveled on Toekin, alert and clear, then quickly returned to a glassed-over stare.

In his head, the plan came together quickly. If they were ready, so was he.

"Don't hurt them." Toekin said. He reached into his satchel, but instead of pulling out the relic, he stepped into a glide, circling the group while he built up the fiercest ball of fire he could. He came to a stop behind Lobo and smashed it into the dog before he knew what was happening. The thick fur at the base of his neck erupted in fire, quickly catching about his head and shoulders. Lobo yelped and ran in circles, pushing his head into the dirt to try and extinguish the flames.

The muscle man with the dragon's blood armor staggered backward, a stream of blood issuing forth from an unprotected spot under his arm. Within seconds, Ezmae had climbed a tree and was sending white light toward Sem. Lua's entire body was radiating blue and she managed to break free from Sem's distracted grip, while Row snapped to attention and pelted Nojento's eyes with a handful of dirt.

Nojento screamed with fury while Toekin ignited the area in patches of explosions and flames as he continued trying to blast Lobo with more fire. The giant, however, had recovered from his initial shock and began swinging. Lua jumped out of the way when his weapon came slamming down, missing her by a hair. Still pulsing blue energy, she grabbed the mace, and wrangled it from the grip of the big man. She swung for his knees, making contact at one of the few places on his body that wasn't covered with hardened Dragon's Blood. The man roared and fell to the ground.

Row looked like he might have had the upper hand on Sem, while Lobo ran, yelping, into the woods. For a moment, it seemed as if victory was in their sight. Then Nojento entered the fray, his eyes burned blood red as he shot white light from his hands. Ezmae fell from the tree and Row was blasted backwards into a trunk, falling into an unresponsive jumble on the ground. Nojento grabbed Lua by the front of her dress and lifted her high into the air.

"I should have killed you long ago," he spat. His voice was thunderous and menacing.

"Stop!" Toekin reached around to his satchel. "I'll give it to you. Just put her down!"

Nojento narrowed his eyes and bared his teeth in what he probably thought passed for a smile, but he didn't lower Lua. "Let's see it," he said.

Toekin pulled it from his bag and held it out for Nojento to see.

Like lightning, a bolt of white light struck Toekin, connecting him to Nojento's pointed finger.

Walk over here and hand it to me. The words came to his mind. It was a show of power. Nojento was trying to frighten him, to make him think a fight was futile.

He shook his head, immune to Nojento's mind tricks. "Lower my friend."

Nojento narrowed his eyes at Toekin, seeming both confused and intrigued. "Interesting," he said bringing Lua carefully to the ground and turning his full attention on Toekin.

Set the relic down, and leave this place. Nojento watched Toekin with great interest, white energy pouring off of Nojento stronger than Toekin had yet seen.

"Stop your mind games," Toekin said. "They don't work on me." Lua had scrambled off to Row's side, patting him gently on the cheek, then laying glowing hands on his head.

"Fair is fair," Nojento said, when she was gone. He held out his hand.

Sem, as soon as I have it—finish them all.

Sem nodded subtly and Toekin looked back at Nojento. He had no idea his message to kill had just been intercepted.

Toekin held the flute out in front of him and took a step forward. Nojento's grin doubled, his eyes widened, and he looked as if he was about to pounce on Toekin and devour him rather than wait one more moment to touch the relic.

It was now or never.

Toekin pulled the dragon flute to his lips, and blew.

Nojento's face fell and Lua screamed, "Toekin, don't!"

It started as a snaking vine of smoke that slithered out the end of the flute through the glassy dragon's open mouth. The red cloud built and billowed, rising into the air, twisting upon itself until before their eyes, Paz materialized. He flew through the forest in a rage, breathing purple flames and snapping trees with his tail before he finally came to rest at Toekin's side.

From afar, it had looked like Paz had great, spiky ridges traveling down his back, but when he came closer, Toekin could see they weren't ridges at all, but people. Bodies grew out of the dragon's back—torsos, arms and heads of nine different people, dead, but not dead, their eyes staring straight ahead. As Paz writhed and waited, they swayed mindlessly, bobbing with every move and twitch from the beast. It was as if the dragon had become a living graveyard of all the people who had tried to control him. The last figure fused to the dragon, more ghost-like and fainter than the rest, was Freya's.

At last, the dragon's eyes fell upon Toekin, full of anger and hate. The black collar he wore offered no comfort. Terrified, Toekin held his piercing gaze, and wondered if Paz might swallow him whole. What was he thinking? This was not a creature to be tamed.

Sem turned and ran from the clearing with the big man hobbling after as fast has his smashed knee would allow. Nojento, on the other hand, stood in awe of the scene before him.

Paz lowered his head, a sign of servitude—Toekin hoped. Fear gripped his heart, but he rushed forward and clambered on before he could talk himself out of it.

"What is thy bidding," Purple smoke swirled out with the dragon's rumbling voice.

Toekin didn't know where to start, but Sem was getting away. "Stop Sem," he said.

The beast rose and Toekin had to grip the spikes of Paz's great mane to keep from falling off. He soared over the trees and then dove out of the sky like an eagle bearing talons, breathing fire onto the fleeing Sem as he went. Sem glided out of its path, disappearing in short bursts and putting distance between them, but Paz wasn't done yet. Toekin felt himself be pulled through the light. Paz could glide. In a blink the great dragon was on top of Sem. Paz spit out the smallest of incendiary plumes down upon the unsuspecting Sem, who screamed out in agony. With his great claws, the dragon snatched him into the air, flew back to where Nojento and the others stood, and dropped him onto the ground.

Paz's claws left gaping gashes in Sem's arms and legs, and the way Sem held his sides told Toekin ribs had been broken as well.

"Circle back and get the other one," Toekin said. This time Paz simply flew down in front of the man with the dragon's blood armor and let out a deafening roar. At once the man turned himself about and lumbered off, back toward the clearing, clearly not wanting the same treatment Sem had gotten.

The next time they entered the clearing Nojento had gone from looking up at the sky in awe, to pulling Lua, Row and Ezmae around him as a human shield with what seemed like a giant glowing rope.

"Get him!" Toekin shouted, "But don't hurt my friends!"

The bodies on Paz's back seemed to wake up and began hurtling streams of red, yellow, white and purple energy toward Nojento.

Toekin! It was Freya's voice. *You don't have much time. Get off the dragon.*

Just a little longer, he thought. *I must defeat Nojento.*

Paz dove and Toekin held on. He found, however, that he wasn't sliding around the dragon's back as much has he had when he'd first mounted. He glanced down and could see scales just starting to creep onto his legs.

Paz dove and reached out for Nojento with his mighty claws, but the blue man ducked and pulled Ezmae on top of him. Beams of light fired out of the eyes and hands of the prisoners riding Paz's back, keeping Sem and the muscle man from escaping. Great blasts exploded at their feet and corralled them, inch by inch, into a thatch of underbrush.

The dragon circled back, swooping down at Nojento, but again, he hid under Toekin's friends for protection. How were they going to get to him? Toekin looked down at his legs. The scales had grown, now covering part way up his thigh. One more pass and then he was going to have to get off, if it wasn't too late already.

He watched, frustrated as Row and Ezmae pummeled Nojento with white light, but he was just too powerful. Suddenly a purple beam from one of Paz's undead hit the ground right in front of Nojento and was followed by a bright flash of blue. The rope that bound them snapped, broken by Lua. Another beam of light plowed into the ground, narrowly missing the lot of them and they used the distraction to scramble away.

"Now!" Toekin said. Paz bore down on the blue man, his fiery breath getting closer and closer. The half dead riders seemed to shoot light out of every orifice, assaulting Nojento with everything they had.

Nojento too, seemed to be reaching for everything he had. Light streaked from him, directed at Toekin and Paz, more dense and powerful than he'd ever seen, even from Espero and Beezul. He panicked, thinking it would be too much for Paz, but the dragon tore through the light like it was smoke in the wind. Toekin could see the look of surprise on Nojento's face, soon replaced with fear as Paz flew past him, bringing his tail around like a battling ram. The crazed man shrouded himself in a tight ball of blue light just before impact. With a crack he flew through the air, splitting a young sapling in two, then slamming hard into a stump.

Gripping his shoulder, Nojento staggered to his feet and light began to swirl around him. "Hold them back Sem!" He shouted, while motioning the large man over to his side. As if by instinct, Lobo came bounding into the clearing, singed almost beyond recognition, and made it to his master's heel just as the light around Nojento's feet surged and engulfed all three of them. They seemed to disappear into a cloud of grey smoke, until it was completely absorbed in the night. The smoke spread, thinning as it went, and when it cleared, Nojento, Lobo and the big man were all gone.

All that remained was Sem, standing guard over the space that used to contain his master. He looked up at Toekin and Paz, who were pulling up hard after circling back for another attack.

Paz dropped to the dirt, hitting the ground fast, skidding through the forest floor and coming to a stop just before plowing over Sem's prone figure. The crash landing should have tossed Toekin, but it didn't. *Hurry!* It was Freya's voice again. *You have to get off!* He planted his hands on Paz's scales and felt a tear and then a rip.

A low growl rumbled through Paz's back and traveled right up Toekin's spine. He glanced back at the riders to find they'd all gone back to their state of open-eyed sleep. He couldn't end up like that. He wouldn't.

Toekin pulled with his might. Finally, one leg came free. And with a little leverage, the second came up even faster.

He hopped off and stepped away from the dragon that huffed in irritation. Sem lay before him, bloody and beaten. His leg stuck out at an odd angle and Toekin wondered where he'd found the strength to stand and protect Nojento's escape—his own abandonment.

"What are you waiting for?" Paz's voice growled. "He is your enemy."

Yes, Toekin thought. This was his enemy. He was dangerous and when whole, nearly unstoppable. He had no doubt that Nojento would eventually find Sem and heal him—maybe turning him into something more dangerous than before. He thought of his hands gripping Lua, dousing her with his dark torture to bring her to her knees. He thought of the darkness he'd caused to come upon him— the feelings and thoughts that were almost impossible to bear—and hatred filled his heart.

Sem rose up on his arm, his cold, black emotionless eyes seemed to beg for quick death. Toekin pulled his dagger from his boot. The handle, made of Seivo Sangue wood, was warm and smooth and fit his hand perfectly. "There's nothing like the wood from the Seivo Sangue," his dad had said when he gave him the knife. "With use, the handle will conform perfectly to your hand, making this knife yours and yours alone."

He flipped the knife around and held it blade down, ready to plunge it into his enemy's heart. He pictured it ripping through Sem's chest while he stood over him, letting his anger build, picturing the killing blow over and over, when a memory came crashing down, taking his breath away.

He and his father stood together over a dead bush squirrel he'd hidden in the woodbox. "I thought it would be fun to see if I could kill him," he'd said through tears.

"Killing always comes with a cost, my son," his dad had said. "You must learn what cost you are willing to live with."

What are you willing to live with? He heard his father's voice ring out in his head. He looked up and saw Lua and Row, they were saying something to him, but the pounding in his head was so loud, he couldn't hear.

What was he willing to live with?

He looked deep into Sem's eyes. Was there a chance at redemption there? Reluctant, he lowered his knife and tucked it back into his boot. The pounding in his head quieted. Sem dropped back down to the ground and sighed with relief. The sounds of the forest returned, and a drawn-out groan of satisfaction came from the long red dragon sitting on the ground next to him. Row, Lua and Ezmae came running.

"Toekin, look!" Lua said.

He turned to Paz just in time to see the last figure in the long line of half-dead riders fade from his back. "You did it! You did it!" Freya shouted before disappearing completely.

Paz shook like a dog shedding water, then blinked in succession. His eyes seemed to smile, appearing brighter, like a thin layer of fog had lifted from them, but when he saw Toekin staring, the hate and fire found their place again.

Toekin turned from the dragon's frightful gaze to see Sem, grimacing through pain, either unable or unwilling to move. "Can you do something for him, Lua?"

She nodded and moved toward Sem as if she were still deciding if it was wise. Her words were reluctant, but they came. "May I?"

Toekin suddenly felt very weak. He pulled the flute from his satchel, observing the relic once more before blowing a single note, strong yet sweet. Paz sighed, lifted off the ground, making lazy circles that grew tighter and tighter until, in a puff of red smoke, he flew back into the flute.

It was over. Toekin lowered himself to the ground and leaned up against a tree.

"Your leg," Ezmae said, pointing.

Toekin looked down to his thigh. His pants had ripped where they'd separated from the dragon's back and in their place were patches of dry, white scaly skin. "Huh," he said, finding it very difficult to keep his eyes open, "interesting."

CHAPTER 21

The Transformation

Toekin's head was filled with so much pressure he could feel it throbbing, and his ribs and lungs felt like they were being crushed. As he came to he opened his eyes and found himself staring down at the backside of legs and heels. Pain and discomfort heightened with every bounce and bob until he was wide awake. "Hey!"

"He's awake," someone said. He was being handled with care, but he squirmed his way free, getting a face full of hair before his feet hit solid ground.

"You okay?" Lua said.

Blood rushed from his head, bringing flashing spots to his peripherals. "I think I'll sit down," he said when he felt his legs almost give out. Sitting was good, and Lua, plopping down next to him, seemed to agree.

Row and Ezmae huddled around them, and as his vision normalized, he noticed a fading blue light around Lua, and how parts of her hair were matted down with sweat.

"How long have you been carrying me?" He said, stretching his aching ribs and back side to side.

Lua was breathing hard. "Long enough."

"We all took turns." Row was quick to point out.

Lua rolled her eyes and Ezmae shook her head just enough for Toekin to take notice. He smiled. Lua had probably been carrying him the whole way, or close to it.

"How are you feeling, Toe?" Row asked.

"Like a sack of beats dragged over a hundred rock piles." He rubbed his back and sat up a little straighter. "Where are we?"

"Close," Lua said. "At least I think so."

"We're pretty sure we've been going the right direction." Row added.

Toekin's head spun. Had he really used the relic to call Paz—and survived? He touched the rough, scaly skin on his leg and instantly the sensation of flying through the air returned. It had happened—all of it. "What happened to Sem?"

The three of them looked at each other. "I did the best I could, but I can't heal broken bones . . . at least not yet."

"I made him promise not to follow us." Row shrugged. "It was the most I could get him to agree to."

"I found a stick and made him a crutch," Ezmae said.

"So he's just on his own?" Sem was dangerous, but he'd been in bad shape. Had they just left him to die a slower death, abandoned in Mato Forest? Maybe it would have been kinder for Toekin to have ended his life? No! Then Freya would not have been saved. Sparing Sem had somehow saved her. It had been the right thing to do.

"We gave him most of our food and water," Lua said. "We had enough for the trek to Triste and back, but . . ." She was still catching her breath, ". . . since we're not going that way anymore, we had plenty to give."

That made Toekin feel a bit better.

"Do you feel like walking?" Row said.

"I think so." Toekin stood but his legs were weak and wobbly. Then he had an idea and sat back down. Crossing his legs, he brought his palms together in prayer form. He didn't know why he did that. It just felt right.

"Uh, Toe? What do you think you are doing?" Row asked.

Toekin cracked an eye open, then smiled at the three of them. He didn't really know what he was doing. But if moonlight could be used to heal, why couldn't he heal himself? It was worth a try. "I just want to try something . . ."

Closing his eyes again, Toekin found the moonlight within. He called upon it, commanding it to heal his body. Suddenly, he felt warmth rush into his head; it moved down his neck and back and throughout his body. It was working.

"Wow," Ezmae said.

Toekin kept his eyes closed but wondered if his spectacular healing was causing his body to glow blue or something.

Strength seeped back into his bones. He sat a little straighter and each breath seemed deeper and more satisfying. He felt the muscles in his arms and legs tighten, and then loosen, as if he was powerful enough to lift Row right over his head. But he kept his eyes closed and decided not to try this.

Then, too soon, the feeling faded. Perhaps he'd run out of moonlight. He could tell he was still weak, but he certainly felt better than he had before. Maybe with some practice he could get better at that.

"That's all I wanted to do," he said, opening his eyes.

Lua came out from behind him, looking even more tired than before, but she smiled as she shared a quick look with Row. "Great job," she said, patting Toekin on the shoulder.

Toekin stood. He was missing something, but he didn't care. He felt loads better. "You guys ready to go?" He asked as he slung his satchel over his shoulder.

Lua smiled, "Ready."

They walked in silence for a while, then Ezmae said, "You think Nojento will come back for Sem?"

"I kind of hope he doesn't," Lua said.

"Why? They deserve each other," Row said.

"I don't know. There was something about him that was different. When I was healing him, something felt, *familiar*. But I couldn't put my finger on it."

"That's weird." Row said.

"And those eyes," Lua said.

"They used to give me nightmares," Ezmae said.

"There was a lot of pain in them," Lua said.

"Well, he *was* in pretty bad shape," Row said. "Burns, missing large chunks of flesh, broken leg, broken ribs, broken ego," Row counted off on his fingers.

"It wasn't pain from his injuries—although that was certainly part of it. This was something else."

"Well, whatever it was, I will be perfectly fine if I never run into him again." Row said.

"Caw!"

Toekin's head snapped up. "Corvo?" High in the sky, a huge black crow circled, then broke into a dive. Toekin held out his arm just in time for Corvo to pull up and execute a perfect landing.

Ezmae cowered behind Row. "What is that thing?" She said.

Toekin laughed. "Remember how you wanted to move to the forest and be friends with the birds?" He said. "Well, this is Corvo—my friend." Corvo nuzzled Toekin's chin and lovingly pecked the bits of sticks and grass from his hair all the way back to their Seivo Sangue tree.

* * *

It was Tessa who saw them first. "They're back!" She ran and jumped into Toekin's arms as they came out of the root entrance, and into the great trunk of the Seivo Sangue.

When the crowd cleared Toekin scanned the room. Row was already telling tall tales to the little kids while Lua was questioning whether or not everyone had given up on chores altogether when she wasn't there to make sure they got done. Ezmae stood back, clearly overwhelmed, watching everything unfold. But Toekin didn't care about Ezmae right then. Let Row or Lua introduce her. There was just one person he wanted to see. And when he saw Força sitting near the fire, watching the scene with great eagerness, but not daring to move, he knew he'd found her.

He walked with purpose across the room until he saw her. Freya.

Her skin was dark now, though not as dark as her father's. Toekin hadn't expected that, but what had he been expecting? She looked nothing like she once had. The pale, withering apparition of an elderly woman had finally been laid to rest.

Freya's hair was black, her skin was smooth and a thin row of freckles ran across her nose and under her eyes. Despite her sunken cheeks and twig-thin arms and legs, Toekin's heart skipped a beat— she *was* the girl from his dreams.

She followed her father's gaze and when her eyes landed on Toekin, her smile lit up her face and took Toekin's breath away.

"Thank you," she said as Toekin approached, gratitude swelling in her eyes.

Força stood up and reached for Toekin's hand, giving it two massive pumps before pulling him into a hug. He was going to need Lua's healing again to recover from this embrace. "Thank you, son," he said. "I didn't expect . . ." He broke off, cleared his throat, then pulled an old cloth from his pocket and dabbed at his eyes.

Toekin regarded Força, then stepped past him and knelt at Freya's feet. "It's really you!" he said, fully aware of how ridiculous it sounded, but unable to think of anything else to say.

She laughed. "You knew it was me before you left."

"Still, it was a little hard to believe."

Freya nodded.

He took her hands in his. "Thanks for helping me back there. Everything was happening so fast, and . . ."

"All I did was tell you to get off the dragon," she said.

"I know, but if you hadn't . . ." Toekin shook his head. He stared into her eyes, still not quite believing that this wasn't a dream.

Força cleared his throat and Toekin dropped Freya's hands. "Why don't you tell me all about it, son." He said, patting a seat on the bench near him, and away from Freya.

He started at the beginning, how they got into his old house, fought with Ezmae's dad . . .

"Who's Ezmae?" Força asked.

"She's over there," Toekin pointed. "I'll introduce you later." He told how Nojento and Sem had come to break things up and the things Nojento revealed about the rebel leader, and his parents.

"Kimnar's in Passo Fundo?" Força said.

"That's what Nojento said. You think we can trust him?"

"I'm not sure," Força admitted.

"What about my parents?" Toekin steeled himself, waiting for the answer he wasn't certain he wanted.

Força narrowed his eyes. "Turbin was always a fighter," he said. "I wouldn't be surprised if he's alive."

Toekin felt warmth spread throughout his chest. The possibilities began to present themselves. Could he use Paz to help find and rescue them? And if so, how soon could he leave?

"Keep going," Força said, bringing him back to the present.

Lua and Row had joined them. Lua sat next to Freya and seemed intent on filling her in on every detail of the last six years. Row sat closer to Força and Toekin and helped tell the story, especially the part about how Nojento had ambushed them, laughed in their face at their poor attempt to be a decoy, and taken them all to use as leverage on the attack against Toekin.

"I heard him, you know, in my mind," Toekin said. "He didn't mean for me to hear, but I did. He told Sem to kill us all as soon as I handed over the relic."

"I don't doubt it," Força said. "He will say and do anything to get his way."

Cheep came over with a hot bowl of meaty stew. "Força trapped some snow rabbits while you were gone," he said. "Kai said you'd be back today, so I had it all ready for your return."

"You're a good man," Row said. Cheep blushed and returned to his large pot.

Lua started to help Freya but she demurred. "I can feed myself now, you know," she reminded her. Lua laughed and let her take the bowl in her hands.

"This might take a little getting used to." Lua hugged her friend again.

Força smiled at the exchange but Toekin wasn't ready to change the subject just yet. "So, what are we going to do?" he said. "Do we act on this information and try and find Kimnar in Passo Fundo?"

"It very well could be a trap," Row said. "And I'm kind of tired of traps right now."

"If it's not a trap now, it could be very soon." Força pointed out. "Nojento has to know that we'll be too curious not look into it."

"So we act quickly?" Toekin said.

"We'll have to," Força said. "We have the relic and everyone will be trying to get it. The longer we sit still, the more of a target we become. Our best chance is to meet up with Kimnar and the rebels, and form a plan to defeat Beezul."

"So, should I even bother unpacking," Row said.

"No," Força said. "You leave tomorrow."

THE END

Thank you for reading!

I hope you enjoyed The Path to Paz: Book One. If you're like me, and one of your favorite characters is Sem, then I say fear not! There will be loads more from Sem in Book Two, where he'll begin taking much more of the limelight.

To find out when the next book in The Path to Paz series comes out, please visit www.jeremythelin.com where you can sign up to receive an email featuring my next release.

As you likely know, book reviews are challenging to get these days. But you, the reader, have the power to help make a book a success— the opposite is true as well. If you have a minute, please leave a link on Amazon. Your review, be it praiseful, constructive, opinionated, or down right rude, is sorely needed. I want and need all types of honest feedback.

Thank you so very much for reading The Path to Paz!

Respectfully,

Jeremy Thelin

Made in the
USA
Monee, IL